FOSSIL COVE PRESS

AXIS OF ANDES
PART ONE

by

D. G. Valdron

THE AXIS OF ANDES

PART ONE

Table of Contents

Axis of Andes
Introduction

This is a work of historical fiction. But it isn't the history that you know.

In our history, the nations of South America were bystanders to World War II, watching in safety as Europe, East Asia and North Africa were consumed by war. The countries of South America were largely neutral, looking to their own affairs.

There were tangential brushes. The Falklands and the Guianas belonged to warring European powers. The Axis' agents and espionage networks were active, particularly in Argentina, Chile, Paraguay and Bolivia, before, during and after the war. In the south, the German warship Graf Spee retreated to Uruguay after the Battle of the River Plate, before finally scuttling itself. In the north, the Colombian navy pursued and sunk a Nazi submarine playing on its shipping. Brazil sent men overseas to fight in Europe. But mostly, South America was left alone.

But it didn't have to be like that, there was the Colombia-Peru War of 1932, followed by the Chaco War of 1932-35, and then the Peru-Ecuador War of 1941. If things had turned out a little differently, everything could have gone very wrong. In our history, the Peru-Ecuador War of 1941 lasted only a month, but its origins stretched back a century. In the story you are about to read, this conflict turns out very differently. This is the history where things went very wrong, and a continent was bathed in flame.

The history of the nations of South America is well worth studying. It's a history of idealism and cynicism, greed and generosity, comedy and tragedy. I commend the reader to study that real history. You will be well served.

This is a work of fiction, we make no apologies. Much has been taken from real history as we know it, of economics and geography, of various historical persons. But I warn you, liberties have been taken with characters and personalities; they may be different in greater or lesser degree than the men who actually lived and died. No disrespect is intended. Here and there, a few persons have been made up altogether, but represent the sorts of personality that turn up frequently and so people very much like them have lived.

Although this is fiction, there may be errors of various sorts in the portions that purport to draw from actual history. These errors are mine and no one else's, and I certainly acknowledge them.

Axis of Andes – Page 3

AXIS OF ANDES

BOOK OF ECUADOR

"The circumstances which bring men to war may be likened to a process of fire. For always there is a spark, and on occasion, this spark will find its way to favourable tinder, there to simmer and smolder, to flash and flare and then blaze until finally it burst into the conflagration which consumes all before it."

Velasco Ibarra, 1967

****

Berlin, December, 1937

Hitler does not stand. Instead, he genially waves the South American visitors to take a seat. The Minister, Velasco, and the Colonel Alba, gingerly settle into chairs at the far end of the long table. The rest of the German cabinet resume their seats, watching the Fuhrer warily.

"I regret," Hitler begins, "that the press of European matters, particularly the struggle of our brother, Commander Franco, does not allow us much time. But be welcome, tell us of matters in South America."

"Thank you, Great Fuhrer," Velasco replies. "Ecuador is a proud country with an honourable history, like Germany itself, but like Germany threatened by a great enemy whose designs would drive our noble people into the sea."

"You speak of Peru, of course," Hitler interrupts, checking his notes, "the fabled land of the Incas."

Axis of Andes – Page 4

Velasco pauses, trying to think how to respond to this. "It is said that the Inca began in the lands of Ecuador, though over time, their conquests extended the length of the Andes."

"Indeed?" Hitler asks with every sign of earnest fascination. "How marvelous, the Inca folk were a remarkable race, superior to the lowly Indians who surrounded them in every way. I hear that they left remarkable ruins behind, strange lost cities and pyramids. And they began in Ecuador you say?"

"Yes, they did," Velasco says. "The Indians of Peru, the Indians who still make up the majority of Peru, were their slaves. When the Inca fell, they were no match for the Spanish. The monuments of the true Inca are found through Ecuador."

"Quite remarkable. I should like to see that for myself sometime. How is the climate in Ecuador?"

"Very moderate," Velasco replies. "European in nature, why much like Berlin itself."

"Really," Hitler asks. "But doesn't Ecuador rest upon the equator? I would think it would be a tropical bath."

"It would be, but we are sheltered by the mountains, and the cold ocean current. Ecuador has the most European climate in South America. Because of that, we have been blessed with a greater immigration of the white races. Particularly Germans."

"Is that so," Hitler beams. He turns to Canaris. "Is this true, Herr Canaris? Is there a little piece of the German nation straddling the Equator?"

"There are many Germans in South America," Canaris answers. "Particularly in Argentina and Chile, but in Ecuador as well. I believe that the largest German communities are in Chile."

"I should wonder then," Hitler muses, "why the Chileans are not here as well? Don't we have connections there?"

"Many of the Chilean Germans are Jews or communists," Velasco says quickly, a light film of sweat appearing on his forehead. "Not all, by any means. But many."

Axis of Andes – Page 5

Hitler looks to Canaris, who shrugs.

"What of Peru?"

"Indians and Bolsheviks," replies Velasco quickly. "And Jews."

"Well," Hitler says, "that stands to reason, where you find Bolsheviks, you also find Jews, and the reverse. It is just as in Russia, the Indians are like the Slavs, a slave race, too easily lead. A simple, childlike race of savages, as Karl May shows us, without the wisdom to see through the lies of communism."

Velasco opens his mouth and closes it.

Abruptly, Hitler's manner changes. He becomes blunt and businesslike.

"What is it that you want from us?"

Velasco nods to Colonel Alba, who begins to stand up. Hitler raises an eyebrow. Alba sit down. He clears his throat.

"We are a small, but valiant nation, preparing to defend ourselves from a powerful enemy. Already that enemy has made war upon our neighbor. Now it seeks to claim our territory. Our-"

"Lebensraum," Hitler offers, "living space. To steal land from the European people, and fill it with Slavs and Bolsheviks."

Alba blinks, but has the wisdom to nod twice. "Yes, exactly. They have numbers and powerful supporters. We need assistance."

"What sort of assistance?"

"Weapons," Alba answers, "and munitions, artillery, armour, aircraft, radio. Perhaps trainers. Whatever you can spare, even trucks."

"And you assume we have vast quantities to spare, to just give you? You assume we are not confronted by true Bolsheviks far more insidious and ruthless than the schemers you face? You feel that we are not troubled by Slavs in endless numbers, Poles and Russians and Ukrainians. That we are not ringed by enemies lead by these selfsame Jews. The German people are not forced to the precipice, standing almost alone in a sea of mongrel races, betrayed from without and within?"

"The Aryan peoples must stand together," Velasco says. "No matter where they are, against the rising red tide. You have come to the aid of virtue in Spain."

"So you see us coming to the aid of our friend, Commander Franco," he asks, "and you think to yourselves, 'ahh, these are just the chaps to save us from the horde of Indians and Bolsheviks?' What of your friends to the north, the Americans?"

"Unfortunately, their business interests are substantially greater in Peru than in Ecuador. And so they favour our enemies."

"And behind business interests, are the Jews," Hitler says knowingly. He glanced around at his cabinet, nodding in affirmation, "You see how it all comes together?"

"We've often thought so," Velasco agrees.

Abruptly, Hitler's manner changes again, becoming businesslike. "We will consider your request," he says. "There are many demands upon our resources, but perhaps we can find something to spare for you. Thank you for your time. Now, you must excuse us, we have a long agenda."

Solemnly, Hitler stands as Velasco and Alba came forward to shake hands. They exchange greetings with the rest of Hitler's cabinet and are escorted from the room.

"One more thing," Hitler calls.

The two Ecuadorans stop.

"Your President, Napoli Bonifaz," he offers.

"Yes?" Velasco replies carefully.

"Is he by any chance related to the famous French General?"

Colonel Alba clears his throat, but Velasco speaks first.

"He has never spoken of it. But many French and Germans came to Ecuador after the battle of Waterloo, finding Europe no longer sympathetic to them. So it is certainly likely."

Axis of Andes – Page 7

"Ahh," Hitler replies, "interesting. Thank you, you may go."

He watches as the two men left, and once they are safely out of earshot he turns to his cabinet.

"What an extraordinary thing," he bursts out suddenly, barking a few short laughs. "I have never imagined such a thing. Why, they were right out of a comic opera!"

There is a round of sycophantic laughter.

"Did you see the Colonel?" Goebbels chuckles. "I was nearly beside myself. With all his gold braid and epaulets, I was almost ready to ask him to carry my luggage."

"Yes," Goering laughs, "I was almost certain that Canaris had hired a couple of actors to play a prank upon us."

"Imagine that," Hitler muses, "a lost country of Aryans on the Equator, amid the ruins of pyramids and temples, facing hordes of Indians and Bolsheviks. Why, it's out of Karl May. No, it's more bizarre even than May would write."

"We should send them to Benito," Himmler offers, "I'm sure he would love them."

"Actually," Canaris replies, "they have already met Mussolini, who indicated that he was quite receptive."

"Has he made a commitment?"

"Not yet."

"Of course he would be receptive," Hitler says thoughtfully, "our friend Benito is hungry for overseas colonies. I'm sure he would love an opportunity to carve himself a slice of South America in some fashion. But make no mistake: things will be decided here in Europe; it would be a mistake to get involved in such a sideshow."

"I do not see any merit in getting involved," Himmler says. "Let the South Americans deal with their own matters. I can see no benefit to us."

"We do have interests and supporters in South America," Canaris suggests. "We have assets there. Perhaps a friendly government might allow us to advance those interests."

Hitler shrugs, steepling his fingers.

"What do you say, Herman?" he asks Goering.

"Like Heinrich," Goering replies, "I see no real advantage in... as you say... being diverted by a sideshow. And to play too heavily there might antagonize the Americans."

Hitler shrugs at the mention of the Americans.

"Our assets in South America," Hitler asks thoughtfully, "do they amount to much?"

"They are small remote countries," Himmler replies, "of no great consequence."

"True," Hitler notes. "But they have come all this way, and their enemies are our enemies. I would not see Bolshevism defeated here, only to have the Jews establish a new fortress somewhere else."

He shakes himself, seeming to make a decision.

"The great battle is coming. Even Spain is merely a sideshow. Still," he paused thoughtfully, "if beggars come to our table, it is only polite to throw them a few crumbs. Let us see if we can spare them a few Reichsmarks and rifles, it might do some good. I'm sure our friend Benito will chip in.... And Heinrich, send a letter to our friend Henry Ford. Ask him to help out. After all, this is America's domain; we should encourage the Americans to choose the right party, not antagonize them. Help, but not too much help. We are here to win victories, gentlemen, not enemies."

Hitler watches for a second as the secretary transcribes notes.

"Very well, now the next item on the Agenda..."

***

Axis of Andes – Page 9

Guayaquil, Ecuador, August 12, 1890

Neptali Bonifaz walks along the docks late at night, heedless. He is a young man, well dressed and far from his usual circles. The night is warm, but he is cold with rage. He has just finished another row with his father. He resolves to leave Ecuador, to find his place in the world. Too long he's been in the shadows of his father, a Peruvian diplomat. He can't stand the man. He is Ecuadorian, like his mother, like his family.

Neptali stands astride two nations, his father of Peru, yet his mother is Ecuador. Ecuador is where he was born. He considers his father's offer to arrange a Peruvian passport for him to travel on. What would his friends say to that? No. Ridiculous. No matter where he goes, he will always proudly carry Ecuador with him.

No to the passport. No to his father. He reaches into his pocket, finds a handful of Peruvian coins, and flings them into the sea. Eventually, he marches back to his home, but the rage, the anger, never quite abates.

The Prelude to War

In South America, the expulsion of the Spanish had gives rise to a succession of quarreling republics, jealous of their territories, protective of their sovereignty, and uncertain of their borders.

Everywhere, poorly demarcated borders become a source of conflict. Between Chile and Argentina, Bolivia and Paraguay, Columbia and Ecuador, Ecuador and Peru, Columbia and Peru.

For the Andean nations, the peculiar topography of the area contributes to tensions. In simple terms, the Andean nations share a sort of layered geography.

To start with, there are the coastal and lowland areas, the lands colonized by the Spanish, the lands of Europeans and Europeanized Mestizo, with cities and towns, ports and roads.

Moving inwards, we come to the uplands and highlands, the hill country, dominated by primarily Indigenous villages and farmers living almost traditional lifestyles, as well as large landowners. This leads to the Andean mountain ranges.

Beyond them lie the vast Amazon jungle, called the 'Oriente' in Ecuador, or the 'Selva' in Peru, but always the rain forest, thinly populated, inaccessible, difficult to hold and reach, extending to the poorly delineated borders of the territories held by Brazil.

It is that rain forest which is often a source of strife. Brazil easily establishes its claims to the interior by following the Amazon River system. The coastal nations of the Andes each claim large inland domains, but have rather more difficulty establishing control over these territories due to the vagaries of mountain passes, trails and river courses. Territories which could be cleanly drawn on a map were often inaccessible or indistinct.

Even today, the interiors remain thinly populated and subject to conflict. Governance is sometimes light. For Colombia, for example, a long standing guerilla movement, FARC, has controlled a large portion of the interior for decades.

Disputes between Ecuador and its neighbors went back a long way. In 1887, Peru and Ecuador submit their territorial disputes to the King of Spain, a process called the Espinoza-Bonifaz Convention. But it falls apart as the Ecuadorans were not prepared to accept the undisclosed decision.

Following this, in 1890, Peru and Ecuador enter into direct negotiations. From this comes the Herrera-García Treaty which gives Ecuador access to the Amazon River, dominion over the Napo and Putumayo rivers, part of the provinces of Tumbes and Maynas, and the Canelos region. The Treaty is favourable to Ecuador, recognizing or conceding its claims to the interior, and quickly proceeds to ratification in 1891.

Peru has just undergone a devastating defeat by Chile in the War of the Pacific, and has negotiated from a position of relative weakness. Consequently, Peru introduces a series of amendments over the next year, which Ecuador rejects. The treaty breaks down.

In 1916, the Munoz-Suarez Treaty is signed between Columbia and Ecuador. At the time, it is a rational agreement, wherein the parties demarcated lands south of the Putumayo, a navigable river, as the boundary. Ecuador makes territorial concessions in favour of securing a stable border with Columbia.

Subsequent events will lead the Ecuadorians to denounce the Treaty as the product of a 'secret pact' between Peru and Columbia.

It will set the nation on a path to war 25 years later.

***

The Saloman-Lozano Treaty

Sometimes you're just walking along minding your own business, and a car jumps the curb, and pastes you.

That must be how the Ecuadorans feel about the Saloman-Lozano treaty between Columbia and Peru, when they learn of it.

Negotiated in secret in March 1922, under the Peruvian dictator, August B. Leguia, the Treaty was another attempt to sort out the issues of the 'Oriente' between the parties. The winding paths of rivers meant that Peru had easier access, de facto access, to territories claimed by Columbia.

In the Treaty, Peru cedes to Columbia a 'corridor to the Amazon' including the town of Leticia, in return, Columbia agrees to the Putumayo river as a mutual border, and concedes the area south of the Putumayo river to Peru. What this meant is that Peru would now literally surround Ecuador, bordering its interior on three sides.

Significantly, the Treaty also saw Columbia recognizing Peruvian claims to territory claimed by Ecuador. Essentially, the Treaty kicks Ecuador to the curb, freeing Peru to deal with the little country at its leisure.

Of course, a secret treaty can't be secret forever. When Leguia is overthrown by Sanchez Cerra in 1928 the Treaty becomes public. The result is fury in Peru, which sees the concession of Leticia as a surrender of Peruvian territory. The Peruvians immediately repudiate the Treaty.

Meanwhile, Ecuador, in outrage, also breaks diplomatic relations with Columbia, argues, with some justification, that they have literally been sold down the river to Peru, particularly given their own treaty with Colombia only six years before.

The fallout from the Salomon-LozanoTreaty will lead almost directly to both the Colombia/Peru war of 1932, and the Peru-Ecuador war of 1940.

****

Ecuador 1920s, Social Divisions and Tension

"South America is legend for its contradictions and the contrary nature of its peoples. We are peoples who seem to flee from victory, who lionize failures; we drive our heroes away mad with frustration, and elevate our monsters to contented glory. If the rest of the world does things one way, then we seem compelled to do it another way.

All of this by way of preamble. It is fashionable to lay at blame for the Andean wars upon Ecuador, to trace the years of blood and suffering that reshaped a continent, to the ambitions and dreams of a triumvirate of scheming madmen, to build an empire on the backs of other nations. But the truth is that the war came about not because Ecuador was strong and ambitious. But because it was weak and afraid."

Velasco Ibarra, 1967

Ecuador, like many Latin American states, originally found its politics divided between Liberals and Conservatives. This is a pattern inherited from Spanish colonial times, and which will divide Latin states again and again. But of course, every state, every nation is unique. The struggles might be common, but in the individual cases, that does not make them less earnest or less desperate. The broad picture might be familiar, but each nation is rich in subtleties and complexities that determine its fate.

The Conservatives are typically the great land owners, called Latifundistas, primarily a class of aristocratic landowners controlling vast estates, known as Haciendas, with patron or semi-feudal relationships to the tenant farmers who worked the fields. The Latifundista are inherently aristocratic and autocratic. There is a huge gap of wealth and political influence between the Latifundista and the common people. The Latifundista estates form nearly autonomous communities, with a high degree of self-sufficiency.

Economically isolated, the landholder class are regional aristocrats or strongmen who rule local economies in an almost feudal manner. They venerate the Catholic Church as a dominant social institution they look towards and ape the manners or European aristocracy. Regressive and reactionary by nature, they are paternalistic to an extreme degree. They dominate the inlands and the Sierra, existing in uneasy tension with the local Indigenous, and with the urban Agro-Mercantile elites of the coast.

The Liberals, on the other hand, are an elite based not on land, but on commerce and trade. They look to America for inspiration and ideology. They are nominally democratic and populist, focusing on export markets and capitalism. They emphasize the development and export of cash crops, and the integration of Ecuador with foreign economies, and some commitment to basic infrastructure as an investment.

Ultimately, the Liberals in Ecuador come under the control of what are called Agro-Mercantilists: Banks, financial combines, wholesalers, and the more industrious planters who manage the gathering, sale and export of cash crops. Essentially, they are a rival elite to the Latifundistas, as wealthy and powerful in their own way as the landed pseudo-aristocracy, but with a completely different orientation and outlook.

The particular structure of Ecuador's economy favours large landowners on one hand, and large commercial export concerns on the other, and relatively little in the way of domestic industry. There isn't a lot of scope for a broad middle class as would emerge in Europe or the United States.

Instead, the Ecuadorian middle class is confined to a residue of professionals: Lawyers, doctors, engineers, teachers, journalists, accountants, etc. They form a relatively small sliver of population, although large in comparison to the elites. Their numbers allow them to dominate the army, forming the bulk of the officer class.

Because of their role as technocrats, the middle class tend to identify their interests with the Liberals, and to support the Agro-Mercantile elites, both politically and economically. Of course, their attitudes vary with their location; the thin sprinkling of the middle class inland, the lawyers and doctors and teachers, tend to be reactionary supporters of the Latifundista. But most of the middle class is concentrated in the cities and towns of the coasts, and so cleave to the Agro-Mercantilists.

Overall though, the middle class are socially conservative, staunch advocates and supporters of the church, and conscious of class and racial distinction and entitlement, particularly their own superiority over the lower classes and races. The middle class, largely impotent on its own, focuses on guarding and advancing their entitlements jealously.

The cacao export booms that took place during the Liberal era after 1895, and in particularly the Arroyo Presidency of the late 1920s, brought a flush of wealth and luxury consumption to elites and middle classes, but had little impact on the poor and working class, who instead endured an onerous and predatory system.

Cacao, the bean used to make chocolate, is the basis of Ecuador's commercial economy, representing 80% of its exports, and 13% of the entire World's production. A booming cacao market creates land-hungry plantations and estates. But increasing production can only be achieved by the expansion of cacao planting, comes at the expense of subsistence and food farming. Massive expansion of estates displaces small holdings as well as tenant farmers and Indigenous. One result is monopolization of local political and economic power in the hands of landowners to an even greater degree.

Those displaced, the small farmers, tenants, the poor, the indigent and Indigenous, often end up as landless agricultural labourers or squatters. Busts in the market lead to unemployment and further displacement, squatters occupy abandoned estates. But in many cases, displaced and landless population drift to the cities and towns.

But things aren't much better there. Cacao didn't require a lot of processing, so there is little in the way of employment opportunities there. There is work for accountants, lawyers, factors, stevedores, warehouse guards, etc.; but little work involved in refining, and therefore not much in the way of economic spin offs.

Without an 'engine' to drive industrialization, most manufacturing is small scale, relatively simplified and aimed at local markets. The middle class and upper classes prefer to import luxury goods rather than buy locally, which undercuts the consumer market, already small in a country of less than two million in 1930. There are significant industrial products in use - telegraphs, railroads, locomotives, but most of the stock, equipment and parts are imported at substantial cost, which makes them expensive and undermines the economic utility of their use.

The result, together with the steady stream of displaced drifting into cities and towns, is a situation where the supply of ready available labour, particularly unskilled or semi-skilled labour, readily exceeds the demand. This is a recipe for extremely low wages, long hours and poor working conditions, all of which comes to pass. To make matters worse, the working poor are almost entirely excluded from the political process.

Of course, economic development requires some skilled trades. Railways, for instance, require specialized and trained personnel;engineers, conductors, brakemen. Shoemakers, bakers, artisans of all sorts form classes of skilled labourers, not middle class by any means, but whose particular training and abilities set them apart from the unwashed masses of the day labourers. Unlike the middle class, they could not afford to entirely ignore the rest of the working class, people from whom they spring, who are their customers and friends, and who in bad times, they might end up rejoining.

An intelligentsia emerges, splitting off from the middle class and skilled trades - intellectuals, thinkers, writers, academics and journalists, union organizers, teachers; hewing to socialism of various brands, from mild leftism of the Christian Socialist variety to outright Communism, looking to European solutions to intractable social problems. Although numerically tiny, they offer leadership and ideas, an intellectual structure and analysis to large numbers of people who find the conventional ideologies to be a poor fit.

All of these groups are essentially excluded from the political process which is essentially a struggle between two groups of elites. Instead, constituencies and classes seek influence through irregular channels.

The middle class tends to throw its support to whichever elite it is most proximate too; as most of the middle class is situated on the coast they tend to support the Agro-Mercantilists. The middle classes domination of the army tends to ensure that middle class values are somewhat represented in the political process. But overall, they are too divided to be a real political force.

The intelligentsia's tactic is promotion, publication and dialogue; attempting to engage the middle class; but also attempting to engage and enlist other social classes. It's an essentially thankless and futile task.

The Indigenous, of course, are excluded entirely, for the most part; they are people of the hinterlands, the Sierra and the Highlands. Almost entirely excluded from Ecuadorian politics, they are a voiceless population, inhabiting the interiors, rubbing shoulders, sometimes uncomfortably, with the great Landholders. Often ignored, subject to racism, sometimes displaced, sometimes hired on as day labourers. They prefer to be left alone.

The urban poor or day laborers found all doors shut to them, and together with skilled trades are a seething volatile mass, people who see the least benefit from boom times and prosperity, who are most frequently victimized by other parts of society, and who are the first to suffer in bad times.

The situation of the rural poor, itinerant laborers, small farmers, tenants and subsistence squatters is almost the same. But the patriarchy of the Latifundistas offers slightly more security and stability; if at the same time exerting a great deal of social control. Still, when the Latifundistas are inconvenienced, it is the rural poor that starves.

The bottom line is that Ecuador is a fractured society. The Latifundistas and the Agro-Mercantiles are equally interdependent and incompatible. As often as not, their goals and priorities are at cross purpose. But neither can fully dominate the other. The middle class is a bottomless pool of frustrated ambitions.

Voting in Ecuador during this period is confined to literate males over the age of 21. In practical terms, roughly 3 to 4% of the country is allowed to vote in elections. As an example, in 1931 in the Presidential election, a total of 68,000 votes are cast in a population of roughly two million. Even assuming one third of the population is under age, that still leaves over 1.3 million potential voters. Even counting only males of voting age, say six or seven hundred thousand, this means that roughly one in ten theoretically eligible 'voting age males' are allowed to participate in one of the fiercest, most open elections of that era.

Of course when you have an electoral process which is so thoroughly unrepresentative from the very beginning, the tendency of powerful constituencies to meddle is irresistible. The Army is frequently the arbiter of elections; the ideological perspectives of the officer class weigh heavily upon, or even displacing the electoral process. Often the army decides how votes are counted, whether votes are counted, or whether results are thrown out entirely. Incumbent presidents or politicians frequently manipulate the vote count, and a number of Ecuadorian elections are tainted by fraud.

Formal politics in Ecuador are a contest, corrupt, exclusive and bitter, between two powerful but unrepresentative elites, with the rest of the country largely unrepresented, unconsidered and thoroughly unwanted.

Beyond that, rural and urban poor, Indigenous, skilled laborers, intelligentsia and other groups struggle to even have a voice, embrace radical ideologies, argue, mount strikes and revolts, and attempt to find channels outside the normal political process to express their aspirations and grievances, or to find a way to force their views and agendas onto the table.

Ecuador is a country drifting steadily towards ungovernability. Stalemates and ambitions, aspirations and revenge, unacknowledged tensions, ideals and ideologies, boiling and simmering, the lubrications of compromise and money, evaporating away.

What could possibly hold it together?

Axis of Andes – Page 19

Ecuador - History - 1830 to 1920

General Juan Flores, a Venezuelan lieutenant of Bolivar's, is the first, third and fourth Ecuadorian President. At this time, Ecuadorian society is already divided between the landed caudillos, who will become the Latifundistas, of the Highlands or Sierra, who establish the capital inland at Quito; and the merchants of the coast, who will develop into the Agro-Mercantiles, centered around the port city of Guayaquil.

Flores establishes himself with the Latifundista class, marrying into the Quito local aristocracy. He proves to be a Machiavellian politician, chiefly interested in maintaining power, skilled at eliminating or co-opting his enemies. He wastes a lot of time and money in territorial conflicts with Peru.

During this time, Ecuador is a nearly medieval society. The Indigenous are largely ungoverned, except for the requirement to pay tribute. Land tenure and debt peonage approach serfdom.

The embryonic society is already dividing along class and regional lines. The Sierra versus the Coast, the landowners versus the merchants, with peasants and urban poor and Indigenous on the outside looking in, applying pressure where they can. Hand in hand with the aristocracy, the church is a major force, a vast landowner in its own right, deeply conservative and controlling.

Flores has a remarkable record of holding on to or finding his way back to power. But eventually, opposition coalesces in the coastal city of Guayaquil, and he is driven off in 1845. He spends the next fifteen years abroad, scheming to overthrow the Ecuadorian government.

This marks a tumultuous period in Ecuadorian society, as liberal and conservative elites struggle for power. The main leader of the period after Flores was vanquished is General Jose Urbina, who comes to power in 1851, rules until 1856, and remains a dominant figure on the political scene.

During this period of relative liberalism, led from the coast, slavery is abolished, the custom of exacting tribute from the Indigenous is ended, and efforts are made to prune back the church. All of which tends to favour the business classes of the coast and undermine the landed gentry of the Sierra.

It also marks the beginning of cacao's (chocolate's) dramatic expansion as an export crop. In 1850, Ecuador produces roughly 6.5 million kilograms of cacao. By 1890 the crop is 18 million kilograms, an increase of threefold, and an increase marked by a massive increase in cultivation, expropriation and consolidation of lands, and shifts from subsistence to cash crop agriculture. During this time, 1850 to 1890, the value of Ecuador's exports goes from barely a million to over ten million dollars, an increase of over 1000%. Essentially, this period sees the steady and erratic erosion of a neo-feudal land aristocracy, and the rise of the coastal business elite dependent on foreign trade.

But the balance of power is hardly stable, and if the landowners are giving way to the businessmen, it is hardly a smooth or even transition. In the absence of Flores, the new rulers of Ecuador cannot agree on anything. They spend as much time fighting with each other, through regional power centers, or simple power struggles, as they spend governing. Stability is rare, and as the late 1850s wear on, Ecuador becomes increasingly ungovernable.

This culminates in an almost complete breakdown between 1857 and 1859, later known in Ecuador's history as 'the terrible year.' It begins with President Robles moving the capital from the mountain city, Quito, to the coastal metropolis, Guayaquil, literally a shift of the seat of government and symbolic power from landholders to business elites.

The landholders don't take this lying down, and revolt by May, 1859, aligning themselves with a new triumvirate centred back in Quito, which included Garcia Moreno. President Robles sends General Jose Urbina to quash the rebellion, and he overruns Quito by June, 1859.

Garcia Morena, ousted from Quito, flees to Peru, which is already deeply involved in territorial disputes with Ecuador over the last few years. Peru provides Moreno with weapons and ammunition. Morena believes he has Peru's backing.

Morena then approaches General Franco, the number-three man in Robles's government, trying to enlist him in a coup. Peru makes a better deal with Franco, who signs a secret deal and makes his own play for power, taking over Guayaquil.

With General Franco now in control of Guayaquil, President Robles then moves the capital to Riobamba, handing the government over to a man aptly named Carrion.

Meanwhile, another member of the former Quito triumvirate, Carvajel, invades from Columbia and manages to take over Quito. A local politician named Pinzano establishes yet another government based in Loja, with local support. It's all fun and games when someone loses an eye.

As 1859 draws to a close, Ecuador is divided between four and seven rival warring governments based in Guayaquil, Quito, Riobamba and Lojas, and suffers meddling and invasions of both Peru and Columbia.

Peru is a particularly noxious party, playing all sides against the middle. From 1858 onwards, it claims vast territories of the Ecuador interior and blockades the Ecuador coast, earning first the supplication and then the enmity of the business classes. Slowly Peru's favour slides from the business class towards the landowners and it declares support for Quito, over Guayaquil.

Preparing to invade, Peru proposes that the Ecuadorians form a single coalition government to negotiate an end to the blockade and territorial dispute. Franco in Guayaquil is the first to meet with the Peruvians.

When Moreno, who has more or less been allied with Peru the whole time, finds out that the Peruvians are also negotiating with Franco, he becomes enraged and breaks off relations. This is probably the best thing he could have done.

Franco, meanwhile, is able to get most of the rival governments of Ecuador behind him as he negotiates with the Peruvians. However, they deny him authority to negotiate away any territory or sovereignty.

The Peruvians land an army, Franco ends up signing a treaty doing exactly what he was forbidden to do.

In the end, this is a disastrous move, uniting all his rivals against him. Garcia Moreno eventually comes out on top, pushing out the Peruvians, overthrowing Franco, tearing up the treaty and uniting Ecuador under his rule. Nationalism, particularly anti-Peruvian nationalism, is Ecuador's first great unifying force.

This sets the stage for what becomes known as Ecuador's Conservative period. A country transitioning from feudalism and landed elites to neocolonialism and business elites, is now ruled by a son of that landed elite. Moreno is a man committed to tradition, fighting the future bitterly every step of the way, ruling with an iron fist from 1860 to 1875. In such a polarized society, it is no surprise that he will die violently, hacked to death on the steps of the Legislature, with dark rumours of conspiracy swirling around.

But Moreno is a man fighting the tides of history and economics. The result is no end of bitterness. Ecuador is a society without compromise. On the one hand, there is Moreno, and behind him, the landholders, highlands and the church, clinging ferociously to power, preserving their entitlements at all costs. On the other hand, there are the liberals of the coast and the business classes, steadily growing richer, Ecuador's economy shifting to cash crops and exports and luxury imports, with demands for infrastructure and education.

During the Moreno era and through the Conservative period, these interests are at war. Ecuador continues to lurch forward awkwardly, Railways and roads are built, schools established, universities reformed, and the army remodeled with Prussian advisors. Conservatives react with social puritanism, brothels are closed, and corruption is purged. During the Conservative period, Ecuador makes the transition to an export-based economy, the liberals steadily eating away at their rivals' power and control.

But the position of the unrepresented classes remains tenuous. The progress which has been made in the 1850s more or less comes to an end by the 1860s. Given the tensions between Liberals and Conservatives, and the slow but bitter shifting of power, neither class can really afford to truly alienate the disenfranchised constituencies. Nevertheless, there are Indigenous revolts in the interior in 1871 and 1884, driven by pressure from landholders, expansion of cacao plantations, the steady infiltration of a cash economy, regional recessions and fluctuations in cacao prices.

What keeps things together, though, is prosperity. Ecuador's economy continually expands, cacao production increases steadily, exports increase dramatically, money flows in. With that money comes a flood of imports and luxury goods. A rising tide floats all boats, and everyone, even the landholders, the poor, the peasantry and the Indigenous benefit, though not quite to the extent of the business classes.

This is the world that Neptali Bonifaz is born into in 1870, a nation riven with tensions, papered over with prosperity. Bonifaz himself is utterly unrelated to the Corsican Bonaparte clan. That would be a little white lie a man named Velasco tells to Adolph Hitler on the spur of the moment. Bonifaz is born in Quito in 1870 to an Ecuadoran mother, and a father who is a Peruvian diplomat; he is clearly a member of the Latin American conservative classes.

From 1879 to 1883, the War of the Pacific between Chile, Peru and Bolivia prove a boon to Ecuador. For one thing, it completely diverts Peru's attention, giving Ecuador a period of stability and freedom from meddling and border tensions. Further, the war means the diversion of trade, with Guayaquil the only significant port on the Andean coast not belonging to a warring party.

It is around this time that Neptali Bonifaz has the falling out with his father, which drives him to embrace radical Ecuadoran nationalism and renounce his Peruvian heritage. The conflict passes, the two men reconcile, and Bonifaz's life continues along its normal track, punctuated only by bouts of loud and sentimental nationalist activism.

By 1895, though, the tenuous balance that sustains Ecuador's society fails. The Conservative Era ends with a series of military rebellions and a scandal over 'selling the flag' – an incident where Chile bribes Ecuadorian officials to put their flag a Chilean warship so Chile can sell it quietly to Japan. The government falls and

Ecuador undergoes a period of chauvinistic nationalism, with Bonifaz in the thick of it.

From 1895, through 1920, the Liberals are firmly in control, and Guayaquil dominates the nation. The railroad from Guayaquil to Quito is finally completed. The legal underpinnings of debt peonage and the semi-feudal system of the highlands are swept away, in an effort to weaken the landowners. The church is stripped of power and privileges, eventually losing its lands and forced from the political sphere.

These initiatives are not accepted lying down. In 1895-96, there is a bloody civil war as church leaders incite followers to rise up against atheists. God turns out not to be on their side. The church is forced to accept a substantial loss of political power and influence, and is pushed almost entirely out of the political mainstream, leaving them to ally more closely with the landholders.

The business interests, or Agro-Mercantile elites, however, are no better friends of democracy than the landholders. Most of their moves are aimed at undermining the power of their rival elite. Ecuador continues to suffer coups and takeovers any time occasional efforts at democracy produce the wrong result. The Indigenous of the interior are disenfranchised, of course, but are left alone. The peasants of the highlands find their condition improved at the expense of the landholders, but only as a means of weakening those landholders. On the other hand, the poor and the workers of the coasts remain poor and marginalized. Again, prosperity papers over the cracks for them, but the seeds of socialism, anarchism and Marxism begin to sprout.

During this period, a decades-long effort to resolve the Peruvian border eventually drifts to failure under the Conservatives by 1890. On the other hand, negotiations between Ecuador and Columbia finally produce a treaty resolving border disputes by 1916. This is the same treaty that will be the seed of later disaster. Border disputes are of little interest to a commercial aristocracy, and are only causes for the nationalist elements of Ecuador when it is convenient for the elites to wave the flag. Anti-Peruvian sentiment is occasionally stoked by remembrance of the abortive invasion and General Franco's traitorous treaty.

Real power in this period inevitably drifts into the hands of a coalition of business and banking interests known as 'la Argolla' (the 'ring'). Through wealth, business deals and loans, these interests work together to control both Ecuadoran business and politics. No politician can succeed without their support, every politician curries their favour. Their loans to the government guarantee influence, which they use to loot the treasury. And of course, they pay their debts by printing their own money. It can only last so long.

****

Ecuador - 1918 to 1929, a decade of turmoil

1918 marks the beginning of the end of Ecuador's tenuous period of stability. Ecuadorian society has never resolved its conflicts, not really. It has gotten by for a long time by ignoring them, using ongoing prosperity to maintain social peace. That is only going to last as long as the money lasts.

Ecuador has been very lucky. Very, very lucky. Throughout the 19th and early 20th century, demand and prices for its main cash crop, cacao, has increased steadily and remains high. Ecuador benefits from the demand and dislocations of the War of the Pacific, remains out of trouble, and prospers during World War One.

But then, in the 1920s, a whole bunch of things start going wrong. The end of WWI produces a worldwide recession, resulting in a decline of both price and volume of cacao sales. To make matters worse, British colonies in Africa begin to grow and export cacao, leaving the Ecuadorans with new and fierce competition. A few years in, new plant blights and diseases strike the cacao plants, further undermining production.

Times are tough for La Argolla. They respond in two ways:

One is by printing more money. Luckily for them, in that era, banks can print their own money. This leads to a wave of hyperinflation.

The other response is to tighten their belts, reducing outlays and demanding increased contributions and taxes from other constituencies. Unfortunately, tightening the belts for the business class means a giant 'screw you' to all the other social classes and constituencies, some already utterly destitute. That doesn't go over well.

The first sign of things going badly is in March of 1920: New agricultural taxes lead to uprisings in Cuenca. Shortly after, in May 1920, revolts against taxes in Chimborazo leave fifty Indigenous dead. A few months later, in August 24, 1920, there is another uprising in Ricaurte against taxes. In a period of recession and hyperinflation, taxes are unaffordable. Unfortunately, the government sees its best options as raising taxes and extending its tax base to previously marginal groups. The result is conflict. May 1921, yet another uprising at Guano, Chimborazo.

In 1922 Juan Manuel Lasso Ascásubi attempts to launch a socialist revolution from the Guachalá hacienda in Cayambe. It is brutally suppressed, but it and previous uprising mark the growing discontent and political agitation of the Indigenous. Excluded from the political process, they make themselves felt through uprisings, demonstrations and direct appeals, which are mostly squashed or ignored.

Socialism and anarchism bursts into full flower. Urban workers have never been in a good position. Population from the countryside tends to flow to the cities. But the cities lack an industrial base, simply being focused on export of cacao beans with little refinement. What little industrial and economic activity occurring is primarily shipping and domestic production. The result is a perpetual labour surplus, leading to most employment being day labour, no job security, low wages and poor conditions. As long as times are good, one can make a living. In bad times, periods of unemployment, recession, hyperinflation, the conditions are brutal.

The recession following World War One is especially brutal. Workers begin to organize. Railroad workers, a skilled and semi-skilled class, organize a strike which spreads. Soon the railroad strike becomes a general strike paralysing the city of Guayaquil.

The government calls out the police and army. November 15, 1922, police forces massacre as many as a thousand striking workers in Guayaquil. The scale of fatalities is astonishing. A thousand people in a country which at the time sports barely a million and a half people.

As appalling as the numbers are, the ferocity and ruthlessness of the massacre is chilling. Unarmed strikers are literally herded up against walls or into alleys and shot. From the balconies and upper floors of houses, the business elites and middle classes open fire, murdering fleeing workers as casually as hunters at a turkey shoot. The back of organized labour is broken. The situation of workers remains bad and continues to get worse, leaving a perpetually angry and discontent underclass.

The massacre does not bring social peace. In September 13, 1923, the army kills thirty-seven Indigenous on the Leito hacienda in Tungurahua. A few years later in 1925, there is another uprising in Azuay. In January, 1926, the Peasant Workers Syndicate of Juan Montalvo, the first peasant-Indigenous organization in Ecuador, leads an uprising at Changalá hacienda in Cayambe over land tenure.

Liberalism in Ecuador, rule by the agro-mercantile commercial business elite of the coasts, spends the 1920s failing. A social consensus built on prosperity is falling to pieces, and so is the country.

In July 1925, the army steps in, led by a group called the 'League of Young Officers' throwing out a particularly corrupt and ineffectual government in a bloodless coup. The Ecuadoran middle class is finally making its play for power. Up to this time, Ecuador's economy has never supported a large or politically active middle class. Mostly, the middle class has provided the backbone of the army and business and government bureaucracies, and it has thrown its minimal political support to whoever it has been closest to. The ongoing crises have pushed the middle class up against the wall. Now, through the army, it is pushing back.

The junta of the 'League of Young Officers' gives way in 1926 to a civilian government under Isidro Ayora, who then sets out to reform Ecuadoran society. Ayora invites an American advisor, Edwin Kemmerer from Princeton to come in and reorganize Ecuadoran government and infrastructure. With Kemmerer's assistance government departments are reorganized, a central bank is established and given control of monetary policy. Technocratic reorganization flushes out the corruption that has become ingrained under la Argolla. The result is a windfall of government revenues. A windfall which surges forward under recovering cacao prices (by 1928 cacao export revenues is up to 15 million dollars) and a reviving export boom.

Neptali Bonifaz, by this time a successful landowner and nationalist, is a part of this movement. The landowners have traditionally been a reactionary lot, emphasizing personal virtue and incorruptibility. Bonifaz has truckled at the institutionalized corruption of La Argolla. Now he steps forward to head the Central Bank, making him a key figure in the success of Ayora's reforms.

Good times are back, and with good times come a period of social peace. The Ayora government enacts a series of progressive social reforms, including civil service pensions and worker protections. Once again, the rising tide is floating all boats. Despite this, the spoils of reform and prosperity are uneven. Once again, the Indigenous see little of it. The working and urban classes remain destitute. Awash in money, most of it goes to luxury and excess, as Ecuador's middle and elite classes gorge themselves on imported goods or travel abroad.

Unfortunately for Ayora, the stock market crash of 1929 is just around the corner.

Ecuador - The Great Depression and Despair

Ecuador's economy and society has always been tied to the outside world. It has been lucky for a long time. That streak has come to an end.

With the great depression, the whole world has gone into the toilet. For Ecuador, the bottom drops out completely. In 1928, cacao exports amount to 15 million dollars. By 1932 it falls to 7 million. By 1933, it is down to 5 million. Exports are below the levels of 1850.

With the collapse of the cacao market goes government revenues. Without government revenues to support social programs, without a viable economy, the tenuous consensus and social peace is gone.

The middle class as represented by Arroyo has failed. The business elites represented by the liberals are discredited. The landowners have no solutions. The underclasses are cut adrift and on their own.

This is a recipe for instability. Any group might try for power. But no social or economic class can marshal the support to hold it. In 1931, Ecuador is a country for which every solution has failed. It is a country ripe for a fascist movement.

August, 1931

Colonel Luis Larrea Alba leads a bloodless military coup against the Isidro Ayora government.

Colonel Alba may have been a member of the League of Young Officers of 1926, but he has never supported the technocratic approach of the Ayora government. Born 1895, and 36 years old by this time, Alba has come from the middle class, which has gone on to form the core of bureaucracy, business and officer corps. Photographs of him from the time show a handsome, thoughtful young man, his clean-shaven features serious and reflective.

But Alba is a little bit more thoughtful than his peers. Witness to the social upheavals of the 1920's, he is perceptive enough to recognize the underlying causes and even have some sympathy for the underclasses driven by them. From his vantage point, Alba perceives the schisms running through Ecuador's society. Alba is far more a leftist than the Ayora group, his views verging almost on socialism.

More than anything though, Alba is a professional. He takes military matters seriously as a calling, studies the art of war, publishes academic papers and even teaches. His views and approach to politics are defined by the history and traditions of the Ecuadoran military.

With the clear failure of the Ayora government brought on by the depression, Alba acts, sweeping aside Ayora and seizing the reins of power on August 25, 1931.

At which point, he discovers that it just isn't that easy.

You need money to be a socialist. The Ecuadoran economy is in free fall, and the government is broke. This isn't a matter of simply retuning and reforming as Ayora had done; the cupboard is bare. There are no resources, nothing to retune or reform.

To make matters worse, Colonel Alba finds himself without support. Too far to the left, neither the landowning elite of the highlands nor the business elite of the coasts are prepared to accept him. He is a bit too radical even for the middle class. And he has insufficient connection to the workers, the peasantry or the Indigenous to rely upon them - these groups, subject to too many army massacres, are wary.

Under other circumstances, he might succeed. But between a rock and a hard place, he has no choice, and he is smart enough to realize that.

By October, Colonel Alba prepares to hand power back to a civilian government and calls an election, the most important election of Ecuador's history...

The Rise of Fascism in Ecuador

The thing you have to understand about fascism is that it isn't an ideology at all.

It's theater.

It's all about dressing up and marching around and shouting in unison. It's about being mad as hell and not taking it, whatever it is, any more. It's about right and wrong, traditional virtues, manly men, womanly women, nervous but alluring sheep. It's simple solutions to a complicated world, the innate superiority of tribe, and fixing the world with a sock to the jaw of some craven Jew/Marxist/Indigenous/etc.

Fascist ideology is almost always a contradiction in terms. What a fascist believes, what a fascist does is self-serving and fluid, fitting the needs of the moment.

There is no real theory. Theory is for eggheads sitting in their ivory towers, contemplating the world, passively studying and forming theories.

Well, while the eggheads sit there and study, the Fascists are about action. They go out and act, and let the eggheads study that. And while the eggheads study, they act again.

Fascism is not about thinking, it is about acting. It is not about reflection or ideology or theory, it is about passion.

It's about the belief in will. Translated plainly, Fascism is all about how, if you believe hard enough, or wish hard enough, then something is becomes true, reality is overcome. Fascism is about force of will overcoming all odds – not force of thinking, not force of planning, just sheer will. Fascists believe that if you clap your hands hard enough, fairies will come alive. Making sense is for weaklings. The true fascist hero doesn't care whether something actually makes sense, his indomitable 'will' can force it to make sense.

It's all nonsense, of course. But Fascism has the advantage of looking good with all its shouting and bluster and appeals to blood and virtue.

Of course, this lack of actual ideas or ideology makes Fascism nicely protean. Mussolini starts off as a socialist. Hitler as a crank. Businessmen, landowners, union leaders, journalists, peasants and workers could all find a home in Fascism's big tent. Fascists can speak the language of socialism, cry for the plight of workers and peasants, and do business with businessmen.

Of course, all that tends not to survive a really hard look. Contradictions would start to pop up everywhere, and incompatible goals and constituencies would inevitably mean that in that big tent, more and more people get the crap end of the stick. The tent would fall in. You could postpone that for a while by lying nonstop. And you can keep the illusion of solidarity by attacking and purging the people who stepped out of line. Sooner or later though, it will all fall apart.

But the depression offers a unique opportunity. Fascism works best on an empty playing field; one where traditional parties and traditional solutions have failed. And the depression is just one big long tall drink of failure. Liberalism, conservatism, liberal democracy, traditional dictatorships, technocracy and feudalism, in a worldwide economic collapse, all of the rival parties and factions are discredited, heaped on the bonfire of failure, their solutions and their ideals exploded. They are all empty suits waiting to be swept away.

In this sort of environment ideologies like Communism and Anarchism gain terrifying power. But these ideologies preach radical reform, not simply upsetting what was left of the apple cart, but throwing it away entirely. These are divisive ideologies, throwing whole social classes on the bonfire.

As a rival to Communism, Fascism offers a bigger tent, more familiarity and stability and the allure of emotional resonance: Storm and blood, virtue, marching and shouting; as opposed to dry dialectics and economic theory.

Axis of Andes – Page 34

So too in Ecuador, we have fascism with the rise of a movement called the National Compact, also known as the Dirty Shirts.

Dirty Shirts? Well, what can we say? Shirts are big in fascism. Shirts are sort of like a uniform, but relatively cheap and easy to procure and wear. Mussolini starts it off with his fascist black shirts, Hitler follows up with brown shirts. Before you know it, in other countries people were marching around as silver shirts, grey shirts, etc., so on down to the 'dirty shirts.'

The National Compact is bankrolled by the Latifundistas, the big landowners of the Sierra. But it is a mistake to see the National Compact as only a tool of the landowners. The Latifundista have seen nearly fifty years of steady decline of power and influence. Although still entrenched, one lesson that they'd clearly learned was that their brand isn't selling.

The path to power is to buy in. The National Compact, as with fascist movements everywhere, is a big tent attracting the angry and the dispossessed, be they peasants and squatters, urban poor, workers and skilled tradesmen and even middle classes. The Latifundistas find their money is welcome.

For a leader going into the 1931 election, the National Compact found... Neptali Bonifaz.

Bonifaz in photographs comes across as a stern but kindly old gentleman. Spare and well groomed, he's the image of genteel aristocracy. In 1931, he is sixty-one years old. He doesn't look like a shouter, and he probably isn't, which makes him an atypical fascist leader.

But Bonifaz has been around for a while. His family were old school landowners, and he is one of the biggest and most progressive. Progressive in the sense of treating plantation agriculture as an organized business undertaking, not necessarily in treating people well.

He has a nasty edge - one of the most famous quotes attributed to him came when a visitor admires his herd of prize horses. He responds that "Each horse is worth twenty Indians." Truthfully, he was a racist regarding the Indigenous, but that's a common attitude back then, particularly among his class.

Bonifaz has the reputation of being a tough old bastard, no nonsense, no bullshit, a damned hard bargainer. He will push your back right up against a wall. But though he drives a hard bargain, he has a reputation for sticking to his word.

And Bonifaz has been around, not just hiding out on his hacienda. In the late 1920s, he steps forward to become the governor of the new Central Bank for the Arroyo administration. He has been a key man in breaking inflation, in the last era of good times the Ecuadorans remember, and he has connections with the technocrats and middle class. Plus he has street cred as a long-time, occasionally radical, Ecuadorian nationalist, even going so far as to diss his father's country, Peru.

His cousin, Ascazubi, founded Ecuador's socialist party and tried to lead an Indigenous uprising. Bonifaz doesn't have much truck with that stuff. But it gives some hope to the destitute and desperate that the old man might somewhere deep down have had a few ideas and sympathies rub off.

So Bonifaz comes forward as the man for all seasons and all times. When the Dirty Shirts march in the streets, it is his name they shout. And when they do the usual fascists tactics, placarding and postering, ranting and demonstrating, vandalizing and harassing, it is on his behalf.

Let's be honest - the political fortunes of the business elite of the coasts, the middle class, the landowning elite, and even the army are shot to pieces. They have all stepped up, had their chance and failed spectacularly. The old rules have failed utterly; the ruling coalition and their backers have failed. The field is wide open.

Come the elections of the 20th and 21st of October 1931, perhaps the first genuinely free elections in Ecuadoran history, Neptalí Bonifaz Ascazubi is elected as President of Ecuador. He is elected by an overwhelming margin, winning 36,000 votes, more than his two rivals, Larrea with 18,000 votes and Modesto, with 14,000, combined. (68,000 votes in a country with 1.9 million population, perhaps not that free after all.) It was a smashing victory. Satisfied, he returns to his hacienda and waits to be sworn in.

There he waits.

And he waits some more.

The trouble is that Ecuador's constitution gives a great deal of power to the legislature, power to obstruct a President. The National Compact is too radical for the legislature, Bonifaz is popular all sorts of places; but not with the conservative elements of the middle class, or with the business elites of the coasts; and between them they control the legislature. Bonifaz is seen as a reactionary Latifundista in sheep's clothes. They don't like him, they don't want him. So they refuse to appoint him, and so he waits while they debate and argue.

Finally, the argument gains traction that Bonifaz cannot be President because he is not a real Ecuadoran. His father was a Peruvian diplomat, after all. He is only Ecuadoran through his mother.

That argument would have a lot more traction if he'd travelled about on a Peruvian passport, as he might have done if he hadn't had his fight with his father. Or if he hadn't a bit of a history as an Ecuadoran nationalist, also as a result of his rebellion against his father.

But the fact remains, he is only half Ecuadoran and his father is a hated Peruvian, a high ranking one. So while not as good an argument as it might have been, but it was what the Legislature had.

Bonifaz has had enough. He warns from his hacienda that if the legislature doesn't shape up, do its job and confirm his election, "there'll be blood in the streets."

August 20, 1932, Bonifaz is disqualified by the Congress of the Republic by 43 votes against 41, accused of Peruvian nationality. Had he been less of a nationalist, or actually been caught with a Peruvian passport from his youth, the margin might have been bigger, say 46 to 38. But as it is, his Presidency stands on the edge.

Velasco Ibarra is one of his loudest proponents. Velasco is a conservative member of the middle class, his father was an Engineer. Velasco studied in France, went into journalism, and honed his skills as a writer and an orator in books and newspapers. At the age of 38, he is starting out on a brilliant political career. He eloquently argues Bonifaz's nationalist bona fides and his credibility. But of course, at this point, it doesn't change the result.

The National Compact, like most fascist movements, isn't just a political party. It isn't even simply a mass movement. It is those things, but it is also a paramilitary. It is a bunch of guys in homemade uniforms who have been practising marching in formation, shouting and saluting, beating up their enemies, stockpiling weapons, and playing at being an army.

On August 20th, they are not about to take this insult to their leader lying down. They are mad as hell. Finally their movement has won fair and square, they had got something. They are just not going to let failed politicians in Congress take that away.

It is on. They are bringing it.

✳✳✳

August 20, 1932 - Guayaquil, Ecuador

"This is an unexpected visit." Colonel Benigno Flores pours two glasses of wine. His hands are shaking. Outside, far off in the distance, somewhere on the streets of Guayaquil, there is a string of popping sounds, almost like fireworks being let off. But they aren't fireworks, they are gun fire.

Colonel Luis Larrea Alba takes his glass; his hands are steady.

"Something needs to be done," Alba says.

"The orders from on high," Flores says, "are that the army stays out of it. Let the legislature and the old man hash it out for themselves. He's a Peruvian anyway."

"Half Peruvian," Alba says, "but he's been a loyal son of Ecuador. And a good man."

"You called him a Latifundista fossil during the election. You remember the election? How it turned out?"

"Not the way I wanted," Alba replies. "But the people chose, that can't be denied. If we don't respect that choice… what was the point?"

"And what about those thugs marching up and down the street? Those Dirty Shirts? The National Compact, are they good men?"

"Rabble," Alba replies. "But they have cause."

"That cause seems to be civil war," Flores says. "They're rioting, here and in Quito, and in other places. People are pulling out guns and shooting at them. They're shooting back. It's getting ugly. I suggest you stay over for a few days, until we see which way the wind blows. Safer that way."

Alba is thoughtful, staring at his wine.

"You're not thinking of getting involved?" Flores asks.

Alba doesn't reply.

"Jesus Christ!" Flores swears and downs his drink.

"I think," Alba says, "that the high command is wrong. The army can't just sit back and let a civil war happen. If we do, what's the point? What's the point of having an army at all?"

"To defend from foreign invasion," Flores replies, "God forbid. And to give young men like us the opportunity to wear clever uniforms and set young ladies hearts to swoon. Seriously, Luis, let's stay out of this one. You heard that earlier? Those were bullets. We could get killed."

Alba's expression tells him this isn't working.

"All right," Flores says, "forget my joking. Are you seriously thinking of going in on this? You have no authority, and if you do this... after the last time, your career will be over. The Generals, they'll drum you out. You'll have to become a cobbler or something."

Flores is referring to something they both knew well. Alba had led a coup to overthrow the previous government. But governance had been a challenge he neither wanted nor fell suited for. Without a mandate, he'd stepped back, and let a civil government move towards elections.

"I'm aware of the risk," Alba replies.

"Then in God's name why are you thinking this mad folly?"

Alba shrugs.

"I don't know. I think I helped to make this mess, perhaps I have a responsibility."

Flores pours more wine into their glasses.

There is a newspaper on the table. Velasco Ibarra on the front page offers a ringing denunciation of the legislature.

"Assuming you throw in," Flores said, "will it make a difference at all? Or just make it worse?"

Alba shrugs again.

"Who are you going to throw down for? The Legislature or the Old Man, they both have a claim. The Legislature unseated him, you know. Legitimate vote."

"43 to 41," Alba replies. "Two votes. And on false grounds, he's not Peruvian, whatever they say. Their claim there was exaggerated."

Alba taps the newspaper, "Velasco Ibarra makes the case I'm not fond of the Latifundista, they're backwards and a drain on the country. And as you say, the National Compact, they're just rabble, a group of thugs. But come down to it, I will repeat: Bonifaz won the election properly. Why have elections if we can't be bothered to honour them? How can we have any kind of government?"

"You'll be court-martialed," Flores says. "The orders from the Generals are very clear. You only got away by the skin of your teeth last time, and odds are, you'll never rise past Colonel. You already have enough enemies."

Axis of Andes – Page 40

Alba nods.

"I know that."

"Bonifaz," Flores notes, "even if you do this, he won't be your friend. Those tight old bastards in the countryside, you know them as well as I. If you don't have the right bloodline, he won't even look at you. You'll have no friends at all. The Legislature won't forgive you."

"I know that," Alba says.

"Then why?" Flores demands. "Why get involved?"

"Because it's the right thing to do," Alba reples quietly.

The two men stare at each other.

Finally, Flores sighs.

"Well," he says, "let's do it."

***

August 20 - 26, 1932, The Six-Day War

The six-day war is triggered by Neptali Bonifaz's insistence on being seated as President and his rejection of the Legislature's decree removing him from office.

In an attempt to pressure the legislature, the National Compact stages marches in Quito and Guayaquil in support of Bonifaz's presidency. The police in Quito order the crowds to disperse, and when they fail to do so, shots are fired. Unfortunately, several members of the National Compact are also armed and return fire, killing several policemen and forcing the remainder to retreat.

Having been fired upon, and having fired back, the crowd turns into a riot, proceeding on a wave of arson and looting. Meanwhile, news of the police assault and subsequent uprising reach Guayaquil, triggering riots there. Running battles with the police break out. As night falls, both cities descend into anarchy.

In response to the National Compact, several rival political parties organize their own ad hoc militias, loosely allied, and nominally in support of the Legislature. A number of prominent personalities, notably Velasco Ibarra call for peace, but are ignored. Ecuador's Generals find themselves unable to pick a side, and order the army to remain in the barracks.

Bloody fighting rages on between warring factions, with frequent sniper attacks, shootings and bombings. Mounted horsemen attack the poorer sections of Guayaquil. In other sections of the city, armed men patrol rooftops and balconies, shooting at anyone they deem suspicious.

After two days, the Army intervenes spontaneously, lead by Colonel Luis Larrea Alba. Alba at the time is detached and has no troops under his command. But he has previously led the overthrow of the Ayora government the year before, and a number of lower commanders and rank and file look up to him, disregarding orders from more senior officers. Guayaquil is put under martial law and curfew, and a cease-fire is put in place between the National Compact and other factions, although neither would consent to disarming. The military also leave their barracks in Quito, taking control of that city the next day.

Although the intervention is expressly neutral, it is clear that the army, or at least the factions of the army that had left their barracks, favour Bonifaz as the duly elected President.

In a contentious session of the Legislature on August 26, 1932, Velasco Ibarra leads a movement to rescind Bonifaz's disqualification on the grounds that it was based on libel, and wins by 44 to 40. This ends the six-day war, and Bonifaz is subsequently seated.

The outcome of the six-day war is a shift of political power in Ecuador from the legislature to the Presidency, and the beginnings of an informal triumvirate composed of Neptali Bonifaz, Velasco Ibarra and Luis Alba, which will dominate Ecuador for the next decade.

****

Interlude – The History We Know

In our history, Bonifaz never had that critical fight with his father and never dramatically threw Peruvian coins into the Guayaquil harbour. He had even travelled under a Peruvian passport as a youth, before eventually committing to his mother's nationality.

In our history, the objections to Bonifaz's Presidency had a little more currency. His connections to the hated Peruvians are more overt, better documented, the Ecuador legislature voted 46 to 38, a larger margin.

The war breaks out and lasts four days, not six. The army, a bulwark of Ecuadoran nationalisms to come to the rescue of a 'Peruvian' President, declines to participate, and stays in the barracks. As a result, the National Compact and their opponents fight it out in street violence. Eventually, the Legislature's factions win. Bonifaz's Presidency ends without him ever taking office. Ecuador's first honest election is a failure.

The result is chaos. Between 1931 and 1942, Ecuador saw a succession of short-lived governments, marked by coups, juntas, fraudulent elections, and conflicts. In order:

** Colonel Luis Alba overthrows Ayora in a military coup, rules from August to October of 1931.*

** Neptali Bonifaz wins the elections in October of 1931 but is prevented from effectively taking office and 'impeached' in August of 1932, following a four day civil war that kills 4000.*

** During this period, October 1931 to August 1932, Alfredo Moreno acts as President of the Senate and de facto head of government.*

** Liberal candidate Martinez wins fraudulent elections in October of 1932, but the legislature blocks all his appointments, effectively neutering him. He lasts until September of 1933.*

** From October of 1933 to September of 1934, Montalvo is a caretaker president.*

** The next election sweeps Velasco Ibarra into power in October 1934, he does not last a year and is ousted by the military in August 1935.*

** Antonio Pons is acting President, August to September, 1935.*

He is replaced by a junta led by General Benigno Flores in September of 1935.

Federico Paez then rules from 1935 to 1937.

General Alberto Enriquez Gallo overthrows the Paez government and rules from 1937 to 1938.

Manuel Borrero takes power in 1938, but doesn't last the year, 'impeached.'

Aurelio Mosquera takes over, from December 1938 to November, 1939, dying in office. Apparently of natural causes.

Carlos Arroyo manages to rule precariously from 1940 to 1944.

Replaced by Velasco Ibarra, in 1944, who rules for two years until being overthrown.

Basically, there are roughly fourteen Ecuadoran governments in a decade and a half. To make matters worse, the Ecuadoran constitution gives substantial powers to the Legislature to block Executive appointments and policies, further contributing to paralysis.

The depression is hell on wheels, and the frequent changes of government are a symptom of economic instability. But they also rob Ecuador of any hope for any competent or concerted approach and leave the state and economy weak and ineffective.

During the historical Ecuador/Peru war President Arroyo kept his best troops and substantial strength in Quito away from the fighting because he fears his political opponents more than Peruvian invaders. Hardly a ringing endorsement of a functional government.

In short, in our own real history, Ecuador was a basket case of revolving door dictatorships and failed politicians, a state incapable of functioning on anything but the most rudimentary levels.

***

The Colombia-Peru War, 1932-1933

"A war without casualties. Nonsense! My friends, this war has had one great victim, it has made a singular casualty. And that casualty is Ecuador!"

Velasco Ibarra, 1933

The Columbia-Peru war comes hot on the heels of Ecuador's Presidential crisis, and more than anything else shapes the policy and history of the triumvirate.

As we have seen, in 1922, Augusto Leguia, the dictator of Peru negotiated a secret treaty, the Salomon-Lozano Treaty. The treaty provided for, among other things, Columbia's recognition of Peru's territorial claims against Ecuador, and a flanking corridor of land on Ecuador's northern side between the Putumayo and Caqueta rivers. In return, the Peruvians conceded a 'corridor to the Amazon' a thin wedge of land deep in the interior, and the towns of Letitia and Tarapaca.

Letitia and Tarapaca had been settled by Peruvians but claimed by the Colombians. The treaty gives these interior towns to the Colombians. But the population remains mostly Peruvian.

But August 1930, Leguia is overthrown by Lieutenant Colonel Sanchez Cerra. The treaty becomes public for the first time. The Peruvians seeing this as giving away not just land, but their own people, react with outrage and Sanchez Cerra abrogates the treaty.

Also crying betrayal, the Ecuadorians expel the Columbian ambassador and break diplomatic relations. But the weak Aroyo government has neither the motivation nor the ability to do much more about it.

Bad feelings all around, but the Colombians continue to hang on to Letitia and Tarapaca.

There is a lot of uncertain border territory in the rain forests beyond the Andes. It is not well demarcated, but then again, it is thinly populated, inaccessible and of no particular value. So mostly the Latin American governments snip and argue with each other, but don't take it much further.

Really, who wants to go to war over a few acres of jungle? For the next two years after the repudiation of the treaty, nothing much happens.

Until one day on September 1, 1932.

The war starts prosaically enough, with a civilian insurrection in a town called Accedes, deep in the Peruvian rainforest. Sanchez Cerra sends troops to quell the insurrection, and then once that is done... Well, suddenly, he has a real force in the area, and the disputed towns of Letitia and Tarapaca are just down the river. So he sends his forces in, expels Colombian officials and administrators, and interdicts river traffic.

Or perhaps a band of loyal Peruvians invade the town of Letitia, drive out the Colombians and then call for the support of Sanchez Cerra, who send troops in support. It's not entirely clear.

Regardless, Sanchez Cerra looks at the situation with cold, cold eyes. The treaty is defunct; the people in these towns are Peruvian by blood. Colombia has a weak army, no navy and no roads to get into the interior.

So why not?

The Colombian government doesn't respond until September 17, probably because they really donn't want to. These towns are deep in the interior, they are hard to get to, of little value, and fighting a war there, even sending an army down there, is going to be hideously expensive with little benefit.

But the news gets out. Peru has invaded. Columbian river traffic is being molested; suddenly the whole nation is up in arms and the government has no choice but to follow along. By September 19, Columbian newspapers have received 10,000 letters calling for war. The same day thousands of students march for war. The Colombian Senate authorizes ten million dollars for the fight against Peru. The nation is seized by a fit of madness, patriotic fervor running rampant.

By the start of October both countries are gearing up for armed conflict, building up armies, stockpiling weapons and ammunition. The Colombians purchase a fleet of old river ships from Europe, and refurbish a series of passenger planes into a temporary air force.

Then they head downriver. Between waiting for the fleet to arrive, provisioning it, and actually sailing an army down the inland watercourses, they finally reach the Amazon by December, 1932, and are approaching the town of Tarapaca by February of 1933. In one sense, that's remarkably fast, in another, it's slow.

By February 1933, at least three thousand Columbian troops face off against three thousand Peruvian troops on either side of the Putumayo River. On February 14, 1933, the Peruvian air force attempts to bomb the Colombian fleet. But it misses. The next day, the town of Tarapaca falls without resistance, as the Peruvians retreat.

Then, somehow, nothing much happens the two sides continue to build their forces and prepare for the conflict. Until April 30, 1932, when President Sanchez is assassinated while reviewing troops. His successor, within two weeks, calls it all off.

The Salomon-LozanoTreaty is adopted. Everyone kisses and makes up. Medals and parades all around.

And so, we have an almost typical comic-opera war. There's a good chance that no one was unlucky enough to actually be killed. There's lots of flag waving, angry letters, waving fists and patriotic fervor. But somehow the actual forces spend most of their time just finding their way into the theatre. Somehow they manage to avoid actually coming to blows. And then, just as suddenly as it flared up, it was over.

But it didn't have to be that way and very nearly wasn't.

Now, the scary thing here is that the President of Peru, Sanchez Cerra, was a genuine badass. In 1914, he was wounded in five places and lost three fingers during the overthrow of President Billinghurst in one of Peru's coups. The fingers went when he grabbed a firing machine gun by the barrel with his bare hands and turned it on the enemy. That's terrifyingly insane.

In 1921 he was involved in an unsuccessful attempt to overthrow another Peruvian despot and ended up shot, injured, captured and exiled. While in exile, he went abroad; he served with the Spanish Foreign Legion in Morocco, where he was wounded yet again. The Spanish legions in Morocco produced General Francisco Franco and his bunch of hard cases, who would later fight and win the Spanish Civil war with Hitler and Mussolini's help. Sanchez Cerra also served with the Royal Army of Italy in 1925, and took advanced military studies in France in 1926.

As late as March 1932, he responded to an assassination attempt by pulling his own gun and trying to shoot his attacker. Here was a man who took war seriously, who studied it as a vocation, who was fearless and aggressive in battle, who had seen combat again and again and didn't flinch.

Looking at the pictures of Sanchez Cerra, you can tell he's one of those mad bastards who are just going to get thousands of people killed. Everything we know tells us that this man was brewing up a great big kettle of bad news, and everything we know about this guy tells us he wasn't going to hesitate to dish it out.

Make no mistake, even if in hindsight the war is a comic-opera farce, the combatants were deadly serious. By March 1933, the Peruvians were taking delivery of a new fleet of Douglas Aircraft delivered from the United States. This is no pretend air force. On April 30, 1933, when Sanchez was shot, he was reviewing 20,000 new troops recruited for the coming war. Those are serious numbers, those are serious weapons.

So here we have a remarkable point of departure. Because sure as shooting, if Sanchez Cerra had lived, there was going to be a real four-star dust up. The Columbia-Peru war would not have been a month's long tussle in the jungle, but a bloodbath on the order of the Chaco war, a history making, border shaking, nation shaping conflict.

But he dies. So it doesn't happen. Instead, the Colombia-Peru War is just a little footnote, in our history and in this one.

****

September 21, 1931 - Three days before the Inauguration of President Bonifaz
Two Days after Columbia Declares War

It is the week of the swearing-in ceremony, and the three men are meeting for the first time, a meeting full of wariness and trepidation. None of them know each other, though they've known of each other. There might have been moments in the small circles that were Ecuadoran society when they may have encountered each other. Luis Larrea Alba has run the country for a few months, Velasco Ibarra is a famous and well read newspaper columnist, and Bonifaz... Well, Bonifaz has been around a long time; he's been the steward of the central bank. But there is no relationship among them.

So even if they don't know each other, they know of each other and they know a lot about each other. Their reputations precede them into the room. What they do not know, is whether they like each other, whether they can tolerate each other. Instead, their minds are full of doubts, of favours owed, of obligations and where they might lead.

There is an initial wariness. The Patrician is full of old world courtesy and grace. The Politician full of chatty warmth. The Soldier careful and polite. Conversation moves awkwardly, with a strangely ungainly quality. At the end of the meeting, none of the men can honestly admit to liking the others.

But strangely, they find that they can work together.

"So, what of Peru's invasion of Columbia?" Velasco Ibarra brings the subject up.

Since September 17, it has occupied the front pages of newspapers all over Latin America. The whole continent is buzzing. The Bonifaz crisis, the six-day war, this is all forgotten. The coming inauguration barely rates a mention. Velasco himself has written of it in a storming editorial.

"Shocking," Bonifaz agrees politely. "Absolutely shocking."

"What should our position be?" Velasco persists.

"We have no love for either side," Luis Larrea Alba points out. "The Colombians' bargain with Peru was a betrayal. They surrendered our territory to the Peruvians? Let them deal with the consequences of their own dishonesty."

"Still," Velasco persists, "Peru is clearly the aggressor. We must choose a side. We must support the Colombians."

"Do you mean go to war?" Luis Alba asks incredulously. "We're not prepared to go to war. We don't have the troops, we don't have the weapons, we don't have the money."

"Obviously," Bonifaz agrees, "war is out of the question. We cannot take sides."

"But your Excellency," Velasco says, "not to take a side is indeed to take a side. To stay silent on a matter of naked aggression by Peru is to countenance it!"

"There's truth in that," Bonifaz admits.

"There is also your own situation," Velasco presses. "It would not be good, given your ... lineage, to be seen siding with Peru. It would raise... questions."

Bonifaz leans back in his seat, staring hard at Ibarra, wondering whether he should be offended.

"You mean because my father was from Peru, people might question my loyalty to Ecuador?" he asks. There's a harsh flat edge to his tone.

"People have," Velasco replies bluntly.

Bonifaz wrestles with his anger. The man before him defended him in the newspapers. He's not accusing him, he's counselling him about accusers. He nods slowly.

"So," he says after thinking it over, "I cannot afford to be seen as to sympathetic to them. Yes, I see your point."

Bonifaz turns to the soldier.

"Luis," he says, "I'd have your opinion. Am I too sympathetic to Peru?"

Alba regards them levelly.

"If you were," he says carefully, "then you would not be President today. And if you are? You will not be President next week."

"Bluntly put," Bonifaz says curtly. Perhaps too blunt. He's not sure he likes this man, Alba.

"My apologies, Excellency."

"No apologies necessary," Bonifaz replies, "I value plain speech. I must go hard against Peru, or my enemies will undermine me. This seems plain."

The other men agree.

"It's not hard in this case," Alba says, "Peru's conduct is criminal. It's naked aggression."

"Will the Colombians win?" Bonifaz asks.

"Too early to tell," Alba says. "They're at a disadvantage. They have no river navy, no paths. They've got their work cut out even to get down there. But their war fever is up, that counts for something."

"And if Peru wins?"

"Bad for us," Velasco replies. "We have our own border disputes with them. If they attack Colombia like this and win, then we will be next. Both virtue and self-interest demands we side with them."

"But our friend Luis there says we cannot join the fight."

"There's other ways," Alba offers. "We can levy a volunteer brigade. We can announce our support and friendship. There are measures."

"As long as we do not commit troops or money?" Bonifaz asks smiling. It's a difficult discussion, and he's still not sure of either, but he appreciates smart men who can have hard conversations. City folk are too often weak.

"We have more of a border with Peru than they do with the Colombians. We may end up fighting Peru first," Alba notes. "If they become too upset with us."

"Really," Bonifaz asks. "Do you think they'd really attack?"

Alba almost chooses to say nothing, he looks thoughtful. "They just did."

***

Ecuador and the Peru-Colombian War

Neptali Bonifaz's first public speech following his inauguration is a ringing denunciation of Peruvian aggression. Within a week, the Peruvian ambassador has left, and Ecuador has broken off diplomatic relations.

Velasco Ibarra announces the formation of a volunteer brigade to fight on the Colombians' side. The Ecuadoran government charters a ship to ferry them to Bogota where they are met by a parade. Ibarra accompanies the brigade on a diplomatic mission, and spends weeks giving speeches, inspecting Colombian war preparations, and quietly negotiating a diplomatic alliance between the two nations.

Returning home, Ibarra leads huge anti-Peruvian rallies in Quito and Guayaquil. The National Compact marches in the streets, saluting Bonifaz's portrait, swearing oaths to defend the sacred soil of Ecuador with their last drops of blood, boasting of forming new volunteer brigades to travel to Bogota when the call comes. Some brag that their volunteer brigades will travel to Lima instead.

Luis Alba, in the meantime, looks to the state of Ecuador's army, and makes careful assessments of the relative strength of the warring parties. Ibarra's reports, the glowing commentaries of a non-military man, are dismissed. But from other sources, Alba charts the progress of Colombia's river fleet. Sanchez Cerra's military build-up in Peru is also observed with disquiet.

Between October and January, the war on their borders creates a kind of holiday for the triumvirate. Ecuadorians have found something that brings them together. A common ground emerges.

The poor remain poor, the working class discontent, the Latifundistas and the agro-mercantile interests in a state of cold war. But everyone it seems can agree on the Peruvian menace, on the justice of the Colombian cause, on the threat on the southern border and on the sanctity of the Ecuadoran nation.

Within that common ground of nationalism, the triumvirate finds the room to negotiate social compromises, buying a measure of peace between business classes and Latifundista, trading for respect for the Latifundista entitlements, quieting the socialists in exchange for slightly more support for the workers.

Neptali Bonifaz, a man whose position was so tenuous that Congress had twice split almost down the middle, for and against him, a man whose election has provoked a civil war, has stumbled upon a winning formula, a way to keep the country together, or at least to keep his enemies at bay and maintain himself in power.

Ecuador is a fractured society. Wealth and prosperity could paper over the cracks. But wealth and prosperity have fled. The new unifying force is a national enemy; it is fear. And it works.

From this point on, every time troubles come, a crop blight, a drop in cacao prices, labor unrest, the Peruvian bogeyman is dragged out.

****

May 21, 1933. End of the Columbia-Peru War

"The fucking Colombians," Velasco rants, "They've sold us out again!"

"At least that madman Sanchez is gone," Alba says easily, "the war is over."

"Their war is over. But our war has been sealed. They've left us on the chopping block. The damnable treaty, that treasonous treaty has been adopted. They recognize Peru's claims against us? Infamous!"

"But at least," Bonifaz points out, "the war is over. And with almost no bloodshed. That should count for something."

"Well," replies Alba. "It's good that the war did not escalate to a full-blown conflict. We would have been a gnat caught between two elephants."

Alba pauses, considering his metaphor.

"Or like Belgium caught between France and Germany in their last war. Had Peru militarized fully and committed to war, there would have been a good chance that we would have been overrun. Or at least, that the Peruvians would have acted to occupy disputed territories."

"It's well then," Bonifaz says, "for the time being. What of the future?"

"The future-" Velasco begins.

"Hush, Ibarra," Bonifaz says. "We know your opinion. I want to hear the assessment of a military man."

"My assessment?" Alba asks.

The two men nod.

Alba rubs his chin thoughtfully.

"Not good. The Columbian concession of the Putumayo in the north means that the Columbians surround us on three quarters of our border, to our south, east and north. Our nation is two million souls and poor. Theirs is six million and rich. They have modernized their army, purchased aircraft, increased their forces by at least 20,000 men. We could not fight them now and win."

"You see!" Velasco begins again.

Alba puts up his hand, interrupting. "They will not fight us now. You see how quick they were to make peace after Sanchez was killed? They do not have the spirit for it, not at the moment."

Bonifaz gives the matter a little more thought.

"The Colombians got the treaty they made, and they got to keep what Peru wanted to take away. It seems to me it can't be said that they lost," he says thoughtfully. "Peru came away with nothing. That concerns me, my friends. The Peruvians are a proud people, they do not take defeat well, and it seems to me that with the Pacific War and the War of the Confederation, the Mapuches, they have been served generous helpings of that meal. Sooner or later, they'll spoil for a fight and be bent on winning. I know them, that's how they are."

Alba and Ibarra glance at each other, acknowledging the older man's tacit admission of his father's heritage. The senior Bonifaz had been a Peruvian diplomat.

"One of the things," Bonifaz says carefully, "which has kept the peace is the balance of powers. No nation is willing to see another become too strong at the expense of its neighbors, lest they become the next victim. In the past, we could rely upon Colombia's support against Peru...Now?"

"Now, they have thrown us to the wolves," he continues. "They have recognized Peru's claims against us. They have essentially promised to take no action, to sit and watch, if the Peruvians invade and steal over half our territory."

"Your diplomatic mission." Bonifaz looks to Velasco. There is a hint of disappointment. "We had hoped it would be more fruitful."

Velasco had spent a month in Bogota, speaking passionately to anyone who would listen about the vital need to repudiate the Salomon-Lozano treaty entirely. The Colombians had been receptive and engaging, everyone had agreed passionately with the justice of his cause. But in the end, they reaffirmed the treaty anyway. He takes it as a bitter humiliation. He no longer trusts the Colombians.

"No. They got what they wanted, and all they had to do was bargain us away. They have made invasion inevitable."

Bonifaz nods.

"What of you, Luis, do you believe that war is inevitable?"

The young soldier considers the matter and then nods carefully. "I do. Not at the moment, perhaps. But sooner or later, it will come."

Bonifaz nods again. "Then we are as one. The question: What can we do?"

Axis of Andes – Page 57

Ecuador and Peru - The Disputed Territories

At issue is the vast interior region of Ecuador, called the Orientale, a thinly populated jungle and rain-forest zone traversable only by rivers. With the endorsement of the Salomon-Lozano Treaty, in which Columbia recognized Peru's claims to Ecuadorian territory, the last major obstacle to Peru has vanished.

The territory in dispute comprises between 40% and 65% of the total land area of Ecuador. That it is thinly populated, almost empty, inaccessible and valueless does not matter. The fact that exploiting it would require greater resources than Ecuador can muster is irrelevant. It is still part of the lands of Ecuador.

This is certainly the way that Ecuador's triumvirate views things. The notion of surrendering or negotiating the territory is never seriously considered. Given the relative inequalities between the two countries, such a negotiation would be one-sided, with the Peruvians bargaining for what they know they can take.

The triumvirate view war as all but inevitable. This comes to underlie every aspect of both foreign and domestic policy.

Latin America and the Great Depression, 1929-1942, Case Studies. Cambridge Press

Like most other Latin American economies, Ecuador, which had moved smoothly from pseudo-feudalism to neo-colonialism, was ill prepared for the Great Depression which began with the American stock market crash of 1929.

Ecuador's economy was based almost entirely on the export of a principal cash crop, in this case a luxury item, cacao, and the import of key products and luxury goods. Ecuador's economy was relatively unindustrialized, with only scattered local or indigenous manufacturing for portions of a small domestic market. Its chief strength, in terms of the depression, was the resilience of widespread and deeply rooted local subsistence economies which allowed many rural peoples to maintain diets and standards of living in the face of collapse.

The Ayora Regime, with its technocratic policies of reform and reorganization, was ineffective in the face of a contraction of the worldwide economy. Fundamentally conservative, the collapse of government revenues meant a retreat of government programs and functions. The Ayora regime thus committed to doing less and less because of financial restraint and budget balancing, at a time when more and more was being required of it.

One can have some sympathy for the Ayora regime. Not only was the necessary response completely beyond their ability to conceive, but it was essentially beyond their ability to implement in any case. Even with full scale implementation of Keynesian economics, a relatively tiny economy like Ecuador was not going to make a significant impact.

One of the first and most unremarked aspects of the Bonifaz regime's economic policies were stability. At first this seems counterintuitive, as Bonifaz's approach to depression conditions was evolving, erratic and at times frankly experimental. But the fact remained that between 1933 and 1944, Ecuador remained under a single coherent government under Bonifaz, which had the luxury to formulate and implement long term policies, and to maintain those policies for extended periods of time.

In contrast, other Latin American regimes which responded to the depression with a series of short- lived governments did far worse. Short-lived governments found it almost impossible to plan or evaluate, they had difficulty developing policies and programs, and what they did attempt was often undermined or entirely abandoned by radical changes of direction or political disagreement by succeeding regimes. Even successful programs were readily abandoned by succeeding governments for ideological or political reasons. As a result, transient short-term governments were completely ineffective in coping with the depression.

Long-lasting governments, while not wholly successful, at least had the luxury to study, experiment and evolve effective policies, and the potential longevity to maintain those policies. For this reason, Ecuador was among the most successful Latin American states of its size and population.

As with other states, the Bonifaz government experimented with a fairly non-ideological grab bag of measures to combat the depression, with varying levels of success. Bonifaz himself was a technocrat and traditional landowner of conservative bent. After Bonifaz, the principal members of the Ecuador triumvirate were a middle class populist and a socialist military officer.

The landowner class, for much of Ecuador's history, were opposed to the coastal business elites who, had over the preceding century, come to dominate Ecuador. With the depression, that business elite lost much of its influence and, for the first time, found itself out of power in Ecuador. Nevertheless, the business class was essential to the economic lifeblood of the country, and the truth of the Bonifaz government was that while it appeared outwardly powerful, it had come into power by the narrowest of margins and survived on a knife edge. It was, after all, a government in the midst of a worldwide depression in a fractured society, and to its credit, it never forgot that.

Governance therefore represented a continuing negotiation and compromise between the interests and wishes of a powerful but out of power business class, and other constituencies and communities within Ecuador. A variety of initiatives were employed, four of which were of particular significance.

The Government took over and centralized cacao marketing in an effort to stabilize cacao price fluctuations. This was driven by a coalition of socialists and landowners, eventually co-opting business interests with a public/private marketing corporation. Among other effects, this allowed the Ecuador government to stockpile cacao surpluses, the sale of which eventually provided a revenue stream during the war years.

Import substitution: Attempting to replace imports with domestic manufactures was a common theme for small and medium sized nations attempting to cope with the depression. Overall, the record of such efforts was usually spotty, and import substitution measures were often counterproductive, as domestic substitutes were often more costly and inferior to imports. Purchasing preferences generally continued to favor imports over domestics. In the long run, import substitution efforts reduced international trade and tended to contribute to the depression.

In Ecuador's case, import substitution worked better than usual, in part because Ecuador's reliance on imports as a neo-colonial economy was excessive, and in part because substitution was not simply an economic policy, but a social policy driven by neo-fascist ideology. Local purchasing was not merely an economic decision, but a nationalist political statement in a society which mandated such statements.

Import substitution measures had a collateral effect during the war years in providing Ecuador with the rudiments of a diversified and industrialized economy, which was able to sustain a war effort to a far greater degree and longer period than one might initially have thought.

Military Keynesianism was another common Latin American initiative. A number of South American states attempted to cope with the depression with military spending. Such spending was often controversial in times of economic reversal, particularly given the military propensity for becoming involved in politics. Latin countries walked a tightrope: Both too little and too much military spending could be dangerous to political stability.

Nevertheless, several countries spent significantly in this area. Peru was notable among these, spending extensively to modernize and upgrade the army, policies that were initiated by President Sanchez before his assassination, but which continued after his death throughout the depression.

In part, driven by continually fanning fears of Peruvian aggression, Ecuador's triumvirate was able to justify and sustain a far greater degree of military spending than would otherwise have been possible. In some ways, Ecuador, with its decidedly fascistic government, came closest to the universal conscription and armament policies of late 19th century European states, although financial limitations constrained this.

Related somewhat to military Keynesian was a variety of infrastructure and economic development projects, ranging from infrastructure commitments to roads, hydro-electric dams, and small business financing and state-driven contracts. Other economic development activities included government sponsored chocolate processing and manufacture, in an attempt to move to value-added refining, and economic partnerships with Henry Ford to attempt to develop a Latin American based truck and auto manufacturing operation, an effort between 1937 and 1940, that was at best only partly successful. At the same time, there were a number of labor protection measures, including working hours and safe conditions, which were acquiesced to by the business community in return for a quiescent labor force and prohibition of unions.

The economic reforms and initiatives did not happen overnight, nor was the path smooth. The Cacao Marketing Corporation came about during a crisis, and even then, it did not command a significant enough market share internationally to fully shield against price fluctuations.

Military spending was erratic, and often a response to transient events and conflicts, frequently taking place outside normal budgeting. Many initiatives were tried often on an erratic basis, and there were frequent reversals, although progress was overall forward. Government expenditures continually outstripped revenues, resulting in inflation and accumulating foreign debt. And of course, no matter what it did, Ecuador could not fully escape the depression which had the whole world in its grip.

Nevertheless, the Bonifaz regime managed to cope with the depression as or more effectively than most of its peers. By 1940, Ecuador was being touted as one of the most robust economies in the region. But there were downsides…

■■■

***

■■■

BOOK OF CHACO

Quito, Ecuadador, July, 1933

"What is the latest?" President Bonifaz asks.

Ibarra and Alba have returned from their latest diplomatic mission to Columbia.

"Mixed results," Alba replies, equably.

"Worse than useless," Ibarra snaps.

"That's quite a disagreement."

Colonel Alba shrugs.

"In terms of trade, in terms of border issues, construction, in a number of respects it went well. The Colombians are accommodating."

"In terms of Peru," Ibarra says, "nothing at all. They were happy to come forth with all the right platitudes, but when it comes down to it, they'll stand by and watch the Peruvians devour us. They won't lift a finger."

Bonifaz nods. "Did you expect anything different?"

Ibarra curses.

"Luis?"

"I concur," Colonel Alba says, "the Colombians speak smoothly. And I have no doubt that they would act if Peru attempted to take all of Ecuador. But as far as the disputed lands are concerned, they will not intervene."

"Hmmm," Bonifaz muses, "so they're content to see us dismembered, but not devoured. Not good enough, I'll see us in Hell before I allow one square meter of Ecuadorian soil to be taken."

Bonifaz leans back in his chair.

"We must fight when it comes," Ibarra says. "If we let the Peruvians take one square meter of Ecuadorian soil, you won't need to see us to Hell. The people will drag us out by our heels and send us down themselves."

"Can we defeat the Peruvians?" Bonifaz asks.

"At this moment? No," Alba replies. "But the current regime there has no stomach for a war right on the heels of this one. We have some time."

"Will we be able to defend ourselves?"

Alba shrugs eloquently. "Given time and preparation..."

"Ibarra?"

"The people, when roused, are unconquerable. We have driven off the Peruvians before, at Mapuche! "

"Indeed," the old Patrician says, "but I gather it will not be easy. It seems to me though, that we must broaden our sights. Colombia has betrayed us, this is true. But Peru has other enemies. If they must guard their other borders, it might discourage them from invading ours."

"Chile," said Ibarra thoughtfully. "Peru wouldn't dare move, if Chile was watching their backs."

"Will they support us?" Alba asked.

"That will be your mission," Bonifaz said to Ibarra.

Ibarra stroked his chin thoughtfully.

"Pity that Bolivia is already in a war, it might have been useful to have them on side. They've no love for Peru."
Axis of Andes – Page 65

"Wars don't last forever," Bonifaz shrugged. "A nation at war needs allies, and they tend to remember who stood by them in their time of need."

"That didn't work out well with the Colombians," Alba noted. "We sided with them. They welcomed us with open arms, but in the end they were all too happy to sell us out."

"That's Colombians for you," Bonifaz replied, "they've no spines, never had. The Bolivians may be different."

"I'm not sure we should bother with the Bolivians," Ibarra offered. "With Colombia, our interests were at stake. We have no interest there, they fight over the Chaco, it's worthless land, nothing to us."

"Then they won't sell us out."

"I agree with Ibarra," Alba said. "I see no advantage to involving ourselves there. Better to try and work with Chile."

"Velasco will go to Chile," Bonifaz said. "You, Luis, I expect you to look into this Boliviano thing, see if there's an advantage to us.

****

The Chaco War - Bolivia vs Paraguay

While President Bonifaz moves towards his confrontation with Congress in August 1932, and as Peru drifts into its war with Colombia in September 1932, another war is shaping up in the south. This war is fated to be far bloodier and more fearsome than either Ecuador's six-day civil war, or the Peru-Colombia conflict.

In late July and early August, 1932, Bolivian forces raid Paraguayan forts in an inland region called the Gran Chaco. The Chaco war is on. Before it finishes it will devastate two countries and leave a hundred thousand dead.

The scale and intensity of the war should not be underestimated. The two combatants have less than three and a half million citizens between them, and are two of the most impoverished countries in South America. Proportionately, the scale of costs and casualties approaches the bloodbaths which exterminated an entire generation of young men in France and Germany during World War One.

And what is the subject of all this blood, suffering and toil?

A largely uninhabited and inhospitable region lying between them, the lower part of the Gran Chaco, known as the 'Bajo Chaco' or Lower or Humid Chaco. This is essentially a flat, hot, arid lowland plain, dry six months a year, a hot dust bowl, with occasional intense seasonal torrential rains. It has some of the highest temperatures in South America. An almost nonexistent gradient causes the little water that falls to drain into swampy flatlands. The flat topography means that rivers shift erratically in their beds, leaving muddy lagoons and empty riverbeds during dry seasons. Much of the underground water suffers from high salinity, making it undrinkable and unusable for farming. Agriculture is unfeasible, European settlement is mostly nonexistent, for most of its history there were no significant natural resources, either biological or mineral, to attract anyone. The lands are so inaccessible and remote that during the War it takes a whole four days for Paraguayans to even reach the area, and twenty days for the Bolivians.

Who could possibly want it, and why?

What makes it worth the appalling expenditure of blood and treasure?

In truth, in the early part of the 20th century, the Chaco seems to have some potential. Standard Oil makes some oil discoveries in the region. But let's face it, that is pretty thin beer. The worldwide demand for oil is a lot lower in the 1920s and 1930s, the prices are even lower, and Chaco oil is inaccessible and expensive. Hell, the United States is still more than self-sufficient in oil, and oil production in Canada and Mexico are already ramping up. In Europe and the Middle East, better oil is more cheaply available in vast quantities.

Chaco oil is, at best, a potential windfall far into the future, expensive and difficult to procure. Still, it's one of those gold rush things, with nothing better to hope for, desperate nationals in both countries get stars in their eyes and oil fever on the brain.

More than that, the Chaco is a salve for a sense of desperation and wounded national pride. What we have entering the war are two nations with their backs against the wall, each with an awful record of losing wars.

Paraguay has, in the 19th century, suffered through the War of the Triple Alliance 1865-1870, where it recklessly fought a coalition of Brazil, Argentina and Uruguay, losing as much as 90% of its male population, and a substantial portion of its territory.

Bolivia in turn, has fought and lost two wars. The War of the Confederation, in which Chile and Argentina destroyed a federation of Bolivia and Peru, 1836-1837, and then the Pacific War, 1879-84, in which Bolivia lost its access to the sea.

Both countries seethe with defeat and humiliation. Both have lost so much and so badly that their very existence as viable nations seem in doubt. For both, the lower Chaco seems the last chance for a genuine future.

In reality, the stakes are no greater or more significant than Columbia's Letitia, or Ecuador's Orientale, inaccessible portions of the rain forest interior, but two things are different.

First, there is a Hell of a lot more riding on it in terms of national pride and survival. Second, this is one of those appalling moments in history when both sides have their acts together sufficiently to commit to a real fight.

Disputes over the Chaco go back all the way to the 1810s, but it really only begins to simmer after the 1870s and 1880s, with recurring border incidents. Still, in most cases these border incidents never really amount to anything. The Chaco is simply too remote and too valueless to the elites of each nation to justify the time and effort, the blood and treasure of a war.

What changes in 1932?

Axis of Andes – Page 68

Most of the blame for the war probably falls onto the shoulders of a man named Daniel Salamanca, the President of Bolivia.

Let's step back a little. Bolivia, like the rest of South America, is divided between elites of conservative landholders and slightly more progressive business interests, with a small urban middle class growing to service both, and a great unwashed mass of Indigenous and labourers whose views no one cares about. It's rather more nuanced than that, but that's the gist.

Bolivia found its way to a measure of prosperity through silver and tin mining; in particular, tin prices have shot through the roof in the first decades of the 20th century. Prosperity, in turn, fuels ambition, flirtation with social programs and social welfare, and rising living standards and more rapidly rising expectations.

Until the depression hits. At which point, world prices for tin collapse, and with that collapse goes the Bolivian economy. Perhaps the collapse isn't quite so profound as the Ecuadoran collapse. Tin is an essential, while chocolate is a luxury item, after all. But it is still hard times. Like just about every other government in the world, Bolivia's regime is caught flatfooted. It doesn't have a coherent response to a world going mad and the global economy failing. Instead, the country is borrowing heavily at exorbitant interest rates, swirling down into bankruptcy.

Meanwhile, the current President, claiming a national crisis, seeks to subvert the constitution to extend his term. Unfortunately, since he is shouldering the blame for a crisis that he has no real ideas for dealing with, this plan doesn't sell. The result is daily demonstrations and the rise of socialist and leftist movements. Inevitably, someone, a student, gets killed. Things escalate from there into a full scale rebellion. Finally, the military takes over. After a caretaker government, elections are held; and Daniel Salamanca rides in to power on a multi-party alliance.

Winning the Presidency is probably the worst thing to happen to Salamanca. To put it kindly, he has no clues. His country is besieged by a massive economic crisis, a crisis exacerbated by his predecessor, but he really has no idea how to deal with it. We can't really blame him; this is a unique situation.

But Salamanca decides that if he can't cope with the big problem, then he'll just go and attack some other problem that he figures he can solve. Although a democratically elected civilian President, he behaves like an authoritarian strongman. Like Bonifaz in Ecuador, he attempts to sidestep an intractable economy by pushing nationalism and national pride for all it was worth.

For Salamanca, this seems to translate into the final frontier, the Chaco. The Chaco becomes an almost mystical prize, the solution to all problems. The resources of the Chaco will rehabilitate the Bolivian economy, new territory, new mines, new lands and farmlands. It will restore shattered national pride. It will be his salvation, transforming him from an incompetent President at the mercy of a crisis beyond any control or reckoning on his way to catastrophic failure, into a national saviour and hero.

When he closes his eyes, he sees two history books - one giving him a trivial footnote as a fool, the other a full and glorious chapter as the man who restored a broken nation. For Salamanca, it is the answer to every Bolivian question. In short, he is busily talking himself into getting lots of people killed.

Neither country is particularly well prepared for war. In 1928 Bolivia had 8000 men under arms, and Paraguay only 2900. By the outbreak of war in 1932, Paraguay is only up to 3300 and Bolivia 21,000 (but only 1200 actually in the Chaco), with both countries in the teeth of the depression.

Although larger and numerically stronger, Bolivia has huge obstacles. The Chaco is much more remote from the Bolivian population centers, and comparatively more inaccessible. As noted, it takes the Bolivians three weeks to even move troops into the region. Long journeys mean long supply lines; long supply lines are costly and unreliable. The Bolivian campaign suffers from handicaps of being slow and expensive. Even worse, the Bolivian soldiers are mostly Highland Indigenous who suffer badly in trying to cope with the tropical lowlands.

On the other side, the Paraguayans mobilize faster, and have shorter supply lines. Within two months of the outbreak of the war, they have 18,000 men under arms and launch a major counterattack.

Logistics tell the tale. The Paraguayans are able to get into the theatre faster and supply more readily. Much of the war consists of a series of Bolivian defeats as they engage in bloody frontal assaults against entrenched Paraguayan fortifications.

Bolivia cannot not get its act together, with Salamanca meddling heavily in strategy, as the army goes through a series of commanders. To be fair to Salamanca, his commanders are a pretty awful lot, but his problem is that he does not grasp military realities. A seasoned armchair general, his approach to command is simply to decree conquest and then blame the underlings for failure to achieve.

It is hideously bad territory to fight a war in. It is an impossibly hot, dry dust bowl in the summer, where men will die of dehydration by the thousands, or fight to the death for muddy brackish water in drying lagoons. In the wet season, the Chaco is a torrential jungle whose water-soaked soil creates a clinging mud that makes movement almost impossible and swallow's wagons and trucks whole.

Still, the fighting is ferocious. The Bolivians continue to pour men into the theatre. Approximately 200,000 to 250,000 Bolivians, some 10% of the population, are mobilized into the Army. That's even higher than it sounds: Exclude half the population who are women, exclude a third of the male population who are children or elderly, and that means that roughly one in three combat-age Bolivian males are inducted into the army.

The Paraguayans mobilize 150,000 men, 16% of the population, which amounts to between one- third and one-half of all combat-age males being drafted. Biplanes fight in the sky, and Bolivian air battles Paraguayan riverboats. Mechanized transport is used to cross the Chaco, and 1920s era tanks and tankettes are deployed.

The scale of carnage was horrendous.

Fought largely in uninhabited country, civilian casualties are minimal. Bolivia suffers 57,000 killed. 10,000 desertions, 20,000 to

30,000 captured, and likely an equivalent number wounded. All told, perhaps 100,000 to 150,000 killed, wounded, injured or deserted, out of an army of 200,000 to 250,000, and out of a population of 2.4 million, of which 800,000 or 900,000 are combat-age males.

On the Paraguayan side, 43,000 killed out of an army of 150,000. Factoring in wounded, even a relatively small number, suggests that the Paraguayans lose anywhere from a third to a half of their army, again in a country with perhaps 300,000 to 450,000 combat-age males. A great many deaths are due to disease, starvation and dehydration; but by any standard, the numbers are appalling.

The first modern war has come to South America.

****

December, 1933. Somewhere in the Chaco

Colonel Luis Alba wipes his brow and takes another swig of his canteen. The water is foul, but it is still water. The air is thick with dust, it is unbelievably hot. A few feet from him, a couple of Indigenous soldiers sit and pant as if unable to catch their breaths. If anything, Alba thinks, they are suffering worse than he is.

Off in the distance, he can hear the steady pop and staccato rhythms of small arms fire, punctuated by occasional bursts of artillery. He's come close enough to get a good look at the deployments. The Paraguayans are dug in deep; his practiced eye runs across trenches and earthworks on the opposite side of a bend in the dry river bed. The Paraguayans have chosen their position well; the Bolivians have to race across the cracked dry mud, hoping for good foot purchase, and literally climb up towards the guns.

He takes a quick count of dead and wounded Bolivians littering the floor of the empty stream. Too many, but it could have been worse. The Indigenous soldiers show little eagerness to charge, even as their officers whip them forward. Alba, with the characteristic racism of his class, has little regard for Indigenous people. But he can appreciate their reluctance; it is the only thing keeping casualties down.

He watches another pointless charge go down one by one. Not enough, he thinks. The only way the assault can succeed is with numbers, hard and fast. But the Bolivians lack the numbers and the commitment. In any event, such an approach is a bloodbath. What's the point of taking that pile of mud if you lose half your men? There has to be a better way.

Is it even necessary to take this fort? Couldn't they bypass it? Alba isn't sure; the flat empty landscape is deceptive. It is hard to tell what is important and what isn't. If anything at all in this hellhole was important.

He takes another swig of the canteen, it is almost empty, swirling the water around in his mouth to cleanse it of the dust. Spitting, he finally straightens up and returns to the staff tent.

General Kundt, every inch a Prussian officer, nods as he salutes.

"Ah, our Ecuadorian prodigal returns," Kundt says, the Prussian commander's Spanish thickly accented. "Did you enjoy your stroll?"

The command staff stand under an open tent erected for shade, beyond the reach of Paraguayan snipers or artillery.

"It was instructive," Alba replies mildly.

"Ah, you hot-blooded Latins," Kundt laughs. "I wager you had to restrain yourself from joining the charge, didn't you? Well, mind yourself. It wouldn't do to send Bonifaz's emissary home in a box. Not before the volunteer brigades arrive, at least."

Alba smiles as the rest of the command staff laugh. Orderlies move among them, refilling water glasses. Everyone drinks water copiously here, it is so dry and hot. The staff wear their dress uniforms, sweating in the heat, following Kundt's example.

"Fill this, please," he asks an orderly, handing over his canteen. Water shortages plague the army, though the command staff does not seem to suffer.

Send volunteer brigades into this hellhole? he thinks. Over his dead body.

The volunteer brigades, now five thousand men, had been organized originally to aid Colombia. They'd never seen combat; their contributions had ultimately been to the taverns and brothels of Colombia. But they'd returned as heroes and Bonifaz had the brilliant notion of immediately sending them to the Bolivian war.

Of course, half of the original volunteer brigades have melted away on return to Guayaquil. It has taken time to rebuild the ranks and there were endless obstacles to reorganization and travel expense. Colonel Alba and a handful of officers, with perhaps an overlarge number of those Bonifaz had deemed least trustworthy, have gone first as military observers and emissaries to pave the way.

Alba's own particular mission is to forge an alliance between Bolivia and Ecuador, in the event of Peruvian aggression.

First, he's met President Salamanca, an effusively confident man, stern, stiff, bold. Salamanca has been very receptive, all but signing a treaty on the spot. Salamanca has spoken glowingly of the Chaco campaign, of the unstoppable prowess of the Bolivian forces, the cooperation of the races in their designated roles, white men providing inspiration and leadership, sturdy Indigenous as foot soldiers. There had been reverses, Salamanca admitted, but these are temporary. Victory is assured.

And once the Chaco is under control, Bolivia would reclaim the path to the sea, from the Chileans, or perhaps from the Peruvians. Bolivia and Peru had once been united, he confided, and so a portion of Peru's southern coast was rightfully Bolivia's.

It is been an inspiring meeting, and buoyed by Salamanca's boundless enthusiasm and confidence, Alba's first reports back are glowing. But soon enough, Alba's doubts begin. As optimistic as Salamanca is, he cannot help but complain about his intransigent officers and commanders. Eager to discuss military matters with a receptive soldier, Salamanca's ignorance is revealing.

A leftist by nature, Colonel Alba pays bit more attention to the conditions of workers, to the screeds of intellectuals, and what he sees and hears does not inspire him. His subsequent dispatches become more cautious.

Bolivia is by far a larger nation than Ecuador. But it is still dwarfed by Peru. And if it seems to have such trouble with Paraguay, what sort of allies would they be in battle with Peru?

In the end, he concludes that the place for a soldier was on the front lines, and makes the hellish three week journey to join Marshall Kundt, to see how the campaign is really going.

He remembered, just before he left, Salamanca's final meeting, the almost pleading entreaty to discuss his experiences on his return, as if Salamanca wants him to spy on his own officers. It was an awkward moment.

"I do not think," Kundt says cheerfully, "that we'll break through here. We must probe elsewhere."

Some part of Alba is repulsed by this. Not here? Then why bother with this battle in the first place? He nods, giving no sign of his thoughts.

"Such is war, my young friend," Kundt tells him, as if he's read Alba's mind. "In the history books, the campaigns of Napoleon and Caesar are clear and obvious. But in the field, nothing is plain; instead, we must push and probe, seeking our point of advantage; and then when we find it, throwing everything in a mighty fist."

Alba thinks that the Prussian is an incompetent butcher.

"War is an art," Kundt continues ponderously. "The tools of our art are the blood and lives of our own men; the monuments we make are of the blood and lives of our enemy. Never be afraid to sacrifice; it is the only way."

Alba nods gravely.

"I will keep your lessons uppermost in my mind," he says diplomatically.

Mostly, it is things not to do. A whole list of them.

And things to make sure of: Organize baggage trains properly; make sure your officers behave decently; choose your targets carefully; dig in and make the enemy rush into your guns; don't waste lives on idiotic assaults.

Alba finds himself hoping that the Peruvians have their own General Kundt.

A new baggage train is joining the camp. Alba is relieved; they are short of everything: Ammunition, food, fresh water. Without the Bolivians baggage train to replenish their supplies, in a few days, the Paraguayans could leave their fortifications to come out and slaughter them at will. Between thirst prostration and lack of ammunition, there'd be nothing to stop the enemy.

An officer resplendent in medals comes marching up to General Kundt, and presents him with a scroll tied in a black ribbon.

Casually, Kundt opens it, unfurling the ribbon and then stretching the parchment, holding it up to the light. A look of shock comes over him.

"I've been relieved of command," he says.

***

The Ecuador Volunteer Brigades

Despite Alba's protests, the Ecuadoran volunteer brigades arrive in Bolivia in January 1934, eventually reaching a total strength of 10,000 by July of 1934. Due to the rainy season, and due to Alba's insistence that Ecuadoran men remain under the command of Ecuadoran officers, the volunteer brigades are not committed to the Chaco until November of 1934.

The Ecuadoran volunteer brigades are not without controversy. Paraguay protests the brigades, and the neighboring states are uncomfortable. All of the countries surrounding the combatants - Brazil, Argentina, Chile and Peru - are officially neutral and most go well out of their way to affirm that neutrality. As a result, Chile is initially reluctant to grant passage through Chile to Bolivia for the Ecuadoran brigades.

This reluctance gives way, as Chile becomes increasingly uncomfortable with Argentina's barely covert support of Paraguay. That support in turn becomes increasingly overt in the form of weapons and ammunition, supplies, military intelligence and volunteers. At one point in December 1933, Argentine forces even invade and occupy a fortress in Bolivian territory, before withdrawing in favor of Paraguay.

In response to Argentina's meddling, in early 1934, Chile begins to permit the movement of Ecuadoran 'volunteer' brigades, across its territory into Chile on a 'humanitarian' non-combat basis. Along with this, Chilean army officers begin to filter into Bolivia as mercenaries. The Ecuador brigades become Chile's arms-length response to Argentina's meddling, and Velasco Ibarra's lone diplomatic success in the region.

Having the Brigades designated non-combat as a condition of entry suits Alba. He has been in the Chaco, off and on for months in 1933 and 1934. Kundt has been replaced by General Penaranda in 1933, who is, if anything, even more incompetent. Alba is forming very definite views of the conflict and reluctant to put his people in danger. Instead, the brigades are deployed to home defense and logistics support, delivering and guarding supplies to the Chaco, freeing Bolivian soldiers for the front. The Ecuadorans gain a reputation for integrity, maintaining supply lines and delivering water, food and ammunition in full amounts and a timely fashion.

The fluid conditions mean that occasionally the Ecuadoran brigades will come under fire, at which point they engaged in combat. These events are always followed by an exchange of diplomatic notes between various countries. Informal linkages are established with the Bolivian officer corps, and with the decidedly more professional Chilean mercenaries.

Elsewhere, Alba sends cadres of officers and observers throughout the battlefield, even attempting to place observers with the Paraguayans. This does not succeed, but on occasion, the Ecuadorians help to negotiate prisoner exchanges. Despite this, the efforts tend to be more symbolic, with minimal impact on the course of the war.

In May of 1933, the League of Nations, facing the first major conflict since its founding, meets and urgently tries to bring the parties to the negotiating table. Neither President Salamanca, who is stubbornly resolute in his efforts, nor the Paraguayans, who are winning a string of victories, are prepared to compromise. League of Nations' efforts continue more or less ineffectually through 1933 and into 1934. In May of 1934, led by Britain, the League of Nations launches an arms embargo to deny the parties the weapons of war.

This impacts Bolivia, although Ecuador and Chile work to circumvent the embargo, with Ecuador acting as the face of arms purchases by Bolivia and Chile allowing transit, 'selling the flag' as it were. Paraguay continues to receive support from Argentina. Bolivia's efforts to import a small number of twin-engine Condor bombers are foiled by Peru, which intercepts the initial aircraft. The remaining aircraft end up in Ecuador, as they aren't allowed to be transported through Chile.

Velasco Ibarra, frustrated by a complete lack of progress in negotiations with Chile, takes over the duties of negotiating with Salamanca, who, as the war progresses, proves to be more and more evasive in committing to any binding alliance, regardless of how secret, with Ecuador, and more and more demanding of assistance. The results in cooperation in arms purchases, and the increase of the volunteer brigades, over Alba's objection. At one point, the two men almost come to blows over the matter. But by October of 1934, Ibarra has joined Alba in having lost all faith in Salamanca.

In November, 1934, Salamanca, tiring of General Penaranda's incompetence and continuing failures, travels to the front to relieve him of command. Unfortunately, it is only the last of a series of misjudgements, as his officers are just as tired of his meddling. Taking him prisoner, they force a resignation. Vice-President Sorzano takes over over. Peneranda continues to be incompetent.

Alba takes the opportunity to withdraw the volunteer brigades from the field, moving them to camps within Bolivia, until the situation clarifies. Ibarra travels to Bolivia to meet with the new President. The redeployment of the volunteer brigades is delayed until January, 1935, by which time; the Chaco has been all but lost. Alba's opinion of General Penaranda is barely better than his opinion of Salamanca, although he cultivates excellent relations with several of the younger, more radical officers.

By this time, Bolivia has incurred significant debts to Ecuador, and incurred more expenses in hosting the volunteer brigade. Negotiations between Sorzano and Ibarra are thorny, as neither party is willing to commit, but each is unable to let go. Ecuador has come to consider its involvement a huge mistake.

Sorzano turns out to be marginally more competent than Salamanca. He finally orders full scale mobilization, but in many ways it is too late. The Paraguayans continue to win, pushing the Bolivians completely out of the Chaco and pressing on into Bolivia and the foothills of the Andes. The oil country is overrun in the battle of Ibibobo, deep in Bolivian territory, in spring of 1935. But this is the last major victory by the Paraguayans.

The shoe is finally on the other foot; the Paraguayans are forced to extend their supply lines all the way through the Chaco during the rainy season. The Bolivians rally and, together with the Ecuadoran brigades, push them back out of Bolivian territory and oil country. Exhausted and nearly bankrupt both countries agree to a ceasefire on June, 1935.

By August, 1935, the Ecuadoran volunteer brigades have returned home. By September, 1935, Ibarra has negotiated an agreement to redeem Bolivia's war debts to Ecuador by acquiring Bolivia's military surplus at cut rates. Despite Alba's bitter complaints about the condition and the quality of material, the Ecuadorans do come into possession of a quantity of artillery pieces, trucks and small arms. Although less than half the material is serviceable, much of what is not usable can be cannibalized for spare parts.

Using the incorporation of the new war materials as justification, Colonel Alba procures Bonifaz's and Ibarra's support for a reorganization of Ecuador's defenses, based on the lessons he and his observers take from the progress of the Chaco war. In particular, Alba pays particular attention to selecting locations for fortifications along the Oriente, which results in frequent border conflicts with the Peruvians.

Finally, in November of 1935, Ibarra is able to finalize a secret mutual aid pact, requiring each country to come to the other's aid in the event of Peruvian aggression. The pact also recognizes and affirms Bolivian claims to a Pacific corridor and the coastal province of Arica.

By this time, however, none of the triumvirate place much faith in the increasingly shaky and thoroughly reluctant Sorzano government, or in the ability of Bolivia to contribute significantly to Ecuador's defense. The treaty is as much for Ibarra to salvage his standing with Bonifaz and Alba as anything else.

Ultimately, Ecuador's tentative participation has made no real difference to the progress of the Chaco War.

But for Ecuador, the impacts are significant, if subtle. Alba has been dead set on keeping the volunteer brigades out of direct conflict; this puts them in supply and service, and provides substantial experience in logistics and movement in difficult conditions.

Alba and his volunteer brigades have their first experience of war and from a vantage point that allows them to learn important lessons, to obtain invaluable training.

BOOK OF CHILE

September, 1933, Santiago, Chile

"Next item on the agenda," President Arturo Alessandri announces to his cabinet. "This fellow, Velasco Ibarra from Ecuador. He has been asking for a meeting with me. What's his story?"

The Foreign Minister shuffles his papers.

"Velasco Ibarra is the leader of the Chamber of Deputies of the Ecuadorian Congress."

"Indeed," Ross, the Finance Minister asks. "So what's he doing here? Why isn't he tending to his business in Ecuador?"

"He's here on authority as the direct agent of Neptali Bonifaz, the President of Ecuador."

"Messy business up there, I've heard. A lot of bloodshed."

"The little backwater states are often violent. So, what does Neptali Bonifaz want with us?"

"It appears that the Ecuadorians wish to forge some sort of alliance."

"An alliance?"

"Against Peru. It appears that they fear that Peru will invade in pursuit of their claims to some worthless patch of jungle, and they are seeking allies to deter or even fight the Peruvians. It seems that the recent Colombia-Peru war has frightened them."

"That? That hardly qualifies as a war. When do they expect this invasion?"

"They did not say."

"They do realize that maniac, Sanchez is dead? The situation is all calmed down?"

"I suppose so, Sir."

"And what precisely do they expect us to do? We have no border with Ecuador. We have no interests there. Why should we care what happens in a far off hinterland of Indians and Latifundistas?"

"I suppose that this is why Ibarra wishes to meet with us."

"I'm not about to send them an army, and I'm certainly not about to go to war with Peru over them. We've barely settled our own border issues with Peru, I'm not about to start that mess over. What's up with this Neptali Bonifaz? He sounds like a frightened old woman."

"Neptali Bonifaz has quite a good reputation, actually. He's one of these highland Latifundista, quite a businessman, reputation as a hard bargainer, but fair. He was governor of the Central Bank during the Arroyo Presidency. By all accounts, a competent man."

"Ayora... I seem to remember him, he wasn't too bad. Whatever happened to him?"

"The Depression, sir."

"Ah, right, go on."

"Bonifaz was actually elected President, back in October, 1931, but for some reason, not seated until August of last year."

"Why so long?"

"I'm not sure. Political enemies, I suppose. You know how these banana republics are."

"There was quite a bit of violence, I seem to recall."

"Yes, Bonifaz supporters and enemies had it out."

"Pfah... banana republics, what can you expect."

"Your assessment of him?"

"Bonifaz? Old school, very traditional Latifundista, smart, shrewd, ruthless. Competent enough if he was running the central bank, it would seem that he has some idea of the business of government. He's associated though, with something called the National Compact, bad bunch, reminiscent of Mussolini's bunch in Europe. Lots of marching and shouting or worse."

"Hmmm," Alessandri silences his cabinet. "This Bonifaz doesn't sound like the type to jump at shadows. What's he playing at?"

"He's half Peruvian, they say."

"Ahh," Alessandri chuckles, "I suspect this has less to do with imaginary threats from Lima, and more to do with politics in Quito."

He pauses.

"So where does this Ibarra fit in?"

"Bonifaz supporter. Perhaps essential to his victory over his enemies during the violence."

"A fighter?"

"No, an orator; he makes speeches, and writes in newspapers."

"An orator!" Allessandri sneers. "That's worse than fighters. A fighter is only a danger to those in reach of his fists. An orator is a danger to everyone in reach of his voice."

"Very true, sir. Apparently, this Velasco Ibarra is quite the rabble rouser; he's got a gift for whipping up a crowd, or writing inflammatory polemics. He had quite a following in the newspapers, and on the radio."

"Have you met him?"

The foreign minister blushes.

"I have not, Excellency, but my secretaries have."

"Their assessment?"

"Thin-skinned, flighty, passionate, quick to anger, dedicated to persuasion."

"Hmmm," Alessandri ponders, "the pieces start to fall into place. I can see why Bonifaz would want a man like that out of the country.

Remember to send the President of Ecuador a thank you note for getting this idiot out of his hair by putting him in ours.”

The Foreign Minister starts to write.

“No!” says Alessandri quickly. “No notes! I was just.... no, don’t write that down,” Alessandri snaps. “We don’t need a diplomatic crisis.”

He pauses, gathering his thoughts.

“Here’s how we handle it. We will show this Ibarra every courtesy, and accord him full respect. What we will not do is meet with him. Not the Cabinet, not myself, not the foreign minister. We will politely make excuses, it will be a matter of schedules, he can make the rounds to secretaries and deputies and assistants and congressmen to his heart’s content.”

“What if the Peruvians complain anyway?”

“Pfft, then tell them we’re not responsible for Ecuadorian politicians and that’s that. I’ll not be dictated to by foreigners, be they Ecuadorian or Peruvian.”

“It may be difficult to avoid Ibarra, at least socially,” the Foreign Minister advises.

“Then we won’t avoid him, we simply will not discuss matters of state in those settings. He can be referred to our offices to make an appointment, and from there we can have him going in circles.”

“He is a rabble rouser,” cautions Ross. “What if he makes trouble? We’ve had our own... unsettled politics, not too long ago.”

Ross was referring to the time between the fall of the Dictator, Ibanez, and Alessandri’s election; a period of roughly a year when Chile had seen fifteen governments, two general strikes and a naval mutiny.

“True. Keep an eye on him. He can talk to whoever he wants, but the first sign of him stirring up things against us, he’s out.” Allessandri thinks for a second. “Make sure he understands not to cross the line.”

Alessandri glances around at his cabinet, seeking signs of dissent.

"Fine, it's settled. Now, on to the next matter of business."

Velasco Ibarra in Chile

Velasco Ibarra's first journey to Chile takes place in September of 1933. Ibarra appears, gives instructions to the Ecuadoran embassy staff, presents his credentials to President Alessandri but does not engage in formal discussions. Instead, he meets with undersecretaries of the foreign office and presents credentials and requests official discussions. This visit lasts a week.

Ibarra's next visit is more extended. Arriving in December, Velasco Ibarra remains in Santiago and environs until early March, with brief trips back to Ecuador or to Bolivia to meet President Salamanca. Initially optimistic, Ibarra is never able to secure a formal meeting with the Chilean President or Foreign Minister, and while the Chileans seemed friendly and sympathetic, a concrete diplomatic triumph remains perpetually out of reach. Ibarra's return home in March, 1934 finds his status with Bonifaz diminishing.

The visit is not a complete failure. Ibarra becomes a popular figure in the salons of the Chilean elite and middle classes. Articulate, witty, cultured and literate, graced with vast charm and passion, he becomes a favourite guest at dinners and parties, a welcome and exotic addition to the nightlife of Santiago. He even goes so far as to submit carefully screened editorials to Chilean newspapers. He establishes social relationships with many important figures in and out of Chilean government.

Among his contacts are Carlos Ibanez, a disgraced former dictator of Chile, and members of the Chilean fascist movement. The Chilean fascist movement in turn has connections with both Italian and German fascists, and provides the Ecuadorians with their first indirect contacts with the European counterparts. Still, success remains out of reach, much to Ibarra's discredit.

His next visits, through June and July, 1934, focus equally on Chilean society in Santiago and cultivating the Bolivian President Salamanca in La Paz. Salamanca is now deemed to be the more realistic prospect for an alliance. Ibarra is able to use his contacts within Chilean society to circumvent the porous League of Nations' arms embargo on behalf of the Bolivians; but essentially, this results in Ecuador assuming risks and costs, with Chile sharing profits.

By October, 1934, however, Ibarra has lost faith in Salamanca, and begins to advocate again for some sort of arrangements with Chile. Between 1934 and 1938, Ibarra visits Santiago a number of times, fruitlessly pursuing an alliance.

Had the 1933 diplomatic initiatives unequivocally failed, then the Bonifaz triumvirate going into 1934 or 1935 would have had to rethink its plans. As it is, success seems to perpetually dangle just out of reach. The Chileans are always friendly and receptive; while being maddeningly noncommittal. The Ecuadorians continue to see enough hope and prospects of success that they continue to seek alliance as a policy goal in and of itself.

***

1890 to the 1920s, the Parliamentary Period of Chile

Between 1891 and 1924, Chile goes through a long sleepy period called the "Parliamentary Period." Following a civil war between Congress and the President in 1890, Congress comes out on top, stripping the Presidency of key powers, and leaving critical authority in the hands of a congress which is dominated by the middle class and elites.

This isn't necessarily a bad thing. During this period, Chile is sitting pretty, relatively wealthy, investing heavily in public works and national development. Ironically, because of the common commitment to state involvement, Chilean politics get slightly muddled. People who are conservatives in the Chilean political landscape would often pass for progressives or even socialists elsewhere. Socialists and Conservatives often found common cause or overlapping interests and views.

Chile undergoes gradual evolution, with power struggles among elites and middle class factions being worked out on an ongoing basis. Leadership is weak, in part because the dominant social consensus is satisfied. Strong leadership is neither desired nor sought. One Chilean President's motto, in response to this, is "99% of problems solve themselves, and the remaining 1% can't be solved at all." That's a hell of a prescription for aggressively doing nothing.

The backbone of the Chilean economy is nitrates. In the 19th century, this is as close to a crucial resource as you can get: The key to gunpowder and firearms, and Chile has a virtual monopoly. Chile is the world's single greatest supplier of saltpetre or nitrates, and the wealth that rolls in is near incalculable. This resource shapes the evolution of Chilean society.

The vast monies accrued are divided roughly three ways. One third goes to foreigners (the British); a third is claimed by the government, and used to subsidize a massive campaign of infrastructure, public works, defence and services; and the final third is reinvested in the nitrates industry.

The wealth brought by nitrates subsidizes a high standard of living for Chileans, particularly the upper and middle classes, and allows Chile to posture and preen on the world stage. In the 19th century, there are three principal dominant South American countries - Argentina, Brazil and Chile. Despite populations comparable to Bolivia and Ecuador, and substantially inferior to Peru, Colombia and Venezuela; the economic, political and economic clout of Chile far exceeds its size.

The nitrates industry, and the disproportionate wealth brought in, has a gravitational effect on the Chilean elites. In Ecuador, geographical and commercial factors made the coastal business elites, and inland Latifundistas (great landowners) two solitudes, interdependent but aloof and suspicious. Things are different in Chile.

The nitrates industry is not dependent on the Latifundistas, it's not about agricultural production or cash crops, and it produces revenue far beyond the wealth of the Latifundista class. Because of this, the Latifundista tend to seek to merge their interests, through marriage and intermarriage, investment and business dealing with the commercial elites. The result is not necessarily a homogenous elite or oligarchy, but certainly a much more unified one than is seen in other Latin American countries. By and large, the struggles for power tend to be more personal, rather than breaking along social and class lines.

The nitrates industry also meant that Chile is much more of an industrial society. You simply cannot carry on large-scale industrial nitrate or copper mining without some industrial capacity. You neede a major investment in plant and infrastructure, transport, labour force organization, a host of skilled trades, from engineers to accountants. Ultimately, Chile is an export economy, pumping out a couple of key products, copper and nitrates, and importing a wide variety of manufactured goods. But by the same token, it is perhaps the most industrialized society in Latin America.

With that comes a large and aggressive middle class, which seeks alignment with and intermarriage to the oligarchy, and a large industrial work force. More fully and effectively industrialized than Ecuador, Chile doesn't experience the massive labour surpluses that make life so unpleasant and perilous for the common man. Labour is often in short supply, wages are usually comparatively good, and bargaining power of labourers is often high, at least at times and in particular trades.

Indeed, labour is in such short supply that the Chileans have large populations of 'guest workers' Argentinians, Bolivians and Peruvians, working in the nitrate mines and industry. This may be an indicator of how horrible conditions are in the nitrate mines, but it also speaks to prospective labour shortages in Chilean society, and a more potentially active working class. This isn't to say that they get better deals, but merely that they are able to exert more pressure.

In a place like Ecuador, a massive labour surplus results in poor negotiating leverage and a relatively weak labour and working class movement, kept docile by occasional violent repression.

In Chile, a more industrialized society and comparatively higher labour demand, produces a much stronger and more active series of labour and working class movements, and quixotically, an even more ferocious level of brutality.

A large part of the problem lies in the skewed nature of the Chilean economy. The nitrates and later the copper mining industries are extraordinary source of wealth, wealth which subsidizes the state and elites dramatically.

Conversely though, the profit incentive, driven by international demand, elites, government and foreign investors, reduce the actual nitrates workers to little better than animals.

Elsewhere, although Latifundista landowners have an almost feudal relationship to their tenant farmers and day labourers. In the end, the mix of ongoing ties and fluidity compels them to some human treatment of and relations with their workers, which one supposes is why agricultural working classes are frequently conservative.

But in the nitrates mines? Workers are literally slaves or worse. They live in company towns, are forced to live in company housing, shop at company stores, are paid in company tokens which cannot be exchanged for real money and are frequently cheated in all sorts of ways. There are stories of foremen whipping the workers at will. Conditions are often dangerous, and at times these are dangers which can be remedied simply and easily, but the company simply couldn't care less. People die; frequently, brutally, horribly, and there is no recourse.

And yet these miners, working like dogs, living in subhuman conditions, enslaved and abused, are the backbone of the Chilean economy; their labour supports a powerful navy, plus railroad and road construction, and ambitious campaigns of public works.

Of course, we see similar conditions and similar brutality in mining operations in places like Appalachia in the U.S., or Cape Breton in Canada, or the Welsh coal mining districts of England. Boxcar

Willy sings "Work sixteen tons, whattaya get, another day older and deeper in debt." He is singing about the near slavery of the mining towns.

Of course, in all these places, we see labour agitation. Keep treating people like dogs, sooner or later they're going to get up on their hind legs and start barking and snapping back. A lot of the most ferocious strikes and labour disputes, and a lot of the most militant labour movements of the late 19th and early 20th century, arise out of such brutal conditions. It isn't pleasant and easy.

But in most places, as messy as it is, there eventually seems to be some compromise and resolution. Possibly, this is because these other economies are larger and more diverse, the importance of mining, or of a single industry, is not overwhelming.

In Chile though, the nitrates industry is incredibly valuable, and the Chilean economy is relatively small, which exaggerates its critical importance. The result is a degree of social repression which is utterly horrific. There's a hidden history of Chile which is nothing but a series of hideous massacres, of women and children being machine-gunned, mass graves, Army officers earning sobriquets like 'Hyena'. A partial snapshot of labour history at the time shows considerable unrest:

* 1890, a national general strike, brutally quashed.

* 1898, another general strike in Iqique, resolved violently.

* 1901, harbour workers staged a sixty day long strike.

* 1902, a Valparaiso strike results in over a hundred dead, the strike spreads, fighting continues for over 40 days.

* 1905, the Meat Riots, resulting from governments artificially inflating the market price of meat to ensure the profits of Latifundista, a wonderful example of how government and wealthy work hand in hand together, the result is a week of urban rioting and casualties of over 250.

* 1907, the Santa Maria School Massacre, a nitrate miners strike, well over 2000 killed, including women and children; entire families machine gunned.

* 1909, another general strike, brutally put down.

* 1921, the San Gregorio Massacre, over 500 killed.

* 1925, the Marussia Massacre, well over 500 striking saltpetre miners and their families are gunned down.

* 1925, the La Coruna Massacre, hundreds killed.

* 1934, the Ranquil Massacre, almost 500 Indigenous and forestry workers gunned down, another 500 taken prisoner.

Some things become apparent. First, there is a dichotomy between the industrializing urban proletariat and the country folk. The urban workers are able to organize and link up more frequently and more effectively. Public works and commerce make for better standards of living, but urban life also creates handicaps: Occasional runaway inflation and shortages. Labour unrest invariably begins peacefully and eventually results in strikes or labour stoppages, and almost inevitably brings about violent state repression. Still, as time goes on, there is considerable social pressure to deal with urban labour issues, and workers' rights.

No such sentiment exists in the countryside. As part of the ongoing national consensus among the elite, agricultural and rural workers are deliberately excluded from any labour or worker protection legislation, in order to cater to the Latifundista.

More dramatically, the elite will not tolerate any interference with the backbone of their economy, and are prepared to enforce absolutely inhuman conditions, and to act with utter savagery. Machine gun a crowd of women and children? So be it. Chile has always seemed to me to be to be among the most advanced and 'civilized' of Latin American nations. But beneath that surface, the ruling classes are all too willing to exercise appalling brutality. The Santa Maria Massacre makes appalling reading. It is so appalling that the Chilean government and Chilean society make an active effort to bury the incident.

Overall, official Chilean society tends to ignore labour massacres and general strikes, either treating them as passing trivialities, or simply omitting them entirely from histories.

It does much to put men like Allende and monsters like Pinochet into context. Underlying the apparent stability of the Parliamentary period is a kind of seething cauldron, the 'Social Question.' Essentially, Chile's stability and prosperity is bought at the price of a suffering and impoverished underclass. Rather than engage in social reform or come to grips with these issues, the Chilean consensus opts for blindness and selectively brutal repression.

The result is a radicalization within Ecuadorian society. It is a radicalization which is somewhat masked by the fact that the leading elements in Chilean society, despite their willingness to resort to brutality, are committed to an activist state; and so to our eyes contain strange elements of progressivism. But it is there. The fact that men like Allende could rise to power in the 60s, or that the brutality of a thug like Pinochet could run rampant in the 70s, the so called 'economic miracle' of the 80s, all have deep roots.

But on the surface, there is drift. Perhaps this isn't the right approach. It may have been that Chile would have been far better off in the long run, if it had made the effort to address its underlying issues. In the end, stability always passes away. The world changes whether we want it to or not.

There are clouds on the horizon as the Parliamentary Period draws to a close. World War I is a huge boon to the nitrates industry. But that is the last big hurrah. After the war came recession, particularly in the armaments industry, which was a major purchaser of Chilean nitrates. Even worse, the Germans manage to develop a synthetic nitrate, vastly cheaper and more effective than the natural product, and so the bottom drops out of the market. As nitrate revenues declined, the Chilean state makes up for it and preserves state functions and a national standard of living by borrowing abroad, mostly from Britain and the United States.

As the twenties wear on, it becomes clear that Chile's economy and society are running on fumes. And then, of course, the depression hits and the bottom drops out.

Axis of Andes – Page 93

Manifested Destiny - Chile in War and Expansion, 19th century

One should, by and large, be cautious about suggestions of national character. To say that Germans are dour and clinical, that Italians are carefree and liberal, or that Americans are optimistic and irrepressible does a disservice to each. Geography, economics, a hundred other intangibles have as great or greater an influence on history than illusions about national character.

And yet, national illusions, treasured and savoured, have affected the course of world affairs. Where would the United States be without Manifest Destiny? The British without the White Man's Burden? Or the French nursing forty years of bitterness over the Franco-Prussian war?

Chile begins as one of the smallest and poorest of the Spanish colonies, a series of coastal outposts on the lower leg of South America's Pacific; it is not particularly blessed with natural resources or bounty. Mostly it's a stopover on the way to and from other places.

With the Napoleonic Wars and the conquest of Spain, many of the Spanish colonies takes the opportunity to seek their independence. Chile is among them and, between 1808 and 1811, declares independence.

The Spanish, once the Napoleonic wars are over, is not inclined to take this lying down. In 1813, Spanish loyalists in Peru begin the 'Reconquista' - the Reconquest. The result is a see-saw campaign between Spain and its loyalists on one hand and the Chilean nationalists on the other, which finally sees the Spanish driven off between 1823 and 1826.

Then in 1836, Peru and Bolivia form a Confederation. Normally, that would just be their own business. But Chile in particular, sees this Confederation as a threat destabilizing the balance of power, and threatening the economic interests of the fledgling nation.

The result is the War of the Confederation, fought between Chile and Argentina on one side and the Bolivian/Peruvian Confederation on the other, and fought mostly by the Chileans on Peruvian soil. Argentina and Chile do not cooperate in the war. The Argentinians, in fact, join the war roughly a year after it commences. By and large, Chile does the heavy lifting. The war lasts three years; in the end, the Peru/Bolivia Confederation is broken. Chile's economic and political interests were secured, and Chile's navy dominates the Pacific coast of South America.

To the south of Chile is Patagonia, a vast unclaimed territory occupied by Auracanian and Mapuche Indigenous. Harsh and unforgiving, by the 1840s, it is perhaps the last great piece of unclaimed or undivided land left in the world. Beginning in 1870, roughly up until 1885, Argentina undertakes a campaign called the 'conquest of the desert'; basically, driving south into Patagonia, pacifying, conquering or exterminating native tribes. During this time, Patagonia is a bone of contention between Chile and Argentina.

But then Chile finds itself embroiled in the War of the Pacific. Fighting Peru and Bolivia, it doesn't need another war or another adversary. The bottom line is that Chile waives claim to half a million square miles of territory in the boundary treaty of 1881.

The truth is that even without the disputed Patagonian territories, which are mostly worthless, in extending south, Chile literally doubles its territory, and establishes its boundaries along the Andes, a forbidding and mostly impassible geographical barrier, which secures it from Argentina.

The big show is in the north. The War of the Pacific, a conflict over far less territory, but one which has far more economic significance. From 1879 to 1884, the War of the Pacific sees Chile once again duking it out with Bolivia and Peru.

In contrast to Patagonia, and the half million square miles, the War of the Pacific involves territories a fraction of that, less than fifty thousand square miles, but containing the most vital and valuable real estate in South America. At issue are the nitrate deposits which will give Chile virtually a worldwide monopoly on the key mineral.

Axis of Andes – Page 95

The war is fought on both Bolivian and Peruvian territory. Once again, the Chilean navy dominates. The end result is the loss by Bolivia of its coastal provinces and Peru of its southern provinces.

The war engenders hard feelings between the principals which endures for a century or better. The Bolivians never get over the loss of their Pacific coasts. The Peruvians nurse grudges for the next half century until there is a settlement and return of the province of Tacna in 1929. Still, even then, relations between the Chile, Bolivia and Peru remain tense, with outbreaks of hostile nationalism.

In 1888, the Chileans, clearly feeling their oats and having the advantage of an active navy, expand out into the Pacific, exerting claims on the Juan Fernandez Islands, Sala Y Gomez; and even Rapa Nui, or Easter Island. Chilean pirates or merchants have been raiding Easter Island since at least the 1860s. While insignificant in terms of population or territory, these acquisitions mark Chile as a colonial power, symbolically more akin to the European powers, rather than as a mere Latin American state.

All of this territorial expansion, both north and south, takes place within few short years, roughly 1875 to 1889. In the end, Chile has more than doubled its territory, acquired an incredible source of wealth in the northern nitrate territories, rules half of the Pacific coast of South America and extends its borders literally to the straits of Magellan, and reaches out into the Pacific laying claim to islands as far out as Rapa Nui.

The Chileans have beaten Spain twice, have simultaneously beaten Peru and Bolivia twice, both together and separately, have conquered hostile Indigenous, have stood off Argentina, built the most formidable navy in South America, have secured a near monopoly of the most valuable resource in the world and established themselves in splendid isolation, with the Andes mountains at their back and the Pacific Ocean stretched out before them.

With a glorious run like that, little wonder that the Chileans consider themselves a breed apart. In a sense, they adopt the incorrigible optimism and insularity of other nations shielded by geography like the United States and England.

The Chileans evolve an extreme nationalism. They see themselves as a breed apart from the rest of Latin America, more European in both character and ethnicity.

The Indigenous populations and mestizo culture that pervade so many other Latin American nations are almost absent, the Chileans has overwhelmed or exterminated most of their natives. Today Indigenous amount to less than 5% of the Chilean population, and as is typical, are historically marginalized.

In contrast, European immigration is encouraged. Large numbers of Basques, of Germans, of Croats, British, French and Italians settle there. Several of these immigrant communities, such as the Germans, form substantial percentages of the population, outnumbering Indigenous and are vastly more influential.

Chilean intellectuals write about the racial superiority of the Chilean people, of the distinctive quality of the Chilean culture and spirit.

In short, the Chileans come to believe in their own natural superiority. It is a superiority based in victory in wars, in unimpeded territorial expansion, in wealth and ethnicity and military superiority, in a dozen ways. But it all comes down to this: they are just better than other people, and they are prepared to admit this to themselves.

On the one hand, the remarkable streak of success and prosperity gives the Chileans a sense of satisfaction and accomplishment, which perhaps underlies the Parliamentary Era that comes about from 1890 to the 1920s. With no new worlds to conquer, no further ambitions or disputes, with unquestioned superiority, comes a national consensus not to rock the boat… at least as far as the elites are concerned.

This may contribute to the savagery with which the elite and middle class assault labour unrest. There's no one so vicious as the righteous. Did the Chileans' utter faith, derived from their history, lead them to defend what they saw as an ordained society with uncommon brutality?

What it all comes down to, is that the Chileans spent most of the 19th century building the sort of national chip on the shoulder that would make life in Europe and North America so interesting for so many nations.

And this conviction of destiny and national superiority makes Chile particularly receptive to the allure of National Socialism.

March, 1934, Santiago, Chile

Velasco Ibarra steps into the meeting hall. It is a large gorgeous building, with elaborate stonework. This is one of the things that strikes him about Chile, the gorgeous public works everywhere. Ecuador has similar buildings, but they are scattered and modest. Here in Chile, they are as common as fleas, all built to impressive stature and quality. The Chileans are, without question, a wealthy and powerful people.

Which makes it all the more frustrating that he cannot persuade them to come to Ecuador's aid.

"Here we are," General Diaz Valderrama says, taking him by the arm. "Let me introduce you to some of the other leading party members."

The General is in his full-dress military uniform, with only the scarlet armband and emblazoned swastika signifying his allegiance. Ibarra allows himself to be led down to the front stage, where a small group of brown-shirted dignitaries and men in suits stand.

"Herr Maree," Valderrama calls, "come and meet our new ally, Herr Velasco Ibarra of the National Compact of Ecuador."

Ibarra ponders explaining that he is not actually a member of the Compact, but then thinks better of it.

A short, swarthy man in a Storm Trooper's uniform steps forward and sticks out his hand. At least he hasn't saluted. "Jorge González von Marées," the man says, "El Jefe of the National Socialist

Movement of Chile. We've heard much of you Dirty Shirts, you are quite the inspiration to us."

"Err... thank you," Ibarra says, shaking hands carefully. "We've heard much of you too."

"We were very impressed by your 'Six-Day War,' you certainly handed out a shellacking to the Communists and Jews. We have much to learn from your example."

Communists and Jews? Ibarra decides not to question it. More importantly: There is a trap here; he's been warned about meddling in politics.

"I guess," Ibarra says helplessly. "I suppose the big lesson was not to start the fight until after the election."

Was that enough?

"President Bonifaz was carried into office by election," Velasco said. "Just like Chancellor Hitler, and President Mussolini, before him."

Maree and Valderrama exchange significant looks.

"Well spoken," Maree says. "Ibarra, is that Germanic?"

"Spanish," I think, Ibarra replies.

"Nothing wrong with that," Maree says, "the Spanish are a noble race. I myself am half Spanish... and half German."

"I see," Ibarra looks around the hall; the huge swastika banners unfurling from the ceiling, the procession of seats being set up, the speakers and the podium. Above the podium there is a tall edifice draped in red curtains but he cannot see what is contained.

"This is all impressive. Is here everyone German?"

Maree and Valderrama laugh. They are joined by a third man, a bespectacled academic with a look of fierce intensity.

"Carlos Keller." As they shake hands, Ibarra decides that the man is not all there. There is something off about him.

"It is only the beginning, my friend," Maree says. "We began two years ago with nothing. Today we have 20,000 members. Soon

Axis of Andes – Page 99

enough, I think, we will follow in your footsteps. Blood and Will triumphs, as the Fuhrer says."

That sounds uncomfortably close to sedition, Velasco thinks. He hopes that there are no Government spies around. He's getting nervous about being in the room. These maniacs are going to get themselves shot, and him expelled.

"Seek victory at the ballot box," he says for the benefit of any spies. "As we did. We did not fight in the streets until after we had won there."

That seems safe enough. With an orator's hunger for the right line, he tries again. "Without the will of the people, there's no victory," he pontificates. "Fight in the election, not on the street."

More men join them. Velasco vaguely recognizes officers from the Chilean army and Navy.

"You have accomplished so much," he says vaguely, "I am sure you will carry on to success in the elections. I hope that we can work together, for the benefit of both our peoples."

"Yes," Maree replies, "for the true Spanish and German peoples, and against those bloody Jews."

Velasco has no idea what to say to that.

"Does Ecuador have Jews?" Valderrama persists.

"I'm not sure," Ibarra replies, blinking rapidly.

"We have some Jews," Keller offers, "but they're not so bad. It's the European Jews who are the problem. Ours are fine. Still, international Jewry is the scourge of mankind. The Fuhrer rails against them; it's quite inspiring."

"Indeed," Velasco says, desperate to be polite, looking around at the Nazi regalia going up, and desperate to change the topic. "Looking at this, I could almost swear that I am in Berlin."

"That's one difference between your Dirty Shirts and us," Maree says, "many of we Chileans are connected by blood to the Vaterland. The Fuhrer is our friend, and the Vaterland provides us with help and funds."

Axis of Andes – Page 100

"Not," Valderrama interjects quickly, "that we disparage your own accomplishments. The Fascist parties must stick together. You've done great things already, on your own."

"Yes," Maree offers, "great things; and greater things are still to come. We are natural allies, you and us. And through us, you will find greater allies elsewhere."

"Have you met the Fuhrer?" Ibarra asks.

"Not me personally, no," Maree says. "But I have a signed photograph, and an autographed copy of Mein Kampf, and I work closely with his trusted men."

The conversation ends soon after. The rally is imminent and there is much to be done. Velasco is ushered to a designated area for honoured guests, where he can watch the Storm Troopers marching back and forth and saluting.

The hall is filling to capacity, a sea of brown shirts looking up at the podium. Maree climbs up the stage to the lectern and stands facing the expectant crowd.

He raises his arm and makes a dramatic gesture.

Above him, the red curtains part revealing a portrait of Adolph Hitler.

"Straight from Germany," Carlos Keller whispers reverently. "He posed for it himself."

And through the hall, the mighty sound rises from a thousand throats.

"Sieg Heil!"

"Sieg Heil!"

"HEIL HITLER!!!"

***

Hitler and the Southern Cross

Ecuador's National Compact, and their Dirty Shirts, are inspired by Mussolini's Fascists and Brown Shirts, no question about that. But basically, they are a cheap local knock off of the Fascist brand.

When you get to Chile though, you actually have people giving the 'Sieg Heil' and saluting portraits of Adolf Hitler. The Chilean Nazis are the real thing, drawing ideas, ideology and imagery straight from Berlin.

As always, to understand fascism in Chile in the 1930s and 1940s, you have to go digging into a bit of history. There were a number of wells that fascism drew upon.

First is the German influence. Germans, including everything from Alsatians to Austrians to Prussians, start immigrating in large numbers to Chile as early as the 1840s. They don't assimilate well, instead forming German communities, publishing German newspapers, and establishing German schools. The Germans, as Chileans, maintain two national identities and real connections to the home country. And of course, they are valued immigrants, literate, professional, often highly skilled.

Chile during this time, is also absorbing Italians and other Europeans in great numbers, some of which assimilate readily, some not so readily. The Chileans can pride themselves as a European people, multicultural to some degree.

What this means is that as fascism takes off in Germany and Italy, there are many in Chile who see these events as news from home, affecting them and their relatives, and not just the doings in a faraway country. Fascist and Nazi ideas and ideals transmit readily through the ethnic Germans to Chile, as if it was just over the border, and not a hemisphere away. The Chilean Nazis can and do actually drink directly from the source.

Of course, not all Chilean Germans are Nazis. Most aren't. In particular, there are quite a few who'd fled Hitler's Germany who are decidedly not Nazis. But at the same time, Nazi Germany, by ideology, pursues a campaign of outreach with its wandering Volk members. So it isn't just a matter of some Chilean Germans getting into Nazism, but also, and perhaps more importantly, Nazi Germany making an effort to come to them, sending agents, money, propaganda, whatever they could.

Italy follows the same track, though less overtly. There are quite a few Italians as well, but the Italian fascists don't quite have the same obsession with Volk and blood that would lead them to be interested and involved with foreign populations far away.

Even so, Germans are a relatively small part of the Chilean nation. Maybe they represent five percent of the population, maybe they have importance far exceeding their representation, but still they are a minority. Same with the Italians.

There were other channels of fascism. One is military fashion. After the Franco-Prussian war rearranged the map of Europe, the Prussians become the 'poster boys' of martial prowess. They've fought Napoleon and won; they've won in 1836 and 1848, they've beaten the Austrians, the Danes and now the French; and they have the British running scared. They have the biggest guns, the most advanced weapons, the tightest discipline and the most uniform goose stepping.

Sure, the British are tops when it came to navies and naval warfare. But the British are a sea power, and they've always been around. They are about native troops and machine gunning hapless spear carrying tribes. The Americans are around, but they have a tendency to go light on the military hardware, gunboat diplomacy aside. The Germans are the new kids on the block, very firmly a land power, and have proved their mettle against Europe's tough customers.

From about 1870 on, Prussian and German military culture gets very big and very influential in Latin America. It is a point of honour to have German officers as military advisers or trainers, or even as officers or generals. The Bolivians, for instance, go into the Chaco War with General Kundt as the Chief of Staff, though maybe they shouldn't have.

And of course, it is a badge of honour for Latin American officers to study war and tactics at the military colleges of Europe. So you have Sanchez Cerra, the maniac of Peru, studying war in France. Another example is Chilean General Ariostos Herrera, who spends part of the 1930s in Italy and comes back as a goose-stepping Mussolini worshipper. Overall, the Chilean military is quite infatuated with the militarism of the European fascists.

Germany, being the dominant power, has the most prestigious military standards, and even the defeat of WWI hasn't diminished that star too much. Indeed, there are now a lot of unemployed German officers and soldiers flooding South America. When fascism arises in Italy and Nazism in Germany, Latin American Colonels and Generals find themselves immersing in a highly politicized military society whose ideology is often alluring and which in the 1930s, seem to offer a successful model.

The inevitable consequence is that Nazism and Fascism are starting to flow quite naturally through the channels of the military cultures of Latin America, especially Chile, whose military culture is powerful, successful and very Europeanized.

Finally, it is vital to understand that in the 1920s, and particularly the 1930s, fascism seems to offer a successful model. Nowadays, we think of fascism, and we think tyranny, atrocity, murderous warfare and aggression, crazed little guys ranting away and losing wars.

But back then, it seems to work. It takes crippled countries like Italy and postwar Germany and seems to rejuvenate them, turning them into powerhouses, imbuing them with spirit and purpose. Their economies hum, the trains run on time, and by God, they get respect.

These things become very important, because when the depression hits, it's just nonstop bad news. Without living through it, it's hard to grasp just how traumatic it is. It is as if the world has fallen apart; the underpinnings of export economies break down as international trade collapses. In America and Europe, millions of people are thrown out of work, factories go silent overnight, there are massive bank failures, currency collapses or hyperinflation.

The old solutions fail; the old politics fails utterly. Parliamentary democracy, liberal democracy, monarchies, progressives, liberals, conservatives, the traditional ways of the Latifundistas, or the business classes, everything fails in the face of the Great Depression. Nothing works any more, no one has solutions.

Well, not quite true. Fascism and Nazism seem to offer a solution.

And just as important, Communism and Socialism offer solutions of their own. Compelling solutions. In the 1930s, we see Socialist and Marxist groups rise to unprecedented heights.

The trouble with Communism and Marxism, though, is that it isn't a big enough tent. Operating on class based analysis, and with sympathies thoroughly on the side of the proletariat, the poor and the working class, Marxism tends to shut the door on the middle classes, on landowners big and small, on the elites. For these groups, the ones that effectively hold the power and the wealth, Marxism offers only revolution, destruction and purges.

So they have to go elsewhere, and the only viable alternative appears to be fascism. Fascist and fascistic political movements spring up everywhere, in Europe, in North America and in Latin America. Mostly, these fascist movements are indigenous, borrowing elements and imagery from the leading fascist movements in Italy and Germany, and giving them a local spin.

The Chilean National Socialist movement, on the other hand, due to a peculiar combination of German heritage, a particular affinity of Chilean nationalism, military indoctrination and economic desperation, channels its Nazism directly from Germany.

Founded in 1932 by General Diaz Valderrama, Carlos Keller and Jorge Maree, the Chileans tap the Nazi spring directly. Not only do they take the name, but they literally borrow the Fuhrer himself, saluting pictures of Hitler, importing Nazi ideology wholesale, even where not particularly appropriate. Carlos Keller, a near mystical academic, is the movement's ideologue, drawing directly from Nazi ideas and ideology.

The direct ideological linkage, the veneration of Hitler and the large German population, all attract the attention of the German Nazi regime, which responds by pouring money and agents in to support this strange offshoot.

In the 1937 election, the National Socialists win 3.5% of the vote, electing three deputies; hardly spectacular, but given the traditional nature of Chilean politics, it is a respectable fringe showing. Given the influence of fascism and fascist ideas in the military, the Chilean Nazis have a potential punch far out of their weight class.

But ultimately the problem is that they hew too closely to Germany. The Chileans are a nationalist people, even arrogantly so. They aren't impressed by the idea of an ideological leader in another country. Moreover, parts of the ideology, such as the anti-Semitism, have no real traction in Chile. As the 1930s wear on, the Chilean Nazi party attempts to distance itself from its German parent, becoming more local and domestic; but many Chilean Nazis continue to have a mystical devotion to the Fuhrer, arguably, their association with the German party continues to hurt them.

In the election of 1938, the Chilean Nazi party merges with the Socialist Union to create the Alliance for Popular Liberty, under the banner of former dictator, General Carlos Ibanez. While not a Nazi himself, Ibanez is prepared to work with them.

***

"Velasco and the Chilean Nazis," Foreign Affairs Quarterly

"..... The Ecuadoran government's association with the Chilean fascist movement was hardly a deliberate or concentrated effort. There is a tendency to envision Bonifaz and his cabal sitting around a table in Quito pulling strings to throw a continent into flame.

The reality is that there wasn't really any master plan. The Bonifaz regime, having persuaded itself that it faced an implacable enemy of overwhelming power and sinister intentions, was desperately looking for allies, and not really finding them.

Certainly the Alessandri government in Chile was not interested. But it was also diplomatic enough not to give Bonifaz's agent an outright 'no.' Rather, it preferred to avoid the issue altogether. The result was that Velasco Ibarra, the number two man in the Ecuadorian triumvirate, spent months hanging around Santiago and Valparaiso, and returned year after year.

Given that the Alessandri government was unwilling to address him directly or formally, he was prepared to speak to anyone at all. Interested in influencing Chile's body politic, any party could have his ear. The National Socialists were merely one of many, and it was circumstance and coincidence that led this alliance to grow.

For the Chilean Nazis, the principal attraction of Bonifaz's National Compact, otherwise to be dismissed as poor country cousins, was simple: Success. They were a fascist movement which had succeeded in forming a government. Association and contact gave the Chilean Nazis a form of credibility, to the Germans, to the Chilean body politic, and to each other. Ideological correspondence did the rest.

Why did the Ecuadorians pursue the relationship? They were desperate. It was as simple as that. During the 1930s, the two fascist parties established various linkages, including informal embassies, exchanges of personnel and information. Many Chilean Nazis travelled to Ecuador on various exchange or support programs. The two fascist movements were also inspired to coordinate and link to other Latin American fascist movements, and these became conduits for German and Italian espionage and covert operations.

The question arises, did the association with the Bonifaz regime have any significant effect on the Chilean Nazi party. The effects, if any, must be seen as subtle. It has been argued that the Ecuadorian influence and example resulted in the Chilean Nazi party moving away from close association with German and German Nazi ideology. This is hardly deliberate on the Ecuadorans' part, but rather a matter of circumstance. Velasco Ibarra, on each of his visits to Chile, was watched by the Alessandri Government, and so was required to be careful and circumspect.

Consequently, to avoid antagonizing his hosts, Ibarra was careful to distance himself from any talk of violence, of coups or putsches and, when these subjects invariably came up, counselled strongly against them. He had little interest in the threat of European Jews; but much to say about the menace of Peru. If the Nazis were animated by racial interest, Velasco was too ready to disingenuously point out that the Peruvians were a mongrel race, contaminated by Indigenous blood.

Between 1935 and 1939, the anti-Semitic trappings were considerably played down or even altogether dispensed with. The mystical veneration of Hitler was also officially played down, though many members clung to it. Arguably, Chile was a nationalist country, and political efforts would have driven the Chilean Nazi party in these directions anyway. But it's also arguable that the Ecuadorian association and example intensified this trend. Velasco Ibarra, wary of stepping over a line, was always careful in dealing with political parties and personalities outside of government. Whenever he dealt with the Nazis, he was always careful to argue against radicalism. He had little personal interest in Nazi ideology, and whenever he had a chance, he preferred to raise the Peruvian threat.

One thing that is indisputable was the adoption by the Chilean Nazi party of anti-Peruvian nationalism, and the replacement of anti-Semitism with anti-Indigenous racism, aimed once again at

Peru. It is not difficult here to see the incessant drumbeat of Ecuadorian propaganda falling on fertile soil.

The Chilean Nazi party took up this gauntlet, publicly repudiating the 1929 treaty with Peru which saw the return of Tacna province, held for over 50 years, and the payment by Chile to Peru of a massive indemnity. This indemnity was blamed, by the Nazis, for Chile's financial woes during the depression.

The 1929 treaty was touted as the 'Peruvian Betrayal.' A 'stab in the back' theme which found widespread support. In 1937, they won almost 6% of the vote.

Of course, this made relations awkward with Carlos Ibanez, who had negotiated and signed the treaty in 1929. But there too, Ecuadorian connections to both the Nazi and Ibanez camps were able to smooth over relations.

It is tempting to wonder, if not for the moderating counsel and advice of Velasco and his peers, how the Chilean Nazis might have acted...."

***

Duel! Alessandri vs Ibanez, 1924-1940

In the 1920s, the long long sleep of the Chilean Parliamentary era is drawing to a close.

In part, history refuses to allow it to go on. Chile has enjoyed decades of uncontested tranquillity, wealthy, secure from enemies, immune from the fluctuations of international markets

But beyond the chambers of Congress in Santiago, the world is changing. World War I has devastated Europe, setting off chains of economic dominos that ripple forth. One of those dominos in particular, the development of synthetic nitrates, will literally knock the pinnings out from under Chile. It will come at a bad time, as the Social Question gathers steam, inflation gallops and various constituencies in Chile, ranging from labour to middle classes to an underpaid military, become increasingly aggressive.

The end of the Parliamentary period comes about through the actions and conflicts of two men, each in their own ways products of this system.

The first is Arturo Alessandri. Born in 1868, the son of an Italian immigrant; Alessandri is definitely not a product of Chile's traditional elites. Rather, he is clearly a member of the Chilean middle class. In 1893, he becomes a lawyer. In 1897, he goes into politics quietly representing a modest rural district for much of the next twenty years.

Alessandri is a bit of a strange duck. Radical, but not too radical. A populist, but inherently conservative in many ways. Aggressive, but timid.

This is the man who would go into the 1920 election campaigning on social reform and the Social Question. He speaks often and charismatically about the working class, and appeals directly to the masses with a new style of oratory. He manages to appeal to provincial elites, to students and intellectuals and to working and middle classes.

But he is far from being a radical. He goes out of his way to assure regional Latifundistas that his reforms will be confined to the cities; but his administration authorizes several of the most savage labour repressions - massacres that kill hundreds, or even thousands of innocent people, that see machine guns turned on women and children.

In short, Alessandri was a radical who was anything but radical. Another Chilean irony.

For the first four years of Alessandri's rule as President, until 1924, nothing much happens. He is headed down to history as merely another Parliamentary President, almost powerless in the face of Congress.

Then, on September 3, 1924, things start to spin out of control. The precipitating incident is the 'sabre rattling' – fifty-four military officers begin a protest against low wages by attending a sitting of Congress in dress uniform and rattling their sabres in their scabbards. It's one of those things that's a lot more impressive when it happens, than it is to write about decades later.

The next day, September 4, 1924, two young officers, Carlos Ibanez and Marmaduke Grove form an officers' committee to 'defend themselves from the government.' ie - from punishment for the sabre rattling incident. The issue is low wages, poor treatment and government deadlock in the face of inflation and economic crisis. On September 5, Ibanez and Grove up the ante by demanding the resignation of three of Alessandri's ministers, the passage of labour codes, an income tax and better salaries. Essentially, Ibanez and Grove are moving towards an open revolt against the government.

By September 8, Alessandri is completely unstrung; events seem to have caught him out entirely. He appoints General Luis Altimarano to run the government, and then tries to resign, believing that he's lost all control of the state. Astonishingly, instead of accepting his abdication, Congress gives him a six month leave of absence, and he flees to Italy. Hardly the mark of a bold and resolute man.

Altimarano goes down in history as being the head of a right wing junta. But among his earliest initiatives are forcing the Congress to pass a series of laws banning child labour, recognizing trade unions, and providing for occupational safety. Nevertheless, after consolidating power, Altimarano begins to move steadily to the right. The coalition inside and outside the army that has supported Altimarano begins to disintegrate. And Altimarano isn't doing all that well coping with the ongoing economic crises.

A few months later, on January 23, 1925, Altimarano finds himself deposed by another military coup, which places government in the hands of Ibanez and Grove.

Paradoxically, Ibanez and Grove bring back Alessandri back from Italy in March, and enact many of his reforms by military decree. Alessandri introduces a central bank, during this time, and initiates a revenue tax. In 1925, a new constitution is enacted by September, providing for a weaker congress and more powerful President. During this period, Alessandri also presides over the Marussia and La Corona massacres, in which soldiers slaughter several hundred workers at the nitrate mines, as well as heir women and children, once again illustrating the brutality that underlies Chile's normal civil society and politics.

Strangely everything seems to happen around Alessandri, but not through Alessandri. He appears to be a kind of charismatic spokesman or advocate for progressive ideas, but the actual legwork, the actual governance. is done by others. Alessandri seldom appears to be the one taking the initiative; he simply reacts to events which seem to run past him, and literally flees until called back.

In contrast, one of the men actually making things happen is Ibanez: Practical, pragmatic, aggressive. With the return of Alessandri, Ibanez goes to work first as Minister of War and then as Minister of the Interior.

At this point, there's a situation. Basically, Ibanez by this time is a kingmaker. He's essentially overthrown Alessandri, overthrown Altimarano, and now reinstated Alessandri. This raises real questions in the public mind as to who is really the power in the country. It certainly raises questions in the mind of Alessandri, whose approach is to once again run away. Ibanez is left in charge of the government, but a coalition of the three congressional parties opposes him. They bring forward a compromise candidate, a man named Figueroa, who wins the election.

But as a sign of just how perverse and contrary Chilean politics is in this age, Figueroa retains Ibanez as Minister of the Interior, which leaves him essentially in control of the Government. By 1927, Figueroa has resigned, clearing the way for Ibanez to finally run for public office.

By this time, Chile's politics are in complete disarray. Ibanez has been a raging bull since 1924. The opposition parties are unable to marshal a candidate and Ibanez runs unopposed, winning 98% of the vote; a rather suspicious number.

After dominating the Chilean political scene for the three preceding years, after winning an overwhelming mandate, and with all his opponents either in self-imposed exile or complete disarray, Ibanez does exactly what we'd expect of him in a situation like that.... he goes full Dictator.

He suspends parliament, rules by decree, appoints people directly to Congress and imprisons his political rivals and enemies, including his old partner, Marmaduke Grove.

And for a while, he does very well. This is a man who, after all, has spent the previous few years learning the ins and outs of actual practical governance. He isn't merely a strutting Caudillo who marches into office, puts his feet on the desk and starts issuing decrees. Rather, he's worked in the mechanics of the ministry and bureaucracy. So he actually has some capacity to get things done.

And he has a spell of luck; the late 1920s see a period of stability, a new boom time before the bottom drops out with the Great Depression. A pragmatic reformer, Ibanez takes advantage of this prosperity, borrowing abroad to maintain Chile's standard of living, while hoping the nitrates market will come back (it doesn't). Among his diplomatic accomplishments are a final resolution of the War of the Pacific, with the return of Tacna province to Peru. Unfortunately for him, the Great Depression hits, and it hits hard.

All those international loans get called in. The nitrates industry has basically failed in its traditional role. The Chilean economy has not found any other footing. Ibanez hangs on, but things get worse and worse, and the ongoing economic crisis discredits him utterly. By July of 1931, Ibanez is forced to abdicate.

With Ibanez gone Chile goes through eighteen months of instability; during this period, we see a dizzy succession of over a dozen governments, the great naval mutiny and two general strikes.

The time is ripe for Alessandri to return. Ibanez, his rival, sometime partner and nemesis, is finally discredited and in exile. Alessandri, on the other hand, remains as the great prophet of social liberalism, the only other political figure of stature, untainted by the Depression.

Alessandri sweeps back into power in 1932, with broad-based support from both the left and right. Quickly enough, Alessandri tilts right, rapidly losing support from the left. During this regime, economic policy seems to have fallen into the hands of his finance minister, Gustavo Ross, who is hated in many circles for his stringent economies and fiscal policies. Under Ross, the Depression is to be fought on the backs of Chile's poor. But at least it will be fought. Ross offers coherent and steady economic policies that make a real effort to address the problems and actually have some impact.

Given Alessandri's peculiar history, one wonders to what extent his 1932 to 1938 government is his, versus Ross's. Alessandri comes across as a charismatic leader, and as a visionary of sorts. He is the man who articulates the nation's grievances and needs, who points towards the shining star on the hill. But he doesn't seem to have a firm hand on actual governance. As we see in the 1920s, he seems prone to losing control to his Ministers. It is tempting to think that Gustavo Ross is the real power, and that perhaps Alessandri provides moderation and some degree of public appeal.

So where is Ibanez during this period? Biding his time. Having gone into exile in 1931, he is back within a few years. But by this time, he is no longer the unstoppable wild man of Chilean politics.

Rather, he has the black marks of his dictatorship and the Great Depression weighing him down.

On the other hand, he remains a live and volatile political force, well connected in the army, a challenger in certain conservative circles. With Alessandri's abandonment of the left, he can push his bona fides there. It's one of the ironies of Chilean politics that apparently diametrically opposed constituencies find common cause. And so Ibanez has doors opening to him from both the Nazi and Socialist parties.

In 1938, Alessandri retires at the end of his term, and his Finance Minister, Gustavo Ross, with the support of the hard right, runs as his replacement. Opposing him is the Radical Leftist, Pedro Cerda. Entering as a third party candidate is Carlos Ibanez, running with a personal party, but with support of both Nazis and Socialists, among others.

Which brings us back to Ibanez. If Alessandri is a man of idealism and beliefs, then Ibanez is basically a man who believes in himself rather than in philosophies. In history, he comes across as pragmatic, his ideas are concrete; he is about practicality not ideology. Having grown up in a Chile which featured a strong activist state, and having come from the military, arguably the most concretely active of state functions, he doesn't fit comfortably into standard definitions of right and left. Indeed, he probably doesn't spend a lot of time worrying about it. He takes whatever worked. Out of power, he is a democrat. Once in power? Well, he already knows the answers. Discussion and dissent is just a waste of time to him.

This combination of ego, pragmatism and a willingness to embrace all sorts of policies, makes Ibanez a maverick, unpalatable to the established political order. He is perennially an outsider, a barbarian at the gates. In power, he is often compared to Mussolini, a comparison he does not dislike.

Axis of Andes – Page 115

Interlude - In the History that We Know

The Chilean National Socialist party begins in 1930, inspired directly by the German party, even to the point of saluting portraits of Hitler. While successful, the party struggles with its identification with the German movement, and the European ideology. In the late 1930s, it does try to downplay this association, but by then it is too little too late.

Nevertheless, the Chilean Nazis does win 3.5% of the vote in the election of 1937, after which they merge with another party, the Socialist Union. In September 1938, the Chilean Nazi Party allies with and supports Carlos Ibanez third-party candidacy for President, in the Election coming up the next year. Ibanez' third-party candidacy is a long shot. Alessandri's designated heir, and the de facto head of government, Gustavo Ross, is ahead of both Ibanez and the leftist candidate, Aguire Cerda.

But the course of the election is utterly derailed by what comes to be called the Seguro Obrero Massacre. On September 5, 1938, a group of 30 young Nazis foolishly attempt a coup d'etat by occupying the Seguro Obrero building; while another 30 occupy a University building. The government responds with force. All 60 are lined up against the wall and executed, after which the bodies are mutilated by bayonet and sabre.

Carlos Ibanez is arrested and placed in jail, as are other prominent supporters and Nazi party members. The crackdown essentially destroys the Nazi party, and ends Ibanez's campaign.

But it also provokes a wave of popular outrage. The Chilean public is prepared to overlook massacres of miners out in remote provinces. But this is a public execution of well-connected young men on the streets of the capital city. Public opinion turns strongly against Alessandri's ruling party and his heir, Ross.

At jail, Ibanez is visited by the left wing candidate, Aguire Cerda, and to spite his right wing opponent, Ross, throws his support to Cerda. With the result that Cerda wins the election, and commenced a rapid program of social and economic reform.

In our revised history, Velasco Ibbara's self serving cautiousness has had an effect, tempering the more reckless impulses and voices in the Chilean National Socialist movement. The Nazis are more careful, the Seguro Obrero massacre never happens. They're never wiped out as a viable party. Ibanez never goes to jail.

Instead, the election goes ahead without incident. Cerda and Ibanez split the vote, and Ross wins, for the moment.

***

Tacna and Arica

Chile wins the War of the Pacific. Bolivia and Peru lose big time. Under the Treaty of 1883, Chile occupies the southern Peruvian Provinces of Tacna and Arica for a period of ten years, after which a plebiscite will determine the fate of its inhabitants.

The way these things go, ten years turn into fifty years. Unable to agree on terms for a plebiscite, the Chileans simply stay and do their best to ethnically cleanse and colonize the region. This leads to breaks in diplomatic relations and more threats of war.

Eventually, the United States is brought in as a mediator. The compromise, arrived at in 1929, is that Chile keeps the province of Arica, with minor concessions to allow Peruvian port access. Peru gets the province of Tacna back and receives a six million dollar payoff (real money in 1929 terms).

The compromise, of course, satisfies no one. The Chileans, stoked on national superiority, are loath to return Tacna. The payment of six million dollars on the eve of the Depression is both a national humiliation and an unaffordable extravagance in a country that will soon go broke.

For the Chilean Nazi party, under the influence of the Ecuadorians, the return of Tacna and the payment of the indemnity amounts to a stab in the back. Chile won the war, the province is its by right of conquest. But somehow, Chile has been forced to return it and pay reparations? It's a raw injustice.

Oddly, this does not create a barrier between Ibanez and the Chilean Nazis. This is largely a matter of realpolitik, since Ibanez had been the one to negotiate and sign off on the agreement. Rather, the Nazis, in allying with Ibanez, took the official position that Ibanez, like the rest of Chile, has been betrayed by Jewish interests in the United States and Peru. Ibanez, rather than being the perpetrator, is reassigned as a victim. Ibanez own position on the subject is fairly nuanced, and becomes more ambiguous as time goes on, eventually allowing him to denounce a compromise he had engineered.

The bottom line was that by the late 30s, early 40s, much of Chilean society has emotionally repudiated the 1929 compromise, though there is little political will to do anything about it. Nevertheless, it remains a flash point of hostility.

Peru, of course, remains unsatisfied, having lost the provinces of Tarapaca and being forced now to renounce Arica. The defeats and humiliations of the War of the Pacific continue to rankle. Once again, there is a lack of political will to do anything about it. But once again, there is a deep seated national and political hostility.

In and of themselves, the fallout of the War of the Pacific, and the Tacna/Arica compromise would not lead to war. No one goes to war over fifty year old grievances, except the French. But in a situation of escalating tensions, the ingrained hostility and unresolved or re-alleged claims brings the threshold of war considerably closer.

***

Ecuador's Failure in Bolivia - 1935 /1937

Following the end of the Chaco War, Velasco Ibarra succeeds in signing a mutual aid treaty between Bolivia and Ecuador, with Bolivian President, Sorzano.

According to the terms of the Treaty, each nation is obliged to come to the defence of the other, if attacked by Peru. The Treaty is invalid if either country attacks first, an incentive against military adventures. The Treaty explicitly recognizes Ecuadorian territorial claims to the Oriente, and defines a Peruvian invasion or occupation of the Oriente as aggression. In turn, the treaty recognizes Bolivian claims to a right to a Pacific coast and the coastal provinces of Antagosta, Tarapaca, Arica and Tacna held by Peru and Chile. Only Tacna is in Peruvian hands, however. The Treaty specifically precludes Ecuador's involvement in disputes between Bolivia and Chile.

Although secret, rumours of the Treaty begin to circulate within a few months. Indeed, the Bonifaz regime itself tacitly spreads rumours to deter what it considers to be Peruvian aggression. To the extent that these rumours reach Lima, they have the opposite effect in encouraging militarism and hostility, and worsening relations with Bolivia.

The crown jewel of Velasco Ibarra's international diplomacy, however, is short lived. By May, 1936, barely six months after the Treaty is signed, Sorzano is overthrown in a military coup by the war hero Colonel David Toro.

Toro promoted a brand of 'military socialism,' advocating wide ranging social reforms, but with little in the way of a concrete agenda.

Ibarra and Alba together, in June 1936, travel to La Paz to meet with Toro, and receive lukewarm assurance that the treaty will be honoured. Despite this, the Ecuadorians have reason to be less than sanguine. Ideologically, the Toro regime is leftist, anti-war, focussed on domestic issues and utterly uninterested in foreign involvement. The promise of Tacna province has lost its lustre. For

Bolivia, and for Sorzano, the promise of a pacific coastline has become a national obsession. But Tacna was unsuited to Bolivian transport requirements, which are mainly through the former province of Tarapaca, now controlled by Chile. And of course, disputes with Chile are outside the treaty.

Nevertheless, Alba's personal relationships with Bolivian officers, particularly Toro, together with sentimental notions of the debt owed to Ecuador keep the treaty intact, or at least, prevent the Bolivians from expressly repudiating it.

Ecuadorian diplomacy has reached an impasse. Entreaties to the United States have proven fruitless. The American government is largely unconcerned and uninvolved with disputes between Latin States. The Roosevelt administration does offer mediation, but the Bonifaz regime, fearing favouritism to Peru, declines. The United Kingdom, previously a major power in the region, has essentially renounced interests. The governments of Argentina and Brazil are largely indifferent. Colombia is unreliable.

Years of searching for a counterweight, an ally, a deterrent, have produced nothing, except a secret treaty with Bolivia.

In July, 1937, David Toro is overthrown by Colonel German Busch. Once again, Ibarra and Alba travel to La Paz, but this time the reception is less cordial. Busch pointedly declines to meet with them, instead providing a written letter, which states in part.

"....our nation shall never forget and never abandon the graces and assistance by our brothers in our time of strife and need. Although divided by distance which cannot be bridged, in God's spirit we shall always be joined. As to the agreements made on behalf of the Bolivian people by the disgraced former ruler Sorzano, be assured that we shall continue to be bound by the spirit of friendship between our nations. As we have seen recently, matters of war must be considered on the occasion which they arise and not before. Only God may know the future."

The letter, together with Busch's refusal to meet directly, is interpreted by both Alba and Ibarra as a renunciation of the Sorzano Treaty, though it is not explicitly terminated.

Ecuador's security deterrent has fallen apart. There are no allies or guarantors to be found in South America, or with the traditional great powers. The mood in Quito is one of despair. Fuelled by a series of border incidents with Peru, there is a sense of impending war.

With Bolivia gone, the last chance to create a working security deterrent is Chile, except that Chile has shown no interest whatsoever. Nevertheless, Ibarra, in August and September is sent on another desperate, fruitless, diplomatic mission.

It is during this mission, that Ibarra renews contact with the Chilean Nazi leader, Von Maree. Through Von Maree, Ibarra is introduced to operatives working out of the German consulate, which brings them to the attention of Admiral Canaris, head of the German Intelligence service. Canaris sees no particular merit, but is reluctant to offend his Chilean contacts who seem so enthusiastic about their brothers in the 'Dirty Shirts,' and so refers the matter directly to Berlin.

***

Berlin, December, 1937

"I regret," Hitler begins, "that the press of European matters, particularly the struggle of our brother, Commander Franco, does not allow us much time. But be welcome, tell us of matters in South America."

"Thank you, Great Fuhrer," Velasco Ibarra replies....

***

THE BOOK OF PERU

Peru - A thousand sunsets - 1880 to 1920

Prior to 1879 and the War of the Pacific, Peru is an essentially feudal caste society. At the top of the Social Order are the Spanish Europeans, or those of their descent. Before independence that caste has been divided further, between those actually from Spain and those born locally. Beneath the Criollo elite are a Criollo middle class caste; below them various grades of Mestizo or mixed breeds of Spanish and Indigenous, the more successful of whom emulate Spanish culture and adopted Spanish language, and then the Indigenous, composted of Quechua, Aymara and Guarani predominantly.

As with other Andean nations, Peru is a layered state. 12% of its territory is a coastal strip, due to ocean currents, much of it is dry and desert like, with fertile areas fed by rivers coming down from the mountains. Today that coastal strip encompasses 40% of the Peruvian population, but most of that is the result of runaway urbanisation over the last few decades.

Beyond the coastal strip, roughly a third of the country is the Sierra - three Andean ranges running north to south, with intervening valleys, hills and table lands, watered by rains and glacial waters, the former heartland of the Inca Empire, and historically home to the majority of Peru's population. Because of the tortured and broken patterns of mountain ranges and the many valleys and hills, transportation and communication are difficult. The trend is towards isolation. Perhaps for this reason, there are as many as 18 dialects of the Quechua language spoken. The Sierra is rich and productive, but difficult to get into and out of, markets tend to be local or regional. Haciendas, export crops and mining operations tend to be small.

Beyond that, of course is the Selva, or the rain forest jungle; half the country, but with a fraction of the population, largely unknown, mostly inaccessible, of little value or economic impact.

In this sense, with minor variations, Peru resembles the other Andean nations we've examined - Chile and Ecuador, and overlaps with Bolivia and Colombia. Unlike Chile, however, which has quickly displaced or extirpated its native population, the Spanish in Peru find themselves ruling over the heartlands of Andean civilization - of which the Inca were merely the latest heirs. The Europeans and their descendants dominate densely populated, agriculturally and culturally sophisticated native populations.

So, while the Chileans can indulge in pretensions of Europeanization, the Spanish in Peru can only impose themselves, creating a feudal caste society, somewhat like South Africa. A minority in their own country the Peruvians maintain the closest ties to Spain and, in fact, is the center of royalist resistance during the wars of independence.

Thereafter, with independence, a Peruvian Spanish elite rules uneasily and ruthlessly over an elaborately stratified, infinitely divided and divisive society. It is an archaic nation, feudal in character, tenuously held together. Which perhaps explains how and why Peru does so poorly in its 19th century wars with Chile. In part, these defeats take place because of the unwillingness of the European elites to risk the sort of social efforts that would disrupt the class structure. They would never put guns in the hands of the Indigenous, for fear of where those guns might eventually be pointed. Indeed, the history of Peru features a series of native revolts, some of them massive, up to the 1930s. In the end, Peruvian elites choose stability over victory again and again.

The transformation of Peru, to the extent it transforms, is not the product of these defeats. Rather, it is the same shift to neocolonialism which is taking place throughout Latin America. International trade, the rise of cash crops and mineral exports, produces an economy based on exports of raw materials and imports of luxury goods. Between 1880, the low point of the Pacific war, and 1920, the value of Peruvian exports increased tenfold, or one thousand percent.

Each Latin state brings its own particular wrinkles to the process. Unlike Chile and its nitrates, or Ecuador and cacao, Peru does not have a single overwhelming cash commodity. Rather, its export products are divided across a handful of mining and farming regions in the interior and the coast; profitable, but not exorbitantly so, and distributed rather than centralized.

Peru's fall into the neocolonial orbit drives consolidation and expansion. Small mining operations are replaced by bigger, more efficient industrial operations; small haciendas are squeezed out by bigger and bigger ones. The subsistence economies of the Indigenous and Mestizo are under pressure. Between 1880 and 1920 over a third of Indigenous lands are taken up by the expanding haciendas, producing protracted conflicts.

One might have expected this will result in some form of civil war or mass uprising. And to some extent, it does. The trouble is that Peru is a difficult place to have a broad-based civil war. Endlessly divided into deserts, and river basins, mountain ranges, valleys, hill countries, it is hard for an uprising to really catch fire and get rolling. Geographical divisions are exacerbated by cultural and linguistic divisions. A third of the nation might be Quechua Indigenous, but as we've noted those Quechua are divided into 18 dialects and regional cultures. Quechua are divided from Aymara, Aymara from Guarani, Guarani from Mestizo, etc.

Instead of the great uprisings (and there has been one in the 18th century, the last gasp of the Inca), the 19th and 20th centuries feature what seems to be an endless smolder. A weak central government largely lets things drift. What you have at times is a sort of Wild West. Rival Haciendas would literally fight their own wars, maintaining private armies of a dozen or more thugs, burning down each others' plantations and buildings.

Indigenous or Mestizo will occasionally rise up, lynching unpopular officials, sometimes taking over a town, but usually going no further. The army will show up, taking things back, imposing a form of order. The uprising population will quiet down, the most hotheaded dying in futile gunfights, resorting to banditry, or simply fleeing over to the next hills, the next valleys, the next towns.

Reading local histories is absolutely amazing. There is the story of a man who becomes wealthy through the expedient of moving into town and marrying a local girl, taking over a local farm, and eventually moving on somewhere else to do it again. It works, when he dies he has eleven wives and ninety-three children at his funeral. You have to think about the sort of society, the sort of nation, where that kind of thing can not only be gotten away with, but even celebrated.

The central government is weak and disorganized. But oddly, that is all right, because within Peruvian society, social resistance is even weaker and more disorganized. More relentlessly heterodox, more diverse and distributed Peruvian society does not see the same sort of polarization between the inland Latifundistas and the coastal mercantile elites that we see in Colombia and Ecuador. This is not to say that it is not there, but rather, that it is not so clear cut, it does not divide so readily into violent class extremes. Rather, local Latifundistas as often as not find common cause with local mercantiles. It seems that there is simply more breathing room.

This seems to permeate Peruvian society. If the Latifundistas and the rise of great Haciendas expropriate vast amounts of Indigenous land and produce social and cultural stress, this doesn't result in as much drainage of migrants into coastal cities, which in turn fails to produce a large urban labour pool with consequent cheap labour and social tension.

Instead, some Indigenous retreat further into the hills and mountains, opening up and cultivating more marginal land. Some become day labourers and sharecroppers in the new regime, others are taken up by local industrial mining operations. Or some simply move, to the coasts, to river valleys, to mountain valleys. Economic dislocations produce population dislocations, but the country is big enough, divided enough, fragmented enough, that it can absorb these dislocations without disruption.

Axis of Andes – Page 127

Although Indigenous are over half the population of the country; although Mestizo are a third; although the European descended Criollo elite is only a fraction; the Indigenous and Mestizo, as with so many other Latin nations, never radicalize, never challenge, and are for the most part, safely ignored. Their grievances are instead expressed in ten thousand acts of small rebellion, none of them ever becoming a raging fire.

Of course, radicalism does come about. As with Chile and Ecuador, it takes root in the coastal cities, where the interface with European economies produces a functional working or urban class, and opportunities for contact with radical ideas.

In Ecuador, a narrow export base, a relatively simple commodity requiring little processing, and a large displaced surplus population produces a working class which was weak, impoverished and desperate. Labour strife, much more desperate, produces massacres.

In Chile, a more diverse export base, more developed infrastructure and processing for those exports, and a relative hunger or demand for labour results in a wealthier. more comfortable working class; but a key commodity also produces a more ruthless government willing to machine gun women and children, and produces massacres.

In Peru, we have a more diverse export base, more inherent infrastructure and processing, the working class is proportionately more comfortable than in Ecuador, but less narrowly based than in Chile. Like the other countries, Peru experiences its periods of strife, including general strikes and the rise of radical socialist or communist movements, but unlike the other countries, at least up to the 1920s, Peru does not exhibit the same level of extreme violence applied elsewhere.

Without aggressive repression, Peru becomes a sort of hotbed of left wing movements and internationalism. Labour unions and labour movements, intellectuals and radical politics find fertile ground for a time.

****

Henry Ford and the American Empire

The Monroe doctrine aside, for much of South America, the dominant economic and military power in the region is Britain, not the United States. American interests and activity seem to concentrate instead in the Caribbean and Central America. Places like Peru, Bolivia and Chile are remote to both American power and interests.

In the early twentieth century, this begins to shift. Andean exports to, and imports from the United States increase dramatically, on average running from around 10% at the turn of the century to 40% by the 1920s. American investment also increases dramatically during this time, as much as ten or twenty-fold.

American investment tends to differ in being rather more aggressive than British investment. There is, in both cases, a tendency to buy not just the product, but the producers; to acquire not just goods but pieces of the economy. Railroads, for instance, are often built, run and owned by foreigners, with leased monopolies of sixty years or more.

By and large though, the British tend to be wary of directly running aspects of the economy. A hacienda or a plantation properly run is a license to print your own money, a feudal kingdom on its own. But it often depends on acute local knowledge and complex pseudo-feudal relationships.

A British overseer could well lose his shirt trying to run one. So British investment is often cautious, focusing on purchasing, on relationships, on selling, and on acquiring the more fungible parts of the economy.

American investment takes things up to the next level. There are a couple of reasons for this. First, the American concerns often have more money to throw around. They can invest on a larger and more aggressive scale. Second, the volume of production, the volume of exports has been climbing steadily and, with this steady increase of production, comes social and economic changes, a weakening of the complex semi-feudal networks, an increasingly organized, cash oriented, production oriented economy. Essentially, the Latin economies have grown and become sufficiently complex that it is becoming viable for foreign concerns to buy, own and operate plantations, mines and domestic production.

To some extent, this displaces or crowds local elites. But the money, and the further expansion of the economy is good enough that they can reliably embrace the American partnership. The middle class, historically a subservient rump, is generally as content to serve Americans as it is Latifundistas or local mercantile elites. No one ever cares what the Indigenous think. The local working classes get the worst deal and are often hostile, but powerless.

Indeed, the major source of friction with American interests is usually with local working classes and labour organizations, which results in a long running American hostility to what it perceives as communism in the region, and the corollary, local resentment of American intrusion, particularly among the left.

But for the most part, the United States, despite its increasing role in the economy and politics of South America, could hardly care less. Europe and Asia are vastly larger and more important trading partners; and Asian theatres have the populations, the politics and the military threats.

To the extent that South American states figure in American foreign policy, it is a foreign policy driven by corporate interests. Americans through the 1900s to 1930s own increasing chunks of Latin America - they own mines, they own plantations, they control vast territories, have timber rights, imports and exports and, when those interests are threatened or confronted, those companies go straight to the U.S. state department.

Not to put too fine a point on it, but American policy in Guatemala is dictated not by the needs, perceptions or concerns of the United States government, but by those of the United Fruit Company. When the American government thinks about Guatemala, the voice it listens to is not Guatemalans, but rather, the United Fruit Company's. So it goes.

What this means was that in American eyes, disputes between Latin American countries tend to be expressed in terms of the relative political weight of American interests in those countries. Standard Oil covertly backed Paraguay in the Chaco War and, in subtle terms, so did the United States.

Going into the 1930s, what this amounts to for Ecuador is bad news. The scale and scope of American corporations in Peru, American investment in Peru, is far greater than in Ecuador. While the United States professes neutrality, the accurate perception of the Bonifaz regime is that if push comes to shove, America will favour Peru over Ecuador. An American negotiated settlement will not be in Ecuador's interests.

The result is a slow but definite chilling in relations between Ecuador and the United States, which culminates in the dispute between Labour Minister Enriquez Gallo, with the American owned mining concern, the South American Development Company, over wages and working conditions for its Ecuadorian miners.

Nevertheless, Ecuador remains a relatively remote and small concern, and the perception of the Bonifaz government as a fascist outpost is only a minor issue to a handful of diplomats.

The 1937 visit of members of the Bonifaz Triumvirate to Berlin and the meeting with Hitler might be a greater cause for concern, in and of itself. The Roosevelt government is becoming steadily more hostile to Nazi Germany, though American commercial interests remain friendly.

However, this chill is blunted by the involvement of Henry Ford in the Ecuadorian economy. Acting in conjunction with, and inspired by German initiatives, Ford focusses on Ecuador as a base for his South American operations. Establishing assembly plants in 1938, Ecuador becomes the manufacturing and distribution point for Ford operations to Colombia, Peru, Bolivia and Chile. The operation is funded partly by reassigned investment from Ford Argentina and Ford Brazil, partly new investment, and partly by funneled Nazi funds. In general terms, it is seen as a good investment, relatively trivial to the Ford Company, low risk, but a big deal to the region.

Ford's pressure on the American State Department obtains government intercession to persuade the other Andean nations to cooperate.

Although Ford Ecuador is, on paper, considered to have more potential than Ford Argentina or even Ford Brazil, it never quite realizes it. Start-up costs and transportation expenses eat into the project's operations. Balancing this, however, is a weak and quiescent labour force.

By 1940, Ford Ecuador is turning out respectable numbers of trucks for local and regional use; and although the Ford Company directly owns the production, economic spin offs ranging from importers, to local parts suppliers, manufacturers, mechanics, servicemen and gas stations are having a major impact on the Ecuadorian economy.

Ford's support also does much to blunt what otherwise might have been a hostile American government which, after 1939, is becoming concerned about potential Nazi penetration of South America - A concern that is beginning to match or eclipse business fears of communism.

Buoyed by this, the Ecuadorian triumvirate becomes ebullient, even overconfident in their dealings with their lagging Peruvian rivals. A recklessness which perhaps contributes to the war.

Despite the significance of the Ford investment, it comes too late and too piecemeal for Ecuador to enter the war as an industrialized or industrializing economy. As a manufacturing base, the Ford investment provides a seed.

Ford's investment produces a brace of trained personnel, organization techniques, machinery, parts and equipment and infrastructural and economic spin offs that through repairs and retrofits extend Ecuador's short-term military potential immensely.

In overall terms, both the Nazi investment and the Ford investment in Ecuador are comparatively tiny. For both the German government and the Ford Motor company, the

Ecuadorian project is relatively trivial in the larger scheme of things.

Nevertheless, although much is made of the German influence, by far the most significant impact is through the investment and political support of Ford.

✳✳✳

The Failure of the Left in South America

The hard Marxist movements of South America actually receive little support from Stalin or from the Comintern. According to Marxist dogma, as expounded by the Soviets, the predicted communist revolutions should come about through the industrial working class. Hence the emphasis is on Europe and somewhat on America, where industrial working classes exist and are seemingly ripe for Marxism.

South America features what is at best an embryonic industrial working class. Mostly the population are various forms of landed and landless peasantry, sharecroppers and subsistence farmers. According to Marxist pseudo-theology, it is just too early. Marxist efforts here would be a waste of time and effort.

The result is that although there were communist or socialist parties throughout the region, they receive little support from the Comintern. Given that world communism in the 1930s was very centralized and under the influence of the Soviet Union, this tends to strangle communist parties in Latin America. If they raise funds, those funds go elsewhere. If they show talent, they get recruited and reassigned elsewhere. Local parties are often burdened with impossible tasks and demands, receive no support, and their failures are pre-ordained.

The result is that the left, in South America tends to be fairly diverse and heterodox, an amalgam of thinkers, journalists, union leaders, intellectuals, radical politicians of varying stripes and ideologies, mostly socialist, but even the Marxists are a diverse group. There is not a lot of firmness or rigour in doctrine, or broad ideological or organizational coherence. Left wing ideology tends to be an urban and European phenomenon and, for the most part, there is little effort to enlist Indigenous or the rural Mestizo.

There are some important left wing thinkers, who bring penetrating analysis to Latin American societies and ideologies, and there are some international movements, but generally it is all weak tea.

Of course, there is a side benefit to this. The relative weakness and diversity of the left wing movements allows some otherwise hostile Latin American societies to co-opt left wing concepts and priorities. So we see the rise of leftist parties within Chile, and even people like Ibanez in Chile adopting progressive platforms; and we see Peronism in Argentina, at least initially, play out as a labour supported movement. Many South American leaders at least flirt with the left.

Unfortunately, in South America, class warfare is very much a real thing for the elites - they have class consciousness, they self-identify, recognize and, in an organized fashion, pursue their class interests, often to the detriment of everything and everyone else.

Other classes simply never achieve that level of consciousness, never pursue their interests as a class or group. Efforts to organize are usually low level and disjointed.

***

Radical Ideology and Ethnic Tension in Latin America, Pilgrim Press, 1972, Ed. B. Aker

.... for the most part, the Quechua, Aymara and other ethnicities which constitute the Andean Indigenous are decidedly apolitical in Western terms. Their existence was primarily organized around village structures, with both the local caudillos or haciendas, and the Catholic Church operating as forces of conservatism and stability. For the Indigenous Andean villages, relationships were local and intensely paternal.

Revolts and agitation were invariably local and sporadic in nature. Frequently they arose in response to local grievances, and were of short duration. Still, political issues could give rise to more broad based uprisings. The imposition of a head tax on Indigenous in 1895 in Peru brought about widespread rebellion until such time as the tax was hastily withdrawn.

Intellectuals, teachers and journalists, imbibing European concepts of socialism or even Marxism tended to remain almost exclusively on the coast, and affiliated with Mestizo or Criollo communities. There they found little support with the middle classes, but were essential in organizing an emerging proletarian class.

Indigenous, however, were both excluded and usually unresponsive to this emerging debate, at least through the 19th and in the early part of the 20th century.

As late 1922 Juan Manuel Lasso Ascásubi, a cousin of Neptali Bonifaz, attempted to launch a socialist revolution from the Guachalá hacienda in Cayambe, Ecuador, failed because of the reluctance of the Indigenous of the hacienda to rise up against their paternal liege.

Nevertheless, although remaining apolitical, the Indigenous peasantry became increasingly restive. Between 1901 and 1930, there were estimated to be over 300 peasant risings in Peru, most short lived. A famous revolt took place in Puno in 1915, led by Teodomiro Guttierez Cuevas, called Rum Maqui, a former soldier and provincial official. Calling upon memories of the Inca Empire and Millennial sentiment, he was able to raise a peasant army which raged for a time before being dispersed.

However, up until the 1930s, peasant and Indigenous agitation remained strictly divorced from modern socialist ideology. The peasants revolted in the interior, animated by both ancient memories and local grievances. The labourers went on strike in the cities, animated by Marxist insight. But the two threads of social discontent had no communication.

Matters began to shift slightly in the 1930s for a number of reasons. Ironically, one of them was the ascension of the neo-Fascist regime of Bonifaz in Ecuador.

Bonifaz was a highly traditional caudillo; his conservatism and racism were well established. Shortly after his consolidation of power, a number of radicals, including his own cousin Ascásubi, were exiled, most finding sanctuary in Peru.

Many of these exiles congregated along the coasts, merging with the local intelligentsia. However, Ascásubi and his followers alienated Peruvian intellectuals by preaching of enlightening the natives. They found themselves unwelcome and marginalised, and were driven into the interior, residing in Mestizo towns.

The radicalization of the Ecuadorian government under Bonifaz and increasing hostilities between the two nations had their own effect on the position of Peru. Peru's ruling oligarchy became increasingly militarized and conservative in nature. A wave of general strikes and labour unrest in 1919 had raised fears of bolshevism.

Now, in the 1930s, with renewed labour unrest and a hostile neighbour, many Peruvian intellectuals found themselves exiled into the interior, often under house arrest, at other times as guests of relatives in haciendas and townships.

Notable among these were Haya de la Torre, one of the seminal Marxist intellectuals of Peru, who while in Mexico in 1924 founded the Alliance for Popular Revolution of America (APRA) which became the dominant left wing political party in Peru through the 1930s. Torre, although a critical thinker, remained in many ways a moderate reformer, and in his writing minimized the role of the peasantry. Relocated to house arrest in the interior south in 1934, he was forced to deal with the Mestizo peasantry.

His chief rival on the left during this time was the journalist Jose Carlos Mariategui. The two, initially close, broke in an acrimonious public exchange of letters in 1928. A revolutionary, as opposed to a reformer like Torre, Mariategui differed in seeing the role of the Indigenous and peasantry as central to revolution. In poor health, however, Mariategui remained on the coast until his exile to the north interior in 1932, when he fell in with Ascubazi.

A third vein of indigenous radicalism came from Bolivia starting in 1935, from refugees, runaway soldiers and native activists. Native enlistment or recruitment in the Bolivian Army during the Chaco war, and under the military socialism of both David Toro and German Busch seeped into the Andean consciousness.

Adding to this mixture was the slow emergence of an indigenous movement which recalled the glories of the old Inca Empire, and a veneration of past accomplishments. What was most remarkable, however, was the apparent failure of these many elements to gel in any way. Despite the presence, deliberate and inadvertent, of many Peruvian intellectuals, they garnered remarkably little in the way of direct followings. No real political consensus emerged during the 1930s, despite various social and political pressures.

For the most part, the indigenous population, while increasingly restive, appeared to continue in its traditional state of political marginalisation and impotence, near-feudal local relationships and indifference to the outside world. The Peruvian government of Augusto Leguia and his successors may be forgiven for continuing to ignore the Indigenous question.

Mariategui was indeed a radical Marxist journalist and advocate of revolution, one of the leading Marxist intellectuals in Peruvian society. Plagued by poor health most of his life, he was injured in 1924 and had to have his leg amputated. A fierce opponent of fascism and an advocate of indigenous communism as practiced by the Inca (in his view), he advocated radicalizing the Indigenous.

Marxist theory and radicalism seems to have failed entirely to penetrate into the Andean highlands or to make much of an impact through the 1920s and 1930s. One intellectual current which does seem to have been active, however, was a vague form of indigenous nationalism, more a form of occasional nostalgia than anything else. Harkening back to the age of the Inca and the notion of indigenous self-government and rule, particularly when the Spanish Criollo were most repressive.

This had underlain the 18th century rebellion of Tupac Amaru II, and showed up from time to time in local sentiments and local rebellions, notably the Puno rebellion of Rum Maqui, a Quechua name that translated as 'Hands of Stone.' Various obstacles, including lack of weaponry, ammunition, logistics, communication, etc., generally prevented such uprisings from getting out of hand. Even the Puno rebellion produced little more than an untrained part-time peasant army, no match for real organized military forces.

Peru - 1904 to 1930, the Era of Augusto Leguia

Barely five feet tall, Augusto Leguia nevertheless dominates the early twentieth century of Peru. One of those archetypal self-made capitalists, through relentless energy and innovation, he makes a series of fortunes in activities as diverse as sugar exporting, insurance, banking, rubber extraction and railway building.

This is during a period of rapidly escalating exports, as the United States replaces Great Britain as Peru's dominant trading partner. Essentially, the market is booming, and if you can get a handle on a key commodity, you can make a fortune. If you can get a lever on the infrastructure that those commodities need - financial or transportation, you can make another fortune. Perhaps as much as brilliance, it is a matter of right place, right time.

Still, Leguia's financial success inevitably makes him a candidate for government. He becomes the Minister of Finance for Jose Prado's government between 1904 and 1908. But then he breaks with his mentor, becoming leader of the progressive wing, and ultimately winning the Presidency between 1908 and 1912. However, his aggressive export-oriented business sensibility does not mesh well with the traditional Peruvian power structure. He is exiled when Prado returns to power in 1912.

1919 and the end of the First World War brings a major recession and economic crisis to Latin America. Peru is no exception. Leguia sits out the gathering economic storm in exile. Consequently, when the Prado regime falls apart, he sweeps in to power on almost universal support, dissolving parliament and ruling as a dictator.

As is so often the case with Latin American despots, his career in power features a steady progression from left to right. In his first years, he consolidates power among the middle and working classes, decreeing reforms such as an eight hour day, minimum wages, initiating public works and employment projects. Between 1920 and 1928, Peru's foreign debt increases by over 100 million, much of it spent on an ambitious campaign of public works and infrastructure, which in turn supports export oriented production and foreign investment.

He manages to defuse mounting tensions in the Sierra by partially recognizing the communal land rights of Indigenous villages, while roads and infrastructure built into the interior allows Leguia to exercise military and political authority against them more effectively.

Under Leguia, Peru moves even more strongly into the American orbit, encouraging and supporting foreign investment. Peruvian owned manufacturing and business remain largely stagnant during Leguia's rule. But foreign investment and ownership increases from roughly 45% of the economy's exports in 1910 to over 80% by 1935.

As time goes on, he becomes an increasingly conservative and repressive autocrat. Leguia manipulates the political system to exclude and marginalise opposition. Rebellions and coup attempts mount. At times, he seems to ride only a step or two ahead of his rivals.

The bottom drops out for Leguia, as for so many other Latin American leaders, with the Great Depression. Within three years, exports and imports have dropped 60%, the state budget drops from 50 million dollars to 16 million; unemployment reaches 25%, major banks close. The spending and infrastructure programs of the 1920s leave Peru with a massive state debt and no more credit to function.

Ironically, Leguia rode into power in 1919, when his exile left his enemies holding the bag for a major economic crisis. But now, this time, he is the man in charge when the bottom falls out of the economy. And in particular, the bottom falls out in those areas of the economy he has most strongly championed.

***

Peru in the 1930s

Leguia's relentless manoeuvring has left him without challengers or rivals in his nation. Most of his opponents are in exile or effectively emasculated. Perhaps this is why he's allowed a rebellious officer, Colonel Luis Sanchez Cerra, with no particular political constituency, to return from exile.

It is a major mistake. With his world collapsing around him, with the key elements of his economic and political power in free fall, Sanchez Cerra, a Mestizo officer, raises a garrison in revolt, and suddenly Leguia is gone.

We've examined Sanchez Cerra and his brief reign, in the context of the Colombia-Peru war. Basically, the guy is one of those hard-core maniacs; fearless, driven, stubborn, the sort of man who gets a lot of people killed.

But within the context of Peruvian politics, he is revolutionary in a number of ways. A Mestizo or mixed blood in a caste-ridden society which has traditionally been dominated by an elite of pure blooded Spanish descendants. In photographs, Sanchez is visibly dark skinned, his features betraying a hint of the stark Inca look. This dark complexion and willingness to campaign in the provinces wins him a constituency among Indigenous and Mestizo.

This is entirely accidental. Cerra does not see himself as embodying the aspirations of Indigenous or Mestizo. He is rather too focused and self-absorbed in the style of the caudillo personality. People follow him, he does not follow them. Still, he does consolidate his following in the provinces with such measures as abolishing the hated forced-labour levies for road construction. Nevertheless, he is something new on the Peruvian political scene. A leader with a genuine mass following, rather than a scion of the oligarchy, ruling for the oligarchy.

In a sense, there is a missed opportunity here. Despite a brief initial flirtation with socialism and with radicalism, Sanchez, having mostly the strength of his own personality but little in the way of actual ideas or ideology, drifts rightward quickly, earning the bitter enmity of APRA, his rival for mass appeal, and becoming a creature of the right and oligarchy.

Still, his relatively brief reign produces two key developments for our purposes. First, his role in and the ultimate resolution of the Colombia-Peru War has left the Bonifaz Regime in Ecuador with no doubts but that they are in extreme danger from their neighbor to the south. At the same time, his preparations and mobilization for the war, a war that ultimately fizzled, sets Peru on the path of militarization. It is a militarization which will only gain force through the 1930s.

After Cerra's assassination in 1933, his lieutenant, General Oscar Benavides takes over. Like Sanchez Cerra, Oscar Benavides has actually seen war in his life; unlike Sanchez Cerra, he's a lot less enthusiastic about it.

In 1911, he commands a coastal army battalion. In response to a Colombian fortification on the Caquetá River far inland, he and his troops march and ride and sail 2000 miles into the steaming jungles of the interior. It is four months of hard travel. Finally, they meet the Colombian garrison, they fight, they win, and two weeks later they have to give it back when a treaty assigns the territory to Colombia. Along the way, he contracts beriberi and his troops are decimated by yellow fever and tropical diseases. Shortly thereafter, he is wounded by bandits, and then shot a second time by friendly fire. For a young idealistic man of thirty-five, it is a bruising indictment of the utter futility of war. Suffering and hardship, disease and misery, ferocious fighting for worthless bits of jungle.

He later writes, "I have suffered so much that the victory obtained and the ovations and promotion conferred on me have not gratified me in the way many assume, as they would have without so much misfortune."

That bitter disenchantment, that conviction of the futility and meaninglessness of war never leaves him.

But the experience makes him a war hero. He receives promotions, honours and parades out of the deal. He goes on to be a scion of Peruvian Criollo society and of the military; a minister, a diplomat, a valued member of the elite, rising to the rank of general. In 1915, he's become President through a coup. In 1930, when Sanchez Cerra takes power, there is literally no one better qualified in all the country to be his second in command. His standing in the army is impeccable. Where Sanchez has a following in the lower classes, Benavides balances the ticket with the gravitas and stability that the Criollo elite crave.

When Sanchez Cerra is assassinated in the midst of turning the Colombia-Peru War into a major bloodbath, it's no surprise that Benavides will have none of it. There is no glory in his mind, only pointless carnage over worthless jungle that the vast majority of Peruvians will never see.

He wraps up the war, makes peace, reinstitutes the Salomon-Lozano treaty and takes the boys home.

After that, he is decidedly and thoroughly uninterested in another war for a few thousand square miles of jungle interior.

And since he is President and War Hero, General of the Armies and favoured son of the elite all rolled into one; he gets his way. At least so long as he is President. In this, however, his position is neither unanimous nor unopposed.

Ecuador's triumvirate, for instance, does not understand that his wartime experience has left him something of a pacifist. Instead, his stature as a war hero and associate of the fire-breather Cerra leaves them, and many others, with the impression that he is another fire-breather himself.

Indeed, in Peru, that impression gives him the necessary credibility and room to end one war and avoid another.

Nevertheless, as a far more traditional scion of the Criollo class, he has difficulty retaining Cerra's populist constituencies. Instead, he campaigns and governs largely as a caretaker on the notion of peace, order and good government. By this time, the worst of the Depression is over, and if Peru is not seeing economic recovery, it is experiencing stability and some degree of function.

Indeed, Peru, despite the devastation to export sectors of the economy, has managed to endure the Great Depression in better shape than most other Latin American economies. In part this is because much of the internal economy in the Sierra Highlands, among the Indigenous and Mestizo, remain traditional and subsistence, and thus not nearly as vulnerable to the vagaries of international capital.

For another, the Peruvian export industry is more diverse than many of its neighbours'. Where Chile and Ecuador are largely single item exporters, Peru's table includes a variety of agricultural exports - rubber, sugar, coffee, as well as a variety of minerals and even a small amount of oil.

But although Benavides' qualifications as a Criollo gentleman and a general are impeccable, he is no economist or technocrat. Fiscal policy remains strictly in the hands of the conservatives, who implement it with a thorough lack of imagination. Any advantage that its more diversified economy gives is squandered. Peru does not pursue import substitution, or any form of Keynesian economics, or any other significant reform.

Rather, it simply imposes austerity, tightens its belt and tries for a balanced budget. That remains elusive. Peru through the depression continues to run both trade and budget deficits, requiring external financing. In return, they allow or encourage substantial foreign investment.

Overall, the Benavides era from 1933 to 1939 is one of relative drift. Peru, as we've noted, is too diverse and too scattered by its geography to be truly governable. With divergent interests in the Criollo elite, the middle class, the army as a constituency in itself, and the emerging though largely ignored voices of the Mestizo and Indigenous, Benavides can do little more than bumble along on the current. A Sanchez Cerra, through sheer force of will, might have dragged the nation after him. But Benavides is no Sanchez.

Under Benevides, the policy of Peru's government can best be described as reactive. Sanchez has initiated a massive expansion and reform of the armed forces which continues under Benavides, though, at times, erratically.

To neutralize political agitation, and counter the possibility of a two front war, the Army is divided into northern and southern commands. An unintended consequence of this, is that the Northern Command became increasingly embroiled in border conflicts with Ecuador, at times carrying on independently of the central government in Lima.

Despite the poor economic performance, hostilities with Ecuador allow the Peruvian military to push for even more money and spark a minor arms race. But in the end, the Peruvian economy, as managed by Benavides and his fiscal conservatives, does not have huge resources to put to an arms race, much less a war.

Left to itself, the military expansion in Peru might have run out of steam on its own; there were enough competing constituencies. But the ongoing hostility and border dispute with the Bonifaz government in Ecuador keeps international tensions simmering. The Peruvian government watches with increasing concern as Ecuador attempts to meddle in the Chaco War and pursues an alliance with Chile. By the late 1930s in the Benavides government, the consensus is not whether there will be a war with Ecuador, but when.

****

Pining For War

The Colombia-Peru War turns out quite well all things considered. But many Peruvians, particularly those in the military, don't see it that way. The real and critical territorial concessions made by Colombia in the treaty and reinforced by the war are overshadowed by the fact that Peru has ceded the town of Leticia, inhabited by Peruvian nationals. This is seen as a national humiliation.

And more, the Peruvian army has not really had a chance to fight. I'm sure that sort of attitude arouses a deep contempt in Benavides. He knows exactly what a real war entails. But try telling that to hot blooded young soldiers and salon generals in the comfort of Lima townhouses.

Nevertheless, the Peruvian military is itching for a fight. The territorial dispute over the Ecuadorian sierra dates all the way back to the Gran Colombia War in 1828. There is a century of military humiliation to overcome. War is on the table.

In this, Bonifaz and his compatriots in Ecuador are absolutely correct about the sentiment in Peru.

Still, Benavides' stature is such that no one is going to challenge him. At least not at first. There will be attempted coups within the Army as time goes on, but there always are.

Ecuador remains a kind of long running irritant, particularly given the border conflicts. And it represents a minor security threat, given its efforts to meddle with countries to the south. But Benavides is not inclined to take action.

The bottom line is that no matter what anyone else might think in Peru, there will be no war while Benavides is in charge.

Of course, in December, 1939, after Benavides leaves and Manuel Prado becomes President, things are different.

Manuel Prado is not a war hero. He's not even a soldier or a military man. He's a banker. The prestige and credibility, the gravitas and persuasion that Benavides possesses as a genuine war hero and general are just not available. Elements in the military who were cautious about trying to push Benavides around, feel less inhibited, and rather more bold, dealing with Prado.

Among these is General Elroy Gaspar Ureta, who has been assigned the Northern Command, one of the two top positions in the Peruvian armed forces. Ureta is Criollo - part of the pureblood Spanish aristocracy, deeply conservative, a stubborn headstrong man, caste-conscious, nationalist. Steeped in Peruvian military lore and prejudice, he harbours generations worth of grudges for lost wars, and a strong resentment of the current Ecuador border situation.

The war, in a sense, is inevitable. Perhaps it has been inevitable in some form or other since 1828. It is certainly inevitable from 1933 onward. The only issue there has ever been is timing.

With the departure of Benavides, and the accession of Prado, the countdown has started.

General Ureta is determined to be the man to start it, and he has too much authority, and too little respect for Prado to ask permission.

And Now, a Word From Bolivia...

The Chaco War ends in 1935, with the ceasefire. It will be another three years of tension before peace is finally signed off. During this period, Paraguay sits on the economic lifelines of Bolivia, and Bolivia in turn rearms in 1937-38, rebuilding its forces to about 35,000 men. It is not until after July of 1938 that Bolivia can really feel at peace.

Sorzano has taken power after the military coup that overthrew Salamanca in 1934. But Sorzano has inherited a bag of hammers: A ruinous war, a complete lack of economic options, and a fractured society. Historically, Bolivia is run by small cadres of competing elites based around the two largest cities, La Paz and Sucre. Most of the population, largely Indigenous and Mestizo, are not invited to the debate. The expansion of tin mining, and before that, rubber and quinine, and subsequently oil production, has created a small disenfranchised, town based, working class. The war has been fairly transformative in rousing the restive and disenfranchised classes.

Sorzano is largely a product of the old way of doing things and of the old elite. His position is essentially hopeless.

By May 1936, he's been ousted by a coup and Colonel David Toro takes over. Toro nationalizes the oil industry, guarantees minimum wages, orders that foreign companies must spend at least 85% of their payroll on Bolivian employees, and supports organized labour. Toro's style of government is called Military Socialism. Essentially, by this time, the Army is one of the few genuine organized forces in Bolivian society, and perhaps the only one with any kind of broad base. He lasts 14 months.

He is replaced by German Busch, another military socialist, a bona fide war hero, but not well educated and not the sharpest knife in the drawer. Busch is a man of conviction and dedication, but often his approach is to issue a decree and hope for the best. He is utterly at sea with the tasks of governance. Sadly, he kills himself in August, 1939. And with him goes Military Socialism.

By this time, Bolivian society is fracturing into three constituencies. There are the Bolivian nationalists; the old guard right wing of the elites; and the rising labour and leftist movements. The old guard, by virtue of traditional business contacts and connections, tends to identify themselves with the interests of American and British capital, and by extension, the Anglo-American Democracies. Despite their appeal to American and British interests and their pretensions to liberalism and democracy, the truth is they are as genuinely democratic as any other repressive oligarchy - say the Saudis or Kuwait.

By default, the Nationalists come to be associated with the Nazis and Fascists, and the leftists and populists with Communists. It's a bit more subtle than that, though. These are indigenous political movements, and the linkages to European or American movements are complex. Some of the Nationalists, perhaps many, find some degree of genuine affiliation or inspiration with European fascist movements.

The left wing takes inspiration from Marxism, European and American labour movements, and even doctrinaire (as it was then) Communism. But these are still indigenous movements which borrow ideas and traits from parallel developments elsewhere.

Fascist and Communist are pretty useful pejoratives for the traditional elite or traditional right to use against their enemies. For one thing, it gets American and British ears perking right up, simplifies the country's narrative into good guys and bad guys for the gullible gringos. Military Socialism, that was pretty close to Communist, or Nazi, as far as Americans were concerned.

After German Busch's suicide, General Carlos Quintanilla takes over. Quintanilla is another Chaco War hero. There is no shortage of them. He was commander of the armed forces in the German Busch administration. And he is plagued by associations with the Nazis.

Even before taking office, Quintanilla's name appears on a list of Bolivians that the British Ambassador is warning of.... "A small body of men who are all impressed by the Nazi regime... it is rumoured that the German Minister is giving his assistance and advice."

The British and Americans are very concerned with Bolivia because it is one of the principal world sources of tin, which is one of many crucial war materials. So the allegation of Nazi affiliation, of course, will get attention in Washington and London. Not surprisingly though, despite being a nationalist, Quintanilla's priority is to keep his foundering country from sinking. His top priority is to obtain U.S. credit, so as to avoid food shortages in the cities. To curry favour in Washington, he undoes a number of Busch's decrees.

Through this time, the relationship with Ecuador is viewed with increasing disdain. The support of Ecuador, and the relationship, has always been the project of a desperate and failing Salamanca. But Ecuador hasn't made much, if any, meaningful contribution to the Chaco War. Salamanca has been replaced with Sorzano, whose entry into the treaty has been a matter of a weak man paying debts. Ibbara's prized secret treaty is practically dead on arrival. Toro and later Busch view it with a mixture of bemusement and mild concern, until Busch makes it clear that Bolivia will not consider itself bound.

Quintanilla, despite rumours of Nazi affiliation, and perhaps some genuine sympathy, has less than no interest in Ecuador, a small country, far away, with no capacity to make a difference to him. Quintanilla might possibly have some affiliation with Chilean Nazis, except that Chile occupies Bolivia's stolen coastal provinces, and is as close as Bolivia has to a national enemy. So, no help for Ecuador there.

Quintanilla is essentially a caretaker government. Under his rule, the traditional right wing assembles under the banner of General Enrique Penaranda. Quintanilla, charged with organizing the election, poses a threat. The socialists are in disarray following Busch's tenure and suicide. However, the nationalists, to the extent that they are an organized movement, coalesce awkwardly under Quintanilla.

It is under these circumstances that the Ibarra-Sorzano Treaty, conceived and signed in secret as a mutual aid alliance in war between Ecuador and Bolivia, becomes a political football. Ecuador's secret weapon against Peru is exposed to the public in February, 1940. The circumstances of the exposure are unclear, but it is certainly a move by Penaranda's supporters to discredit Quintanilla.

Ironic, as Quintanilla certainly has nothing to do with the treaty and may not have known of it. But Quintanilla's alleged fascist sympathies are already a major handicap, particularly in the eyes of America and Britain. The apparent association with Andean fascism puts an end to any possible Presidential aspirations.

In the larger sense, it is a tiny scandal, even by Bolivian standards. A ginned up, phony outrage that occupies a weekend's discourse in La Paz and Sucre then is quickly forgotten.

In Bolivia at least.

Outside Bolivia the ripples travel far. Ecuador, humiliated, simply denies everything, a denial that does not succeed and only engenders further humiliation. Ibanez, in Chile, expresses outrage at the indirect assault on Chilean sovereignty. Certain passages in the treaty appear to recognize and support Bolivia's territorial claims against Chile. However, beyond heated denunciation, there is little further action. Ibanez threatens to close the border to Bolivian coastal trade, but ultimately does nothing.

Peru denounces the secret treaty and breaks diplomatic relations with both countries. The nation is agog over the exposure of a conspiracy against it on both borders. Anti-Ecuadorian sentiment rages, and there are marches in the streets of Lima and Trujillo demanding war. Bolivia under first Quintanilla and then Penaranda clearly and unequivocally repudiates the treaty. But this does nothing to quench the furious rage against Ecuador.

Indeed, from the viewpoint of the Peruvian military, this increases their fervour. The exposure of the treaty humiliates and discredits Ecuador. It ends any hope of a diplomatic resolution, and creates a textbook casus belli for war. Peru can attack, claiming pre-emptive defence from planned aggression, as set out in the Treaty. Bolivia's repudiation of the treaty means that Ecuador's only possible ally and Peru's only possible deterrent is gone from the field. No one else will come to Ecuador's aid in the circumstances.

Things fall out quickly after that. The treaty is exposed in February of 1940. By March, Quintanilla publicly abandons any further political ambitions. In April, Penaranda takes power in Bolivia.

With Penaranda's ascension, the last shred of a barrier is vanished away, and Peru's General Ureta is now free in May to issue his ultimatum. A month later, fearing that the perfect political moment may pass, General Ureta decides to attack. The invasion is on.

****

Chile in Turmoil, 1939

Within a year of his election in August, of 1938, Alessandri's chosen man, Gustavo Ross, has squandered his credibility. Formerly the Finance Minister in Alessandri's government, Ross emphasized fiscal rigor without the softening measures that had been required by Alessandri. Initiating a series of further austerity reforms intended to put the Chilean economy on a firmer footing, Ross repudiates the neo-Keynesian economics of the Radicals, and of his own patron.

The effects are disastrous, the Chilean economy contracts. Up and down the country, strikes break out in mining towns, put down by a new round of massacres. In Santiago, the housewives strike, bringing a new round of police repression. Ironically, in a country which turns a blind eye on machine gunning hundreds of women and children in remote industry towns, the deaths of four middle class women is a national scandal.

Although he lost the election to Ross, the worm has turned and Ibanez comes to the fore. Ibanez is the last remaining independent voice. Ross's Conservatives are disgraced and Cerda's radicals are in disarray.

Allying with Ibanez, the Nazi party rises dramatically, recruiting large numbers and organizing street demonstrations. At points, running battles break out between members of the military and the Chilean Nazis.

During the disastrous year of Gustavo Ross's Presidency, Ibanez is arrested twice, but released each time after massive Nazi-organized demonstrations. These signify not only the debt that Ibanez owes but also the capacity of the Nazis to resist, in the event of a falling out.

For Ibanez, his association with the Nazis is proving to be as much a liability as an asset. In particular, the Chilean military is deeply hostile to the Nazis and suspicious of his affiliation.

An open conflict, if it ever materialized, would have been a one sided affair. The Nazi party claims membership in the hundreds of thousands, but based on attendance at the rallies and demonstrations it organizes, the true cadre of Nazi party members numbers at best in the low tens of thousands, and the effective paramilitary arm somewhere between a few hundred and a few thousand. They lack military training and discipline and would pose little more than an irritant to the police or military. And in fact, the military finds them profoundly irritating.

Politically, the Chilean Nazis have failed to score any significant electoral success. Their true strength comes through acting as a rallying point in an increasingly chaotic environment. So despite their shortcomings, Ibanez needs them at least as much as they need him.

Eventually, Ibanez finds a way to turn this to his advantage, presenting himself to the Army and Navy as the one man who can control these uncouth radicals. He even hints in private meetings that his return to power will mark the end of the Chilean Nazis as a radical political force. Something very like Hitler's own 'Night of the Long Knives' is in the offing.

Despite his promises to the military, untangling himself from these allies will prove a complex matter.

Finally, following votes of non-confidence in the Parliament, and a refusal of military forces to obey orders, Gustavo Ross has had enough. He leaves the country, traveling to Brazil, and from there to France. The Chilean legislature then passes a motion accepting his resignation, though it's not clear that he actually offers it.

In the ensuing crisis, Ibanez steps forward and is appointed President by way of a military coup, in August of 1939.

Ibanez has become President in the manner of dictators. But he's also

come into power on a popular movement, and his supporters represent… everyone, the rich and the poor, the left and the right, the urban middle classes, the rural landowners, the radicals, the military. He owes everyone.

For Ibanez, attaining the Presidency is the beginning, not the end of his problems. His position is extremely precarious. He's been put in power by the military, but lacks control over it.

He owes huge debts to the Nazis, who continue to maintain disproportionate influence through massive rallies and demonstrations. Both the radical parties of the left and the conservative parties of the right are suspicious and hostile. Everyone supports him, but each constituency is just waiting to turn on him, should he not satisfy their demands. And of course, there's no way to satisfy people whose interests are diametrically opposed to each other. He is a king without a constituency.

An energetic and persuasive man, this does not stop Carlos Ibanez, who proves to be an agile politician. To the satisfaction of the Army and Navy, he manages to steal much of the thunder from the Nazi party, appearing in actual military regalia, organizing his own rallies or co-opting the Nazis'. The Navy he placates through a campaign of military spending. The Army is neutralized through a series of promotions and redeployments.

With almost no support from conservative constituencies, he abandons them, appealing directly to the masses with public works programs, promises of social reform, and radical rhetoric, actually winning support from communists and socialists. Cerda is enlisted in his cabinet as the first socialist Finance Minister. But of course, such rhetoric alienates military constituencies, which forces him to immediately declaim more right wing platitudes.

Chilean political cartoons at the time depict Ibanez as all manner of circus performers: In one cartoon he is a clown stuffing a carriage full of warring cats and dogs; in another, he's a tightrope walker; in another, he's a juggler; in yet another, he's a carnival barker. There is a counter-wave of political cartoons depicting him as a circus strongman or fire eater. The Ibanez regime is nicknamed 'The Circus.'

Ibanez as a politician desperately needs a common ground, and he finds it in Chilean nationalism and anti-Peruvian sentiment. A public cornerstone of his policy is the repudiation of the Tacna betrayal, characterized as an insidious national humiliation and the author of Chile's financial ruin. Every public speech he gives rails against Tacna.

In private, of course, he is much more pragmatic. As far as Ibanez is concerned, a new war with Peru is as desirable as a war with the Moon. He disparages Tacna province as a worthless desert, at one point dismissively suggesting that it be given the Bolivians.

The Graf Spee Incident

Commissioned in January, 1936, the Admiral Graf Spee is a heavy cruiser, nicknamed a "pocket battleship" of Nazi Germany. The ship engages in blockade patrols during the Spanish Civil War in 1936-38. Immediately prior to World War II, it is sent to the South Atlantic to raid shipping. Once war is declared, between September and December, 1939, the warship sinks nine vessels.

On December 13, 1939, the Graf Spee is confronted by three British cruisers, Exeter, Ajax and Achilles, at the Battle of the River Plate. In the ensuing battle, all four vessels takes heavy damage. The Graf Spee breaks off the engagement, and puts into port at Montevideo, Uruguay, for seventy-two hours to effect repairs.

The British cruisers maintain watch, but are in no shape to give further battle. Instead, they issue false radio messages suggesting that a British aircraft carrier and heavy cruiser are proceeding into the area to engage. At this point, Hitler orders the Graf Spee to return to the waters and fight to the death, or to proceed to Argentina, where the ship and crew will be interned. The final option is to scuttle the ship.

Commander, Hans Langdorf, suspecting a ruse, opts to break out. The Graf Spee once again enters the Atlantic, but does not offer battle to the British cruisers, opting to flee instead. The cruisers are in no shape to pursue effectively. But the Graf Spee is in poor shape, most of its ammunition is used up, and several key systems are jury rigged, instead they make for Argentina. Meanwhile, the British government exerts considerable diplomatic pressure on the

Argentine government. Attempting to come into port at Buenos Aires, the Graf Spee is denied access. With its location pinpointed, unable to return to Montevideo and unable to fight, the German warship has no option except to continue fleeing south, to Chile

Chile's active Nazi movement has deep connections to Hitler's Germany. Jorge Maree, the head of the Chilean Nazis, has been appointed Ibanez's Minister of Culture. Although the British again exert diplomatic pressure, the Reich's Admiral Canaris is able to counter this by reaching out to Maree. Maree in turn enlists Admiral Jose Encelada, Minister of the Navy, who is very interested in acquiring a state of the art German warship for the Chilean navy.

On January 6, 1940, the Graf Spee sails into the territorial waters of southern Chile, to be interned at the southern naval facilities. The crew are interned, but released upon applying for Chilean citizenship. These new citizens will eventually be reassigned to the Graf Spee. Germany formally renounces ownership of the craft, in exchange for financial considerations which are never paid.

On January 31, 1940, the ship is renamed the Toro, after Policarpo Toro, the naval officer who acquired Rapa Nui (Easter Island) for Chile. By this time, it has become clear that the Chilean government has acquired a pig in a poke. The Toro has sustained massive damage in the Battle of the River Plate, and is barely seaworthy. It will require a massive investment to repair and refit the ship to make it fit for duty - money that the Chilean government does not have. Even with the impetus of the war, repairs are slow and the Toro is not fully operational until 1941.

Diplomatically, the incident causes a major breach between Britain and Chile, which persists through the remainder of the war. Less obviously, there is considerable consternation in the American government which sees the incident as clear evidence of collusion and cooperation between the Ibanez regime and Nazi Germany. They have a point. This will complicate Chilean-American relations for years.

***

Ibanez on the Eve of War

Despite constant war talk, Ibanez takes no real steps to act on it. Indeed, he is quick to resolve any border disputes or incidents. Ibanez even goes so far as to privately assure Peruvian diplomats of his peaceful intentions and signs a non-aggression pact with General Benavides in November, 1939. Historically, this is viewed as evidence of his duplicity, but there is much to suggest his sincerity.

The irony is that had Ibanez actually been bent on war, a coalition of his supporters would have assembled to stop him, and it would have been the end of his career. Instead, he is completely uninterested in war, simply cynically using sabre rattling to keep his coalition together.

However, events are rapidly outrunning him. The public revelation of the Bolivia-Ecuador Pact in April, 1940, has touched off a firestorm of outrage in Lima and has become a continent-wide scandal.

Ibanez denounces the treaty and the practice of secret treaties as an outrage. Ironic, since he's signed his own secret treaty of non-aggression with Peru only months before. However, despite an inflammatory speech or two, he takes no other action, and does not even curtail Bolivia's use of Chilean ports.

The Peruvians, tiring of constant border tensions and incidents with Ecuador, and convinced that they have neutralized possible adversaries in the south, then proceed to launch an invasion of Ecuador. The long simmering northern front of Peru finally breaks into war on June 2.

Peru and Ecuador are at war and Ibanez doesn't care. All that matters is how it can can advantage him at home.

***

Order of Battle - Peru

Population 6 million

Area: 1,171792 square kilometres; 452,432 square miles.

Armed forces: Peru has compulsory military service, however, the actual conscription is carried out only on a limited scale. The military has been divided into five districts, but in 1937, due to tensions with Ecuador, this is consolidated into two commands: A north and a south. In particular, the northern command operates almost independently of the Peruvian government.

The army's composition in 1940 is as follows: fourteen infantry regiments, six artillery regiments, seven cavalry regiments, four sapper battalions, one anti-aircraft battalion, and one signalling battalion. The army's personnel officially amount to 3500 officers and over 70,000 other ranks.

Armour and Artillery consists of 48 Czech-era tanks, and 150 artillery pieces, a mixture of Czech, French and British, with another 200 support vehicles, mostly trucks. Like other Latin American militaries of the era, Peru continues to maintain a horse cavalry, consisting of 2500 horses. An additional 5000 oxen, horses, burros and llamas remain in use as draft animals.

The police and gendarmerie, collectively have 15,000 personnel by 1940 (including civil guards and mounted police). The civil guards field 11 cavalry regiments, one infantry regiment of four battalions, one independent battalion, and one machine gun battalion.

The air force consists of 30 bombers acquired in 1933 by Sanchez Cerra, plus an assortment of fighters. Aircraft vary from WWI biplanes up to late 1930s metal sheathed aircraft. The Peruvian air force was distributed among the five military commands, and is now divided between two, with approximately a third assigned to northern command.

Of the total Peruvian military forces, the Northern Command, under General Ureta, holds a strength of perhaps 25,000 to 35,000 men, with 20 Czech tanks and roughly sixty artillery pieces.

The Peruvian navy had been utterly destroyed in the War of the Pacific, and although Peru has rebuilt and modernized its fleet, it is unable to compete with the wealthier Chile. Warships are an expensive item, and their operation and maintenance requires a lot more sophistication and infrastructure than simply conscripting a bunch of Mestizo and sticking them on a parade ground somewhere. The Peruvian navy never reaches the scale of the Chilean Navy, nor does it acquire the degree of autonomy or status that the Chilean force does.

Still, rivalry with Chile dictates that Peru invest in a significant naval presence as a deterrent to Chilean forces. Most of the capital ships of the Peruvian navy date to the period between 1906 and 1915. These pre-World War I ships have been upgraded periodically, but are a far cry from fully modern.

Following the ascension of Benevides in 1933, slightly more attention has been paid to the navy, as a way of subtly reducing the influence and resource of the army. This becomes significant in 1936 when the Benavides government goes further into debt to outbid Ecuador on some 1910 destroyers. Nevertheless, despite this effort and a significant increase in naval power, the army continues to dominate and direct Peru's military culture.

By 1940, the Peruvian navy consists of three cruisers: Almirante Grau and Coronel Bolognesi, both built in 1907, and the Aguire, a surplus British warship built in 1910.

These are supplemented by the destroyers; Rodriguez, built in 1909 and acquired from France, two former Estonian ships built in 1915, Guize and Villar; and the former British ships, built in 1907 and 1919, respectively Garcia and Palacios.

In addition, the Peruvian navy operates five submarines, a transport ship, an oiler, patrol boats, motor launches and various auxiliary and support craft. The principal submarine base is offshore from Lima, and other naval facilities are distributed along the coast.

Unlike Ecuador, which has a single significant seaport area in the Gulf of Guayaquil, the Peruvian coast offers more numerous harbours and coastal cities and towns. The sort of shoreline defence that Ecuador tries to build up around Guayaquil and

Puerto Bolivar is not viable. Instead, the air force is deployed to port protection, and bombers and are assets are distributed to cover the coastline.

Unlike the Chilean navy, Peru, with its vast rain forest interior, operates a fleet of six river gunboats and accessory river craft. The river fleet is technically assigned to the Peruvian navy. Its counterpart in Ecuador is operated as an adjunct to the army.

****

Order of Battle - Ecuador

Population - 2.4 million

Area: 449,000 Square kilometers; 180,000 square miles.

Armed Forces: Ecuador also has universal military conscription, widely enforced during the Bonifaz regime. In the Bonifaz regime, the military is strictly unitary, operating under a single command with a joint Chiefs of Staff, headed by Colonel Alba as de facto, though not de jure commander. Alba is head of strategy and operations, technically under Benigno Flores; but for all intents and purposes, he is supreme commander. There is also a parallel civil guard or civil militia, which act as military reserves.

The army's composition in 1940 is as follows: twenty infantry regiments all under strength, four artillery regiments, five cavalry regiments, two sapper battalions, one anti-aircraft battalion, and one signaling battalion. The army's personnel officially amounts to 2,000 officers and over 25,000 to 30,000 other ranks.

Armour and artillery consists of 36 tanks and tankettes, including 6 ton Vickers. Much of Ecuador's armor is obtained after 1937 and includes Czech, German and Italian tanks and 120 artillery pieces, with another 100 support vehicles, mostly trucks.

Like other Latin American militaries of the era, Ecuador continues to maintain a horse cavalry, consisting of 2,000 horses. An additional 10,000 oxen, horses, burros and llamas remain in use as draft animals.

Ecuador, from 1933 on, has gone through a concentrated campaign of military expansion, but lacks the resources to fully match Peru's own responding build up. Ecuadorian military policy is therefore contingent on long-term construction of defensive emplacements, balanced against rapid mobilization

The largest and most difficult ongoing military buildup is the Oriente, thinly populated and difficult to access. Here there is a typical network of military bases with stored supplies. Plans are to assign up to 8,000 men to the area, and have another 8,000 as reserves, but this target is never met. Efforts to relocate personnel from the Coast and Sierra to the Oriente meet numerous obstacles, including staff resistance and tropical diseases. The decision is made to supplement military personnel with local part-time recruits, leading to a nominal strength of 3,000 to 5,000; with a more substantial commitment to reserves. An insubordinate general is assigned to local command.

Beyond that, there is substantial investment in the provinces of El Oro and Loja, and the coastal city of Guayaquil; but there, strategy focuses on rapid mobilization of reserves among the civilian population.

Approximately 10,000 Ecuadorians see service in the Chaco War, at least half remain in the Ecuadorian army and the other half remain in the reserves.

The 'Dirty Shirts' remain an active paramilitary of approximately 15,000, but are mainly equipped with small arms, and have been designated as a military reserve.

As with Peru, the air force is a mixture of wooden 1920s and metal 1930s era craft. The Ecuadorian air force sports very few bombers; most of its aircraft are fighters or ground support. Since 1937, the Ecuadorian air force has been significantly upgraded with the addition of German and Italian donations. Many of the pilots are German 'volunteers.'

Ecuador's navy is not a significant force in the early 20th century, but has been the subject of some investment. The Ecuadorian navy consists of two destroyers and two frigates, and twelve river gunboats. The destroyers and frigates are older, cheaper ships, considerably inferior to the Peruvian warships, with less experienced and competent crews. Most of the river gunboats have been commissioned and built since 1933, and six more are on order. The river boats are significantly inferior to the Peruvian gunboats, more lightly armed and armoured, with smaller motors, but are more manoeuvrable with shallower drafts. In addition, there are nine river barges, testifying to the commitment to hold the Oriente.

For the most part, the Bonifaz triumvirate shows relatively little interest in naval affairs. Given the small size and relative poverty of the Ecuadorian state, the notion of investing in significant naval ships is seen as a reckless and unnecessary expense. Alba becomes a proponent of air power as an answer to Peru's navy, and funds are expended for coastal defence batteries, particularly around Guayaquil and Puerto Bolivar.

****

The Peruvian Attack

June 2, 1940 - early in the morning, the Peruvian 5th and 7th Cavalry Regiments, the 6th Artillery Group, the Army Tank Detachment and First Light Infantry, assembled at the Peruvian town of Tumbres, invade the coastal Ecuadorian province of El Oro, overrunning the town of Huaquillas. They advance through Puerto Bolivar, and reach the town of Machata by June 8.

Peruvian forces rely on close air support for strafing and reconnaissance. Much of the Ecuadorian air assets are destroyed on the ground at their airfields. Meanwhile the Peruvian navy enters the gulf of Guayaquil, blockading the harbour and supplying coastal support.

Ecuadorian forces, despite years of preparation, are taken by surprise, fighting an intense rearguard action. The Ecuadorian Montecriste battalion is overwhelmed. The Cayamba battalion retreats up the coast towards Guayaquil, re-establishing in Puerto Bolivar and then retreating to the town of Machate. The Cordova battalion and the Mariscal Sucre Artillery battalion do not give battle but retreat towards the inland province of Lojas.

Meanwhile, Alba issues a general mobilization on June 3, and begins moving forces from the towns of Cuerca, Riobamba, Puyo to counter the offensive. The city of Guayaquil is placed under martial law. Air forces from as far north as Quito and Portoveijo are mobilized and sent south, to aid in the defense of Guayaquil.

Although scheduled to begin simultaneously, Peru's northern strike does not begin until June 3 and 5, when the Army Jungle Division under the command of General Antonio Silva, advances south, up to and crossing the Napo River and attacking on the northern border in the Amazonian territory. Meanwhile, further to the south, Lieutenant Colonel Victor Rodriguez with the Chinchipe Army detachment and 33rd Infantry Battalion strikes west in a broad band along the river Maranon, attacking towns and outposts.

However, the offensive along the Maranon and Napo rivers in the east and north meets spirited resistance from well-established jungle battalions dug in. Seaplanes taking off from and landing on rivers give the aerial advantage to the Ecuadorians. The attack from the north fails, and General Silva is killed during the fighting. The Peruvian forces fall into disarray, and are overwhelmed by Ecuadorian fighters, who advance into Peruvian territory, sweeping up to the Putumayo River and the Colombian border.

As the war opens between Ecuador and Peru, the Peruvian Navy is a major part of General Ureta's invasion plans. On June 6, 1940, the cruiser, Coronel Bolognesi, and the destroyer, Villar, along with a troop transport and support vessels, enter the Gulf of Guayaquil with the intention of blocking shipping, shelling defensive emplacements and seizing port areas.

The Ecuadorians are able to put up surprising resistance. The Ecuadoran gunboat Calderon encounters the Peruvian destroyer, Villar, on its way to Puerto Bolivar, on June 7, 1940. The Calderon opens fire at the Villar while retreating. The Villar pursues, the two ships exchanging fire all the way, until the Calderon is able to retreat into local river channels where the Villar cannot pursue.

Axis of Andes – Page 163

The Villar proceeds on its way, to Puerto Bolivar the next day, with troop transport following, but takes fire from shore batteries. The shore batteries are reduced, but the situation is deemed such that a landing and occupation is not feasible, and further action is left to Ureta's ground forces.

Meanwhile, the Coronel Bolognesi proceeds to Guayaquil, entering the harbour and reducing shore batteries with heavy firepower, on June 9 through 12. A demand for surrender, however, is ignored. Ecuador deploys bombers and air attack fighters. Although no hits are scored, some of the explosions are close enough that the Coronel Bolognesi, seeing no further achievable objective, and withdraws from the harbour.

From this point on, the Coronel Bolognesi and the Villar hold position outside aircraft range in the Gulf of Guayaquil to implement the blockade and interdict shipping.

Further south, Peru's Lieutenant Colonel Rodriguez, leading a Chinchipe Army detachment, penetrates deep into the interior between the outposts of Jaen and Nauta, marching past Concordia and advancing as far as Itutu in the Interior. However, Rodriguez outruns his supply lines and, in the face of reinforcements by Ecuador, is forced to retreat. Rodriguez's line of attack becomes ragged and breaks apart.

They are confronted by the Ecuadoran Oriente Command, a distributed command based out of Zamorra and Andoa, well within Ecuadoran territories. Nominally these are led by General Enrique Blandon, based in the village of Andua deep in the interior. Blandon is an 'old school' officer, and fierce critic of Alba; and is assigned to the interior to keep him far from political infighting.

The Ecuador's Oriente force consists of a series of distributed and supplied garrisons located in the Ecuadoran interior at what were estimated would be the limits of Peruvian advance where their supplies ran down. The predetermined strategy being to attack the advance at its weakest. It works.

By June 15, Peru's Chinchipe Army detachment dissolves into four separate uncoordinated units, three of whom are in retreat. By June

16, the Ecuadoran Oriente Command takes Concordia and vanquishes one of the segments.

By June 18, the Ecuadorians cross the river at Jaen and take the town of Bagua.

Ecuadorian river and jungle forces then proceed down the River Ucayali from the east and the Maranon from the west, pushing the retreating remnants of the Chinchipe south.

General Blandon leaves Andua, in order to take direct personal command of the rain forest front. Progress is slow, and the war in the Amazonian hinterland is on its own calendar. On July 14, the two forces meet at the Peruvian town of Yurimaguas, where the Ecuadorians win decisively. General Blandon arrives on July 16.

Ecuador's expansion from its own Oriente into the Peruvian Amazon is largely an accident. A consequence of well supplied and organized Ecuadorian forces pursuing disorganized and retreating Peruvian forces. There's no Ecuadorian plan to conquer the Amazon or even to keep it, though they may seek security in territorial concessions beyond the Napo in the north.

Keep in mind that the numbers of forces engaged here are comparatively small, and operating mostly independently from the main theatre. The Jungle War, as it evolves, becomes a picturesque theatre of war all its own.

Meanwhile, on the coast in the El Oro province, the Peruvian Navy has retreated to the outer regions of the Gulf as a result of heavy aerial attack. Aerial dogfights between Ecuadorian and Peruvian air forces take place as both sides attempt to bring up aircraft fuel and prepare landing strips.

Eventually, the Ecuadorians bring superior numbers to bear locally, and by June 24, dominate regional skies. Peruvian anti-aircraft batteries prevent this advantage from being decisive, but Peruvian mobility is impaired and reconnaissance eliminated.

Peruvian Czech tanks prove consistently superior to the Ecuadorian Vickers 6-ton tanks and tankettes. In addition, the Peruvians bring greater numbers to bear in local battles. Several of

the encounters involve single or pairs of Vickers facing as many as
a half dozen Peruvian tanks.

In an effort to assemble a fighting force, Alba orders his remaining
tanks and tankettes to retreat without giving battle, to the town of
Machata, where he struggles to assemble a coherent armour force,
just a few miles from the town of Puerto Bolivar. The Peruvians
have taken the town of Puerto Bolivar on June 8, and pause to let
their supply lines catch up. Meanwhile the Ecuadorians are
desperately fortifying the town of Machata.

On June 14, the Peruvians attack, encountering fierce opposition.
The battle of Machata continues until June 20, with heavy
casualties on both sides. By the time Alba retreats from Machata on
June 21, Peruvian forces are decimated.

During this time, however, Alba has begun to redeploy forces from
the Province of Loja, cutting off supply lines. The Peruvian army,
at this point, is seriously overextended. When Alba begins a new
offensive, flanking both Machata and Puerto Bolivar, the Peruvians
are forced to abandon their hard won territory and retreat from
both towns.

By June 24 the retreat is a rout, as the Peruvian army begins
running out of gasoline to operate tanks and vehicles. The
Peruvians start to leave tank and infantry units in rearguard posts as
the main army withdraws. But Alba ignores these stationary units,
merely establishing pickets and continuing to harass the retreating
Peruvians.

Finally, near the Zamilla River in the border of Peru and Ecuador,
Alba choses to give battle, and the exhausted Peruvians surrender
after a morning of hard fighting on June 28.

In retaliation, the Peruvian Navy once again enters the fray. The
Coronel Bolognesi enters Guayaquil harbour and commences to
shell the city heavily, taking minor damage from aerial bombing.
On this second incursion, the Ecuadorians commit their air power
more aggressively.

Although several Ecuadorian aircraft are shot down or disabled,
worsening conditions persuade the Coronel Bolognesi to withdraw

from the harbour and rejoin the Villar, which has better anti-aircraft armament.

There matters stand until the Chilean battleship, Almirante Latorre, and two destroyers, the Aldea and the Hyatt, enter the Gulf of Guayaquil, ostensibly to protect shipping, on July 7, 1940.

The two naval forces confront each other but make no hostile moves. No foreign ships enter the Gulf. The commander of the Coronel Bolognesi requests permission to withdraw from the Gulf in the face of superior force, but General Ureta countermands this. The perception at the time is that the Chilean provisional declaration of war is a bluff. Withdrawing from the Gulf would be a significant political concession. The warships remain, although after making repairs on the Bolognesi, support craft are permitted to withdraw.

For the Peruvians, the first phase of the war, while initially triumphant, ends disastrously. The Peruvians lose all the amour and artillery deployed, much of which is later reconditioned and added to the Ecuadorian arsenal.

Casualties are extremely high, with an estimated 5,400 Peruvians killed, 3,800 wounded, and as many as 4,000 prisoners. As few as 5000 Peruvians, mostly the reserve forces of Colonel Salazar and Colonel Morozs, manage to return to Peru. The jungle campaign into the Ecuadorian Oriente is been a complete failure and the Ecuadorians have actually penetrated deep into the Peruvian Selva instead.

Despite delays and missteps, the Ecuadorians do better. Casualties are high: Roughly 2,800 Ecuadorians killed, including 300 civilians in the shelling of Guayaquil. Another 4,500 Ecuadorians are wounded in the fighting. Prisoners are negligible.

For the Peruvians, July opens to widespread shock. While General Ureta struggles to reassemble his forces and begs for reinforcement from his fellow regional commanders, the Peruvian government enters a state of paralysis where it seems unable to marshal a response.

Taking advantage of this, Colonel Alba plays his boldest gamble, and while the Peruvians reel, he opens the second phase of the war - the infamous "March on Lima."

Interlude - In Actual History

The real Peru-Ecuador war began a year later on July 5, 1941, and ended on July 31, 1941. There had been no secret treaty to expose, and therefore no casus belli in 1940.

Although inevitable since the Salomon-Lozano treaty of 1922, and the Colombia-Peru war of 1932, the war itself is entirely the creature of the renegade Peruvian General Stanley G. Ureta, commander in the north. Ureta has no respect for President Prado, and simply opted to attack on his own, following a series of border incidents on each side. There is an ongoing dispute over who started the war, but it is clear that the Peruvians were simply seeking a pretext. The attack is far too massive and organized to be ad hoc. An operation such as the one Peru performs takes both planning and preparation.

Peru attacks on July 5, 1941, with 13,000 men and a force including Czech tanks, invading the coastal and highland provinces of Lojas, El Oro, as well as the disputed territories of Oriente/Amazon the rain forest, attacking from multiple directions. They meet and sweep aside a bare 1,800 Ecuadoran defenders, unprepared, poorly armed, and ineffective. Peruvian paratroopers capture the port city of Puerto Bolivar. The attack includes coordinated aerial bombing of Peruvian towns and the invasion of the Guayaquil harbor by Peruvian warships. One Ecuadoran gunship manages to exchange fire with a Peruvian destroyer, eventually retreating up a river.

Ecuador is completely outmatched and unprepared. Ecuadoran forces barely reach 18,000, with only a handful of artillery pieces and no tanks. In contrast, the total Peruvian military was almost 50,000, two dozen tanks and over 120 artillery pieces.

Over the last decade, Ecuador has been a revolving door of fraudulent elections, coups and counter-coups. The most recent ruler, President Arroyo has only taken office less than a year before, in September, 1940, and insists on retaining the bulk of Ecuadoran forces in Quito to guard against yet another coup. Safeguarding his position is more important than defending the country.

Arroyo requests a ceasefire which is granted on July 31. By January, the parties agree to the Rio Protocol which surrenders the larger part of the Ecuadoran Oriente. Nevertheless, disputes continue for decades into the 1990s.

As with the Colombia-Peru war of 1933 before it, the Peru-Ecuador war goes down in history as one of those 'harmless' Comic Opera banana republic wars that Latin America seems so famous for; a startlingly brief, largely harmless conflict over marginally worthless territory, with minimal casualties or consequence.

Nevertheless, a thousand Ecuadorans lose their lives, as do perhaps a couple of hundred Peruvians. The war is only fast and bloodless because the contest is so terribly unequal. Ecuador is a nation a quarter the size of Peru, bankrupt from the depression and the collapse of its single major commodity, with barely a military, a revolving door series of regimes and a government more interested in preserving its shaky grip on power than on actually fighting. Peru, while battered during the Great Depression has overwhelming advantages and moves aggressively.

But it didn't have to turn out that way. A stable Ecuadoran government, steeped in nationalism, with a decade to prepare for an inevitable conflict, might have done much better. In changed circumstances, the comic opera war could have been the real thing...

***

Aftermath of the Failed Invasion

Despite the disastrous invasion, Peru remains committed to war. Perhaps even more so given its humiliation, it begins a national mobilization.

Both sides are well aware of the huge disparity in population. Having walked into disaster, Peru clings to the idea of victory through eventual numbers. On the other side, the Ecuador Triumvirate doesn't believe that their nation can survive a protracted war with a nation three times their size. They have to knock Peru out early, and thus the March on Lima.

Ecuador's advantages at this point are a faster, earlier national mobilization, better training, and a much better handle on logistics. With this in mind, Colonel Alba commences his 'March on Lima,' roughly 700 or 800 miles away. The objectives are to force Peruvian surrender or peace terms. Failing that, to do so much damage to Peru's military that they will be unable to effectively prosecute the war.

In terms of movement, Alba's expeditionary force is using a large number of draft animals, horse cavalry and pretty much all the mechanized transport he can pull together, including captured Peruvian assets. Most of his mechanized transport are 1930s era vehicles, Ford production, basically truck chassis. Alba's has perhaps a thousand, give or take. Some of the trucks have been locally up-armoured, and a number have been modified with machine gun platforms, and others as artillery platforms or haulers.

Weather conditions are reasonably clement. The force is moving across Peruvian all-weather roads, by no means double wide, asphalt-paved American road surfaces. But they are reasonably sturdy, packed gravel or rock faced roadways over many portions, mostly coastal roads between significant towns and villages. Real roads for the most part. Alba's done his homework, has a good idea of the roadways and options, including the various resources (like gas stations), risks (like bridges), and potential Peruvian deployments. He's got advance units which can move quickly to scout or secure key points.

Under these circumstances, Alba is able to move his forces an average 20 to 30 miles a day, not counting actual combat time, with short bursts of more rapid movement lasting a few days here and there.

Alba can't and won't hold territory per se. The Ecuadorians are overrunning and occupying adjacent coastal Peruvian provinces, notably Tombes, but that's a very different thing. Peru, even coastal Peru, is simply too big and populous for Alba to take and hold, and even if he holds territory all the way to Lima, that still leaves 3/4 of the country ready to mobilize and roll him up.

Alba's strategy therefore is equivalent to a giant raid. He intends to penetrate deep into enemy territory, carrying supplies and resupplied by convoys, destroying or scattering enemy forces along the way before they have time to organize. The objective is not conquest, but to knock Lima out of the war.

It's a reckless gamble, but given that Alba's without allies and facing a country three times his size, with four or five times the territory and an even more disproportionately larger economy... Well, any conventional strategy is going to be doomed. So the Ecuadorians are forced to roll the dice.

As for the Indigenous, they're mostly in the Sierra - the Andean highlands and valleys, and they'd really rather be left alone. Alba finds no local allies, though he's not going to encounter a lot of opposition in small villages and towns.

***

America Takes Notice!

[White House Cabinet minutes, June 3, 1940.]

[declassified September 1, 1990. names redacted]

OFFICER #1 - ....next order of business. War has broken out between Peru and Ecuador.

[General laughter.]

OFFICER #2 - Seriously, where is Ecuador?

OFFICER #3 - It's a small country in South America on the Pacific coast, between Peru and Colombia. Typical banana republic.

OFFICER #1 - Any strategic value? Do they produce anything important?

OFFICER #3 - Cacao beans mostly.

OFFICER #2 - Cacao beans?

OFFICER #3 - Chocolate.

[General laughter.]

OFFICER #3 - And we've been looking at the Galapagos islands as a possible naval base.

OFFICER #1 - Where are those?

OFFICER #3 - A remote area of the Pacific, off South America. Basically desert rocks. Turtles and iguanas, nothing much else. It's not really critical.

OFFICER #1 - How far along is that?

OFFICER #3 - We're just looking There are no negotiations, it's not anywhere.

OFFICER #4 - How serious is this war?

OFFICER #3 - Probably not very. The usual pattern with these Latin types is that things flare up, there's a lot of marching and shouting, someone takes a few pot-shots at a fort in the middle of nowhere, then everyone goes home and holds parades and gives each other medals. Banana Republic stuff.

OFFICER #4 - What are they fighting over?

OFFICER #3 - Apparently there's a long running dispute over interior borders. They're both claiming the same jungle territory.

OFFICER #1 - Is it worth anything? Are there mines there? Oil?

OFFICER #3 - Nothing, it's worthless. No resources, inaccessible. It's just barren jungle. Howler monkeys and headhunters and that's it.

OFFICER #2 - Nothing?

OFFICER #3 - Well, yellow fever, beriberi, malaria. Things like that.

OFFICER #4 - So they're fighting to see who has to take it?

[General laughter.]

OFFICER #2 - Why are we bothering with this? How is this important to us? Two banana republics having a pretend war over worthless jungle. This isn't cabinet level stuff. Send it back to the State Department, let some Undersecretary deal with it.

OFFICER #3 - They're Nazis.

OFFICER #2 - Who?

OFFICER #3 - The Ecuadorians, el Presidente Bonaface and his bunch. Dyed in the wool Nazis. Even went to Berlin and palled around with Hitler. We've got a report on it. The Germans have put some money and arms into them.

OFFICER #4 - So they've attacked Peru for its jungle? We're going for goosestepping howler monkeys?

[General laughter.]

OFFICER #3 - Actually, Peru has attacked them.

OFFICER #4 - So someone's invading the Nazis? Only in South America.

Axis of Andes – Page 175

[General laughter]

OFFICER #2 - What a mess.

OFFICER #1 - Do we have any significant interests in either of these countries?

OFFICER #3 - Well, there's chocolate...

[General laughter.]

OFFICER #3 - We have some business and mining interests in Ecuador. There's been some disputes there. They don't get along. We have a lot more interests in Peru. Much larger country overall. Ecuador's just one of these little fly spit places. Peru's got mines, oil, coffee, sugar.

OFFICER #4 – Sounds like they're the team we should back?

OFFICER #3 – Peru is about four times the size of Ecuador, they'll win without us.

OFFICER #1 - I've heard enough. We can't support aggression, even against Nazis. But I'm not going to support a fascist government anywhere. It doesn't sound like this is going to amount to anything. Give it back to State. We have important things going on in Europe... Next agenda item...

***

Berlin, June 4, 1940

Hitler is having tea with Goering and Goebbels when Himmler walks in.

"Sir! Peru and Ecuador are at war!"

Hitler pauses in sipping tea, holding the cup genteelly between two fingers and waits expectantly. After a second, he raises an eyebrow.

"Peru...," Himmler says haltingly. "Ecuador...."

Hitler waits.

"This news just in, sir. Peru has invaded the nation of Ecuador," Himmler pauses to gather his thoughts. "You will recall that a few years ago, a delegation from South America..."

"Oh, them!" Hitler says. "Yes, yes, I remember now. The quiet gentleman dressed as an elevator operator, and his wild-haired companion with the sash."

Hitler nods.

"You know, I never did manage to decide which one was supposed to be the monkey and which the organ grinder," the great dictator smiles slightly at his witticism. Goering guffaws, while Goebbels titters behind his hand. "So they finally decided to get off the pot, have they? About time."

"Yes, my leader," says Himmler. "I thought you should know."

"Well, it's all very nice, but we do have important things to think about. Still," Hitler pauses thoughtfully, "we should show appropriate courtesy. Do up a telegram. What was the name of the leader of the Peruvians again? He didn't show up here did he? Bonaparte something? No that's not quite it...."

"General Bonavides is the President of Peru," Goering offers. He's had a casual discussion about South American politics with Canaris a few months back. Dreadfully boring, but the name has stuck in his mind. Bonifaz, Benavides, all these tedious Latins tend to run together.

Axis of Andes – Page 177

Hitler snaps his fingers. "Yes! That's exactly it. That's the one who sent those delegates. Yes, we'll send them a telegram...."

Hitler clears his throat...

"To General Bonavides of Peru, we have received news that you have finally decided to strike boldly against our mutual enemies. Strike without mercy, blah blah blah, we're all in this together, blah blah blah, death to Ecuador, yours truly, Adolph."

Himmler writes furiously.

"Got that?" Hitler asks.

"Yes, Sir," Himmler replies, a bit embarrassed at being used as little more than a personal secretary in front of his rivals.

"Good," Hitler smiles. "I'm sure you can find the appropriate words to fill in the blanks. Oh, and maybe tell them politely that we cannot provide them any further aid... did we provide them any aid to start with? Never mind, just so they know the cupboard is bare."

Himmler hesitates. It looks like he is about to say something.

"Excellent," Hitler says. "Off you go."

Hitler turns his attention back to tea. Goering, he notices, looks stricken. "Is something wrong, Herman?"

Goering appears to think quickly. Was he really sure? What had they discussed way back then? And with whom? He wishes he'd paid more attention to Canaris.

"Nothing, just a bit of indigestion, Sir,"

"Have some more tea then, it's good for your bowels. Now, as I was saying, I absolutely adore Bavarian pastry..."

***

America Looks Down: American Foreign Policy During the Andean Wars

Ed. Keith Chalmer, Yale Press, 1970. Excerpt

It is not clear whether the Roosevelt administration was even informed of the outbreak of War in Latin America. If it was, it does not seem to have been taken much time. This is understandable given the relative remoteness and unimportance of the area, particularly when compared with trials like the Great Depression and the escalating wars in Europe and Asia.

For the most part, initially at least, the war was dealt with at the Embassy level and through the lower levels of the State Department. America's initial position was neutrality and calling for a ceasefire and negotiated peace. American diplomatic efforts amounted to attempting to coordinate other Latin American nations in supporting the peace effort.

Events tended to outrun America's diplomacy. The Anderson Peace Plan was presented to an international conference on June 20, proposing the division of contested territories 1/3 to Ecuador, 2/3rds to Peru. This is hotly contested by Ecuador, with vocal support from Chile. However, within days of this plan, the Peruvian invasion was falling apart. Support for the Anderson plan evaporated.

A week later, a revised peace plan authored in Washington was presented, offering to freeze borders at the respective lines of conflict. However, the State Department had not realized that by this time Ecuador had overrun Peruvian territories. Peru was not receptive.

The next proposal, hastily put together by local ambassadors, was for a regional ceasefire and return to original borders. This failed as these borders remained in dispute. Finally, this plan was cobbled together again and presented with the proposal that boundary issues be resolved by an American- led arbitration. However, this was rejected by Ecuador, fearing that the United States was not truly impartial.

During this time, the war continued to escalate dramatically, with both Peru and Ecuador mobilizing rapidly. American diplomacy was continually taken by surprise, as with Alba's 'March on Lima.' American policy was characterized by drift and vacillation during this key period.

It is entirely possible that aggressive American diplomacy or military action could have resolved matters decisively at this early stage. But this was not to be.

June 7, 1940 - Who are the Real Nazis?

(translated from the Spanish, taken from one of Santiago's daily newspapers)

The world has been shocked by the unprovoked act of aggression by the Peruvian tyranny upon the unsuspecting and peace-loving peoples of Ecuador. The barbarism on display in Europe has come to Latin America.

Here in Chile, the streets have been filled with Jorge Maree's National Socialists, joined by many Chilean patriots, marching to demand that Chile lend its formidable strength to come to the aid of our brothers in the north. Among many, there is concern that this Nazi agitation will lead to a greater war.

But we must ask ourselves, who are the real Nazis at this moment in history? Is it Jorge Maree and his followers who, though they derived much inspiration from Germany have abandoned anti-Semitism, chosen to pursue their fortunes at the ballot box and accept the results with a distinctly Chilean grace and fortitude; and who have shown themselves to put the good of Chile ahead of their own ideology by cooperating with socialists and Communists in the Ibanez regime?

Or is it the aggressors to the north? Consider the conduct of the parties.

In Europe, we have Mr. Hitler in Germany, who first bullies his way into territory, the Sudetenland, which his nation rightfully forfeited in war. His neighbour, France, has every right to keep the Sudeten, but defers in the interests of peace. But this only incites his gluttonous appetite, and the next thing you know he is nibbling away at Czechoslovakia, stealing lands from that country as well, for which he has not the shadow of a claim. He rearms in violation of treaties in the midst of the Depression's hardships. Encouraged by success, he eventually launches an unprovoked war against Poland, and has now plunged the rest of Europe into flames.

It seems that the Peruvians have read Mr. Hitler's infamous book and have found it to their liking. What have they done? They have built up their arms and armies, while too destitute to feed their own people. They have first bullied their way into territory, Tacna Province, which they rightfully forfeited in war.

We had every right to keep Tacna, but deferred in the interest of peace. A gesture that President Ibanez now acknowledges as a mistake. But as with Germany, this has only made Peru more ravenous. For their next step was to seize and steal lands from Colombia. And now, they have cast Ecuador in the role of poor Poland.

Clearly, Peru is following the example set in Europe. But this compels us to ask, what next? For Mr. Hitler did not stop in Poland, but immediately turned to his habitual enemy, France. It is of a certainty that once Ecuador falls, the Andean Jackal shall turn to face its historic rival and victor, and once again, we shall be forced to contend with the guns of Peru on our borders.

In this matter, morality and self-interest are as one. If we do not defend the weak against aggression, then sooner or later the battle will be brought to our shores. Jorge Maree and the crowds which fill the streets have it right. There must be war!

July 2, 1940 - The State of War

Ibanez stands in the Presidential offices, surrounded by his Ministers and generals.

The Peruvian ambassador stands at attention, while the Chilean President reads the prepared announcement.

"As a result of the pre-meditated and unjust aggression of the Republic of Peru, against the innocent and helpless nation of Ecuador, the Chilean people have no choice but to affirm that a provisional state of war exists on the South American continent. On behalf of the nation of Chile we have no option but to demand that all hostilities cease immediately, and commit to a negotiated settlement, or accept consequences."

He presents the letter to the Ambassador. The Ambassador reads it carefully.

"I don't understand," he asks finally. "Is this a declaration of war? Has Chile declared war on Peru?"

"No," Ibanez replies. "It is an acknowledgment that a state of war exists."

"But Peru is not at war with Chile?"

"Nevertheless," Ibanez says, "Peru is in a state of war and this is intolerable. Therefore we must demand an immediate ceasefire and withdrawal of all parties."

"Relations between Peru and Ecuador are matters internal," the Ambassador retorts stiffly. "Peru has no designs or hostilities against Ecuador or its legitimate lands; we are merely addressing the issue of wrongful occupation of Peruvian territory, nothing more. Chile has no place in these matters."

"We disagree," Ibanez replies. "We will not tolerate aggression against friendly states."

The Ambassador stares at the Chilean President.

"The Republic of Peru hereby acknowledges the position of the Republic of Chile. I must ask: Is Chile intent on engaging in military action against the people or lands of Peru?"

"No," Ibanez replies. "The Republic of Chile will not undertake military action against Peruvian territory. But we will respond immediately and with overwhelming force against any attack upon our territories and citizens."

"I see," says the Ambassador doubtfully. He speaks carefully. "Does Chile propose to intervene directly in the dispute between Peru and Ecuador by placing naval or military forces at the disposal of the Ecuadoran government?"

"Not at this time," Ibanez replies. "Chile will reserve the right to engage in correct actions at the appropriate occasion."

"I understand," the Ambassador says, but really doesn't, "and will ensure that your message is conveyed to Lima."

"See that you do," Ibanez tells him.

The Ambassador, followed by his assistant, bows and departs the Presidential offices. Once they are safely in their car and returning to the Embassy, only then does the assistant speak.

"What did all that mean?" the assistant asks.

"It means that Ibanez is trying to thread a needle," the Ambassador says curtly. "It means that this asshole Ureta better wrap things up quickly, so that everyone can calm down."

***

Chile on the Sidelines

Ibanez's first act is to denounce the Peruvian act of aggression and to call for an immediate ceasefire, putting himself forward as a mediator, on June 5, 1940.

But events are now running out of control. The Peruvian invasion quickly becomes a disaster. Colonel Alba's forces are far better prepared and dug in than expected. The Peruvians suffer heavy losses all along the front, and are thrown back in many places. By the beginning of July, the Peruvian invasion has failed and Ureta is pushed back across his own borders. Ecuadoran forces occupy Peruvian border provinces. Ureta is demanding manpower and munitions for a further campaign, even while Alba is preparing for the next phase of the war.

Meanwhile, the strongly pro-Ecuadorian Nazi party of Chile responds with new rounds of demonstrations and rallies in support of their northern allies. With every success of Alba, the star of the Nazis rises higher, and Ibanez's bleating for a ceasefire seems weak and impotent. Something like war fever grips the nation. Even the senior naval officers begin to support war.

At the same time, the senior generals of the Army, as well as the Socialist and Liberal parties are equally opposed to war. There are counter-demonstrations, street battles, and even bitter arguments within his own cabinet. The fragile coalition that Ibanez has put together is in danger of coming apart.

Finally, with no real choice, under pressure from the Nazis and with a need to appear in control of events, Ibanez issues an ultimatum. The Peruvians must agree to a cease-fire and a negotiated border recognizing the bulk of Ecuadorian claims, or he will declare war. Peru, in turn, rejects both proposals.

On July 2, 1940, one month after the commencement of hostilities, Chile announces a provisional state of war exists, a move falling short of a declaration of war. Still, despite threats, Ibanez is reluctant to follow through in any material way.

Instead of attacking Peru, or sending troops to Ecuador, he delivers a strongly worded message to Lima, setting out a ceasefire proposal, and implying that military hostilities might commence if genuine peace negotiations do not begin immediately. He also expressly refuses to mobilize the Chilean army, correctly assessing that this will be taken as a sign of imminent military action.

To satisfy the war factions, Ibanez assigns the Chilean battleship, Almirante Latorre, and two destroyers, the Aldea and the Hyatt, to the Gulf of Guayaquil, ostensibly to protect shipping. The warships are under strict orders not to take any overtly hostile act, and not to engage the Peruvians, unless fired upon. The warships arrive at the Gulf on July 7, 1940.

The Chilean warships encounter Peru's Coronel Bolognesi and Villar in open international waters. Neither naval group makes any hostile moves. Despite the 'protective presence' of the Chilean fleet, no foreign ships enter the Gulf, and there is no effect on Peru's de facto blockade.

The naval standoff serves only to raise tensions further, and incite war-mongering tensions in Chilean society, and in Army and Navy units. In particular, a number of low level officers in the Army feel slighted that it was the Navy that has been given the task of confronting Peruvian aggression, and feel emboldened that the Navy has been so ineffective.

By apparently declaring war but expressly promising to take no real steps, Ibanez is playing a dangerous game, attempting to placate all sides while retaining his freedom of action.

He finds himself struggling to hold together an increasingly divided Chilean populace. On the other hand, the international reaction is poor. Several states, notably America, Brazil and Argentina, react poorly to his efforts to intervene. Ecuador at first welcomes his initiatives, but rapidly loses faith. Chilean relations with Peru worsen. This only confirms, for the Peruvians, the strategic urgency to win against the Ecuadorans in order to free itself to deal with its possible enemy in the south.

Events rapidly move beyond Ibanez's control, and his efforts to manage the situation actively make things worse.

***

Order of Battle, Chile

Population: 5 million.

Area: 756,096 square kilometres; 292,000 square miles.

Armed Forces: Chile's army is based on a national militia system that emphasizes total mobilization of the country's manpower. All citizens capable of bearing arms are required to serve in the armed services in case of a general mobilization. On full mobilisation, the strength of the armed forces can theoretically reach 750,000 troops.

By the war's outbreak, there are four military districts which are obligated to raise a whole division in case of hostilities. The army consists of four cadre divisions of the military districts and a cavalry division (each division included three brigades).

By early 1940 these five cadre divisions include the following units: 12 regiments and four mountain infantry battalions, six cavalry regiments, four field artillery regiments, one heavy artillery group and six mountain artillery groups, four engineer battalions (pontoons, sappers, and communications), one regiment of railway troops, one regiment of heavy bridge engineers, two mixed detachments, and other units.

Beginning with the ascension of Carlos Ibanez in 1939, there is considerable effort made to rapidly modernize and upgrade the army. This is due more to Ibanez's precarious political situation and need to procure the support of the military than to foreign considerations.

In 1939 the first motorized divisions are established. The principal tank supplier is the United States, which sells a number of its 1920's and 1930s era tanks and support vehicles as it begins to commit to a policy of expansion and upgrade. By the outbreak of war, Chile has taken delivery of 28 of a proposed purchase of 42 tanks. It has also obtained an additional 14 armoured vehicles. The Chilean army's complement includes over 200 trucks and transport vehicles. Spare parts, ammunition and training will be major obstacles.

The air force undergoes considerable expansion beginning in 1939, fielding four air brigades of mostly American-manufactured planes. Each military district has an air brigade permanently assigned to it. Again, spare parts become an issue, but with redeployments and cannibalisation, Chile's air force retains a high degree of effectiveness.

Overall, unlike Ecuador or Peru, Chile has made no real preparations for war, and Ibanez vacillations have thrown away a lot of initial advantage. Their armour and aircraft divisions are both very new and somewhat underdeveloped, so Chile's definitely not punching in its weight class yet and won't be for some time.

Chile's geography is unique in that the entire country is effectively a strip of coastline, extending 2880 miles north to south, but only 265 miles wide at its thickest point. The border with Peru is approximately 106 miles long.

The crown jewel of the Chilean armed forces is its navy, which operates as a separate and independent command from the army.

The flagship of the Chilean navy is the Almirante Latorre. One of two ships commissioned from Britain in 1913, the Almirante Latorre was intended to be a super-dreadnought, a next generation battleship, bigger, badder and more powerful than anything in the British fleet. World War One breaks out, and the Almirante is requisitioned by the British government, serving out the war as HMS Canada. It is eventually transferred to Chile, where it is modernized in 1929 and then again in 1937. In its day, it is arguably the single most powerful warship in South America. By 1939, it is showing its age, despite upgrades of torpedo blisters and anti-aircraft guns. Its armour is inferior, its big guns short range. But it is still a psychologically potent symbol of Chilean power.

Two other battleships remain in service, both of them much older and arguably approaching obsolescence. The Almirante Cochrane was built in 1874, and was due to be scrapped in 1937; however, the ascension of the fascist government in Ecuador, and the consequently altered political situation of Peru and Bolivia, persuade the Chilean government of Alessandri to simply mothball the ship rather than scrap it entirely. It was reactivated and given an overhaul in 1938. Much inferior to the Almirante Latorre, the Almirante Cochrane is assigned to Chile's southern fleet. The other battleship is the Capitan Prat, built in 1890, and also scheduled for scrapping in 1936; however, the Capitan Prat is seen as very much necessary, and is kept in service and scheduled for overhaul for 1940. The Capitan Prat is assigned to the northern or southern fleets as occasion demands. The 'pocket battleship,' the Toro, formerly the Graf Spee, is heavily damaged and under repairs for the immediate future, but is potentially the most modern and advanced weapons platform in the navy.

Below the battleships are the cruisers: Blanco Encelada - commissioned 1893; Almirante O'Higgins – 1897; Chacabuco - 1898.

Beneath them are eight destroyers. The older ones, Almirante Lynch and Almirante Condell, date from 1912 and 1913. But the remainder, the Serrano class, comprising Aldea, Hyatt, Orella, Riquelme, Serrano, Videla, have all been constructed in 1928 and are close to state of the art. These, even more than than Almirante Latorre, represent the true martial strength of the Chilean navy.

Chile also maintains a fleet of nine submarines, some quite modern for the time. In addition, there are two coastal defence ships, a surveying ship, a submarine depot ship, two oil tankers, and miscellaneous training and auxiliary vessels.

There are several naval bases, at Valparaiso, Coquimba and Talhuanco, mostly near the center of the country. The depot ship, oil tankers and other auxiliary vessels give the Chilean fleet substantial mobility. The capital ships can operate far afield for extended periods with auxiliary ships providing resupply.

If there is an acknowledged weakness, it is that the Chilean naval strength is concentrated near the center of the country, near the population centers, rather than at the more thinly populated marginal regions of the north and south. To maintain the fleet in those locations isn't an option in the situation of the Depression.

The unacknowledged weakness of the fleet, of course, is to air power. The Chilean navy only slowly adopts anti-aircraft guns on its warships, and is even slower to top-armour its ships from aerial attack. This will have consequences.

As between Peru and Chile, the naval advantage goes to Chile. and it is almost as overwhelming as Peru's naval advantage over Ecuador. The Peruvians have no answer for the Chilean Almirante Latorre or the older battleships. The cruiser/pocket battleship Toro alone, when it finally returns to service, will be a match for the whole of the Peruvian Navy. Without the Toro, there is rough parity in cruisers, three for three, with the Peruvian cruisers being slightly younger than the Chilean ones; but the Chilean vessels are more effectively maintained and modernized. In destroyers, the score is five to eight, but all of five of the Peruvian vessels are turn of the century, compared to only two from Chile. More tellingly, six of the Chilean destroyers are from 1928, and far more modern and deadly. Even the older Chilean destroyers have been modernized more effectively. In submarines the ratio is five to nine, though arguably the nature of submarine warfare makes them closer to equally dangerous.

BOOK OF ALBA

Ecuador - The March on Lima, Part 1

July 10 - Colonel Alba begins the March. He leads a force assembled in the Provinces of Loja and El Oro, into Peruvian territory, quickly routing disorganized local Peruvian military units with a combination of surprise and overwhelming numbers.

Alba conquers and establishes skeleton garrisons in the towns of Tombes, Talara, Sullana and Piura; and takes the provinces/administrative regions of Tombes, Piura and Lambayeque. Reinforcements from Ecuador's main force are directed to follow and occupy the provinces, fortifying against a possible counterattack.

Taking coastal roads, Alba proceeds with minimal resistance, until Chiclayo. The force, consisting of a mixture of cavalry, draft animals and truck transport carrying troops and artillery, moves quickly. Averaging approximately 20 to 30 miles a day with mechanized portions rapidly leaving behind the pack animals.

The March has two objectives. The first is to degrade or destroy Peruvian military capacity in the north, to hinder Peru's ability to carry out the war, and to encourage them to negotiate or accept a peace settlement. The second is to directly attack and capture the seat of Peruvian government in Lima in order to bring an end to the war.

Alba's starting force is huge, consisting of almost 20,000 men. These include approximately 10,000 infantry, 2,500 horse cavalry, 3,500 armour and artillery, and 4,000 support and others. Transport includes over 800 motorized vehicles, including 10 tankettes, a number of truck-mounted artillery and machine guns, and troop transports. In addition, roughly 4,000 horse and oxen carry supplies. This represents between 30 and 40 percent of the entire ongoing Ecuadorian mobilization to date. Many of the infantry personnel are involved in logistics support as well.

The size of the force is its own defence along the coastal roads. Towns and villages offer no resistance. For their part, Alba's forces are under strict orders to give no offense. Gasoline, trucks and vehicles, food and water, are purchased where available.

When sporadic resistance is encountered, horse cavalry units, or mounted artillery or machine gun platforms are dispatched to deal with it, with the balance of the army continuing to march

****

Chile - False Start at Tacna

On July 11, 1940, local units of the Chilean armed forces, inspired by the Alba's bold invasion of Peru in the North, and allegedly acting on their own initiative, invade the Tacna province in Peru. The local Peruvian garrisons retreat without fighting. The invasion is a bloodless affair.

Ibanez is dismayed. Reports of the invasion rock both Santiago and Lima. While elements of the Chilean Nazi party celebrate and look forward to war, the overall social reaction is muted. War talk is one thing, actual bloodshed another. The consensus of Cabinet is that such a local action is tantamount to mutiny. Ibanez orders his troops to withdraw back behind Chilean borders, which withdrawal is completed by July 14.

Ibanez sends a secret letter of apology, and again offers to mediate a cease-fire of all parties, emphasizing his influence over the Ecuadorians and his personal relationship with Ibarra (truthful), Alba (marginal), and Bonifaz (false). There are several border incidents, and tensions are rising, but along most of the Chilean/Peruvian frontier, there is little sign of war.

****

America Takes a Stand

[White House Cabinet minutes, July 15, 1940.]

[declassified September 1, 1990. names redacted]

OFFICER #1 - This thing in South America has turned into a mess. What the hell is going on there?

OFFICER #3 - We expected it to be one of these little brushfire things. Over practically before it starts.

OFFICER #2 - So what happened?

OFFICER #3 - We're not sure. The Ecuadorians kicked Peru's ass. The Peruvians saw blood started mobilizing. Now the Ecuadorians have invaded them, and Chile's declared war.

OFFICER #1 - What the hell is their stake in this? The Chileans, I mean. Are they Nazis too?

OFFICER #3 - The Nazis are heavily into Chile. The Ambassador reports a lot of German activity there, and they're pretty influential. But the country is run by a man named Ibanez, former President, one of those strongmen types of the old school. He's not really a Nazis, he's just relying on them a lot.

OFFICER #1 - So he works with Nazis, but he's not one himself? I don't like the sound of that.

OFFICER #3 - Well, that's pretty harsh when you put it like that. But we've dealt with him before. State's divided on him, but we think he's someone we can work with.

OFFICER #1 - Except that he invaded Peru?

OFFICER #3 - There is that. But...

OFFICER #1 - But?

OFFICER #3 - But then they apologised and went home.

OFFICER #1 - What?

Axis of Andes – Page 194

OFFICER #3 - That might be more local politics than anything else. He's got a lot of dogs barking at him in his capital, some for war, some against. He tried to push a peace settlement, but when that didn't work, he declared war. But then didn't do anything else. We think maybe he's trying to push Peru into a cease-fire.

OFFICER #1 - You seem to be more impressed with this man than I am. All this over some worthless patch of jungle? Appalling.

OFFICER #3 - I'm just relaying...

OFFICER #1 - We don't need this distraction. How do we go about resolving it and getting these people to settle their differences.

OFFICER #2 - Easier said than done, sir. No one down there seems ready to listen to reason.

OFFICER #4 - Can we send troops down there, sort it out for them?

OFFICER #2 - Possibly. But it's not as simple now. Before this all happened, the Illinois National Guard would have been sufficient. Now? Best information from Ecuador is that they've got 60,000 men on the march, and maybe 100,000 before the year ends. Peru, is half that again, and Chile, who knows.

OFFICER #4 - But they're just Latins.

OFFICER #2 - Yes, but there's a lot of them, and they're gearing up for a real war. They're no match for us. But getting involved now might take a lot more men and a lot more time. We could get dragged in longer and deeper than we counted on. My dad said never stick your hand in a dogfight.

OFFICER #1 - Given circumstances in Europe, I don't think we should become distracted.

OFFICER #4 - What did your Dad say to do about dogfights?

OFFICER #2 - He'd say let them have it out, and when they're done, kick 'em both to show them who is boss.

OFFICER #4 - Is that your suggestion here?

OFFICER #2 - We could do worse.

OFFICER #1 - Leave them alone. We cut them off: No oil, no weapons, no nothing. Let them come to their senses or throw sticks at each other. The British will follow our lead.

OFFICER #3 - Well....

OFFICER #1 - Out with it.

OFFICER #3 - Chile's our main copper supplier. We need that. And we need tin, and most of that we get from Bolivia, and they ship through Chile.

OFFICER #1 - And this is the country you let the Nazis get into?

OFFICER #3 - Well...

OFFICER #1 - Stop. Let me think. So, diplomacy hasn't worked?

OFFICER #2 - Not so far.

OFFICER #1 - And you're not recommending military intervention.

OFFICER #4 - Sir, it would be foolish to get tangled up in a petty squabble while the big fights are going on.

OFFICER #1 - So, we have Nazis in South America, and some of these Nazis have stuff we need. But they didn't start the fight, they're the defenders in a war of aggression. And basically, we can't really do anything about it right now. Do I have that right?

OFFICER #3 - That's the size of it.

OFFICER #1 – At least we don't have to deal with Communists.

OFFICER #3 – Well…

OFFICER #1 – Well, what? Out with it.

OFFICER #3 – Ibanez has Communists in his Cabinet. And Socialists.

OFFICER #1 – Excuse me?

OFFICER #3 – It's some sort of coalition, national unity government. He's got all the parties in there. He hasn't given the

Communists any important positions, just minor cabinet posts. Public works, things like that.

OFFICER #1 – Communists and Nazis in the same government? Jesus Christ!

OFFICER #2 - Only in South America.

OFFICER #1 - All right. We stay neutral; we encourage them to settle their differences. We embargo the combatants: No oil, no weapons. We'll trade but only civilian, humanitarian goods. Meanwhile, I want you to see about getting the German infiltration there under control.

OFFICER #3 – Yes, sir!

***

America Looks Down: American Foreign Policy During the Andean Wars

Ed. Keith Chalmer, Yale Press, 1970. Excerpt

The United States had been viewing developments in Latin America with escalating concern. What had started off as a petty regional war had continually escalated, superseding peace efforts.

The original peace process proposed by America had sought a cease-fire between Peru and Ecuador, and the resolution of the interior territorial border issues, with significant concessions by Ecuador. That had fallen apart even as the invasion had fallen apart.

Alba's March on Lima, and his stunning series of successes, had shocked American planners. The State Department had put together a plan guaranteeing both nation's borders, and recognizing Ecuador's claims to the Oriente. Without realizing it, the Ecuadorians had come within a hair's breadth of actually winning their war by American fiat.

But as Alba moved through Peru, it appeared that there might not be a Peruvian government to work with. Instead, Washington had held its breath and waited, Ibanez had entered the war, provoking American hostility. Peru had rallied and Alba had retreated.

The speed and degree of mobilization had shocked American leadership. Armies of a few thousand had grown to tens of thousands. By 1941 and 1942, hundreds of thousands of men were under arms, and the fighting was serious. This is not a typical lackadaisical Latin war of shouting and shooting but nothing much going on. America would have no qualms about intervening militarily in such a Potemkin war. This war, however, would require a serious commitment. More of a commitment than the United States was prepared to make, given isolationist sentiment and the state of affairs in Europe.

Instead, American policy shifted to one of economic sanctions to discourage combat. In cooperation with the British government, oil and weapons were prohibited to the combatants. The United States continued to require Chilean copper, and Chile was a point of export for Bolivian tin. A complete embargo was therefore not in America's interests. Instead, legislation for a modified embargo was initiated, allowing neutral shipping - primarily American and British tonnage, to trade 'humanitarian' or 'non-military' supplies with the combatants.

In practical terms the fascist powers, Ecuador and Chile, were the big losers in the arrangement. Ecuadorian exports were mainly cacao, and although this was still technically an export commodity, British and American demand dropped, as did the price. British colonies tended to replace Ecuador in the cacao marketplace, a process which had been going on for a decade but which had now accelerated for political reasons.

Ecuador's revenue declined, and as existing oil reserves and weapons stockpiles were used up, in late 1940 and early 1941, the state began to run increasingly large deficits, supported only by extensive borrowing from Colombia, Venezuela and Brazil.

In particular, Colombia, the only practical land neighbor, became a primary trading and borrowing partner, supplying weapons and fuel at ruinous prices. Ecuador retained defensive capacities, but increasingly found offense more difficult, after mid-1941.

Chile's key commodities remained in strong demand with the United States and Britain. This demand only increased as the world situation worsened. Chile enjoyed further revenue as transshipment for Bolivian trade. However, the oil embargo hampered the Chilean war effort and economy, Chile having no real oil production capacity of its own. Nevertheless, Chile retained sufficient industrial capacity to manufacture arms and ammunition.

As with Ecuador and Colombia, Chile found a temporary ally and benefactor in Argentina. Argentina's financial situation was desperate, and it was more than willing to earn foreign revenue by selling war material to the Chileans. However, Argentina's oil production capacity was insufficient for the country's own needs. This left Chile in an increasingly difficult situation.

Peru endured the embargo best. Its domestic oil production allowed it to continue to operate despite the embargo. Although hampered by prohibition of weapons, this was rather more casually applied than for the Axis powers. Peru was allowed to import trucks, truck engines, steel for armour plating, machine tools and production equipment which supported the escalation of the local industrial base and an indigenous arms production industry.

Of course, it would take time for these things to work their way through. The prognosis over time, was that gradually, the balance would shift as Ecuadorian and Chilean finances and military and energy stockpiles degraded, and as Peruvian war production was established and ramped up.

Although Peru's mobilization was relatively slower than its enemies', and its fractured caste structure meant that it would have difficulty mobilizing as great a fraction of its population; the long term advantage was with Peru. What would make the difference would be oil and war production.

***

Ecuador - The Battle of Chiclayo

July 19 - Colonel Alba meets the remains of General Ureta's Northern Command as it is assembling and rebuilding at the town of Chiclayo. Although Ureta is aware that a force was moving out from Ecuador, he does not credit either the size or the speed. Alba's arrival takes General Ureta completely by surprise.

In the ensuing battle, General Ureta and his staff are captured and their correspondence examined. From this, Alba learns much of the state of military deployments along the coast. The Peruvians are mobilizing rapidly. Alba establishes a garrison to control an airfield, sending out reconnaissance flights.

Alba's march has traveled approximately 300 miles.

Alba waits a few days, until July 27, allowing his supply column to catch up with him.

[Battle of Chiclayo - Peru has roughly 7,500 men under arms with Ureta, minimal armour or emplacements. In the battle, 3,500 Peruvians killed or injured. Approximately 600 Ecuadorians.]

July 30 - A relief convoy leaves Tombes to resupply Alba's forces, making good time, and meeting no significant resistance. The force is made up of freshly mobilized troops called up in the last few weeks, together with requisitioned, reconditioned or manufactured motor transport. The object of the relief convoy is to maintain effective supply lines along the roadways. At this point, Alba's original force remains entirely self-sustaining, and is continuing to accrete supplies from the countryside. But Alba foresees bottlenecks. The secondary force setting out in his wake is intended to cover that.

The relief convoy consists of approximately 10,000 men, including less than half infantry and half supply and support personnel. The convoy amounts almost entirely to new mobilization, lightly armed, with minimal artillery. The objective is entirely resupply.

On the road ahead, Alba will face his first major challenge, the battle of Trujillo.

****

After Chiclayo

General Benigno Flores sits back on his bunk in the command truck, wrestling with a cork. With a grunt, he pulls it loose, and then pours a measure of wine into a mug.

"Pour me one, would you," a voice comes. Colonel Alba climbs into the back of the truck, flopping onto his own bunk.

"We missed you at the officer's briefing," Flores says, pouring wine into a second cup and handing it over. "You could at least have dropped in long enough to accept the congratulations."

Alba tastes the wine and makes a sour face.

"What is this shit?"

"Something from that village we passed. Paid for it with my own money."

"You were robbed."

Flores grunts. "You're the one who insists we pay for everything. I'll tell you right now, that's not going to work for long. Even with Ureta's treasury, there's not enough gold to get us all the way."

Alba shrugs. "Doesn't matter. For now, we pay. It's too early to be leaving angry peons behind us."

"What does it matter what they think? They're peons."

"It makes things easier," Alba replies. "These people, they're not soldiers, they're not nationalists. They live their whole lives in their little villages, maybe they travel twenty miles from the spot where they're born. They just want to be left alone. We pass through, we make no grudges, it makes our progress easier, going forward and coming back."

"You're just a peon-lover," Flores laughs, "full of sentimental attachments. You should have joined the Socialist party. How you became a soldier…"

Axis of Andes – Page 201

Alba laughs.

"So where have you been so late?"

"Quartermasters," Alba replies.

"Quartermasters," Flores says, "always the quartermasters. You inspect the artillery, you watch the infantry, but you can barely spare a moment for your officers,"

"That's why I've got you," Alba says, "to look after the officers."

"But all the time, you're with the quartermasters. I change my mind. You're no socialist, you're an accountant. I bet you can tell me to the last litre how much gasoline we have left."

"We're very good there," Alba says.

"You see!" Flores waggles a finger at him.

Alba holds out his cup. "And you can tell me to the last dram how much wine we've got."

Flores pours a measure.

"I have my priorities." He pauses. "But seriously, the quartermasters? Let them do their job and keep track of the mules and the gas, the spare tires and the rounds of ammunition."

"You were with me in Chaco," Alba says. "Did you learn anything from that maniac Kundt?"

"All sorts of things," Flores replies. "Mostly, I learned that war is no place for a soldier. I mean, think on it: People shooting back at you. A man could get killed like that. It's unhygienic."

"Speaking of..."

"The latrines? Yes, I made sure that was taken care of."

"One thing not to worry about then," Alba says. Flores wrinkles his nose with disgust.

"No," Flores continues after a sip, "war is no place for the soldier. It is a foolish and romantic misapprehension of civilians that we're somehow meant to fight each other."

Flores gives a mock shudder. Alba sits back with a half-smile. He's heard it from Flores before.

"So what are we meant for?"

"Why, to shoot civilians. A superior undertaking in every way. They don't shoot back, I'll point out to you."

"That's rather unsporting."

"Oh it's excellent sport," Flores claims. "But that's beside the point. I ask you, what is our purpose as soldiers? Why, to maintain order. But what order, you ask? Well, I say, the order God intended, farmers farm, shopkeepers keep shop, milkmaids churn, brothels.... er broth, doctors heal and landowners run things. There is a place for everyone, and everyone, high and low, holds their place. That is order."

"The danger to order, that's not from other countries, other armies. They usually keep to their place, they have their own order to maintain. No, the danger to order is civilians. Sometimes they feel untidy."

"Untidy?" Alba asks.

"Farmers decide they don't want to farm for landholders, coal shovelers decide that they do not want to work for starvation wages, someone's always got a grievance, there's not enough, there's too much, someone else has more."

"Even if those grievances are legitimate?" Alba asks.

"All grievances are legitimate to those who bring them, selfishness is the human imperative. I do not ask myself who is right or wrong. I'm a soldier, not a lawyer or a priest or a judge."

"You just shoot them?"

"If they disturb order? Of course. That's my job. When you were in Chaco, sometimes I was with Velasco in Santiago. He wanted a real soldier around to make him look good, I suppose. While there, I met the Hyena of St. Cristobel."

"I haven't heard that?"

"Charming fellow actually, quite educated, very forthright. It turned out that it was not his mother who named him Hyena."

"Oh?"

"No, he earned it turning a machine gun on a group of striking miners, and on their wives and children. Killed a few hundred. He got the name from them. And he got a medal. As it happened, I had passed through that village on an occasion."

"And?"

"They lived like dogs, those miners. They lived worse than dogs. Endless poverty and misery. I saw the foreman whip them. They were right to rise up."

"And the Hyena?"

"He did his job, he was a soldier, not a priest. If there's justice out there, it's not for soldiers to give. We just keep order."

"You're quite a cynic," Alba observes.

"And you're a Socialist," Flores replies, smiling. "If you believe in a better world, all power to you. Until it comes about, in this life or the next, I just live in the one we have."

Flores holds up the bottle. "Empty. Damn. And it's too late to open another bottle."

"I don't look forward to shooting people," Flores says, "on principle, I'm against the notion. You go around shooting people, sooner or later, you run into someone who shoots back, and suddenly you're in a war."

"Which brings us to here and now."

Flores shrugs.

"Well," he says, "someone has to keep track of the important things for you, while you obsess over gallons of gasoline and rounds of ammunition."

"Like the wine?"

"To the last drop."

"Maybe you should open another bottle?"

"No, it's too late."

"So," Alba asks, "how are the officers faring?"

"After this?" Flores laughs, "Oh they're in love with you. They think you walk on water. I mean, you had their respect, these last few years. But I think a lot saw you as an upstart or a strange duck. But your star rose up when you put the invasion down. And now…"

Alba sighs. "We're just starting. It's a hard road."

"Yes," Flores replies, "so you have to count every gallon of gasoline. I get that. Still, this fight has given you a lot of credit among officers and men. Use that."

Alba nods.

Flores considers for a moment, "thinking on it, maybe don't get too close with the officers. Right now, you're a hero in the distance…"

"And familiarity breeds contempt?"

Flores shrugs.

"So have you finished going through Ureta's papers?" Flores asks.

"For now."

"Assessment?"

"They're all like him, I think. Condescending, arrogant, obstinate. For all their education and position, they're brutal thugs who don't see further down the road than they want to."

"Typical soldiers then?" Flores says.

Alba starts laughing so hard he chokes. Flores leans forward to pound him on the back.

"Oh don't do that, my friend, give me some warning before you fire a round like that. You'll kill me next time."

"They're still running about like chickens with their heads cut off. Ureta wrote whole tracts blaming everyone from Prado down to the latrine keepers for his defeat. They're all pointing fingers at each other, making demands."

"That's good, then."

"It won't last," Alba says dourly, "and the requisitions. They're calling up thousands. They're mobilizing fast. Even led by fools, there's going to be a lot of them."

"We're mobilizing faster."

"Not fast enough, and in the end, we're a small country. They're large, and much richer."

"Maybe we should have stayed home, throw up some walls, fortified, and let them come to us."

The old discussion.

"Do you really believe that?" Alba asks, as he lies down on his cot.

"It's tempting," Flores waves a hand dismissively, "and if it was equal numbers, I'd put our soldiers up against anyone. Peruvians, Americans, Romans, Spartans, anyone. But it's not going to be equal numbers. If we wait for them..."

He pauses, thoughtfully.

"If I thought simply defending would work," Flores says, "I'd be back home, defending Ecuador from the comfort of that brothel in Quito. But it won't. Time is not our friend."

He sits morosely.

"Do you think we can win? Really, just between us? Or is this some mad venture?"

From Alba's bunk comes a slow snoring.

Flores listens for a moment, and then rouses himself to cover his friend with a blanket. Then he heads out; perhaps somewhere there is a bottle already opened and waiting....

***

July 31, Yurimaguas, Peru

General Enrique Blandon lifts his head at the sound of distant rifle fire, and looks out over the streets of Yurimaguas. He is not happy. The town, such as it was, is larger than Andua, a more fitting command center. But there is something desolate about it.

The civilians have all left, of course, fleeing with the defeated Peruvians. There are burned buildings, pits from explosions, bullet holes everywhere. The place is much more battered than Andua.

This was the final campaign of the Oriente, where his men crushed Ureta's Chinchipe detachments. Dozens had been killed, dozens more surrendered, and the rest fled into the jungle. It has been a great victory.

Of course, he wasn't there to see it.

"Oscar," he orders his lieutenant, "go and see what that rifle fire is, and be quick about it! If it's just foolish soldiers getting drunk and popping off, I'll have someone whipped."

Blandon slaps at an insect, and wipes sweat from his face. It is ungodly hot and humid. He loathes the rain forest. Having been stationed there, he is of half a mind to give it to the Peruvians. Never, of course! He is a loyal Ecuadoran, and he'd die for every centimeter of his beloved country. But all in all, he'd rather die for some other part.

He returns to the letter. So the 'Great Pretender' Alba is steamrolling his way through Peru? As it turns out, the Peruvians weren't much of a challenge, given how easily the Chinchipe regiments had been bloodied.

He isn't actually in the chain of command for dispatches, but he still has friends in Quito. He and a great many senior officers consider Alba a pretentious upstart, and a Socialist. They have no regard for him. It rankles that he'd advanced by climbing into the old man's lap.

Most officers keep their opinions to themselves. But Blandon is old school, he believes in honour and probity, in traditional values, so while he isn't insubordinate, his views are clear; and while he hasn't been rebellious, he has insisted on the proper way of doing things.

He can never decide if the Andua commission had been a reward or a punishment. Certainly, only a brilliant man would be assigned to defend the entire Oriente. But sitting in that little jungle village, Andua, he'd had the sense that the war was passing him by. He was informed, but not actually consulted on the deployment of Oriente forces; or the strategies that were commissioned. Understandable, most of these deployments had come after he was in Andua, and communication had been so difficult. But it almost seems like he was sidelined; as if the Oriente defense was set up to proceed without him.

He's done his best to order his command. But ultimately being in Andua was worthless. He decided to move closer to the front. As it turned out, the battles were all won before he arrived.

Undeterred, he spends two weeks in Yamaguas, turning the evacuated town first into a garrison, then into a fortress, concentrating most of the manpower and supplies directly underneath him in and around this village. No more shitty little outposts in the jungle; he is building a mighty fist to smash the enemy, should it try again.

But it is unsatisfying. He crumples the letter. That prick, Alba, is getting all the glory. And for what? Slaughtering some Peruvian cattle? Blandon is certain that he could have done it faster and more cleanly. Hell, he knows a dozen officers in Quito, two dozen, that could show that blowhard up.

But it is all politics. Alba has his nose up the old man's ass, and Bonifaz, bless him, knows no better. He doesn't recognize the upstart for the shopkeeper's son and social climber that he is. So real soldiers, real talent, are cast aside to suffer in silence.

Oscar returns. Blandon looks him over critically. Even the short walk has left the man sweaty and dirty. Disgraceful. But then, conditions are appalling. He decides to overlook it.

"What was it?" Blandon demands. "More drunken soldiers?"

"Uhm..." Oscar wavers. "No. No, General, Sir. Undetermined. We think it's the Peruvians, just hangers on, leftovers. We've sent men in, but... the jungle... It's of no matter."

"Hmm," Blandon says thoughtfully, "so they're still out there?"

"Nothing significant. Probably farmers. Or locals. Nobodies really."

Blandon looks at the letter. Alba marching through Peru, like a puffed-up jackass. Here he is, having won territory himself, here in the Oriente, the whole point of the war...

"Not nobodies. Peruvian forces," Blandon corrects, "still out there, scouting, sniping, setting up a counterattack. We're going to have to go after them."

"But, Sir," Oscar protests, "...orders."

"And those orders were correct," Blandon agrees, "and they've taken us this far. But now it's time for new orders. The war's not over. Not on the coast and not here. If we're to protect what's ours, we can't leave the enemy out there, preparing his next attack. We have to take it to him."

Oscar seems confused.

"New orders," Blandon snaps. "We're going after the enemy, even if we have to chase him all the way south!"

Let Alba have his march. Blandon will do what real soldiers do, win where it counts.

***

Ecuador - The March on Lima - Trujillo

August 1 - Alba arrives at Trujillo, attacking the Central Army Command at Trujillo. The Central command is taken by surprise, but the position is fortified.

Alba initiates battle with a series of air raids from the Chiclayo airstrip, catching Peruvian air on the ground and strafing barracks. He then proceeds to flank the Central Army, cutting it off from supplies.

After three days, the Peruvians are running out of ammunition, and Alba commences his attack. After days of fighting, the Peruvians ask for terms, on August 5

Alba accepts the army as prisoners, strips them naked, burning their clothes and confiscating their boots and sets them marching to the village of Otuzco, approximately 50 miles inland by August 11. It is a major humiliation, which the Peruvian army will not forget.

Alba has travelled approximately 400 miles from Ecuador

[Battle of Trujillo - Central army command recruitment and training centre. Approximately 24,000 men, but 40% are recruits in basic training. Fortified garrison, but not well supplied. Peruvian casualties 9,000 dead or wounded. Ecuadorian casualties 2,500]

****

Chile - The Drift to War

Even while Ecuador's troops march across the north, Ibanez's own efforts to maintain some control of the political situation at home steadily disintegrate. For once, both the Nazis and the two branches of the military, army and navy, are in agreement that the current 'phony war' situation is not acceptable, and that the war must be prosecuted.

A major factor during this time is Alba's military successes in the north. Each time after the battles of Chiclayo and Trujillo, public sentiment, led by the Chilean Nazi party shifts harder against Peru. Initially, the Peruvians are reviled as aggressors, but the public sentiment grows more contemptuous after each battle. With the Peruvians increasingly seen as weak, evil and incompetent, pressure mounts on Ibanez. Peru cannot manage against little Ecuador, and yet Chile handed Tacna over to them and paid reparations barely a decade before. And worse, little more than a few weeks ago, Ibanez forced Chile's own soldiers to back down. The word 'coward' is being bandied about behind Ibanez back, and he's well aware of it. It's only a matter of time before it's said to his face, and after that...

Sentiment within both branches of the military has also shifted to war. The Navy is engaged in a standoff in the Gulf of Guayaquil and champing at the bit. In the Army, the consensus is evolving that while the ad hoc invasion of Tacna was wrong; withdrawing in humiliation afterwards was the greater wrong.

Ibanez advisors in the Nazi party, and more importantly, his generals and admirals in the army and navy are unanimous that the Peruvians have proven themselves to be paper tigers. If they can't handle a single army column from little Ecuador, then it is guaranteed that they will be no match for Chile's professional forces. The Peruvians will collapse like a house of cards, particularly in the face of a two front war. The conflict will be over in days. Even the Socialists and Communists agree that this might be the best way to bring things to a conclusion, provided that Chile is properly generous and enlightened in administering victory.

Ibanez continues his increasingly desperate efforts to arrange a cease-fire or peace treaty. But the Peruvians, disorganized and occupied by Alba's invasion ignore him. Finally, with the assurance of quick, decisive and nearly bloodless victory, he bows to pressure from his Cabinet and the public.

On August 8, in a public pronouncement, Ibanez repudiates the Tacna treaty, asserting rightful claim to the province and demands the return of monies paid as reparations. He then orders troops to occupy Tacna.

✱✱✱

Chile - Battle of Tacna - August 8-13, 1940

Unfortunately, Ibanez's

continuing indecisiveness proves disastrous.

The Peruvians, with their territory invaded from the north, are now taking the matter very seriously and are well into a national mobilisation. The Ecuador War had begun as General Ureta's private project, but it has become a series of disasters that is rousing the whole nation.

In the south, particularly, Peru has been humiliated by the abortive invasion of July 11, 1940, and warned by the 'cold war' Ibanez threatened. It has rapidly invested considerable manpower and resources into mobilizing and fortifying its southern border, particularly the province of Tacna.

The result is that when the Chilean forces again cross the border on August 8, 1940, the outcome is far different. Instead of encountering undermanned and under-equipped conscripts without orders or effective officers, the Chileans encounter a series of heavily manned, well-equipped defensive installations.

On the other side, the Chilean incursion is poorly organized and suffering from extravagant optimism. The Chilean army genuinely expects only a short, glorious battle against an ineffective and inept foe, essentially a repeat of July 11.

Axis of Andes – Page 212

Unfortunately, that is not what they meet.

Resistance is stiff initially, and the Chilean forces begin to take heavy casualties. Chilean officers refuse to change battle plans or acknowledge difficulties, with the result that more and more troops move into the line of fire, breaching Peruvian defences in some places with sheer numbers.

After five days, of minimal progress, and devastation to the assigned battle groups, the Chilean attack is called off, and forces retreat to the adjacent Arica province. The Chileans take three thousand casualties to the Peruvians two thousand. Chile has suffered their first major military defeat in a century on August 13, 1940.

The response to this national humiliation is war fever, and a furious demand for vengeance. Ibanez is forced to fully commit the Chilean Army to the cause of victory. Buoyed by superior numbers and equipment, the Chilean forces again push their way into Peruvian territory along a narrow and fiercely contested frontier.

***

Chile - Battle of the Gulf - August 16, 1940

In revenge for the August 13, defeat in Tacna and the invasion of Arica, President Ibanez orders a naval force in the Gulf of Guayaquil into action

On August 16, 1940, the Almirante Latorre opens fire on Peru's Coronel Bolognesi. The Bolognesi returns fire, retreating along the gulf until it is pinned to the coast. The two ships exchange fire, but the Almirante Latorre has better armour, bigger guns and better range. Latorre pounds the old cruiser until it starts to burn. Firing is briefly suspended to allow the surviving crew to abandon ship, and then resumes until the burning hulk sinks. The survivors surrender to the Ecuadorian army on shore and are taken into custody.

When hostilities commence against the Coronel Bolognesi, the Villar makes a break for it, exchanging fire with the Chileans as it makes for open water. The Peruvian destroyer is faster than the Chilean battleship and soon outruns its guns.

As the Villar makes its escape, the Hyatt pursues, the two ships exchanging occasional barrages, while the Aldea supports the attack on the Coronel Bolognesi. When the Coronel Bolognesi is trapped against the coast by the Almirante Latorre, the Aldea breaks off the attack and goes in pursuit of the Villar. The Aldea and Hyatt, both Serrano class destroyers from 1928, are significantly faster than the Villar. On the Peruvian coast, the Villar is trapped between the two Chilean ships. Refusing a demand for surrender, the Villar races onward. The Chilean ships opens fire, disabling it. At this point, Villar's crew scuttles their ship, the survivors are taken into custody aboard the Hyatt, and remain prisoners of the Chilean navy for the duration of hostilities.

The news of the naval battle is greeted with hysterical joy in Quito and Guayaquil and celebrated throughout Ecuador. In Chile, the battle wins the navy unabashed acclaim, and parades are held in several cities. The victory at sea is a welcome reassurance in the face of hard fought and increasingly desperate battles in the northern provinces.

In Peru, the battle is called the 'Treachery of Guayaquil Bay," crowds take to the street, and newspaper editorials ring angrily with denunciations for what is considered to be an unprovoked attack, notwithstanding the state of war and the eruption of fighting in the south.

For the Peruvian military, the battle comes as an appalling shock. Principally a land-based force; the Peruvian command has little grasp of naval warfare. The almost instantaneous loss of a quarter of Peru's naval strength, with no damage at all to Chilean ships, is stunning. Suddenly, they are looking at the possibility of the obliteration of their entire naval force and Chilean dominance at sea.

***

Ecuador - March on Lima

August 18 - largely oblivious to the battles at sea and in the south, Alba proceeds along the coastal road through the towns of Chimbote and then turns east and inland, proceeding up through the town of Cazma to the town of Huarez, avoiding contact with the assembling Peruvian military.

News of Trujillo has reached the Peruvian command, and forces are being assembled inland. A gathered expeditionary force proceeds onto Alba's trail, following him towards Huarez.

Digging down in the town of Huarez, and establishing an airstrip, he waits for the relief convoy while Peruvians assemble their forces. His supply train catches up with him slowly. Aircraft reconnaissance allows him detailed knowledge of Peruvian troop movements.

Alba is approximately 550 miles from Ecuador by now

August 23 - determining that the relief convoy is only days away, Alba conveys instructions by airdrop and leaves Huarez, travelling back along his road to give battle. Peruvian forces are caught between Alba's main force and his relief convoy. After two days of hard fighting the Peruvians retreat in disarray on August 26.

Alba's combined force is roughly 24,000 men

[Battle of Huaraz - Peruvian forces are approximately 25,000. Casualties are high, Peruvian losses are 15,000 killed or injured. Alba loses 6,000 killed or injured]

***

After Huaraz

"Cheer up, my friend," Flores claps Alba on the back. Most of the other officers are wary around the remote Colonel Alba. Only Flores dares take such liberties.

"They're calling you the new Napoleon," Flores says; "you should bask in the glory."

"I recall how Napoleon turned out," Alba replies.

"I'm glad you presented a better face to the officers," Flores teases. "I'd hate to have them see you mope. But seriously, how can you be so dour? We've won every battle so far."

"We're moving too slowly," Alba complains. "I think that the pack animals were a mistake, they slow us down."

Flores makes a sour face.

"That again? We didn't have enough trucks for our needs. So the choice was go with fewer men, or wait and hope to requisition enough motor vehicles."

"It slowed us down."

"It was a trade off," Flores says, "and I notice you've grabbed every motor vehicle the Peruvians have left lying around, even civilian ones, which you pay for... Why? I have no idea."

"That'll end soon enough," Alba says. "The treasury we took from Ureta is all but gone, and they were clever enough to leave no spoils at Huarez. The road is going to get rougher."

"We're moving fast enough," Flores says, "and we can ditch the animals and move faster when we need to. Meanwhile, you've got your spotter planes watching where the Peruvians are. It's not quite the plan we set out with, but we've done well along the way."

Alba grunts.

"They're mobilizing faster than I expected. You saw the size of the army at Trujillo? They had the numbers on us. And again at Huarez, a brand new army, out of nothing! How many will they have in a month? They'll drown us."

"So we'll move faster," Flores shrugs. "As I see it, you're making two mistakes."

"Only two? I count dozens," Alba says, and then huckles. "What two?"

"Trujillo," Flores says, "kill a man, but never shame him. You shamed the entire Peruvian army, stripping them naked and setting them off barefoot. They'll never forget that, and never forgive. I'd have given my right arm to see those generals in Lima react to the news, I can imagine their faces. But they'll have it in for you from now on."

"We had no place to put them," Alba says. "I couldn't accept their parole, so it was either render them harmless and send them off, or kill the lot of them. What was I supposed to do?"

"I know," Flores says, "murder to kill them all, it was a pretty pickle. I don't know what else we could have done. They were going to be shamed no matter what. And a shamed man with boots is immeasurably more dangerous than a shamed man without. I can't think of anything better."

"So it wasn't a mistake?"

"It certainly was. Just because there's nothing better to do doesn't make it a good thing. But I'll tell you, we'll end up having to kill four times their number in the end, because of it."

"Fair enough," Alba says.

"And my second mistake?"

"You're too good at killing Peruvians."

"How so?"

"So far, you're fighting idiots. Those educated ignorant thugs, as you are so fond of calling them. Soldiers, I call them. But I can't really disagree with you. The point is that Peru, they have the numbers."

"And those numbers are starting to show."

"Yes, numbers. But no brains. They're led by stupid men. Now after Trujillo, stupid angry men, which is not a bad thing. But you're killing them too fast."

"I am?"

"Oh, yes! Keep killing stupid men at this rate, and sooner or later someone clever is going to end up in charge. Clever like you, my friend. And when that happens, we're in trouble."

"Sounds daunting."

"Well, we're lucky in that Peru has vast wells of stupidity, but at the rate we're using them up, sooner or later they'll run out."

"What do you suggest?"

"Two things. Move faster, and make the best use of our advantages while we have them"

"My plan as well. And the other?"

"Simplest thing in the world. Tell our soldiers to aim for their smart ones."

✳✳✳

Peru - The Naval Battle of Coquimbo

The Chilean Guayaquil expeditionary force, comprising the battleship Almirante Latorre and the destroyers Hyatt and Aldea, remains in the Gulf of Guayaquil until August 24; at which point the destroyers Serrano and Videla arrive to relieve them. The capital ships begin the long journey back to their home base at Coquimbo in central Chile.

Axis of Andes – Page 218

At this time, roughly between August 20 and August 28, the Peruvian offensive in the south is pushing into Antofagasta, and much of Chile's political and military attention is concentrated on repelling the invasion. Elements of the Chilean navy are principally engaged in offshore shelling of Peruvian forces, and maintaining control of the coastlines.

Around this time as well, Colonel Alba's March on Lima is ongoing. The March has proceeded along the coast through the battles of Chiclayo and Trujillo, and through the July and August, Bonifaz has requested Chilean naval support. Ibanez has dithered, considering Alba's March to be a foolhardy and likely doomed venture. By August 18, Alba has marched his forces inland, to the town of Carmaz and is proceeding towards the Huarez on August 23, and the question of Chilean naval support is moot.

At this point, the Chilean navy has essentially run out of targets. Having scored its quick and decisive victory in the battle of Guayaquil, with no interest in and then no ability to support Alba, and attention diverting rapidly to the southern theatre, its role is simply to support the army on the front and to suppress the Peruvian navy, should it choose to show.

On the Peruvian side, however, the events at Guayaquil on August the 16 and the military successes on the southern front over the next couple of weeks produce a strange combination of panic and giddy aggression. Having been crudely awakened to the inferiority and vulnerability of their fleet, but emboldened by success in the Antofagosta, the Peruvian military command rapidly conceives a reckless plan of attack.

On August 21, the surviving cruisers Almirante Grau and Aguire, and the destroyers Palacio, Guize and Garcia, as well as four submarines, together with oil transport and support ships, are dispatched for an attack on the Chilean navy at Coquimbo. This is almost the entirety of the Peruvian navy. The only ships not joining the attack are the destroyer Rodrigues and a submarine, both undergoing refitting.

The flotilla sweeps far out to sea, avoiding the battle zone of the southern frontier. The Almirante Grau develops mechanical problems and falls a half day behind. The destroyer Garcia hangs back to accompany it. On the morning of August 28, under a cover of heavy fog, the first part of the fleet enters the harbour at Coquimbo opening fire on the ships and harbour defenses. The Coquimbo port authority has been anticipating the return of the Almirante Latorre and its destroyers and so does not initially react to the appearance of the ships.

At this time, the Almirante Latorre, the Hyatt and Aldea are still in transit. The Serrano and Videla are posted to the Gulf of Guayaquil. Of the remainder of the northern fleet, the cruiser, Blanco Encelada, is assigned for coastal assault.

In harbour at Coquimbo are the battleship Capitan Prat, the cruiser Chacabuco, the destroyers Orella and Riquelme, the destroyer Almirante Lynch diverted from the southern fleet, and three submarines, as well as more than a dozen auxiliary vessels, including both oil tankers. By luck and circumstance, all of these ships are in the harbour for provisions, refitting or reassignment, and are taken by surprise.

In the ensuing battle the Almirante Lynch and Riquelme are sunk. The Chacabuco is disabled and beached, and will eventually be scrapped. The Orella is able to return fire, but takes heavy damage and requires extensive repairs for a year before becoming seaworthy again. The Capitan Prat also fires its guns, but catches fire on the return barrage and takes heavy damage. Due to parts shortages and difficulties with repairs, the Capitan Prat is out of commission for the remainder of the war and eventually scrapped. By mid-day the Almirante Grau and the Garcia arrive on the scene, adding to the carnage and overwhelming the defender's efforts to rally. Two submarines are sunk, the third disabled. Both oil tankers are sunk and most of the auxiliary vessels are destroyed.

The battle is not without consequences for the Peruvians. The Palacio and Guize both take damage, the Guize somewhat heavier. The Aguirre is hit, but this does not impair any functions and there are no casualties.

The fleet then leaves the harbour and proceeds up towards the war zone. There they catch the Chilean warship, Blanco Encelada, engaging in support work and sink it after a quick encounter. The Peruvian's Guize, previously damaged is disabled and ultimately scuttled. The remainder of the Peruvian ships scatter to open sea, in order to avoid the Almirante Latorre and its destroyers, who have received the news and are heading south for revenge. They successfully avoid the Almirante Grau and take shelter at Callao. On the return, one submarine develops mechanical problems and sinks.

The battle of Coquimbo is a major shock to the Chilean nation, coming literally in the midst of the hotly contested battles of Arica. In the aftermath, the principal Fleet Admirals retire or are replaced and a number of positions are shaken up. The navy is reorganized, and the northern and southern fleets are dissolved in favour of a unified command. Talhuanco becomes the primary base of naval operations. In the short term, the loss of the oil tankers in particular and of many of the auxiliary vessels cripples the long-range capacity of the Chilean fleet. Arrangements have to be made with Ecuador to support the destroyers and Guayaquil, and the ability to carry operations on the Peruvian coast is briefly interrupted.

As of September 1, 1940, the respective standings of the two fleets are:

Chile:

Battleships: *Almirante Latorre and Almirante Cochrane*

Cruisers: *Almirante O'Higgins, and Toro (still in repairs)*

Destroyers: *Aldea, Hyatt, Serrano, Videla, Almirante Condel*

Six submarines

Peru

Cruisers: *Aguire, Almirante Grau*

Destroyers: *Rodrigues, Palacio, Garcia*

Four submarines.

Ultimately, the battle of Coquimbo fails to cripple the Chilean navy, or to enable a Peruvian breakthrough on the land war. The destruction of the Blanco Encelada, or the temporary crippling of coast attacks makes no real difference to the land war.

In reprisal, the Almirante Latorre shells several Peruvian coastal towns and cities, partly as reprisal and partly to draw Peruvian naval forces into battle, before finally being driven off by aircraft.

In Lima, the battle of Coquimbo is seen as a masterstroke, provoking public celebration, and irrational exuberance in Benevides' government. The truth is that it was reckless, stupid and succeeds only with astonishing levels of luck.

Coquimbo arose from a combination of factors:

> (1) Ignorance - as noted, the Peruvian military and high command is army driven, they don't have a good grasp of naval matters, the navy's status and influence is comparatively less, and so the high command could opt for it without fully appreciating the difficulties and risks involved;

> (2) Panic - as noted, the battle of Guayaquil and the instant loss of a major chunk of naval power sends the Peruvian high command into a tizzy; they didn't truly appreciate naval warfare;

> (3) Irrational exuberance - Peruvian Army is still steeped in 18th and 19th century military doctrines that advocate bold, even reckless action. There's a history accessible to them of this sort of shenanigan working on land and sea. And right at the moment, reckless boldness seems to be working for them as they overrun Tarapaca and push into Antofagasta (actually, it's superior preparation, but that kind of thing often gets overlooked). And Alba's March on Lima is again a matter of reckless boldness working. Against them, in Alba's case, but it seems to prove the principle.

Ultimately, under the circumstances, there are really only two choices left to the Peruvian Navy: Basically pull into harbour and wait it out; or try something reckless like this. Do nothing safely or do something dangerous. The Peruvian military culture since Sanchez (restrained only by Benevides) was very much the 'do something' crowd. These guys were eating their Wheaties and feeling their oats, and doing nothing just wasn't sitting in their belly - that was the reason they invaded Ecuador in the first place. So odds were, they were inclined to try a stunt like this; it's really the only active option.

After that, it's simply luck - no one spots them in advance, they come in under cover of fog, the harbour master and watchmen don't realize what they are till the attack begins, etc. No excuse for any of that except that in real history it happens a lot more than you'd expect and succeeds a lot more than seems plausible. Basically, what's going on is that basically most naval engagements are slugging matches and numbers and quality tell the tale. And mostly numbers and quality are on the same side. Those are brutal equations, and there's not that many ways to dodge around them, what with the sea being bereft of mountains, valleys, and useful geography. So really, the only way to really screw with the equations is to seize the initiative boldly - to indulge mass pre-emptive attacks and nail the other guy before he can get his mojo on. So, as I've said, long history of this kind of shenanigans, and for whatever reasons, it works more often than it ought to.

In the end, Peru remains overwhelmingly outgunned both in numbers and quality at sea.

✳✳✳

March on Lima – Battle of Calao

September 5 - Alba reaches to the town of Calao outside of Lima without further incident. Peruvian forces have marshalled there. After an exchange of fire, Alba retreats, leaving the Peruvian forces to follow. A few miles from the town of Huaral, Alba chooses his field of battle. The Peruvians, in hot pursuit, allow their line to become ragged and fall into a trap. Alba defeats and destroys a force three times his own size, advancing to the outskirts of Lima by September 8. He establishes pickets on the main entries to the city.

Alba has travelled approximately 750 miles from Ecuador

[Battle of Calao - 50,000 Peruvian conscripts versus 18,000 Ecuadorian recruits. Peruvians lose 12,000 killed or wounded. Ecuador's casualties are 3,000]

September 10 - President Manuel Prado appoints General Oscar Benevides, the former President to negotiate with Alba.

Chile - The Battles of Arica

August 15 - Peru attacks Arica, crossing the border from Tacna at several points. The Peruvians employ overwhelming numbers, supported by the Southern Command's armour.

August 20 - Peru overruns Arica. Peru mobilizes faster. Peruvian forces number 15,000 but are increasing rapidly, as Bolivian border detachments are reassigned. Chilean forces are roughly half that and overextended. The Chileans are making desperate attempts to increase their numbers.

August 24 - Peru pushes into Tarapaca using superior armour and artillery, launching attacks on Antofagasta, deep into Chile. Chile begins mass mobilization. Approximately 20,000 Peruvians oppose 14,000 Chileans, which include horse cavalry and reassigned paramilitary police detachments sent to combat. The desperate effort to mobilize has come at a cost, however. Chileans have outrun their supplies and are forced to retreat as fighting extends into Antofagasta.

August 28 - Chilean forces receive reinforcements and counterattacks. The overextended Peruvian line is at the limits of its supplies and forced to retreat slowly. The barren Tarapaca province provides little sustenance. Through the first weeks of September, the Peruvian forces are pushed back steadily.

September 20 - Chile's forces retake Arica after heavy fighting and press on to Tacna. The Peruvians withdraw to fortified positions in Tacna. Peruvian supplies and manpower are being diverted to contend with Alba, who has reached Lima. The subsequent coup and ascension of General Ramirez is also sewing confusion and undermining the Peruvians.

September 30 - Village to village fighting in Tacna, with a hostile population resistant to the Chileans. Peruvians consolidate and push back. Chileans fall back to Arica.

***

Axis of Andes – Page 225

The War in the South, Early Stages....

Why does Peru perform so well and Chile so badly in this theatre, when by rights, the advantage should be with Chile?

A large part of this is the relative degree of preparation by the respective parties. The Ibarra-Sorzano treaty between Ecuador and Bolivia is now common knowledge in Peru, and although Bolivia's Penaranda has repudiated it, relations are still poor. Further, Velasco's prior diplomatic efforts and connections with Chileans are known, and there is reasonable apprehension that there might be a secret treaty in place there. Thus, as General Ureta issues his ultimatum to Prado, by letters he notifies the southern commands of his intention, so that they can go on alert in case of action by Bolivia and/or Chile

Therefore Peruvian forces in the south on both the Bolivian and Chilean frontiers are prepared to mobilize for war when Ureta begins his invasion. Peruvian forces in the south remain at a high state of readiness even as Ureta's invasion falls apart in the north.

Later, in his memoir and other writings, Ureta repeatedly attacks his fellow commanders for 'hoarding their guns' - not providing him with troops and weapons, which he claims, crippled his effort.

Following the failure of the Ecuador invasion, when Peru commences general mobilization, the disorganized Northern Command, reeling from high casualties and demoralized by failure, is almost completely unable to take full advantage of it, and put together an effective force against Alba. The Central Commands have to gear up for war in addition to absorbing conscripts and coping with Alba's March on Lima; in the short term performing both functions poorly.

However, the Southern Commands on the frontiers are already geared up for potential war and are already at maximum readiness. They are able to absorb, arm and train the new conscripts much more effectively. Peru has divided itself into relatively autonomous commands. This has allowed General Ureta, on his own initiative, to plunge the country into war. But it also allows the southern command generals, Marin and Odria, to maintain themselves at a high state of readiness, unaffected by disaster or turmoil elsewhere.

On the Chilean side, there has been a general failure to prepare, which related to Ibanez's domestic political situation.

In particular, Ibanez's support in the Army and Navy respectively is quite divided, with the Navy's attitude distinctly lukewarm and inclined towards Congress. In 1890, a civil war between the President and the Congress had resulted in the Army and Navy each supporting a different faction. The outcome of that war had seen the emasculation of the Presidency and the beginning of the Parliamentary era.

The Navy, smaller but more professional and with substantial firepower, is not reluctant to go up against the Army. Ibanez is therefore handicapped in military deployments. He has difficulties directing both branches and has to be wary of antagonizing either. In particular, with the Army he has to be careful of deployments or mobilizations that the Navy might see as a provocation. Or that the Army might see as meddling.

Thus, for most of the time he has been in office, less than a year, he'd had to focus on currying favour of two jealous siblings. There has been very little in the way of appointments, no transfers, and no military movements or deployments except where demanded by obvious necessity.

Even after the declaration of war, much of the Chilean military does little to prepare or advance to a war footing. Senior commanders are informed and agree to the declaration as a negotiating tactic, and there is a general consensus not to act on it.

Initiative, when it comes, is haphazard. In Santiago and Valparaiso, the Nazi party stages mass pro-war rallies demanding Chile's own March on Lima. The military bases are besieged by young men attempting to join. In response to public agitation the Chilean Navy prepares plans for a limited naval action to break the naval blockade of Ecuador, for humanitarian purposes, to which Ibanez cautiously accedes.

In response to that, rogue Nazi-influenced elements of the Army, not wanting to be one-upped by the Navy, independently and without authority launch their own attack on Tacna. This puts Ibanez in the position of having to walk them back. The result is confusion and indecision, and a certain amount of frustration in army ranks that cannot be placated by the Senior Command Following this, Ibanez finds it increasingly difficult to contain war fever among the lower ranks; but despite this, there is no organized military consensus and no commitment to preparation. The Chilean Army and Navy decline to coordinate.

Chauvinism and even racism play a part. The Chileans have fought two successful wars against Peru and Bolivia together. In fact, Chile has an unbroken run of military successes, while Peru has yet to win a war with anyone. The Chilean perception is that they are a modern European people, while the Peruvians are a half-breed race, backwards, poverty stricken and mired in the 19th century. The full expectation of the Chilean public and media is that the war will be swift, sharp and therapeutic. This is an opinion shared by both branches of Chile's military, which leaves a feeling of lack of urgency towards preparation.

The end result is that Chile's mobilization to war footing lags at least one to two months behind Peru's. While the Chileans will regain their bearings rapidly, it will take a number of weeks for the two nations to reach an even footing.

Indeed, Chile performs so poorly in the opening months of their war that only two factors really save them from complete disaster.

One is the poor logistic capacities of the Peruvians. The northern provinces of Chile are thinly populated and at times desolate. Invading Peruvian armies cannot live off the land, but have to bring their own supplies. The further the Peruvians push into Arica and Tarapaca, the longer and more tenuous their supply lines grow and the shorter and more compact the Chilean's.

Initially, the Peruvians are able to compensate for this by reassigning the Bolivian frontier's command to the Chilean front, providing a stream of fresh supplies and reinforcements. Unfortunately, the Peruvians do not take advantage of this bonus by developing or reinforcing their supply lines. They only begin when the resources of the Bolivia Command are approaching exhaustion. This is a critical mistake.

The Chileans, for their part, initially have very poor supply logistics as well. Although they can successfully push the Peruvians out of Tarapaca, by the time they are marching through Tacna, they are overextending themselves badly and are vulnerable to the inevitable renewed assault. The war becomes a seesaw as each side competes to rush men, weapons, artillery, cavalry and supplies into the area, with momentary advantages translating into large military swings.

The other factor that works in favour of the Chileans is Alba's March on Lima, which from mid-August onwards, consumes increasing attention by the Peruvians. Alba's ensuing siege of Peru in mid-September, and the consequent Ramirez Coup disrupt reinforcements and resupply for the south, as most effort is diverted into repelling Alba.

***

September 9, 1940 - Lima, Peru

Colonel Alba once again checks his uniform. Is everything straight? He notices a loose thread. There isn't time to fix it. He is afraid he looks shabby.

General Benevides steps into the room. Alba and Flores stand, the men salute each other.

There is a cordial exchange of greetings.

"So what is it that you want?" Benavides asks bluntly.

"An end to the war."

Benavides barks a laugh.

"Well, we're agreed on that much. What terms do you propose?"

Alba glances at Flores and licks his lips. He hasn't expected the old general to be so forthright. There is a disturbing candour in his eyes. Benavides is a man who has abandoned illusions a long time ago.

Alba takes a breath.

"Recognition of Ecuador's claims on the Oriente."

"The Oriente? How much? I've heard of the massacre at Pucallpa. How much are you claiming?"

"General Blandon has exceeded his remit," Alba replies. "This happens in war. We have no designs on, and no claims against, Peru's territory. We are prepared to withdraw, both here and in the jungle."

"So just the traditional claim? That patch of jungle in the north?" Benevides says. "You can have it. It wasn't worth the lives it cost either side to fight over."

"I'm sorry that General Ureta did not see it that way."

"Ureta is a fool and a thug looking for a place in the history books."

Alba isn't sure how to respond to that. Luckily, he doesn't need to. Benevides continues.

"I would propose an independent third party be agreed upon to resolve boundary issues."

"My position is not negotiable," Alba says stiffly.

"And I'm conceding on this point, but there are always details with boundaries. We don't need to start another war over it."

"Ahh," Alba says, "agreed."

"I want a return to the rest of the borders. Tombes, Piura, Lambayeque, we take it all back."

"Yes," Alba says, "that is agreeable."

"Remove your army from our lands. We may agree in principle, and I'll sign my name to it, and you'll have our word as gentlemen. But it's not an official peace treaty until you're back where you belong," Benavides says.

"Agreed," Alba responds.

"And General Blandon, running around in the jungle?"

"He will be recalled immediately."

"Excellent."

Alba nods. "We will require free passage back, unmolested. And resupply and provisions."

The old man rubs his chin.

"Done, as to the first. To the second, don't press your luck, but we'll see what can be done to speed you out of my country. But as consideration for that favour, you will immediately grant free traffic in and out of Lima while we hammer out the details. There is no need to make more inconvenience."

"Granted," replies Alba, "so long as there are no further military operations or preparations during the same period."

"It's not as if they've given you much trouble, boy, but agreed," Benavides thinks for a moment. "Reparations?"

"None demanded, none offered."

"Good enough," Benavides stands and holds out his hand.

"We'll have peace, then. There are a thousand details to work out, but we have the essentials. I'll waste no more time now. I will have to consult with Manuel."

Manuel? Alba realizes that Benavides is referring to the Peruvian President. He stands and shakes Benevides' hand. Flores stands up hastily.

"It was good to meet you, sir," he says.

"I'll be back this afternoon, and we can start the real work of it."

The old man marches out, followed by his retainers. He pauses at the door.

"I am glad to see," he tells Alba, "that you are both an honourable man, and a reasonable one. The two often do not go together."

Then he is gone.

Alba suddenly finds he is shaking slightly. He sits down quickly to mask the trembling in his knees.

"My God," he says, "how long was that?"

"Not fifteen minutes," Flores says.

"Fifteen minutes and it's all over?" Alba whispers. "Astonishing."

It seems impossible. All those years of waiting, of preparing and planning, training, all of Ibarra's diplomacy. For seven years, this war has haunted him, has consumed him with its looming presence. When it had finally come, when Ureta's troops crossed the border, his emotion had been a sense of relief. Now it is all over. Now he feels empty.

"We should have demanded reparations," Flores is saying. "He gave in way too easy. We could have gotten more out of him. Tombes or Piura. A few more border adjustments. Maybe a cottage or two, perhaps some dancing girls. I would not have said no to a pension."

Alba laughs a little hysterically, Flores joins him.

"You've won the war, my friend," Flores says.

"No," Alba replies, "we've won peace."

****

Profiles in History, The Napoleon of the Andes

One of the most romantic figures of the Andean Wars is Colonel Luis Larrea Alba, the so called Napoleon of the Andes, who fought for Ecuador. Much is made of Alba's brilliance as a commander, but in his early life, there was little evidence of it.

Until the outbreak of the Andean War, Alba has been unremarkable, most notable for his interventions in Ecuadoran politics in 1931 and 1932. This has led some to question Alba's merits. Is he really that good, or is he simply lucky?

The historical consensus is that while he is lucky, he really is that good, for four principle reasons.

> 1) Although Alba received conventional military training in Ecuador, his time with Kundt in the Chaco war is a strongly formative experience. Out there, he encounters the remains of literally entire battalions that die of dehydration because water isn't being delivered, and watches Kundt hammer futilely at mud forts indistinguishable from other mud forts to no particular effect.
>
> From this, he becomes obsessed with logistics and supply lines. Obsessed to the point that his fellow officers consider him a bit neurotic on the subject. But it allows him to organize very large forces and move them very quickly and maintain them at a high level of effectiveness.
>
> Indeed, he astonishes his opponents with how quickly he can move parts of his forces. Again, a legacy of the organizational foul-ups he witnesses in the Chaco. Alba's focus on logistics and movement allows him to come at his opponents days before they expect, or to arrive at a point earlier and take the time to hunker down and prepare.
>
> Finally, he learns from the Chaco to choose his targets, and his ground very carefully. His obsession with logistics is well known. But he is equally, if less obviously, devoted to reconnaissance and planning.

During the seven years leading up to the war, he personally travels the Peruvian roads his army would later be marching on; he accumulates a very detailed set of maps, picks up a lot of intelligence on Peruvian officers and commands, and continually sends scouts ahead to prepare the way and survey the ground. One of his innovations is that he keeps sending up aircraft with trusted trained officers to survey the countryside and keep tabs on where his opponents are. The flights take off from well behind the lines and they convey their information by having the ride-along officer drop his notes from the air.

2) In general terms, the Ecuadorians have been preparing off and on for the last seven years. They've been fairly systematic about it. And they've managed to acquire some decent hardware from the Germans, with time to get good at it. Henry Ford's truck factory has also been effective at imparting a useful set of skills and equipment as well as transport vehicles. Alba's expeditionary force has a lot of veterans of the Chaco 'volunteer' brigades and, while they had mostly avoided the fighting, they had received training in the field, providing him with a hard core of veterans who were particularly well acquainted with logistics and field movement. He also has the blooded veterans who have just fought off Peru's initial invasion; they have learned fast and their morale is high. In terms of sheer quality of force, Alba's troops are experienced, trained and motivated; far superior to the Peruvian conscripts.

3) His opponents are poor. Alba describes them as 'educated ignorant thugs' and that's not too far off. The Peruvian generals are not stupid men, but they are products of their social caste - Criollo with a historical sense of entitlement, somewhat racist, deeply conservative, far better at politics than tactics or strategy. They're the products of an elitist ruling class in a rigid, hierarchical and very traditional society. The results are personalities and command structures that are deeply conservative, very inflexible, and traditionally used to operating with deployments of static or stable forces in a civilian environment. They're not

experienced with moving large numbers over open country, they haven't been particularly concerned with logistics, and their knowledge of contested battles is mostly academic or historical.

Essentially, as a group, the Peruvian Command, at least in the initial stages of the war, are far better at plotting coups or unleashing their forces on civilian strikers than they are at running an organized campaign. They've set conscription in motion, and are raising up huge armies. But they're struggling to arm and train these forces and really don't have a handle on what to do with them. And they continually underestimate Alba, particularly how fast he can move, and how well he selects his ground. They are almost invariably blundering into meeting him on his own terms.

This is not to say that the Peruvian forces are particularly backwards. They are well aware of what goes on in the world, have had contacts and training with Italian, German and American militaries; and they have the budget to buy modern ordnance and tactics ranging from tanks to paratroops. They've even read the instruction manuals.

But their military culture prevents them from appreciating the new toys on anything more than a superficial level and, collectively, there isn't a sufficient level of insight or flexibility to make skilful use of their assets.

4) Alba is lucky. People make their own luck, and Alba's basically done almost all his stuff right. He's made mistakes, but they haven't hurt him. On the other side of the coin, his opponents have basically done all their stuff wrong, and the failure of the invasion has unstrung them, leaving them disorganized at crucial times. Ibanez declaration of war and moves in the south has distracted them. The Generals are fighting among themselves and President Prado isn't really leading. So basically, the breaks are consistently going Ecuador's way.

Axis of Andes – Page 236

Coup in Peru

September 12 - President Prado is overthrown, and both Prado and Benevides are killed in a coup organized by members of the Peruvian armed forces, led by General Antonio Rodriguez Ramirez. Ramirez sends messages to Alba protesting confusion and requests additional time to consider terms agreed by Benevides, while at the same time deploying troops through the city and summoning waiting army divisions.

September 14 - Alba learns by airdrop that Peruvian armies are on the move, coming from the south, north and interior. He has only finite time before he's trapped. He gives General Ramirez an ultimatum; and when no response is made by noon, orders the shelling of the city. Cavalry and armoured car sorties come under heavy fire. Alba is short of armour and unwilling to attempt a battle for the city with the numbers and resources at his command. There's also the matter of approaching Peruvian reinforcements.

September 19 - After attacking Lima for four days with artillery, Alba is no closer to taking the city from its defenders. The Peruvians reject all further offers of negotiation and refuse to discuss terms of surrender and cease-fire. Meanwhile, the Peruvian fleet is shelling from the coast and Alba's air cover has been picked to pieces by the Peruvian air force. The Peruvian army is assembling large forces to the north and south. If he remains, he will be crushed between Lima's defense forces and the armies marshalling against him.

It's time to leave.

***

Outside Lima

"It's getting harder," Jose Moreno says. Technically, Jose is a lieutenant in the Ecuadoran army, but the airman wears none of the trappings of an officer. His leather flying cap, not his officer's bars, is his badge. "We've lost six planes. Four in the last two weeks, the Peruvians are catching on."

Alba nods.

"Sooner or later, we knew they would."

"They're not doing air reconnaissance yet," Jose says. "They haven't figured out that part of it. But it's getting more dangerous to go near their bases. They send someone up to say hello, and we have to run away."

"You are equipped?"

"Yes, machine guns," Moreno replies, nodding towards his biplane. Alba's forces hold a mile-long stretch of reasonably straight and well maintained road outside Lima as a makeshift landing strip. It has been the latest in a series of improvised landing strips and drops. "But I prefer to leave, not to fight. There's no advantage to getting in a dogfight. You never know what you're going to meet up there."

"What about mobile units?" Alba asks.

"Easy to spot, and they don't send anything up. If you buzz them, they scatter like chickens and fire rifles. If you don't buzz them, they don't pay much attention. Maybe down there they look at you and then say a prayer to Madre de Dios that you're not dropping a bomb on them."

There've been too many occasions where Peruvian air forces have dropped bombs on Alba's column. Thankfully, the Peruvians have not been terribly accurate and have done little harm. When they fly low enough to do harm, they become vulnerable to ground fire.

And on occasion, Alba's been able to arrange a surprise for them from some of Jose's friends.

"Don't buzz them," Alba says. "Just watch them. It's going to be hard enough dealing with them, without giving them too much warning."

Moreno shrugs. In his experience, senior officers' advice falls into two categories. The obvious things that he was going to do anyway, and the ludicrously stupid things he has no intention of going near.

It is a measure of Alba that most of the things he says fell into the blindingly obvious rather than the ludicrously stupid, as far as Moreno is concerned.

"Understood," he says. "You know, I could take one more fly around, see if anything's moved."

"No," Alba replies, "no need. I can already guess that General Odria's coming up from the South. Thousands more conscripts are coming down by the rail from Cuzco and Ramirez is trying to pull his army back together in Lima. I don't need more air reconnaissance to tell me that."

He pauses.

"As for what's up ahead," he says, "the road is clear for now. No significant opposition is forming."

"Things change, though," Flores notes.

"Which is why we don't want to be here," Alba replies. "The Peruvians are getting their act together, and if we stay..."

"But they still have assets up ahead. Fortresses and bases, battalions, and their navy," Flores argues.

Alba nods.

"Fine," he said. "Your orders are still to return to Ecuador with the reports and orders. We need General Gallo to lead a relief column out. But follow the road; if you see something of concern within.... two hundred miles... fly back and make a drop."

Jose rolls his eyes. Flores notes this and squints hard, but without effect. These airmen are immune to discipline.

"As you say," he comments. "You know, it's getting harder. The age of the biplane is just about done for. It's done in Europe. Your German friends were giving us cast offs they had no more use for. These newer planes, they are not easy to deal with if they catch you."

"How do you manage?"

Jose shrugs. "Don't get caught. I'm slower, but far more able. Fly low to the ground. As I said, the Peruvians, they have some good planes, but they don't use them so well. Those monoplanes, they don't land so good, so they need good airfields. They don't travel as much."

"Are you sure you'll be able to get home?" Alba asks.

Moreno laughs. "Assuming the forward bases are still there? A couple of stops, and I'll be in Guayaquil. Gallo will be on his way. We'll even send you back a couple of planes for reconnaissance. Maybe one of these fast new single-wing ones, the monoplanes."

"If God wills," Alba replies.

Moreno smiles. "I don't know about God," he teases, "but the men, they say that a certain Virgin has a bit of a crush on a certain young Colonel."

Alba blushes.

"That's enough, I think." He stands.

Moreno and Flores stand in turn. Moreno tries an awkward salute, which is returned. Alba extends his hand, and Moreno, after a moment's hesitation, shakes it. Flores copies the gesture.

"We'll see you in Guayaquil," Moreno says.

"Guayaquil," Alba and Flores echo.

Moreno turns about. Alba sits back tiredly on an empty crate, watching the airmen climb into their biplane.

"You couldn't get me into one of those things for God or money," Flores says.

Alba shrugs. Flores sits down next to him.

"The men keep calling you our new Napoleon," he says, "but I think you must feel like Hannibal. Fighting your way to the gates of Rome, but unable to enter."

"Hannibal? Hannibal traveled from Carthage, the length of Algeria, through Morocco and Spain; he crossed the Pyrenees with elephants and made his way through Italy. As for Napoleon?" Alba shakes his head. "These comparisons shame me. By those measures, all we've done is a walk down the coast."

He stares thoughtfully, as the plane engines revs and it taxis to its run.

"And it's been hard enough. I can't imagine how they did it. They must have been giants in their day."

"Don't be hard on yourself. This last battle at Callao, you vanquished a force what? Three times? four times our size?"

"Raw conscripts just off the rail from Cuzco. Half of them didn't know how to button their uniforms or which way to hold their rifle. How many of them did not even speak proper Spanish?"

Flores laughs out loud.

"Luis," he says, "when this is all over, let me write the story of the campaign. The way you have it, we'll not get a loaf of stale bread from a shopkeeper for the tale."

"As you wish, Benigno," Alba replies, smiling.

"You just make sure we have enough gasoline."

Alba nods.

They watch the plane take off.

"So it's over now," Flores says. "We go home. Too bad it didn't work."

Alba shakes his head.

"It's not over," he replies. "Now it's the hard part. Now we have to survive the journey."

Axis of Andes – Page 241

Ecuador - The March on Lima - Part IV

Battle of Lima - Four days of artillery shelling and sorties. Peruvians 4,000 killed or wounded, 3,500 of them civilians. Ecuador 1,000.

September 20, 1940. Unable to extract a surrender, and unwilling to commit to urban warfare against an increasingly entrenched enemy, lacking armour and with supplies dwindling, Alba orders a retreat.

From the south, General Odria is moving up the coast with battalions formerly held in reserve for the Chilean front. Meanwhile, the shattered Callao army remnants, which have retreated from Lima, are being rearmed and reorganized. In the interior, massive conscription is underway and troops are being readied to ship by railroad to the coast. In the north and centre, army units are struggling to reorganize and link up. As this is going on, the Peruvian navy haunts the coast, looking for opportunities to launch shells inland.

Alba's last actions are an attack on the railroad to the interior, and the looting of Callao for all available resources, notably gasoline, motor vehicles, ammunition, food and other perishables. Anything that has military potential that cannot be taken is destroyed. A number of buildings are detonated in order to block roadways.

On the road, Alba employs a scorched earth policy to slow pursuit, destroying towns and villages, looting wherever possible, and driving refugees into the country or up the road ahead to obstruct his enemies' possible movements. Resistance is minimal, and full military force is employed where it does occur.

Moving up the coast, speed is premium and unnecessary supplies and broken equipment are destroyed and jettisoned. The arrangement of vehicles is continually revised. Draft animals are pushed to their limits; many die or are jettisoned along the way.

Alba has now traveled roughly 850 miles since leaving Ecuador.

September 21 - A second Ecuadorian supply convoy, led by General Enrique Gallo, leaves Tombes, aiming to unite with Alba's forces at Cajamarca. The Convoy consists of roughly 12,000 to 15,000 men, with substantial armour and artillery. More than half of it consists of infantry.

September 26, Alba has reached the town of Barranca. Harassed by Peruvian offshore shelling, and wary of the possibility of a naval landing, he moves inland, avoiding contact with an army group assembling at Huanaco with Indigenous conscripts, led by General Ernesto Montagne Markholtz.

October 4 - the rape of Huaraz. Alba passes through the town of Huaraz, sweeping aside remnants of the Peruvian army. He holds the airstrip for a day, looting the town of supplies and burning it behind him.

Alba's expeditionary force has now travelled approximately 1,000 miles since leaving Ecuador.

Meanwhile the army group at Huanaco, and another at Lima led by General Boaz pursue, but are a week behind. The Generals, Markholtz and Boaz are eager for the credit of destroying the retreating Alba and refuse to cooperate with each other. Markholtz races ahead, instead of waiting for Boaz to catch up.

October 8 - General Ramirez undertakes a nationwide public radio address, accusing Alba of war crimes against the civilian population, namely the 'Shelling of Lima,' the 'Rape of Huarez' and conspiracy to foment war. He demands the immediate and complete surrender of the Ecuadorian government, the cessation of all hostilities and standing down of all foreign forces, both Ecuadorian and Chilean, within Peruvian territory. He also demands the Chilean withdrawal to previously agreed borders and payment of reparations. He demands the handing over of both President Neptali Bonifaz, Colonel Luis Alba, Congressional leader Velasco Ibarra and unidentified others for trial for war crimes against the Peruvian people. He promises the destruction of enemy forces within days if these demands are not complied with. This marks the beginning of Peru's 'total victory' position with regards to Ecuador, though the position with Chile remains more moderate.

October 10 - The second Ecuadorian convoy led by Gallo arrives at Cajamarca, taking over the town. It has seen very little fighting during the journey.

October 14 - Alba's forces arrive at Cajamarca, where they dig in, uniting with Gallo's relief column. He waits for battle.

Alba's combined forces now total 24,500, more than half of it exhausted, the remainder fresh and unblooded.

General Markholtz's command consists of roughly 20,000, including remnants from Huarez and Trujillo, reorganized and incorporated into the command, as well as fresh troops.

General Boaz's command consists of roughly 30,000, with the backbone mainly drawn from the professional Lima army garrisons, with the bulk being filled out by the remnants of the battle of Callao, re-armed and re-trained.

Alba's force has now travelled almost 1,200 miles since its departure from Ecuador.

Through the campaign, Alba's expedition has lost men and struggled to replace them with reinforcements. Alba's starting force was about 20,000 men. At the Battle of Chiclayo, he loses 600; the Battle of Trujillo, he loses 2,500; Battle of Huarez, he loses 6,000. His original force is reduced through attrition to approximately 10,900.

But at Huarez, the relief column caught up to him. That starting force was about 10,000 men. Roughly 2500 were deployed in the border provinces, holding down captured territory. So overall, he's down 9,100, but up 7,500, which leaves him with roughly 18,400 men to continue marching towards Lima.

Battle of Callao, he loses 3,000; Battle of Lima, he loses 1,000. Combined, that is roughly 4,000 more men. Which means that he arrives at Cajamarca with a maximum of 14,400 men.

That's 13,100 in losses overall. But actually, it's higher than that. Factor in about 10% overall for the whole campaign for attrition for diseases, accidents, desertions, and ongoing local resistance, that's about 2,000 to 3,000. Which means that when he arrives at Cajamarca, his effective force is as low as 11,400 to 12,400.

But actually it's a little better than that. Casualties include killed and injured. Some of the injuries are permanent or serious, taking the soldier entirely out of the war. Some are recoverable within a period of days or weeks, allowing the soldier to return to the field. A total of 13,100 casualties means8887 between 3200 and 3900 'wounded but still able to fight.' Which means that in a pinch, factoring in his walking wounded/recovering wounded, his viable fighting force may be between 14,600 to 16,300.

Of course, he's had to deploy forces to protect his supply lines. In point of fact, he's had to leave detachments behind to maintain airstrips and communication for his biplanes. Some of these he's hoovering back up as he returns. But some represent losses; some he hasn't gotten to yet, so basically, ballpark that as 1,000.

Which puts him somewhere between 13,600 to 15,300, when he settles in at Cajamarca. Let's ballpark it at roughly 14,000 to 14,500.

The second Ecuadoran relief column arrives at Cajamarca. It started out at 12,000 to 15,000, which should put Alba back up to 25,600 to a max of 30,300. Or ballparking, 26,000 to 29,500.

But the second relief column's been suffering its own attrition. Let's say, given shorter time period and shorter distances, less than 5 percent. More significantly, the second relief column's job is to cover the retreat. So they've been laying pickets and depots, and establishing road control along the way. So let's say between 10 and 20 percent get assigned the important job of covering the return road, defending it, making sure that supplies are in place and ready to give warning.

There may also have to be backups put in place on alternate roads, in case of disaster or enemy action. So the total chopdown is between 15 and 25 percent, which means anywhere between 3,000 to 3,750 at 25 percent loss of 12,000 to 15,000 (leaving 9,00 to 10,1250). Or 1,800 to 2,250 at 15% loss of 12,000 to 15000 (leaving 10,200 to 12,750). Let's give it a ballpark of 10,000 to 10,500 to ride to Alba's side.

Which means that as he goes into battle at Cajamarca, Alba has roughly 24,000 to 25,000 soldiers under his command.

Alba on the retreat has been pursuing a scorched earth strategy; there's no longer a need to avoid inciting civilians. He's not doing total burnt earth in the sense of sowing the ground with salt. But he's basically out of money to buy goods. He's not expecting to see these towns again. He's got an enemy on his tail. And he's on the down side of his supplies.

Although he's expressed a little bit of snobbery about a lot of the troops defeated in the last battle not speaking Spanish, it is meaningful. The enemy have a lot more problems co-ordinating operations and passing down orders than they should.

The army has traditionally depended on the Indigenous and Mestizo for its basic infantry conscripts. There's been quite a cat and mouse game going on over the decades, with hill country people avoiding conscription, and conscription officers chasing them down. Over the years, a lot of second or third sons, wife beaters, petty criminals and unpopular types end up getting caught and conscripted, people the community has decided it can do without.

Now with the war on, there's a huge conscription effort going on throughout the country. The middle class is doing its best to avoid enlistment. Employers in vital enterprises (and all employers think their enterprise is vital) are protecting their workers. The unemployed or semi-employed urban and coastal under classes are feeling Pedro Conscript's heavy hand. It's also coming down very hard in the Sierra, where the poorest landless class peon class, or the displaced landless, are being scooped up like never before.

The conscripts are being funneled to the centre of the Sierra, from north and south, where they're given rifles, uniforms but little in the way of training, as they get shipped down to Lima. The plan is to properly train, equip and organize them in or around Lima.

But Alba shows up way too early. They aren't expecting him to move so fast, or to cut through so many defenders. So in a panic, they basically throw this giant army of poorly trained conscripts at him as cannon fodder, holding their better troops in a reserve. It's not bad as spur of the moment plans go, but it turns out as disastrously as you'd expect.

It does, however, illustrate that there's a huge gap between the Peruvian infantry and grunts and the NCO, Officer and technical classes. Basically, the high command is pretty reckless about wasting the lives of common soldiers.

One important development is that while Peru's suffered some pretty heavy casualties, it's not all grunts sucking up bullets. There's been some stiff attrition among NCO and field officer classes. And while you can always raid the villages to get more grunts, where do you get your replacement officers and sargents?

Chile - War in the South - the Trench War Forms

October 9 - A new Chilean offensive overruns Tacna, reaches Moqueguera, and attempts to establish a front along the road to Lake Titicaca. Once again, the Chileans are overextending themselves, as the Peruvians prepare a new assault. Approximately 30,000 Chileans face 24,000 Peruvians.

October 12 - Chile attempts to pre-empt a potential Peruvian counterattack, with raids on Arequippa province. This is the furthest reach of Chile during this phase of war. They are badly overextended.

October 18 - Peruvians counterattack. Chilean offensive collapses. Chilean forces are split into three groups. One surrenders. The others retreat, pulling back to Tacna with casualties. Peruvian numbers rapidly building up to 35,000.

October 21 - Peruvians push to Arica. Chileans desperately reinforce rushing men and munitions to the front.

October 30 - Border stabilizes at Tacna. Roughly 40,000 on each side; trench war begins to develop.

Through the month of October, Peru's Central Army Group absorbs and deploys the majority of fresh conscripts and material deployments, diverting them from the south. This despite the fact that Alba is in retreat back to Ecuador and barely willing to give battle. It is only after the northern front stabilizes in November that the worsening situation in the south begins to reoccupy the High Command in Lima.

Their respective advantages squandered, Chile and Peru can only pour increasing numbers of men and weapons into an increasingly congested battle zone until; finally, by December a stabilizing frontier begins to emerge, of trenches and expanding earthworks. The war in the south drifts towards stalemate.

By November 10, 1940, there are roughly 50,000 men on each side. 100,000 men facing each other over along a 106 mile frontier. This means that each mile of the front has 500 men on each side. For literally each five feet of front, two soldiers face each other in war, continuously for over a hundred miles.

And more are added each day, together with a steadily expanding supply train carrying food, water, sandbags, barbed wire, bricks, mortar, shovels, munitions, weapons, artillery and shells and weapons of war.

As each side builds up, the networks of trenches extends and deepens. Behind the trenches, increasingly elaborate fortifications spring up, roads are reinforced and expanded, airstrips carved, telephone and telegraph lines are run, generators are installed, gasoline and supply depots built.

Freedom of movement dies away; the mobile war has passed. The sheer increasing volume of troops concentrating along a relatively short stretch of border precludes that. Instead, the southern front becomes static: An increasingly brutal no man's land of sudden futile charges, bursts of gunfire, artillery barrages and air raids.

The resemblance to the western front of World War I is not lost to either side. It gives the war in the south an erratic quality as both sides, alternate long periods of quiet with minimal combat across the front; and increasingly futile and antagonistic peace talks, punctuated by periods of extreme violence as one side or the other seeks to break the stalemate.

***

Ecuador - The First Battle of Cajamarca, October 20, 1940

Night is falling; the temperature is dropping rapidly. The air is still humid, the damp rains of winter are passing slowly as September passes and October wears on. But the skies remain cloudy and overcast.

From the top of a sloping hill, well back from the enemy's artillery barrages, Alba and his commanders watch the battlefield. A roil of smoke, shouts, flickering fires and shifting clusters of men; only practice enables him to understand the underlying order, the cut and thrust behind the madness.

Beside him, Flores coughs as the wind blows a mist of cordite stink towards them. The smell is thick in his nostrils; he can feel it against his skin, like tiny pinpricks. Bad as it is, the other stenches of battle, the offal smell of excrement and blood that come from exploded and torn bodies, hovers just under it. Unmistakable.

There is a booming chatter, and a flare of intense light further back from the battle, staining the sky: Markholtz's artillery.

"What's he doing now?" Alba asks, rhetorically.

Flores swears.

"Maybe he's planning another sortie," one of the staff officers suggests.

"No," Alba says, "he's committed all his reserves. He's got to be trying something else."

"I don't think he's got enough flexibility left to make it work, whatever it is," Flores says.

Markholtz has set his artillery too far back, Alba decides. Too tightly clustered, which makes it easier to organize and direct, of course. But too vulnerable to attack. To compensate for that vulnerability Markholtz has them set up further back. But then that blunts their effectiveness. Alba guesses that a goodly fraction of Markholtz's shells are falling on his own men.

Alba has divided his artillery, setting it down in four groups. Two he's let loose shortly after the battle has begun, once Markholtz's infantry enters their overlapping kill zones. Bodies have disappeared into red mist. Screams of terror and pain ring out over the battlefield.

Markholtz has sent his tanks in, his one major advantage over Alba. The tanks proceed towards his artillery posts. Once in range, Alba's third and fourth batteries open up with barrages, catching the armour and wrecking much of it. The surviving tanks pull back. Alba's disappointed that they didn't get them all.

Alba expects Markholtz to retreat as the initial artillery exchanges finish. He sets his troops going forward. But Markholtz surprises him by committing his own infantry in an advance. Alba rapidly backpedals, pulling his forces back to prepared lines. It is either reckless or brilliant on the part of Markholtz. Alba's not sure, and he feels the gut-clenching terror and uncertainty that is his constant companion on the battlefield.

But then, Markholtz answers that question, failing to establish his own line; simply pouring men at Alba's positions. Alba's response is a withering hail of fire all along his line, churning Markholtz's men into red stew. Astonishingly, Markholtz continues to push his soldiers forward, despite appalling casualties.

Thousands of Peruvians have died, their bodies everywhere, the stench of wrecked corpses thick, blood flowing into pools of red mud. Thousands more are injured, crawling for safety, screaming in pain and agony. The worst ones are those for whom no aid is possible, trapped out, blown to pieces, their cries shrill in horror at their ruined bodies.

His men have casualties. Many. Thousands. But nowhere near the numbers of the Peruvians. They've fought well, and they hold the ground, they hold to cover.

Axis of Andes – Page 251

The battle has been going on since noon. Alba judges he still has the field. His men occupy a low ridge paralleling the road, and a long line built up. It's a neat crossfire, and Markholtz has been marching his men into a bloodbath all day.

Markholtz isn't completely stupid, he's been trying to flank the ridge, but it's hard ground; and his flanking forces have had fire rained down on them If it had been him, Alba thinks, he'd have saved his armour and committed it to flanking, rather than this disastrous direct assault. There's an appeal to it, of course; had Markholtz's tanks actually made it to the lines, they'd have driven straight through and his infantry would have followed, splitting Alba's forces. As it was, Markholtz's increasingly desperate attempts to flank are lowly splitting his command.

"Look," Flores says. A line of fire comes down deep in the enemy center. "That's the forward battery."

Alba and the other staff officers train their binoculars on the area, trying to make out detail. Alba's gaze sweeps. The forward battery is too exposed. It's come under attack twice, and the field commanders have to fight the enemy back.

"They're under attack again," Alba says. "Send a message to Diego, tell him to move his men and take up position on the forward battery. They need reinforcements."

"I think we caught Markholtz," Flores says, "forward Battery walked a line right through his command post."

The officers are cheering. Under a tent on a makeshift table, orderlies struggle to draft orders.

Forward battery is too deep, Alba thinks. It is a calculated risk, vulnerable, but capable of doing far more damage. Alba had thought that Forward battery might be deployed against Markholtz's batteries. That is a mistake. Markholtz's batteries are concentrated and further back, out of range. Markholtz's bigger guns can reach forward, but not vice versa. Only Markholtz's relatively poorer accuracy has saved them.

Alba's artillery has been parked for more than a day at their sites; they've had time to work their ranges out.

Axis of Andes – Page 252

Yes, Alba thinks. They're right. Markholtz's command post has been hit. There's a flurry of activity as the Peruvians struggle to adjust, to put together a new command. Has Markholtz been killed? How bad is it? No way to tell until later.

He signs an order, scrawls in a further note about withdrawing the men from forward battery if and when they run out of shells. Without shells, the guns are only useless steel on the battlefield. Recover them later, if there is a later. The men can be redeployed to the other batteries. Soon, copies of the order are on their way on horse couriers.

The remnants of his horse cavalry have found use as battlefield messengers. Runners go behind them with backup orders. A man on horseback is the fastest thing on the battlefield. But a man on horseback is also a target. Alba is surprised at how many of them have managed to stay away from a bullet, skirting the edges of fighting, staying as far away from the enemy as they can, finding nonexistent cover. They deserve medals, Alba thinks.

A horse messenger runs up.

"Sir," he cries, "Rondel reports tanks coming up the ridge, just past the tree line."

Then there's a new round of thunder, for a second, Alba's and Markholtz's batteries are all firing simultaneously; the sky grows harsh and flickering shadows jump this way and that. The sound is overpowering. A wind blows a thick tide of blood and excrement and spilled intestines, and for a second they all want to gag.

"We need to move," Flores calls out. "His lines are getting too close."

The sound of gunshots comes in waves, peppering the countryside. Very close. Alba nods. His line is dissolving, Markholtz's men are climbing for the Ecuadoran's positions, what's left of them. The fighting is becoming disorganized, at least on this part of the front. They do need to move; pull in behind a firmer line. But not yet.

"How many tanks?" Alba demands.

"Rondel says four," the horseman shouts.

Only four? Alba reckons Markholtz has eight. Where are the rest? Is he holding them in reserve? Using them elsewhere? Will they follow in against Rondel?

"What else?" He demands.

"Two battalions infantry, following them," the horse rider says. "Rondel wants orders. Hold or retreat?"

Insane to think that Rondel's men have a chance against tanks. There's nothing they're holding that will even scratch the armour. Markholtz has set his flanking manoeuver very high. If he has the manpower, Alba's whole line will collapse. If he doesn't have the manpower, he's wasting his tanks.

Alba's spyglasses search the battlefield as he tries once again to second-guess Markholtz, to calculate numbers from writhing shapes, estimates of casualties, guesses as to who is where. No surprise, the grounds are clearer in the artillery fall zones. Soldiers seem to have an instinct to be somewhere where the shells are least likely to fall. The ground is a patchwork.

Alba pulls the cavalry man back, grabbing the rein as the rider bends forward to hear. Even so, Alba almost has to shout. "Tell Rondel to hold as long as he can, then fall east. I'll keep the ground clear and send him what backup I can. Tell him to keep moving east until he reaches Ramos's position."

Ramos occupies the centre of the battlefield, the line of assault has flowed around him. Ramos needs support. Alba was going to send Pascale from behind. But his inspiration is to leave Pascale in place.

There's a gully past the tree line. The tanks can't go much further. So they'll either hold position, or follow Rondel down. If they follow, they'll cross one of his batterys' fire zones. If they hold....

"You're splitting our line there," Flores says.

Alba shakes his head.

"He wants me to pull the whole line," he shouts. "He's bluffing. He hasn't followed it with the men he needs to take them."

I hope, Alba thinks.

If he's wrong, a lot of good men will die. But if he's right, and he pulls the whole line, many more might die. The sun is very low on the horizon, the skies are darkening. Come night, Alba thinks. Come quickly. With nightfall, real movement becomes impossible. Alba's forces are in position, Markholtz's are not. Night catches them, it's all over.

Markholtz's effort to flank is terrible. Not unless he's got far more infantry to shore up with than he's shown. He's set his tanks out too far, too deep, where they're wasted and at risk.

The cavalry man rushes off, the mad, mad fool, heedless of bullets. His lieutenants are struggling to scrawl copies of the orders, another horse rider, runners. Each set of orders slightly different, scrawled by a different man in the confusion of the moment. Maybe some will make it, maybe one, maybe none. Maybe Rondel will throw them away, their moment having passed, and seek his advantage as desperation dictates. The battlefield is madness, have even half his orders been received and acted upon? No matter, enough of them have that the fields of blood has shaped themselves to his hand.

Flores makes a gesture. Hand out, palm flat. Alba stares in confusion, against the background peppercorn retort of gunfire. He doesn't understand. His lips work, forming a question.

And then it hits him. He puts his own hand out, expectant. Feels the droplets.

It's starting to rain....

***

Axis of Andes – Page 255

March on Lima, Cajamarca

October 20 - Huanaco Army Group under the command of Markholtz arrives at Cajamarca four days before the Lima force. The General decides to immediately give battle, assuming that Alba's forces are exhausted, but without fully reckoning on his reinforcements from the second convoy. The Peruvians' attack is premature, without securing either their flanks or their command structure.

During the battle, Peruvian command breaks down altogether. Markholtz's command structure is destroyed, but Markholtz miraculously survives. Markholtz's effort to flank with armour fails. In the confusion, Alba holds his forces in place and commits his reserves. The Huanaco forces are decimated and flee.

Alba pursues, hoping to destroy Huanaco as a force before the Lima army arrives. Alba doesn't feel like he has much of a choice. He can withdraw and make for Ecuador, with a fresh army on his heels, and the risk of being caught on the run. That would be a disaster. And it is a pretty likely disaster. Or he can follow up on the victory and take the fight to Boaz, essentially keeping the initiative. He knows the ground that Boaz will have to fight on, having passed through it.

1st Battle of Cajamarca – Peru's Huanaco army under Gernal Markholtz totals 20,000. Casualties of 7,000. Ecuador loses 2,000.

October 24 - the retreating Huanaco army meets up with the Lima army. Approximately 2,000, have deserted. Markholtz's force is down to 11,000 exhausted men by the time they join with Boaz. But together, Markholtz and Boaz's combined forces are roughly twice Alba's.

Boaz halts, going into a defensive posture. Alba has shown a knack for chewing up Peruvian armies; including Markholtz bare days ago, and Boaz has no intention of being reckless. This is a mistake, which neutralizes his advantage of numbers, and leaves the initiative with Alba.

Alba attacks aggressively, and attempts to flank, but sheer numbers foil the Ecuadorans. Alba moves his artillery far forward, accepting risk to compensate for the greater range of Boaz's big guns and raining down fire on Boaz's and Markholtz's infantry. Boaz is killed by a sniper's bullet. Markholtz takes command.

After two days of inconclusive battle, both sides disengage. Alba burns Cajamarca behind him as he withdraws. The combined Lima/Huanaco army pursue slowly.

2nd Battle of Cajamarca - Combined Huanaco and Lima forces total 41,000. Ecuador's totals 22,000. Casualties on the Peruvian and Ecuadorian side are roughly 5,000 each killed or injured.

Despite Alba's apparent victory, the advantage is to the Peruvians. Boaz's forces are still relatively fresh, while Alba's troops are tired. The ground isn't optimum for the Ecuadorans. The casualties are just about even on both sides, which is ugly, since Boaz has twice as many men. Alba will not survive a war of attrition.

On the other hand, Alba has succeeded in his objective of crippling the movement capacity of Boaz's forces. One of the reasons his casualties are proportionately high is that he was specifically targeting transport, mobile armour and, to the extent he could hit it, logistics. It isn't just cowardice that keeps Markholtz parking on the way to Chiclayo; he really has lost a lot of movement capacity.

October 27 - Alba retreats from the ruins of Cajamarca. General Markholtz slowly re-occupies the town.

***

Correspondence

"And now, having tasted the lash, the Ecuadorian dog runs back to his hole to lick his balls. The Coward Alba has turned his tail, as I knew he would. All out of tricks, and treachery, his true nature reveals. I say to you, Colonel Alba, stand and be as a man. Or flee back to your country and grovel like the worm you are."

Excerpt from an open letter published by General Ernesto Montagne Markholtz, broadcast on radio, October 27, 1940.

"My Dear Friend, I am glad to see you speak with such passion and bravery. From our encounters, I had thought your taste for battle entirely absent, and am pleased to see that it has returned. Meet me in Chiclayo, between the 30th and the 1st we shall settle our issues. Yours Truly, Colonel Luis Larrea Alba"

October 28, 1941

March on Lima, Home

October 28 - Colonel Alba's forces march rapidly across the Peruvian countryside, passing through Chiclayo only briefly.

October 29 - General Markholtz's pursuing force halts at the town of San Pedro, ostensibly for purposes of resupply.

November 2 - Alba reaches the captured Peruvian town of Jaen near the border, receiving further reinforcements.

Colonel Alba's forces have travelled almost 1,400 miles

November 3 - General Markholtz's combined army reaches the town of Chiclayo, remarkably untouched. On arriving at the town, Markholtz learns that Alba has left a sealed letter for him. The content of the letter is unknown; it is rumoured that it consists of a single word. Markholtz burns the town of Chiclayo.

November 6 - Alba arrives at the Ecuadorian town of Lojas, in the province of same name, to a hero's welcome.

The March on Lima is over. In three months, Alba has traveled almost 1500 miles; and has fought six major battles, winning crushing victories in four, with two ending inconclusively; and leaving a trail of death and destruction behind him. Only the battle of Lima can be counted a defeat. He has consolidated a reputation as a latter-day Napoleon, the most heroic figure in Latin America since Simon Bolivar.

Despite this, Alba has utterly failed in the Ecuadorian's key objectives. The first was to force a surrender or peace on favourable terms from the Peruvian government. If anything, this has backfired spectacularly.

The Peruvian army, already reeling from the fiasco of its failed invasion, has been completely humiliated by Alba's March. The generals are out for revenge. General Ramirez, in a Public Radio Address on September 15, calls for the complete and utter destruction of Ecuador, the razing of Quito, and the trial of

Bonifaz, Ibarra and Alba for conspiring to wage war and commit crimes against humanity. In this, Ramirez is at one with the senior generals of Peru. Markholtz in particular has sworn an oath, and takes command of the northern command. General Ureta retires in disgrace. The limited objectives of resolving disputed territorial claims have been abandoned.

The second goal of the March on Lima was to destroy or so badly cripple the Peruvian military so as to force Peru to the negotiating table, or to at least allow Ecuador a viable chance to defend itself. While it is true that Peru has experienced appalling losses, both in its infantry and in its non-commissioned and field-officer classes, these have been overwhelmed by unprecedented massive conscription. The Peruvian army is larger now than at the start of the war, though its ethnic composition has changed considerably.

The total Ecuadoran expeditionary force for the march, including Alba's initial command and the reinforcements was 42,000 men, the larger part of Ecuador's military strength, particularly artillery, armour and support vehicles. Of this force, approximately 18,000 have been killed or wounded as casualties, with disproportionate losses in artillery, armour, ammunition and supplies, and support vehicles. The Ecuadoran military has been bled white on a bold and reckless gamble to throw Peru out of the war.

That gamble has failed, and now the Bonifaz triumvirate is desperately struggling in a race against time to finance the rebuilding and rearming of its military, and the recruitment of tens of thousands of new troops before Peru's inevitable next attack.

*****

New Perspectives on the Andean War, 1989, Cambridge Press

.... perceptions shift with time. Certainly, this is true of many of the seminal events of the Andean War. Who were the heroes? The villains? What were the blunders? And which acts were heroic? What were the true pivots upon which events turned?

A classic episode subject to continuing reinterpretation has been Colonel Luis Larrea Alba's infamous 'March on Lima.' After 45 years of scholarship, there are almost as many versions of the March as perhaps there were soldiers. We cannot pretend to cover the full range of opinions, but we can offer a survey of some of the most influential views, with a few comments.

As to the basic facts of the March, there is little doubt. Early in July, 1940, following the failure of the Peruvian invasion, Colonel Alba led a force of approximately 20,000, in an invasion of Peru. Alba's force was enhanced by relief convoys of roughly 10,000 and 12,000. Between July and November, Alba's forces fought six major battles, arguably winning four conclusively, with qualified victory for one more, and a stalemate over the last, before returning to Ecuador, having failed to take it's ultimate objective.

Those are the facts. Let the debate begin.

Triumphalism - The initial reports and the position of the Ecuadorians themselves was one of abashed triumphalism. Luis Larrea Alba and his cohorts were photogenic personalities, it seems, and there was a clear element of David and Goliath in the conflict. Alba's often crushing victories and the steady progress of the March lent an allure of glory to the proceedings. The March was followed avidly by newspapers throughout Latin America and even covered in the United States.

The Grand Failure - Ironically, this assessment was popularized by Alba himself in his writing following the war. As Alba describes it, he set out with two objectives: to win peace, and/or to destroy

Peru's war capacity, and he failed to accomplish either. The most critical military objective, the Battle for Lima, was doomed from the outset, as Alba never had the weaponry or resources to conquer the city.

The Disastrous Quest - popularized in 1954 by Professor Steve Hofstetter, following on Alba's own writing. Hofstetter's argument is that the March was not simply a failure, but a disaster in its own right. During the course of the March, Ecuador's forces suffered casualties as high as 14,000 men killed or injured, almost half of Alba's combined force, and a significant portion of Ecuador's total mobilization. In addition, Alba's March sacrificed almost all of the draft animals and cavalry; resulted in the loss of a significant fraction of the motor vehicles and artillery available; and expended vast quantities of fuel and ammunition; none of which Ecuador could truly afford. Hofstetter points to the fuel dislocations which occurred later in the war and Alba's own complaints that there were no draft animals to take up the slack because so many had been lost on the March.

A Trivial Excursion - promoted hard by the Peruvian government, and adopted in the 1960s in avante-garde historical reviews, places the March as an extravagant sideshow, a distraction without real consequence to the course of the war. Thankfully, this view is all but abandoned by serious historians. It was not persuasive when the Peruvian government promoted it, it certainly did not improve with age. From the Peruvians' point of view, the March was an unending string of disasters for them; basic manpower losses sustained by the Peruvian army were hideous. Casualty rates among field and non-commissioned officers decimated the Peruvian military structure. Senior generals were killed or disgraced. The Peruvian government itself fell in direct consequence to the March, and almost the entirety of the early Chilean campaigns, including the decision to proceed with the war were directly influenced by the March.

In this paper, we offer yet another interpretation: That of a qualified success. In our view, too little attention is paid to the failure of the objective of forcing the Peruvian government to peace, and far too little attention is given to just how close it came to succeeding.

Careful examination of the historical record demonstrates that there were at least three occasions where the March came within a hair's breadth of achieving a resolution. There was, of course, the Chilean intervention, and a period when the generals seriously debated making peace in the north in order to defend against the enemy in the south.

Declassified cables suggest that on more than one occasion, the United States almost intervened to force a peace.

And of course, there is the famous Prado/Benevides concord, displaced by a coup.

It's certainly impossible to characterize the March as a doomed or disastrous effort given how very close it came to achieving its primary goal.

As to the secondary goal, a reappraisal leads us to a provocative conclusion. Alba's March arguably succeeded in its secondary objective. Very clearly, Alba devastated Peru's army, particularly in the north.

When Alba crossed the border, Peru's General Ureta was in process of gathering forces for a second invasion. By the time he returned to Ecuador, Alba's forces had killed or wounded a number equivalent to the entire Peruvian army, pre-war. The officer cadres of the northern command were utterly devastated. The loss of material, of tanks and artillery, of ammunition of war materials left the Northern Command paralyzed and ineffective for years. While Peru's generals vowed revenge, the punishing experience had left them extremely cautious, even timid.

Although Peru did launch its second invasion attempt in 1941, it is clear that this effort came several months after it was planned. Caution dictated a significantly larger force, but one deployed with considerable timidity. Structural and leadership problems persisted in the army of the north, literally until the end of the war. It was out of the question that the Peruvian military could be permanently put out of commission. But any fair reading of the record leads inexorably to the conclusion that Alba's March crippled the army in the north for years.

Although the infamous criticism still holds, that Ecuador and Chile, despite fighting a common enemy at the same time; were consistently unable to coordinate, the effect of Alba's March should not be overlooked. It is fashionable to see the trench warfare which congealed in the south as inevitable. But during Alba's March, that southern theatre was fluid, and at critical times, what could have been critical strategic victories by Peru were undercut by troops diverted north. Without Alba's March, and particularly during his retreat, things could have gone much worse for Chile.

Finally, it's generally acknowledged that one of the reasons for Chile's commitment to the war Ecuador's string of successes. Wit hout Chile in the war, there would be nothing to stop Peru from bringing overwhelming forces to crush Ecuador. But instead, the Peruvians were forced to concentrate energies in the south, leaving them little left over to attack north, delaying and undermining northern campaigns.

BOOK OF WAR

The River War

While Alba engages on his futile March on Lima in the north; while Ibanez blunders into a trench war in the south; while navies engaged in one-sided battles in the Pacific; a fourth theatre of war continues almost unknown under the guidance of General Enrique Blandon.

Both Peru and Ecuador are nations of the coast, with large parts of their populations, and much of their economies, situated along thin coastal strips. Beyond the coasts are the towering Andes ranges, home to the balance of the populations of these nations, mostly Quechua and Aymara Indigenous, living as they had for centuries.

Beyond that, there is the interior - a vast rain forest, called the Oriente in Ecuador, the Selva in Peru; network of jungles and rivers, impassable except by water, flowing from the foothills of the mountains themselves and merging seamlessly into Brazil's vast hinterlands.

The ice caps of the Andes Mountains produce run-off, which finds its way into a series of rivers and streams: the Napa, the Putumayo, the Pastaza, the Maranon, the Caquetá, the Ucayali, the Purus, the Jurua, the Javari, the Japura, the Guaviare all eventually leading further and further inland, to one by one merge with the Amazon. These rivers are erratic, shifting in their banks, dividing into streams and tributaries, most of which are unmapped and unmarked, merging with or crossing each other. The region is inaccessible, occupied mainly by indigenous populations of hunter-gatherers, with only occasional missionaries and explorers passing through.

Off of these main rivers are endless and innumerable streams, some charted, some not, some navigable, some partially navigable, and some not. Maps are unreliable, explorers might travel several hundred miles with no clear idea of which river they are on, or even which country they are in.

Travel in the area is treacherous; the rivers and tributaries swell or dwindle with the seasons, with the result that during low water periods, large sections might be impassible, tributaries and streams inaccessible. Hazards are everywhere, and risks range from diseases such as malaria and yellow fever, to hostile natives, and simple difficulty finding one's way. Even reaching established places within the territory can take weeks.

The towns or river stations include Iquitos, Leticia, Rio Branco, Cobijo, Cruziera do Sul, Yurimaguas and Pucallpa.

This, the larger part of Ecuador's Oriente is what two nations have gone to war over.

Here, initially, Peru holds the advantage, with a fleet of six river boats, armed with heavy-caliber machine guns, small artillery pieces and powerful engines. As part of his planning, General Ureta manages to procure three of the river boats for his invasion in June of 1940. This is supported by requisitioned river barges which serve as troop carriers and supply ships.

Against these the Ecuadorans establish an 'Army of the Interior' under the nominal command of General Enrique Blandon. The interior town of Andua is designated as the Center of Command for a vast region, encompassing over fifty percent of Ecuador's land area. This command amounts to a notional strength of 5,000 men, with another 5,000 reserves; but in practical terms, somewhat less. It features a fleet of small craft, mainly shallow-bottomed motor boats and steamboats with fixed machine guns bolted on; and cargo space assigned for fuel and ammunition. Secondary vessels include barges used for provisioning and supply depots, and large canoes which can field even shallow streams or be dragged through portages. This is supported by a network of heavily fortified supply depots. Native populations and their canoes are pressed into service as couriers and scouts.

Initially, the Peruvian invasion goes well. However, the offensive along the Maranon and Napo rivers in the east and north meets spirited resistance from well-established jungle battalions dug in. Seaplanes taking off from and landing on rivers give the aerial advantage to the Ecuadorians, both in terms of reconnaissance and strafing or bombing attacks.

One of the Peruvian riverboats becomes mired, and is unable to move; it attempts to hold a defensive position while the supporting flotilla withdraws, but is overwhelmed. The attack from the north fails, and General Silva is killed during the fighting. A second riverboat is captured during a night attack, and the remainder of its flotilla is sunk or captured.

Further south, Peruvian forces penetrate deep into the interior between the outposts of Jaen and Nauta, overrunning Concordia and advancing in the Interior. However, the invasion outruns its supply lines and in the face of reinforcements is forced to retreat. By June 15, the Chinchipe Army detachment has dissolved into four separate uncoordinated units, three of which are in retreat. By June 16, the Ecuadorians retake Concordia and vanquish one of the segments.

By June 18, the Ecuadorians have crossed the river at Jaen and taken the town of Bagua. Progress is slow, and the war in the Amazonian hinterland is on its own calendar. On July 14, the two forces meet at the Peruvian town of Yurimaguas, on the Rio Huallaga, where the Ecuadorians win decisively.

There Blandon remains for two weeks, concentrating and redeploying his forces, before launching an unauthorized new series of offensives into the largely undefended northern areas of the Peruvian rain forest.

June through December is the dry season for the Amazon, and the river systems are at their lowest ebb. The cusp of June is selected by Ureta as the latest feasible time for an invasion of the Orientale, or the Selva, as Peruvians call it. This is a mistake. Water levels drop through the month; and by the beginning of July, the heavier

Peruvian craft find movement increasingly difficult, and are confined to the largest rivers. In contrast, Ecuador's lighter, flat-bottomed, boats move easily up and down tributaries enjoying superior mobility.

Through late June and early July, the remnants of the invading Peruvian forces, their supply ships, depots, bases, towns and missions, are steadily outflanked, outmanoeuvred and overcome. The scattered remnants of Peruvian forces either withdraw or are taken.

The vast majority of the population in the region are Indigenous, who have little idea of what the war is about. At first Blandon, traditionally racist, is wary and suspicious of the Indigenous communities, but sees little importance in them. As he proceeds into what were, for him, uncharted territories he begins to see the usefulness of retaining native guides, and cultivating local support. He begins to bestow gifts on native villages. His arrivals are often matters of pomp and portent, where he offers incomprehensible and poorly translated, but enthusiastically bombastic speeches.

Blandon renames the captured Peruvian riverboat Matilde; it sails down Rio Ucayali, where it sees combat several times against its former owners. The Matilde, continually re-armed and refurbished, becomes one of the most heavily armed platforms in the Selva. It also becomes Blandon's personal command center, and the flagship of a fleet of light craft, supply boats, native auxiliaries and air support which steadily pushes into Peruvian territory, parallel to Alba's March on Lima.

Due to communication obstacles, Peru finds it difficult to adequately respond to the incursion. The Ecuadoran jungle campaign steadily chews its way through the river systems, moving south. During this time, the principle resistance is low-level sniping with bows and arrows by native populations. As a result, the Ecuadoran expedition takes to arming its native auxiliaries with firearms.

By late July, the Benevides government opts to assign its remaining river fleet and a small army detachment to the town of Pucallpa, as staging for a counter-attack.

Pucallpa is originally founded in the 1840s, on the Rio Ucayali one of the largest rivers in the region. Between the 1880s and 1920s, there have been several attempts to build a railroad into the area. But even by 1900, the population of the town is only about 200 people. Starting around 1930, Peru undertakes a project to build a highway from the coast into the town. Still only partially completed in 1940, there is at least a partial road access, and the town's population expands to several hundred.

Battle of Pucallpa

September 2, 1940 - Pucallpa is the staging area for Peru's three remaining riverboats, a flotilla of secondary support craft, and over two thousand Peruvian soldiers, with another thousand irregulars, and another thousand temporary workers.

The Matilde and her fleet are known to be approaching, but there is little clear idea of where exactly the force was. By this time, the Ecuadorans are well known for aerial reconnaissance but no planes have been spotted since August 14. Exploratory trips up the river by small craft have been fired upon by native auxiliaries. The local military consensus, however, is that the Ecuadoran force is unlikely to mount an attack, given the overwhelming defences and firepower stationed at Pucallpa.

The consensus is wrong.

On the evening of September 2, at approximately 4:00 am, the Matilde comes steaming down the Ucayali towards the harbour and opens fire. The first Peruvian riverboat is caught at dock and mercilessly pounded, catching fire and sinking. Of the other two, one is at dock, but is able to ship off under fire, where it attempts to engage. Meanwhile, the third boat, which had not been docked, but a little further down the river at a refueling station, returns to action. The three armoured riverboats exchange fire until the second begins to sink under the Matilde's bombardment. The third boat remains, taking fire but providing cover for the crew of the second to abandon ship. Following this, the third boat comes under secondary fire from the Matilde's support craft, at which point it is forced to withdraw further down the river, to avoid pursuit.

Meanwhile, the town of Pucallpa is under attack from a concerted landing of the Matilde's support fleet. Approximately 1,100 Ecuadoran soldiers and some 400 native auxiliaries are brought to bear against the town's military contingent. Taken by surprise, they are unable to mount a concerted defense. This difficulty is compounded by the burning of the main docks and widespread arson and looting. With the withdrawal of the third river boat, the Matilde turns its heavy guns on the town, and morale breaks.

The remaining defenders are routed, fleeing for the partially constructed and semi-passable road inland. Others surrender en masse. During the confusion, there are several small massacres of prisoners conducted by either native auxiliaries or Ecuadoran irregulars. By morning, the town is in Ecuadoran hands.

The following day, the survivors of the attack regroup on the road. A portion of these assemble for reconnaissance and counterattack on the town, but are easily driven off. Eventually, prisoners of war are put to work scavenging the town's valuables and war materials. They are released and sent down the road a few days later.

Because of the existence of the partially completed road, it is judged that the town cannot be held. The Ecuadorans remain a further five days and then depart, stripping the town of all weapons, ammunition, fuel and other supplies, and burning whatever cannot be taken. The Peruvian retaliation expedition arrives and finds only ruins.

The remaining Peruvian river boat, badly damaged, limps to the town of Atalaya where it puts in for repairs.

Virtually the length of the Ucayali river basin is effectively abandoned to Ecuadoran control, although the Matilde's forces do not range significantly south of Pucallpa. Effectively, the Rain Forest campaign has not only successfully defended the Oriente, but manages to conquer as much as half of Peru's Selva.

Axis of Andes – Page 272

Empire in the Interior

The success of the Oriente campaign exceeded all intentions and expectations in Quito. There was no plan to invade the Peruvian jungle regions. The strategy was simply been to repel invaders, defend territory and, at best, to take and hold strategic positions.

That it went beyond this, is perhaps a result of the difficulties in communicating and travelling through the region. Radio communication proves extremely unreliable; messages are principally transmitted by couriers travelling up and down the river from one supply station to another. It will take days for messages to reach a command post capable of giving orders, weeks for each to reach Quito.

The difficulty in getting messages in and out means that Blandon, rather than remaining in Yurimaguas, eventually opts to relocate his command to the cutting edge of the interior campaign. A skeleton staff of field officers, all of them junior to Blandon, are left at Yurimaguas, their duties being simply to maintain supply lines, comply with Blandon's demands, and relay messages and reports to Quito.

The encroaching dry season, however, makes travel tricky. Many of the minor tributaries and streams become steadily impassible. This means moving up or down the river is confined to major tributaries and rivers, which complicates navigation. Inevitably, possibly inadvertently, the conflict extends into Peruvian territory.

Initially fearing counterattack, Blandon pushes deeper and deeper, rolling up outposts, and engaging, sometimes peacefully, sometimes violently, with native populations. Due to the nature of the rain forest and its rivers, contact with the enemy is erratic. One might go a week or more without any sign of enemy activity; even then, that sign might be no more than a rumour. Blandon becomes convinced that there is a major Peruvian force in the region and reports this back to Quito. On his own initiative, he pushes deeper, searching.

Over time, his perspective shifts and his self-appointed mission evolves. As Alba's March on Lima proceeds Blandon's objectives move towards a parallel 'March through the Selva,' motivated by jealousy and competition. Military ambition merges with personal ambition. Blandon is senior to Alba and, like many of the senior officer class, he resents the upstart Colonel.

This in turn evolves into the 'Conquest of the Selva,' through which Peru's Selva could become a negotiating counter, the return of which, would come at the concession of all Ecuador territories and Ecuador's eternal security. An achievement as decisive and significant as the 'March on Lima.' At least in Blandon's mind.

In fact, given Blandon's perspective of his stunning victories, why concede the Selva at all? Why not re-negotiate the borders of the interior in a more decisive way? Why not retain some of what was conquered? Or by rights, all of it? In Blandon's mind, Ecuador could become heir to an inland empire of rivers and jungles second only to Brazil.

Blandon's mission creep comes to Quito only occasionally in the form of reports and dispatches, suggestions and proposals, initially tentative, but steadily more ambitious. These are received with some degree of confusion. Attempts to rein him in, or refocus his efforts are tentative, and largely ignored. Blandon's principle relationship with his masters is to demand a steady stream of supplies through specific requests. Requests which are difficult to refuse. Requests are not confined to military supplies, trade goods for the natives become an increasingly significant component; and in return, Blandon organizes a small but steady trade.

The numbers are small. Less than 5,000 men had been assigned to the command originally, and perhaps as few as 3,500 are actively involved in the campaign. Of this, only indefinite portion accompany Blandon into the Selva. Added to this are indigenous auxiliaries, armed and unarmed, amounting to fewer than 2,000 troops at any time. Actual combat usually produces relatively modest casualties, and there are many occasions of so-called hostile forces cooperating, in the delivery of or sharing of medicine, for example. Deaths through disease, illness, accident and natives far exceed combat casualties.

Axis of Andes – Page 274

The greatest advantage of Blandon's rain forest campaign is Peruvian distraction. Between July and November, Peru is simultaneously struggling with Alba's March on Lima, and Ibanez's war in the south. There is very little attention or resources left over for conflicts deep in the interior. Instead, the matter is left for local commanders to address piecemeal, with inadequate communications, manpower or even ammunition. Local outposts are often barely more than police stations. The few military forces in the region find it impossible to communicate with each other, and are barely able to navigate.

The sacking of Pucallpa, however, persuades the new Ramirez Junta, that there is indeed a problem in the interior that needs to be addressed. In late October, 1940, rebuilding is commenced on Pucallpa, establishing a well-fortified outpost, which becomes operational in January, 1941. Plans are drawn up for a new mission to the interior as the dry season draws to a close. The wet season will result in rivers and tributaries once again flowing deep, and with it, a new season of navigation.

Meanwhile, drunk with success and ambition, Blandon continues to press further down the Ucayali river, sending portages to the Purus River and following that channel deep into the jungle. At this point, October of 1940, Blandon has taken literally the whole of Ucayali province, and 3/4 of the Peruvian Amazon, leaving only Madre de Dios province in Peruvian hands.

****

The Pause - November, December, 1940

Alba's return to Ecuador from the March on Lima, on November 6, 1940, marks a pause in the war. The Ecuadoran mission has failed, and so now Quito focuses on entrenching its position, and consolidating its hold on captured Peruvian territories.

In the north, the Peruvian command, and Peruvian armies, are too shattered to mount any kind of offensive operations, focusing instead on rebuilding for the next push. General Markholtz sets about making the army his own.

In the interior, the Oriente and the Selva, General Blandon reigns supreme on his armoured river boat, de facto ruler of a vast swathe of territory, overextended, and unthreatened.

At sea, November 18, 1940, the unstoppable Chilean battleship, Almirante Latorre catches the Peruvian cruiser Almirante Grau and the destroyer Palacio in open waters heading to the Gulf of Guayaquil. The Palacio escapes the Almirante Grau is sunk.

Thereafter, the Peruvian navy remains close to its home ports, and the Chileans begin to aggressively implement a naval blockade, albeit one which does not interfere with American shipping. With the resources of the contenders considerably diminished, the naval war enters a subtle phase, as air power and submarines come to dominate the sea.

In the south, mobility has largely come to an end, though both sides continue to build up elaborate networks of trenches and earthwork fortifications. Numbers at the southern front have climbed to 65,000 Peruvians facing 75,000 Chileans, by December 31, 1940, with both sides continuing to mobilize.

Despite this, there is relatively little fighting on the southern front. Relative, of course, being a relative term. Throughout the balance of November and December, there are regular artillery barrages and duels, occasional sorties, and a scattering of air raids. Each side tests the other's defences. But the experience of the Great War in Europe is too fresh in both parties' minds, and neither side is prepared to throw lives into a cauldron recklessly. At times, a strange sort of peace seems to settle across the frontier, with soldiers calling out to each other across the frontier.

***

Chile - The New Year's Offensive

This quasi peace is broken on January 9, 1941, with the 'New Year's Offensive.' An addition of 15,000 fresh troops to the front inspires the Chilean generals to launch a human wave offensive against the Peruvians. Fighting a force half again as large as their own, with inferior weapons, training and equipment, the Peruvian army holds on grimly, making no offensive moves, but bitterly contesting every inch of ground. The New Year's Offensive is supported by Chilean naval elements along the coast, and by Chilean fighter and bomber aircraft, as well as sustained artillery.

Nevertheless, it fares poorly. Casualties are appalling. By the end of the offensive on January 21, Chile has lost 13,000 men. Artillery and air have proven to be of little use to the Chileans. Meanwhile the Peruvians have deployed their limited air resources against Chilean ships, severely damaging the destroyer Aldea. The battle ends with minimal gains and the removal of the General in command of the front.

During this time, the Chileans demand an Ecuadoran offensive in the north, to divide Peruvian attention and energies. However, this demand comes late and with insufficient detail. The Ecuadorans fail to advance beyond their captured provinces. Only Blandon, in the interior, carries out aggressive operations.

The north remains quiet. General Markholtz, who has replaced Ureta, concentrates on building up Peruvian forces at Trujillo and Cajamarca, and on perfecting his transportation and communication systems. There is considerable tension between Markholtz and the command in Lima. Lima continually demands action; Markholtz continually demands more and better troops and equipment.

At sea, Chile achieves naval dominance, but this turns out to be of little value. For the most part Chile's navy finds it dangerous to approach the Peruvian coast. Peru mobilizes aircraft wherever possible to attack Chilean naval assets. Many of these are shot down.

But on February 21, the Almirante Latorre is struck by several aerial bombs, forcing it to return to Valparaiso for repairs.

The blockade proves ineffective. Shipping to Peru shifts from Lima to secondary ports, and the Chilean navy does not have the resources to interdict it all. American shipping is a particular concern, with Chilean naval vessels reluctant to accost the Stars and Stripes.

Only the jungle war remains active, with General Blandon's riverboat navy penetrating deep into Peruvian territory with seasonal flooding.

***

Girding For Battle

Internally, each of the parties undergoes considerable evolution.

The primary beneficiary is Carlos Ibanez, taking and holding power through a shaky coalition; the erratic progress of the war and the frequent defeats and stalemates undermines the prestige and influence of the Chilean army and navy. As the country shifts to war footing, Ibanez's power and influence consolidates and grows. Supplanting civil institutions, Ibanez's rule becomes increasingly autocratic and arbitrary as he gathers power under himself. He moves forward energetically with plans for the reform of the Chilean military; and Chilean economy and society as a whole. Chile increasingly becomes a genuine fascist dictatorship on the European model.

Meanwhile, in Peru, under the stewardship of General Ramirez, a different society is taking shape. Ramirez is only one among several generals and senior officers in Lima, and Lima is only the center of a network of generals and senior officers, including generals who command large numbers of troops in both the north and south. Peruvian governance has become thoroughly militarized, but without a clear central command. Rather, it is run through a sort of committee. Ramirez is not the autocratic dictator that Ibanez is becoming, but rather merely the head man at a large and often squabbling table.

Peruvian society is rapidly militarizing. The generals might squabble, but on certain matters there is consensus. They all need more troops, they all desperately need more troops. They need more and better equipment at any prices. Conscription and armaments cost, and that cost must be paid. This is made up, de facto, with a combination of increasingly high taxes, confiscations and borrowing, both at home and abroad. The Peruvian economy experiences contractions as the government diverts available investment capital from the economy, in the form of taxes and borrowing, and makes up shortfalls by printing money. Inflation begins to take hold, developing into hyperinflation late in 1941. The response to increasing economic dislocation are a series of piecemeal and ad hoc measures which see the Peruvian government increasingly taking control of the economy, sometimes by instituting wage and price controls, sometimes by directly ordering or placing military advisors in businesses.

The Peruvian generals have long experience in running a country. However, the truth is that they were never particularly good at it. They understand command and control, tactics and strategy, and the running of military hierarchies, in a satisfactory 19th century manner. But they are not especially skilled with, and have no insight into actual governance. Their fiscal and social policies tend to be stringently conservative in nature. Thus, although they are stumbling blindly into a form of military Keynesianism, they lack the intellectual tools or the consensus to use it effectively.

Rather, their approach is to simply increasingly militarize the population and the economy; in particular to recruit increasing numbers of Indigenous and mestizo, and even to use them to fill out the rapidly depleting lower officer class. The consequences and blowback of these actions are addressed only when it becomes a problem, and then usually in the most short-sighted and ad hoc fashion.

Further north, Ecuador finds itself at a crossroads. The triumvirate of Bonifaz, Velasco and Alba remains intact, their policies and attitudes in place. The only real difference is that the background level of internal dissent from Congress, from unions, media and other constituencies, has faded out entirely. The war, long warned of, has finally come. The triumvirate has led brilliantly, and the nation has united behind them.

But here, at the threshold of, if not victory, then success, the triumvirate has lost its way. Now that the war has come, they really have little idea of what to do next. The invasion has been defeated, they have fought their way into Peruvian jungle and coastal provinces; they have even fought their way to the gates of Lima and destroyed the Peruvian military in the north.

But peace has failed to materialize. Negotiations are not resulting in progress. The next step is not obvious.

During this period, a variety of options are argued within the nation. Some voices call for the annexation of captured territories, or at least significant border adjustments. Others demand withdrawal to original borders and offering terms. Still others advocate standing pat, holding on to captured ground as leverage for peace negotiations.

The triumvirate settles on something equivalent to a status quo, holding territories and signaling a willingness to make peace. The Ecuadoran economy shifts more smoothly to a war footing than either Peru's ad hoc floundering or Chile's radical reforms. Rationing and state direction of the economy increase, but Velasco and Bonifaz are careful not to tinker with the money supply or to raise taxes dramatically, thus avoiding the hyperinflation that will plague Peru. Instead, the Bonifaz administration prefers to accumulate debt or to seek financing from regional lenders and elsewhere.

The result is a small trickle of German and Italian money, and diplomatic and financial missions to Colombia, Venezuela, Brazil and Mexico. The triumvirate even seeks financial assistance from England, where it is turned down, and from private lenders in the United States, where it finds some success.

However, hostility from the American government makes direct financing difficult. Increasingly, loans and funding are funneled through Colombia, and Colombia becomes Ecuador's primary banker. Major civilian infrastructure projects are initiated to link Colombia and Ecuador by road and rail, paid for with Colombian money. For its part, the Ecuadoran government secures Colombian loans through pledging of tax revenue and eventually the selling of royalty rights and property licenses, primarily in the contested jungle interior.

Ironically, even as Colombian influence and involvement is growing, Chilean and Ecuadoran cooperation and relations continues to fail to gel.

The Chile continues to maintain a pair of warships in the Gulf of Guayaquil and Ecuador assumes the costs of support. The attempted raid by Peru's Almirante Grau and Palazzo has demonstrated the continuing need for protection.

But beyond that, there is little scope for cooperation. Neither state is willing to supply the other with significant numbers of troops, nor does either have munitions or arms to spare.

An initial attempt to enlist support by coordinating attacks falls flat - Chile's New Year's offensive, organized and launched on an almost ad hoc basis, allows far too little time for any meaningful cooperation. Chile makes demands, but provides little in the way of notice or concrete information. By the time Ecuador gears up to participate, the campaign is over. The results are recriminations on both sides for lack of coordination, particularly by the Chilean military who are desperate to shift blame anywhere to anyone.

Internationally, the world finds little consensus in its approach to the Andean war. Colombia, as noted, finds itself in the role of Ecuador's banker, funnelling third party money, and securing an increasing interest in the Ecuadorian economy. Brazil maintains a watchful eye, but takes no position and expresses little interest. Argentina's policy is one of ambivalence, driven by personalities, alternately supportive of or hostile to Chile, but otherwise so focused on its own issues that it takes little care.

Germany and Italy have little role in the proceedings. German capital and German espionage remain in place, but for the most part, their efforts are token. Ecuador and Chile are considered friendly states, which limits freedom of action. What German or

Axis interests remain in Peru are confiscated. Only in Bolivia and Argentina do the Axis powers play anything like a significant role in the politics or among the players of the nation.

Still, the smell of Nazis is in the air. Britain, fighting for its life, holds its nose and maintains trading relations with all the Latin states. It defers to emerging American policy in the region.

American policy in the region, however, is stuck dithering. The United States clearly sees Nazi Germany as an adversary and rival, and Nazi efforts at influence in Latin America are very unwelcome. Ecuador's and Chile's Nazi connections predispose the Roosevelt administration to be hostile.

But there are complications for American decision makers. Ecuador and Chile are not the aggressors. The war has been started by Peru, and then to make matters worse, it has been badly prosecuted by Peru; which makes the Peruvians less than ideal allies, neither just nor competent and America wants at least one of the two. Peru has gone from bad to worse; a civilian democratic government in Peru has been deposed on the threshold of peace, and has been replaced by an autocratic military regime which seems unwilling to entertain the notion of a peaceful resolution.

Within the halls of power, divergent American economic and financial interests argue and bicker on behalf of their respective interests in different countries. Coffee interests argue for Colombia, Mining investments plead for Chile, and so forth. The morality of the conflict takes second place to who owns what investments where, and how they should be protected.

The Andean war, despite its connections to the European conflict, is an unwelcome sideshow. The Roosevelt administration's foreign policy through 1941 is almost entirely focussed on the European and Asian conflict. To the extent that the Roosevelt administration has a position on the Andean conflict, it is a pox on all their houses.

The American position comes down to the following elements: 1) Ceasefire; 2) Return to original borders; 3) International (American and British) adjudication of territorial disputes; 4) Elimination of Nazi influence and compliance with overall U.S. policy, particularly with respect to access to vital resources, such as copper and tin; 5) Embargo of oil and war material.

Progress on these fronts is erratic at best. America is most successful in terms of accessing vital resources, and all of the combatants maintain extensive trade with the United States, often offering preferential terms and discounts to curry American favour.

The Embargo is incompletely applied, and all of the parties at one point or another slide in, though Peru benefits most. Ceasefires take place frequently, but without much in the way of consistency, America's nominal favourite, Peru, is all too frequently the most belligerent of the combatants. The situation refuses to admit resolution, but on the other hand, American interests and priorities are respected.

Ucayali River - December, 1940

"For the love of God, Montresor," General Enrique Blandon swears.

The river shore is packed with natives, almost a hundred by his reckoning. Men, women, children, all of them brown-skinned and naked, or nearly so. His eyes linger on the women; some of them aren't bad to look at. A few of the men carry spears or bows and arrows, but make no hostile move. Not a rifle to be found among them. They simply watch. Blandon smiles and waves at them.

Somewhere around here there are villages of primitive huts.

"Sir?" Montresor asks. His name isn't Montresor, that is simply an affectation, a name Blandon bestows. He has no idea what it means. The brown-skinned man wears a few shreds of uniform, and bears a lieutenant's commission, although he probably can't find Ecuador on a map. But he speaks the native languages, and that makes him useful to Blandon.

The Matilde's engines are off to save on gasoline. Drink it in, he thinks, smiling at the natives. The most magnificent engine of destruction you have seen in your lives. Light armour decking, proof against gunfire, an artillery piece, four heavy machine guns.

Out in the world, it isn't a flyspeck against a battleship, or even a destroyer. But here in this green world, it makes him feel like a God.

It was one of six, but he's destroyed the other five. But this one, his darling Matilde, he has saved, captured and made her his bride, his pride, his flagship and his command center.

Behind him comes the flotilla, an assembly of smaller boats, steamboats, flat barges, rafts and canoes. The complement comes to a couple of hundred. A fraction of the forces he has scattered about.

"Who are these people?" Blandon asks. "Have we encountered them before?"

Montresor shouts to the people on shore, a swirl of native gabble. Some of them shout back.

"Ashaninka," he says, "from the interior. Not close, they have come far to see. They heard tales of the great fleet. They are good Christians."

Blandon nods. He grins at them and waves.

"You tell them," he orders, "that I am the good man, here to free them from their oppressors."

A good man, that was the nearest the natives can understand. A good man is a great man.

Greater than that fucking clown, Alba. All the way to Lima, and then he'd just sat there with his thumb up his ass, waiting to be told to go home. Ecuador needs real soldiers, not some socialist accountant with his tongue up old Bonifaz's ass. He swears under his breath.

Montresor glances at him. Some of the things Blandon says are hard to translate.

"Tell them that I am mighty. That I command the lightning and the thunder. Where my hand falls, there is fire and death to my enemies. But those who follow me, they receive gifts and plenty."

"You want them to follow you, sir?" Montresor asks, puzzled. Where? For how long?

"Not literally," Blandon says. "I don't need more dogs begging for scraps. You know what I mean. Good friend, bad enemy, powerful master. Say that."

Montresor nods, he raises his rifle, and shouts out once more.

This time a rousing cry comes from the throng, the crowd on shore raises up their arms. In answer, a series of ululations rise up the fleet behind, they don't know what is being said, Blandon doesn't, but they can all sense the enthusiasm. Blandon raises one arm high, but does not roar. When the calls die down, he lowers his arm.

One of the natives shouts.

"What was that?" he asks.

"The man there," Montresor says, "he says he will give you his finest daughter, in exchange for a rifle."

Blandon looks to the shore where the man has shouted; three women are beside him. Which is his daughter? He hopes it was the good looking one. It is almost tempting.

"Tell him my gifts are only for the worthy," he orders. "But perhaps someday, I will judge him worthy."

Montresor shouts back the answer, receives surprisingly enthusiastic cries.

But now the gunboat is approaching the bend in the river. The crowd will pass out of sight. He wonders what they will do? Return to their villages with tales of wonder? Will some of them follow? One or two might make a pilgrimage to one of the stations. If so, he'll figure out what to do with them. There are always natives hanging around the stations. Some of them can be made useful.

They are moving downriver towards the camp. Blandon isn't entirely sure; he reckons another twenty miles or so.

"I am thinking, Montresor, that perhaps it's time to sack Pucallpa again. We can't have too many supplies, and the Peruvians, they've been very good about handing them to us," Blandon says.

"They're building it back up pretty fast," Montresor says.

The great sack, as Blandon calls it, has been incredibly productive. There was so much loot that Blandon's fleet had to make two great expeditions and a dozen minor ones to carry it all away. There'd been thousands of rifles, machine guns, hundreds of thousands of rounds, belts, cartridges, slings, the contents of a machine shop, an apothecary, dozens upon dozens of barrels of gasoline and kerosene. Even the sunken gunboats had been picked over, liberating a workable field piece, a pair of machine guns, and a brace of engine parts.

The haul has been scattered across stations up and down the river, hauled up barely navigable tributaries. He has entire crews reconditioning the rifles, teaching and training the natives. He now has over a thousand armed native auxiliaries, kept under control by officers who are judicious with the deployment of ammunition.

He still demands supplies and armaments from Quito. Why not? Best not to let them know how well supplied he is. Besides, he still needs supplies; the country provides food, but not so well. There are trade goods, medicines.

Even after the sack, Pucallpa is still lucrative. He's gone back, or sent forces back, a few times, to run off the few Criollo who keep returning. The trouble is the damnable road. A pipeline all the way to Lima that might carry thousands, tens of thousands of Criollo, a Peruvian tide to drown them all.

"We should do something about that place," Blandon says, "burn it once and for all."

Montresor shrugs. He's heard it before.

"The rainy season will wash away the road," Montresor replies. He has no clear idea about the significance of the road, but he's heard it enough times to repeat it back.

"Yes," Blandon says. "Let them build up, then when the rain washes the road away, and they are caught, then we'll crush them."

The natives on the shore are far behind now, but still in Blandon's mind.

"This is a forgotten land, Montresor," he says. "Forgotten even by those who live here, an entire country asleep and waiting to wake. This is our mission, Montresor, we bring war, and in its footsteps, civilization will grow."

****

Peru - The Selva Campaign

The rebuilding of Pucallpa proceeds rapidly beginning in October, 1940, well into the rainy season, up to late February, 1941. Blandon's forces stage several successful raids in October and November. In early December, 1940, a major firefight erupts, after which Blandon discontinues further attempts.

The Ramirez Junta accelerates construction of the road, but there are limits to the pace of construction. The road will be completed by 1943. In the meantime, the utility of the partially completed road declines seriously in the rainy season as large sections are eventually washed out or flooded.

Nevertheless, by early January, Pucallpa is an impregnable rain forest fortress, splitting Blandon's forces above and below the reaches of the Ucayali.

At the same time, the Ramirez Junta persuades General Markholtz to establish secondary fortresses in the town of Tarapota and Lamas, far in the north, in the Selva Baja (the cloud forest). Although in the north, this is well away from the coastal areas of Ecuadoran control. The high elevation of Tarapota, and waterfalls have secured it from the war.

The secondary sites pay dividends when the Peruvians are able to recapture the town of Yurimaguas, which had been overrun by Ecuador and held since in July 15, 1940. This has the effect of partially severing Blandon's expeditionary forces from Ecuador, now splitting it in three groups, and potentially opening the Oriente to a new invasion.

Instead, of proceeding into the Oriente, however, the Junta opts for a conservative strategy: Eliminate Blandon's expedition above Pucallpa, and preferably Blandon himself, if he is there. If not, move downriver, roll up Ecuador's stations and crush Blandon somewhere between Pucallpa and Tarapota. Finally, move into the Oriente, hopefully in conjunction with a renewed offensive by Markholtz.

There are three principal problems with this strategy. One is the Matilde, which alone or with her accessories is by far the most dangerous fighting platform in the Amazon basin.

The second is that the Peruvians have badly misjudged the evolution of Blandon and his forces during their eight months in the interior. The expectation is that Blandon has suffered a continuing attrition of manpower due to disease, accidents and ongoing combat operations, that his extended supply lines are delicate and thin, and that he is running out of supplies and even food. Instead, Blandon has steadily made up and overcome his losses by recruiting, training and arming native auxiliaries. As to supplies, he has relentlessly confiscated Peruvian resources up and down the rivers, including the sack of Pucallpa, and has no significant supply issues.

The rainy season has come. Constant heavy rains pose challenges to both sides, reducing visibility. Rivers swell, bursting their banks, Pucallpa is cut off. Areas below Lamas and Tarapota become inaccessible. Tributaries everywhere become navigable; even areas which had been dry land become river channels of varying navigability. The rains and the new water drainage change currents, creating new hazards and concealing known ones. The result is a landscape that literally changes day by day.

With the rainy season, Blandon's forces are no longer bisected above and below Pucallpa. Instead, there are numerous channels above and below the fortress which allow his expedition to bypass the Peruvians. Nor are supply lines from Ecuador significantly impacted by the Peruvians; the rainy season provides routes around that, although it does pose its own challenges.

As a result, Blandon's expeditionary force retains free movement throughout the region, particularly local mobility. However, conditions require Blandon's forces to disperse. The Matilde and larger craft are still not suitable for many of the changed rivers and tributaries. Flatter, lighter boats have much more freedom of movement, including crossing in and out of river systems. Local guides and auxiliaries are invaluable in making sense of the rapidly shifting river systems, and a degree of communication is maintained through light canoes and mail drops. One advantage lost is that the float planes are no longer able to fly in the rainy season, and retreat to airfields in Ecuador, which eliminates aerial reconnaissance and attack.

Faced with these conditions, the Peruvians have no real choice, except to pour their own men and boats into the region and simply try to wear Blandon down, literally boat by boat. A steady stream of small lightly-armed craft are retrofitted and sent into the waters.

The Selva Campaign enters a new and dangerous phase, one in which visibility is sometimes nonexistent; every stretch of river contains unknown and unforeseen hazards ranging from hostile natives, to running aground, underwater obstructions, disease, natives or worse, Ecuadoran armed native auxiliaries and, potentially enemy boats with live weapons. The war becomes an endless series of games of cat and mouse, with both sides blindfolded, their roles changing constantly.

Through the rainy season, Peruvian losses are high. But the Peruvians have one advantage, attrition. They can keep pouring men and resources into the field. Compared to the demands of the southern or northern fronts, the requirements of the Selva are trivial. Although Blandon has replaced his losses with natives, and has accumulated a considerable war chest, his resources are not unlimited. Eventually, Blandon will run short of men or bullets. And then he's finished.

The Peruvians, around March or April, learn to concentrate forces locally, wiping out Blandon's men unit by unit.

In response, Blandon shifts tactics, avoiding futile battles, and using superior mobility and communications, and local knowledge to avoid the enemy until they can be lured into an ambush. As the Peruvians flood the region with men and boats, Blandon moves his forces further and further down river, and the theatre of war expands considerably. The further down-rivers the battles go, the more difficulty the Peruvians have beyond local supply lines, and the more effective Blandon's ambushes are.

Inevitably, sometime in April or May, both forces begin crossing over the Brazilian border into the Amazon districts. This is probably not deliberate, not initially. In rainy season conditions, guides are sufficient for local navigation, but it becomes impossible to tell where you are, sometimes within margins of well over a hundred miles.

By the time the rainy season gives way to the dry season, in June, 1941, the rain forest has become a diffuse battleground extending over three countries. Blandon's command is now centered across the border in Brazil.

***

The Second Northern Campaign, March and April, 1941

March 1, 1941

Ecuadorian forces - 65,000

Peruvian forces - 180,000 (75,000 on the northern front, 105,000 on the southern front)

Chilean forces - 120,000 (90,000 on the southern front)

Although the March on Lima has ended with Colonel Alba's return to Lojas and from there to a hero's welcome in Guayaquil and Quito, Ecuador remains in control of the adjacent Peruvian coastal provinces of Tombes, Piura and Lambayeque.

With the Tacna front stabilizing, and neither Peru nor Chile able to pursue a definite advantage in the South, Peru turns its attention to the north, and to a new offensive campaign.

The Second Northern Campaign is the brainchild of General Markholtz, whose first victory, following the New Year's offensive, is to persuade Lima and his fellow generals to give him the equipment and manpower to launch a major offensive. Despite the hard fighting of the south, and the threat of future offensives, Markholtz argues successfully that the southern front has stabilized. There is no progress to be made there; the parties are both dug in too deep, the frontier too well fortified.

Success, if it is to be found, will be in the north. If Ecuador can be knocked out of the war, Peru can employ its full strength. While Ecuador remains a factor, Peru will fight Chile with one arm tied behind its back.

Consequently, Markholtz is able to procure the lion's share of new recruitments, as well as bolstering his ranks with conscripts rotating out of the southern front. Markholtz's demands are ceaseless: More armour, more artillery, more supplies.

Meanwhile, relations between Chile and Ecuador reach a nadir by late February. February 20, Ibanez agrees to a ceasefire. Within the next week, the United States arranges two negotiating tables, between Ecuador and Peru and Peru and Chile separately, to attempt to build a long-term peace.

The Northern Campaign proceeds on March 4, 1941, with a concerted attack by the Army of the North, commanded by General Ernesto Montagne Markholtz and 75,000 strong. The Army of the North mobilizes two-thirds of Peru's available tanks and mechanized transport.

The assault at first succeeds. Markholtz starts out from Trujillo and Cajamarca and proceeds in two coordinated columns. Lambayeque and Piura province are taken. Tombes is bypassed in favour of a strike through Ecuador's El Oro province, advancing on Guayaquil.

However, by March 26, 1941, Alba counterattacks from mountain strongholds in Lojas towards the coast. After fierce fighting, the Markholtz is driven back, but retreats in good order, towards his supply lines. On April 4, Markholtz counterattacks ineffectually with an inconclusive battle. He then retreats to Piura and then Lambayeque, procuring reinforcements.

Alba attempts to flank him, but by this time, Markholtz's supply lines are short and Alba's are long. Alba allows himself to be driven back, retreating towards Tombes and attempting to trap Markholtz between his own reinforcements coming from Lojas. By April 11, Alba is counterattacking and inflicting heavy damage.

During this time, seeing an opportunity, Ibanez, in Chile, citing Peruvian intransigence ends the ceasefire and initiates a new campaign on the southern front on April 7, 1941.

Taking and inflicting casualties, Markholtz retreats, breaking out of the trap, on April 13. On April 16, 1941, the campaign ends as Markholtz disengages and focuses on consolidating his position. Ecuador remains entrenched in Peruvian territory. But Markholtz has made territorial gains, and more critically has recovered the oil-producing territories of Peru.

Unknown to Markholtz, the Ecuadorians have reached the end of their tether. Widespread fuel shortages have brought the Ecuadorian armies to a halt. Alba is unable to bring in fresh troops, and most divisions are reporting a few day's ammunition left, if that.

Had Markholtz persisted, perhaps even a few more days, he would have overrun the Ecuadorian frontier. This would still be far from overrunning Ecuador or even taking Guayaquil, Alba had prepared defence in depth. But potentially, Ecuador could have been forced out of the war.

The question is whether Markholtz could have continued the offensive at all, or whether he'd reached the limits of his capacity.

Nevertheless, at the end of the campaign on April 16, 1941, Markholtz has recovered substantial Peruvian territory and has kept his forces in good order, but has failed to capture Guayaquil. In turn, Alba has failed to destroy Markholtz's forces or his capacity to wage war, but has maintained a defensive position. Both men claim victories of sorts, but the advantage is clearly to Markholtz. Alba needs to score a knockout blow, while Markholtz can content himself with grinding his enemy to pieces.

At the time though, matters are not so clear. The campaign is almost the end of Markholtz. He's failing to knock Ecuador out of the war, he's wasting vast quantities of men and munitions, and he's stolen badly needed resources from the southern front. General Rodriguez on April 20, 1941, issues a directive relieving Markholtz of command and demanding he return to Lima. Markholtz ignores both orders, retaining his northern command.

[Casualties - 25,000 Peruvian killed and wounded. 16,000/3500/5500

[Casualties - 14,000 Ecuadorian killed and wounded. 6000/4000/4000

The Second Northern Campaign illustrates the limitations of Ecuadorian and Chilean cooperation. The Chileans provide naval support, a key reason why the Peruvians made no effort to take Tombes, which was vulnerable to offshore shelling, and provide limited air support. But the Chileans are unwilling to coordinate an attack in the south to divert or take pressure off.

When Chile chooses to attack, the tide of battle has already turned in Ecuador, and Ibanez is clearly attempting to take advantage of what he properly perceives as confusion and disarray in the Peruvian command.

Due to oil and weapons embargoes, the Ecuadorans are beginning to experience fuel and ammunition shortages. Many of the remaining Ecuadoran tanks are acting as fixed artillery, and rationing is in effect throughout the country. Chile can provide little help. It too is experiencing fuel shortages.

In order to sustain itself, Ecuador, in its hour of desperation, turns to Colombia, importing fuel, ammunition and necessities from the north. As the bottleneck of approaches a crisis point, Ecuador's negotiating position becomes desperate. In the end, Colombian fuel and munitions don't arrive in time to alleviate the crisis. For two weeks, Ecuador's military is so thinly stretched that a good shove could have taken it.

But of course, Markholtz has already lost heart and is fighting disgrace. The shove, in the form of a Third Northern Campaign, does not commence. It is a near thing, though, and as Ecuador rebuilds its stockpiles, it desperately resolves not to be put in this position again.

In the aftermath of the Second Northern Campaign, Velasco travels to Bogota to negotiate and reinforce supply lines, including overland and coastal routes for oil, coal, ammunition and weapons. To pay for this, Ecuador trades both current and future agricultural and mineral production, mortgaging itself increasingly heavily to Colombian and indirectly to American interests. In turn, Ecuador is able to rapidly rebuild and expand its armies to an unprecedented degree.

It is, however, a two way street. As Ecuadorian debt to Colombia steadily increases, Colombia finds itself increasingly unable to disentangle its affairs from Ecuador, and is increasingly concerned about what Ecuador's fall will do to its own financial interests.

***

Axis of Andes – Page 295

The Trench War in Tacna, April through June, 1941

The failure of the New Year's Campaign results in the disgrace of several of Chile's senior generals. In the resulting power vacuum, President Ibanez, himself a former general and commander, moves decisively to consolidate power.

Taking direct command of the Army, he reshuffles military positions and announces a general mobilization. A significant portion of Chile's military strength has been withheld from the front, stationed in cities and towns to maintain both social stability, protect against possible threats from Argentina and, most importantly, to neutralize any possibility of a counter coup against him.

The housecleaning leaves Ibanez with unchallenged command of the army. Demoting, reassigning and at times simply cashiering potentially disloyal commanders, Ibanez is able to tighten his grip on both military and civil society. This gives him a lot more flexibility for deployment. He literally has a spare army to use.

At this point, late January or early February, his personal position consolidated and unassailable, Ibanez is prepared to make peace. He accepts the American ceasefire and agrees to a resumption of original borders, with both Tacna province and the Ecuadoran Oriente to be subject to international arbitration. His sole divergence from the American proposal is a demand for reparations and indemnities. Ibanez is confident that he can obtain favourable terms and enlist American support.

The fly in the ointment is Ecuador. There is in Santiago by this time, substantial enmity towards Ecuador as a result of widespread belief that they 'stabbed their ally in the back' by failing to support the New Year offensive with their own. This isn't realistic, but the Chilean military is desperately in need of a scapegoat.

Bonifaz responds to Ibanez's peace plan with approval in principle, but the Ecuadorans fail to withdraw to their own borders as proposed, and, in particular, General Blandon in the Amazon interior continues military operations beyond the control of anyone. Relations deteriorate.

Markholtz's Northern Campaign of March 4, throws the peace process into disarray. It is not entirely clear that the government in Lima has authorized the offensive, although they were definitely aware of it. Ibanez accuses Lima of bad faith, and asks the United States to intervene directly, but takes no action himself. Peace negotiations deteriorate steadily through the rest of March.

By April the 11th, it's clear to all observers that the Second Northern Campaign is floundering badly. Ibanez, seeing an opportunity, repudiates the ceasefire and launches a massive attack across the front, promising victory in ninety days.

The initial phase of the attack is preceded by coordinated air attacks on enemy artillery positions, and deployment of heavy artillery barrages on select points on the front. Thereafter, Ibanez deploys his armour against these points, followed by mass infantry to exploit the breakthrough. It is classic World War One tactics, and it almost works. By April 22, despite heavy casualties, the Chileans have overrun four of six objectives. By April 29, the Peruvian forces are split into three groups.

Peru responds with massive reinforcements, hastily conscripted and thrown recklessly into the field. The Peruvian submarine fleet, along with the remnants of the navy, attempts to challenge the Chilean coastal and naval forces. The tide begins to turn; by May 4, the assault has run out of steam and Peruvian units have managed to reform their ranks. The Chileans have penetrated deeply but unevenly into Tacna.

The Chilean gains are pyrrhic. The advance positions are so far into the new Peruvian lines that they are often caught in Peruvian crossfires. The Peruvians pour so much firepower into these enclaves that the Chilean nickname becomes the 'Hellholes.' Ibanez, however, is unwilling to surrender these gains and insists that they be held at all costs.

****

Axis of Andes – Page 297

Santiago, April 27, 1941

"We're going broke," Carlos Ibanez rants. "We're going broke. We can't even borrow money. The Germans can't lend, the Americans won't, the British don't have a pot to piss in, and the Argentines are worthless."

"We have some credit with Brazil. And we can print money," Cerda, his Finance Minister points out. He isn't nearly as distressed as he ought to be.

The socialist has been full of ideas, more so than that fool Gustavo Ross. Ibanez doesn't necessarily agree with, or even understand, all that the man comes up with. But he is more or less inclined to trust him. Socialism and war, it turns out, make good bedfellows.

"Sure we can print money," Ibanez growls, "until it's worthless. That will only get us so far. If I try and raise taxes again, I'll have riots in the streets."

"What I want to know," he demands, "is how those bumpkins in Lima aren't going broke. I've met those fuckers; some of them I wouldn't trust to run a vegetable stand. And those pricks in Quito, how are they managing it? Why are we the only ones going broke? Are the Brazilians financing them too?"

"Quito is being floated by the Colombians," Cerda replies.

"As to Lima..." he shrugs. "I think they're in a bad way. Maybe they just don't appreciate it."

Ibanez swears.

"All I know is that every time we put a soldier up on the front, they put one up, sometimes two. It's been going like that for a year now. The bastards are bleeding us dry."

Fontaine, the florid Italian, who he's appointed as Minister of Public Works, pipes up. "I've heard that the Americans may be funding Lima on the sly, pretending neutrality. Perhaps we should tighten the blockade, at least until we get fair treatment."

Ibanez stares. He knows where the man had heard this nonsense: During one of Ibanez's own drunken rants. It galls him to have his words fed back to him.

He leans back into his chair.

"Tighten the blockade?" he muses. "Admiral, what do you think of that notion?"

"I would recommend against it," Admiral Encelada says stiffly. "American shipping moves freely, for us, for Peru, for Guayaquil. We depend on the revenue of American shipping, as our friend Mr. Cerda tells us. And to be honest, the Chilean navy is not currently in the best position to make a contest with the American navy."

Not currently, Ibanez thinks to himself, the old fossil is deluded if he thinks that his ships were ever a match for the American navy. No, intercepting American shipping is the fastest way to lose the war, and get Santiago shelled by the battleship New Jersey, or some such.

The Americans need Chilean copper and Bolivian tin from Chilean ports, and that should have been enough to settle them on Chile's side. But the trouble is that they have their fingers in too many pies, and for every gringo in Washington who speaks up for them, there's some prick piping up for that idiot Ramirez.

Washington is happy to sit back and watch us all slaughter each other, as long as it gets to suckle at everyone's teats like a hungry piglet. But woe to the fool who takes a teat away, that will be the end of it.

And stupid as the bastards in Lima are, they aren't that stupid.

So here we all are, Ibanez thought, stuck in some stupid war that doesn't even involve us, foisted on us all by young shit-for-brains bravos. He glances at Jose Maree, the Nazi leader, sitting quietly, representing the Ministry of Culture. He wishes the man would say something so he could tear a strip off him. But alas, he's stuck the man in the most inoffensive portfolio he could think of.

"We shouldn't have broken the ceasefire," he grouses. He glares at General Robelledo, the Minister of the Army. Ridiculous in wartime to have two Ministers, one for the Army and one for the Navy, and neither one worth spit. "This is your fault."

The general knows better than to argue. Technically, it was Ibanez's idea, buoyed by frustration and Ecuador's latest success. He's bullied his military staff into preparing a new offensive. Strike them while they're bogged down in the north. It had seemed perfect.

Of course, nothing happens overnight. It takes time to mobilize and position troops for a new offensive and, in the meantime, the fight in the north wound down. The Ecuadorans could never hold their end up. But Chile had gone ahead with the offensive, and now it was turning into a mess.

"What I want to know," Ibanez says, "is how come we end up flat-footed on our asses every single time. But somehow, that prick, Alba, chews up one army after another. He waltzes all the way down to Lima, like he's on a sightseeing trip, and then saunters home, tucking a few provinces under his arm, like loaves of bread. Seriously?"

His voice rises.

"You know what they call him? The Accountant! I've met the slimy little ass kisser, tagging along after that shit, Velasco," Ibanez snarls. "How does—"

"I think that was Colonel Flores," Robelledo suggests.

"I don't care!" Ibanez roars. "Flores, Alba, they're not the point. They're provincial rubes who can barely button their pants correctly. But somehow, they've done a thousand times better than the finest fighting men from the most advanced nation on the continent! What the hell is wrong with this picture? Explain!"

"Well," Maree offers; he looks like he wants to be hiding under the table. "It's about movement. Ecuador's front offers substantial freedom of movement. Our border is narrow, and so..."

Ibanez is preparing to tear a strip off the quivering Nazi, when the old fossil, Encelada, speaks up thoughtfully.

"He's right," the old admiral quavers. "As long as we play their game, we'll be stuck battering ourselves bloody against a stone wall."

A navy man sticking up for a Nazi, Ibanez thinks, what's the world come to?

"It's not like we can drive around through Bolivia," Cerde says.

That would solve a lot of problems, Ibanez thinks. But the Bolivians are like jelly, you can't trust them. And if you do it without their say-so, well then you have two wars on your hands, and we can't pay for the one war we are already fighting.

"No," says Encelada. "We don't have to go through Bolivia. Remember, we still have the most powerful navy on the continent. The Almirante Lattore or the Toro, either them alone could sink what's left of Peru's fleet."

"And then get bombed by airplanes," Robelledo smirks.

"Shut up," Ibanez says thoughtfully.

To Encelada: "Where are you going with this?"

"As I was saying, the Almirante Lattore..."

"Blah blah blah," Ibanez says. "Yes, we have the mighty Chilean navy. Boon to Quito, glorious victories at sea, except for the time you got it up the ass at Coquimbo. But it hasn't done us fuck all good on land. Are you proposing to shell the trenches from the sea?"

"No Sir," Encelada mumbles; the man is rattled but stubborn. "I propose we take the whole of the navy, all of it, and as many small craft and landing craft as we can gather, and use it to land an army up the coast, beyond the frontier. The Peruvians are entrenched; we come at them from behind, crush them on both sides. The stalemate is broken, we're no longer bottled up, we have mobility and the Criollo army of the South is destroyed. We can march straight into Lima."

"Hmm," Ibanez reflects thoughtfully. "A sea landing. That's just infantry and small arms. What are they going to do against tanks and artillery?"

"That's the key, Sir," Encelada replies. "The Navy provides cover. We can shell the coast, we can shell miles inland, if we're close enough."

"Only miles though," Ibanez asks, "what about past that?"

"Once we've got a bridgehead we can set up and offload heavier equipment easily."

Ibanez nods.

"Airplanes?"

"Troublesome, but with the full force of the Navy, there won't be enough and they won't be able to do enough damage to effect the outcome."

Encelada falls silent. Thoughtfully, Ibanez drums his fingers on the table, thinking it over.

"I like it," he says finally. "Is this just beer hall bullshit? Or have you been looking into it?"

The man stiffens.

"Sir," he says, "sea landings have been a part of our naval heritage since the war of the Pacific. We've maintained capacity, and improved since..."

Since the mutiny of 1931, Ibanez thinks. So, the old fossil has been keeping a few cards up his sleeve. They learned a lesson in 1931, and clearly, they've put some thinking and planning in, just in case.

"I see," Ibanez says quietly, still thinking. "This sort of landing, though, it would have to be on a heroic scale, not just put down some sailors to overrun a town or city in the night. You'd need to land an entire army, ready to fight. That's a tall order."

"I think we can do it, sir," Encelada replies, "with the assistance of the army."

Axis of Andes – Page 302

Robelledo bristles. Ibanez lifts a hand slightly, the message clear: Settle down. He is a general himself; he can imagine what Robelledo's response will probably be. Something along the lines of the Navy being a taxi service. He doesn't care. This is a serious discussion, he doesn't need them going at it like cats and dogs.

Robelledo catches the gesture and restrains himself. So, he's not completely stupid, Ibanez thinks.

"I'd have to confer with the Admiral about details," Robelledo says carefully, "but it seems feasible..."

That is enough.

"Fine," Ibanez barks. "Cabinet meeting is dismissed. All other business is tabled. Gentlemen, Admiral Encelada, General Robelledo, put your heads together. We meet tomorrow; you have..." he looks at his watch, "thirty hours to come back with an operations plan. Whatever you need, from whatever department, they're at your disposal; confiscate every fishing boat and rowboat in Chile if you need to. If it can be done, I want it done yesterday. Every day wasted, the sons of Chile are dying, remember that and let it speed you."

***

The Chilean Navy

The Chilean navy is easily one of the most powerful in South America, almost rivalling those of Argentina, a country with almost four times its population, and Brazil, a country with ten times its population. It is a vastly expensive and oversized navy, given the size of the country, or its relative wealth.

Partly, this is explained by Chilean geography. It's a long spaghetti string of a country, fifteen hundred miles in length, but in many parts no more than a hundred miles across. For a country like that, a navy may be as or more effective than an army. But there is more to it.

Historically, Chile has always been connected to the sea. It was an important stopping point for ships plying the South Seas or rounding the Cape. Anyone going from the Atlantic to the Pacific, or vice versa, heading to or from places far away, often stopped in Chile. Whalers and sealers plying the South Seas often put into Chile for fresh water and recreations. For the Chileans, the sea is a close neighbour, never more than a day or so away, full of bounty and treachery.

From the age of sail onwards, Chile is a nautical nation. Chile's military conflicts, particularly the War of the Confederation and. most importantly, the War of the Pacific, were principally naval wars and it is Chile's navy which wins these wars.

The War of the Pacific, in which the Chilean Navy performed spectacularly, cemented the status of the navy. Sea power was essential to the war, had destroyed of the Peruvian navy, made the invasion of Peruvian home territory possible and won new provinces in Antofagasta, Tarapaca, Arica and Tacna.

Of course, the Chilean navy's status takes a bit of a dip less than a decade later in 1891, when it backs the wrong side in the Chilean civil war - supporting the President.

The ensuing 'Parliamentary Period,' an era of weak Presidents and of congressional domination might have been bad for the navy. But as we've said, the navy is deeply entwined with national pride. For a time, Chile was the dominant naval power in South America.

A naval arms race between Argentina and Brazil erodes that dominance, relegating Chile to second and then third place. But this also provokes national pride and deepens security fears; and so parliamentary qualms notwithstanding, Chile joins the naval arms race in the 1890s and early 20th century, which ensures both massive levels of funding and continuing high social and political status.

The civil war, however, does demonstrate a clear division in Chile's military. The army and navy are separate components, separate communities, separate cultures; and they view each other with wariness and skepticism, if not considerable rivalry. As is the case in Latin American militaries, the branches are not hesitant to dabble in politics when the occasion calls for it.

The point is that Chile's navy is not merely a weapon, or series of tools. It is a political force and a focused constituency, a voice, within Chilean society.

The Parliamentary period, a happy interlude of drift, comes to an end in 1925. Carlos Ibanez becomes dictator for the first time, and for a few years rules happily while spending like a drunken sailor. Not a good idea; Chile's economic fundamentals have taken a bit hit when the nitrates industry declines, Ibanez sustains things by borrowing, but when the depression comes to town the bottom of the whole country just drops out.

The government is caught flat footed. It isn't terribly stable to begin with. Ibanez is turfed on July 26, 1931, and replaced by a fellow named Montero. On August 20, Montero is replaced by his vice-president, Manuel Trucco, so Montero can run for election. For Trucco and Montero, austerity is the rule of the day.

In 1930, there is a 10 percent pay cut to navy salaries. In 1931, one of Trucco's bright ideas is to chop navy salaries by another 30 percent. The Chilean government is reeling, it is floundering like a drunk drowning in a bathtub, and one of the ways it has decided to cope is to cut naval pay by an accumulated 40 percent.

The Chilean navy by this time has evolved into a fairly strict caste society. There are the officers, drawn from the social elite, and there are the enlisted men. They don't talk to each other. One orders, one obeys that is it.

The military, despite their prestige, suffers chronically low salaries during the Parliamentary period. The salaries of the enlisted men, the low caste, are particularly low. Things improved for a while under Ibanez, but in those two years, enlisted men's salaries, never high, drop 40 percent To make it worse, bonuses previously earned and owing are unilaterally cancelled.

In the context of the navy, the particular combination of high status, strong cultural cohesion, low caste and brutal financial suffering produces a radicalisation among the enlisted men.

The result is a mutiny on the battleship Almirante Latorre on August 31, 1931, while the fleet is in the port of Coquimbo. Many of the senior officers are on shore attending a boxing match (seriously), Within a day the mutiny has spread to the other thirteen ships of the fleet at Coquimbo. Within a couple of more days the mutiny has spread to the naval base at Talhuanco, and to the ships of the southern fleet, as well as the navy's remaining mainland bases and facilities. By this time 26 ships are now part of the mutiny, including all of the big bads - the battleships, the cruisers, the destroyers and submarines, and the key support ships.

It is amazing. It is a radical populist movement that spreads like wildfire. These men have not coordinated their uprising. In fact, such coordination would have been impossible. Rather, what you have is a naval underclass that was extremely cohesive, radicalized by circumstance and adversity, and is spectacularly pissed off. The revolt, buoyed by initial success, spreads with the force of an explosion.

It spreads so fast, so far and so hard, it literally outruns its leadership. Suddenly one of the most lethal war machines in South America, a world class juggernaut of death and destruction, a force capable of flattening countries, is in the hands of an angry host of rebels....

And at this point, they are all sort of looking at each other nonplussed, having no real idea how they got there and no idea of what to do next. On September 1, 1931, the de facto leader of the mutiny, a petty officer named Ernesto Gonzalez, cables the government to reassure them that the movement is not political, and demands their old salaries back.

Seriously? Talk about not thinking it through. The Chilean military, as with the sabre rattling incident (a spat in the 1920s where young officers banged their sabres noisily in Congress to protest low wages) has a history of loudly demonstrating its grievances.

But this isn't a demonstration. This is mutiny on an utterly shocking scale. This is trials and prison sentences and lots of death penalties level stuff. This is bombing and shelling and civil war. These guys have precipitated a literal civil war, and they are still nattering on about wage scales. Astonishing.

The result is a sort of paralysis as the mutineers struggle to play a game of intellectual catch-up, trying to adjust their demands to the magnitude of their actions. The eventual result is a series of twelve demands, and an expansion of radicalism. Some within the mutineers just want their goddamned money. Others see an opportunity to make fundamental changes to Chilean society: Social revolution, agrarian reform, branching out and enlisting groups on the mainland like the Communist party.

Of course, there isn't a real consensus, and there is no real leadership to build that consensus. There are leaders for the mutiny, of course, but mainly these are guys running ahead of the tidal wave. It is going, they just happen to be in front, that's all.

It is very much within the boundaries of possibility that had the naval mutiny lucked into leadership, had it proceeded swiftly and expeditiously, instead of succumbing to paralysis and dithering, that it might have won out and taken the country. But the dithering is fatal. Within five days, the government manages to regain the initiative.

On September 5, 1931, the Army attacks naval facilities at Talcahuano, taking it after heavy fighting. More interestingly, the naval mutiny sees the first clash between air power and naval power in Latin America. At first, air forces are used to attempt to prevent the southern fleet from joining up with the mutineers' main force. Unfortunately, that fails, they can't find it. Humiliated, Commodore Ramon Vergera, Commander in Chief of the air force, settles on attacking the fleet itself.

The results, to put it kindly, are inconclusive. The plan is to bomb the Almirante Latorre, but only one bomb lands anywhere near it. Only one mutineers' ship, a submarine, is actually hit, with a single fatality. In turn, five air force planes are shot up by return fire, and a sixth is so badly hit it goes down over sea.

But that is it for the mutiny of 1931. With their mainland forces overrun, with very little consensus as to their action, and with an actual though relatively bloodless battle undermining resolve, the mutineers decide to throw in the towel. As anyone might predict, a number of them are tried and sentenced to death or prison.

The fallout of the mutiny is a major reduction of power and prestige for the navy. The enlisted men and the officers find themselves the subject of repeated purges. In 1933, the Almirante Latorre, flagship of the fleet and national symbol, is mothballed, and a number of capital ships are scrapped or retired, ostensibly for age or economic reasons; but almost certainly an underlying motive is to prune back the navy. Only the heightened tensions in the region, including the Peruvian military build-up, and the Ecuador/Peru cold war, save the capital ships from being scrapped entirely.

But coming into 1940, what we have in the Chilean navy is a proud constituency, still feeling the effects of the reduction in standing and prestige resulting from the 1931 mutiny, and, if not desperate, then at least looking for a way to regain its former standing. For the navy, a repeat of the War of the Pacific with Peru seems like just the ticket.

As Ibanez's political efforts drift, and a phony war is declared, the Chilean navy finds itself increasingly on side with the Nazis that they loathe, in coming to the view that the phony war must become real.

So, despite the Army's failure to prepare; in Navy circles, the fantasy of intervening decisively to end the Ecuador/Peru conflict with a crushing naval victory.... the so called "Rescue of Guayaquil" plan takes root and becomes increasingly popular, to the point where admirals are promoting it to Ibanez.

Ibanez is nowhere near the weakling that President Prado in Peru is. But he's come into office at the head of a divided and quarrelsome assembly of constituencies. Unlike Prado, his generals and admirals could not issue an ultimatum and then proceed to war without him. But the pressure grows increasingly to appear strong by taking a decisive role in events. And in particular, the pressure is strong to commit the fleet to some kind of decisive action, which ultimately means committing the country.

And so, Chile finds itself at war once again.

But if the Naval Mutiny of 1931 provides a vital underlying element which drives Chile into war with Peru in 1940, it also provides a major strategic lesson everyone overlooks - the emerging dominance of air power over sea power.

In truth, the actual performance of air power against the Navy in 1931 has been underwhelming. And the culture of the navy is such that the strategic implications will be overlooked and ignored, or explained away. But it is a lesson that the Chilean navy will be schooled in at its cost through 1940 and 1941, as Peruvian aircraft prove an increasing threat to warships.

This humbling lesson is obscured due to an even greater humiliation. The Battle of Coquimbo has been a disastrous blow to the pride of Chilean sailors. They have been caught flat footed, and have taken serious damage.

The Chilean navy of 1941 has endured over a decade of abasements. It is an organization and culture desperate to regain its status and dignity. Again and again, in reviewing the mistakes of the mutiny one failure has stood out.

Despite overwhelming firepower, the navy was defeated, rightly or wrongly, for lack of a ground capacity. It was unable to land troops quickly and effectively, or to provide effective cover. For a decade, in the cloistered reaches of naval procurement and planning, the admirals have been studying and trying to quietly develop a capacity for ground-force landing.

Now, with the army humiliated and stalemated in trench warfare, the admirals of the navy see an opportunity to regain their former glory and prestige, and once again win the war for Chile.

As of May, 1941, the Chilean naval forces stand as follows: The terrifying battleship Almirante Latorre, damaged in November, but repaired; the Toro, formerly the former German pocket battleship Graf Spee, finally repaired and returned to service as Toro; the ancient but still formidable battleship, Almirante Cochrane; the ancient cruiser Almirante O'Higgins; five destroyers, Almirante Condell, Aldea, Hyatt, Serrano, Videla; five submarines, and a number of auxiliary vessels. Although Coquimbo has been devastated, the Navy's southern shipyard has gone untouched.

***

Chile - The Landing Land and Sea Battle- May 26

Using the bulk of the Peruvian navy as cover and shore assault, Ibanez deploys every ship, boat, auxiliary craft and civilian watercraft he can assemble or requisition to launch a massive landing against the shores of Arequippa province, behind Peruvian lines. Within the first day, 5,000 troops are landed. Initially, the landing is without resistance, but by May 28, Peruvian troops and local militia are engaging.

By May 29, the Peruvians are committing most of their remaining naval resources, including their submarines and most of their aircraft, to trying to dislodge Chile's beachhead in the last major sea battle of the war.

During the Battle of the Landing, the Peruvian destroyers Rodriguez and Garcia are sunk, and the cruiser Aguire is disabled and forced to withdraw. At least one Peruvian submarine is lost to enemy action. The ferocious sea battle breaks the back of the Peruvian navy.

The Chilean battleship, Almirante Cochrane, is hit with multiple air strikes; no longer seaworthy, the ship beaches itself near the shore and continues to fire its big guns to provide cover for the landing force. The Chilean destroyers Hyatt and Videla are also heavily damaged and rendered incapable of action, mainly from aerial fire. The Videla is eventually scuttled. The Hyatt is in repairs for the remainder of the war. The rest of the capital ships take minor aircraft damage, but are protected by smaller craft retrofitted with anti-aircraft defences.

Relatively few of the requisitioned ships and boats are landing worthy, or capable of modification for landing. These are the first wave and many are scuttled. Modified barges are towed towards shore and are deposited as makeshift docks, allowing ships incapable of landing to dock and disembark soldiers or offload motor vehicles and heavier equipment. In order to maximize the force, all of the capital and support ships are packed with infantry. As the small craft disembark their soldiers at the makeshift docks, they return to the capital ships to pick up more human cargo. A number of soldiers drown in the transfer process, and many of the smaller ships are damaged or scuttled, but the operation proceeds quickly.

The sea battle marks the end of Peru as a naval force. Its capital ships are reduced to a couple of operable warships and submarines, none of which are a match for the Chilean battleships and cruisers.

Chile's victory at sea, however, has come at a terrible cost; several capital ships have been lost or damaged. Worse, however, they have been shown to be ineffective. Save submarines, all of Chile's ships are vulnerable to air attack. They cannot attack Peruvian cities or ports; they dare not come within range of ground-based airfields. The best they can offer is a blockade. But the navy dare not interfere with American shipping, which makes a blockade worthless.

Nevertheless, the Landing continues; by May 31, the Chileans have landed almost 24,000 troops. These numbers, however, are recklessly large. The force is almost entirely infantry, little artillery has been landed, and only a handful of vehicles. Food and water are in short supply, and only two-thirds of the force have sufficient ammunition. As many as half of the boats and auxiliary craft have been beached or damaged in the landing and are no longer usable.

The navy can offer only limited fire support from the capital ships. Low on just about everything, and desperate, Chile's only option is a rapid forced march down the coast towards the rear of the entrenched Peruvian positions, even while the Peruvians are organizing a pursuing force. Over the next few days, it is an open question whether the Chilean landing force will be crushed between the jaws of its enemies.

It is estimated that as much as half the landing force are casualties. However, by June 4, at least some of Ibanez's plans come to fruition. The landing force, supported by the navy, attacks the rear of a section of Peruvian lines. The Peruvian line, under attack from three sides, collapses in this area, but withdraws in good order inland, where they reform.

Hard fighting continues until June 16, at which point the Peruvians dig in to a new zigzag line that now extends over 180 miles. Ibanez has made substantial gains in Tacna and publicly proclaims sovereignty over the whole of the province. In Chile, propaganda depicts the battle as a glorious victory.

The gains have come at an appalling cost and the new battle lines have left Chilean forces far more vulnerable. Ibanez has expended far more resources on land and at sea than he can afford.

The Peruvians, comparatively, do better. Their casualties are heavy, but they have fought largely on the defensive and manage to preserve a good portion of both their assets and their order. This is largely due to the experience and professionalism of the southern command generals and officers, who are fighting on terms they understand, as well as vast numbers of Quechua Indigenous conscripts, whose mountain agrarian lifestyles and tribal cohesion, makes them resilient soldiers in this theatre.

Ibanez anticipates a Peruvian collapse once significant portions of their line have been broken. But again and again, the Peruvians are able to recover and reform. The rout he hopes for does not arrive.

Intermission

June 16 is the end of major operations, but small engagements off and on continue for the next couple of months, as the Peruvians push the Chilean forces back along sections of the front.

Overall, the trench war of Tacna remains comparatively less violent and casualty rates lower than the European theatre in WWI.

There are a number of reasons for this: The combatants have relatively fewer resources to waste; the gigantic WWI battles of the trenches had been expenditures of vast wealth. Chile and Peru simply do not have the money to spend, or for that matter, the manpower. At the same time, officers and soldiers on both sides are well aware of the European example and are generally unwilling to commit so recklessly.

Despite this, the Trench War remains the most brutal theatre of the Andean wars: Between April 11 and July 1, 1941, the campaign has seen 73,000 Chileans killed or injured, and 45,000 Peruvians killed or injured.

Even these numbers have been overrun by the ongoing mobilization and conscription. By July, 1941, with almost a year of war, Chilean army has reached 220,000 strong, the Peruvian Mobilization is at 280,000 and Ecuador's defence forces are over 100,000.

Of the three, Ecuador is reaching its physical and demographic limits of manpower and the capacity of its economy.

Both Chile and Peru are implementing plans to scale their forces up to a half million each. Economically, both countries are experiencing bottlenecks of money, munitions and oil that slow mobilization. Chile is in a better position. But Ibanez's act of aggression has alienated the American government; and while the Roosevelt administration is not prepared to excuse Peru's own bad conduct, it is increasingly prepared to look the other way on Peru's behalf

At the end of this second phase of the war; peace seems a remote prospect. While Ecuador will be increasingly desperate for peace, both Ramirez in Peru, and Ibanez in Chile have by their separate political routes come to the point where the only option available to either man is victory absolute and total. Victory at any price.

IN THE NEXT VOLUME

NEW WORLD WAR
Axis of Andes, Part 2

Book of Bolivia,

Book of Argentina,

Book of Quechua,

Book of Ending,

Chronology of Campaigns

NEW WORLD WAR

Part Two of AXIS OF ANDES

By D.G. Valdron

Return to Table of Contents

AXIS OF ANDES
Chronology
(Altered History in Bold)

1810 -1820s - Wave of Revolutions see Latin American independence.

1818-1831 - Gran Colombia established, comprised of Venezuela, Colombia, Panama and Ecuador.

1828-1829 - Gran Columbia-Peru war, largely over the interior territories which would be claimed by Ecuador.

1836-1837 - War of the Confederation. A Peru/Bolivia Federation is embroiled in a war with Argentina and Chile separately. Loses. End of confederation.

1859 - "The Terrible Time" of Ecuador. Four-way civil war, and brief invasions by Peru and Colombia.

1865-1870 - War of the Triple Alliance between Brazil, Argentina and Uruguay on one side, destroys Paraguay on the other.

1879 – 1883 - War of the Pacific. Peru and Bolivia engage in a war with Chile. Lose badly. Chile controls nitrates.

1881 – Chile, embroiled in a war with Bolivia and Peru, signs a treaty with Argentina, giving up claim to a half million square miles of Patagonia.

1890, July - POINT OF DIVERGENCE. Neptali Bonifaz, a young man of mixed Peruvian and Ecuadorian parentage, has a huge row with his father, causing him to reject a Peruvian

passport and subsequently occasionally involve himself on an intermittent basis with Ecuadorian nationalism.

1895 - "Selling the Flag" Scandal, a Chilean destroyer reflagged for Ecuador, for sale to Japan. End of the Conservative Era. Beginning of the Liberal period of Ecuador.

1916 - Munoz-Suarez Treaty between Ecuador and Colombia demarcates the Colombian/Ecuador border at the Putomayo river.

1918 - End of WWI. Worldwide Post-War Recession affecting Latin America, destabilizing governments.

1920-1922 - Recession, depression and hyperinflation in Ecuador. General strikes. Uprisings among natives and in urban locations. March, May and August 1920, uprisings in local areas. May 1921 another regional uprising. July, 1921, attempted Indigenous uprising. November, 1922, a thousand workers massacred in main city, Guayaquil.

1922, March - Salomon-Lozano Treaty between Peru and Colombia, made in secret, recognizes Peru's claim to Ecuadorian territory, cedes northern lands allowing Ecuador's claims to be flanked on three sides.

October, 1922 - Europe - Mussolini takes power in Italy. Italy's fascist government becomes relatively influential with Latin American military officers in the 1920s and 1930s.

July, 1925 - Ecuador. League of Young Officers - overthrows corrupt government.

1925, Ecuador - Isidro Ayora government takes power, initiates reform. Brief boom period ensues.

1925- July 1931 - Chile - Carlos Ibanez is defacto dictator of Chile. Ousted because of the depression, he will struggle to regain power.

1929 - Peru/Chile -Treaty between Peru and Chile results in return of Tacna province to Peru, and Chile's payment of a six-million dollar indemnity.

1929 - Stock Market Crash in the United States. Great Depression begins, worldwide. Collapse of Latin American export economies.

August, 1930 - In Peru, President Leguia is overthrown by Lieutenant Colonel Sanchez Cerra. Sanchez will shortly become President and new dictator.

September, 1930 - Peru/Ecuador – Salomon-Lozano treaty becomes public, much to the outrage of Peruvians, who see it as a disgrace and capitulation. Ecuador's public is also shocked at the betrayal, the 1916 treaty is considered a conspiracy. Colombia's Ambassador to Ecuador is thrown out.

August 31, 1931 - Chile - Naval Mutiny. It ends badly for all concerned by September.

August-October, 1931 – Ecuador - Colonel Alba overthrows Arroya government. Unable to put together a coalition. Resigns in favour of elections.

October, 1931 - Ecuador election. Semi-Fascistic organization, the National Compact, with its 'Dirty Shirts' lines up behind Neptali Bonifaz, who wins the Presidency by an overwhelming majority.

July-August, 1932 - Chaco war begins between Bolivia and Paraguay.

August, 1932 - the Six-Day Civil War in Ecuador, between supporters of Bonifaz and supporters of the Parliament. 5,000 dead. Won by Bonifaz with the support of Colonel Alba of the military and Velasco Ibarra in Parliament. Beginning of an informal triumvirate of Bonifaz, Alba and Ibarra. Result is a stable long-term Ecuadoran government through the depression, instead of the revolving door governments of our timeline.

September, 1932 - April, 1933 – Colombia-Peru War. Big fizzle. On the path to being bloody, until President Sanchez is assassinated. General Benavides replaces him. War is resolved with acceptance of Salomon-Lozano Treaty.

September, 1932 - Ecuador - Ascubazi, a leftist revolutionary and cousin of Bonifaz, in Ecuador, is exiled and goes to the Peruvian Sierra, living among the Indigenous. This begins a trend of exile of leftists and radicals from Ecuador. Concurrently, Peru imposes internal exiles, first under Sanchez and then under Benavides.

Leftists and revolutionaries are exiled to the inland Sierra, away from the Spanish Criollo-dominated coasts.

January, 1933 - Europe - Hitler and the Nazi Party take power in Germany.

May, 1933 - Ecuador's triumvirate assesses the outcome of the Colombia-Peru war and concludes that an attack or invasion by Peru is inevitable. Colombia has thrown them to the wolves. America will likely not help. Decision is made to prepare and defend.

June 1933 - Ecuador's armament, part of a general economic strategy, will spark a mild arms race with Peru.

August/September, 1933 - Ecuador's triumvirate, seeking alliances against Peru begins to support Bolivia in the Chaco War.

October, 1933 - Ecuador's Velasco Ibarra makes his first diplomatic venture to Chile.

December, 1933 - November, 1934 - Ecuador sends military observers and a 'volunteer brigade' eventually reaching 10,000.

1933 – 1940 - Ecuador/Peru border conflicts emerge frequently in this timeline. Conflicts occur in our timeline with both frequency and severity. The number of conflicts and intensity increases. Relations between the two countries are extremely poor.

January, 1934 - Ecuador's Velasco Ibarra goes to Chile seeking a diplomatic/military alliance to restrain Peru. The Allessandri government wants nothing to do with him. Ibarra eventually becomes involved with disgraced former dictator Carlos Ibanez and with the Chilean Nazi Party.

March, 1934 - Ecuador - pursues diplomatic initiatives with Argentina and Brazil, again seeking to restrain against Peru. These initiatives continue, but by 1936 it is clear that they are fruitless.

March, 1934 - Chile - Connections between the Ecuadorian fascists and Chilean Nazis evolve. Effect is to moderate the anti-semitism and volatile extremism of the Chilean Nazis. Also, transmit anti-Peruvian and anti-Indigenous sentiments. Nazi rejection of Tacna treaty of 1929 as a 'stab in the back.' However, the Nazis remain a marginal Chilean party, and Ecuador has no tangible benefit.

1935 - Peru - Lima expresses concern and discontent with respect to Ecuador's involvement with Bolivia and in the Chaco War. Peru has also become aware of and concerned with Ecuador's attempts to establish diplomatic and military alliances.

June, 1935 - Paraguay and Bolivia agree to ceasefire. Ecuador's involvement in the Chaco war has made no real difference to the outcome.

August, 1935 - Ecuador and Bolivia agree to settle Bolivia's war debts with military surplus equipment.

November, 1935 - Ecuador and Bolivia agree to a Secret Treaty, mutual aid and assistance.

May, 1936 - David Toro and German Bush overthrow the Bolivian government to introduce military socialism.

July, 1936 - Europe - Spanish Civil War begins. Hitler and Mussolini intervene on behalf of Franco.

1936 - Peru - General Benavides in response to tensions with Ecuador, and potential threats from Bolivia and Chile divides Peruvian forces into 'Northern' and 'Southern Commands.' General Ureta is eventually in charge of the Northern Command. Many in the Peruvian military favour war with Ecuador as a way to wipe away the perceived humiliation of the Peru-Colombia War.

July, 1937 - German Bush overthrows David Toro, becoming sole ruler of Bolivia.

September, 1937 - Ecuador's Alba and Ibarra travel to Bolivia on a diplomatic mission to confirm the Secret Treaty. Bush's

response, while polite, makes it clear that the treaty, their only real success, can no longer be relied upon. Ecuador is all out of diplomatic options on the continent.

December, 1937 - Ecuador's Velasco and Alba, through the assistance of the Chilean Nazi party, and via Admiral Canaris, meet with Franco, Hitler and Mussolini, seeking aid and assistance.

1938 - Ford Motor Company, as a result of support and recommendations from Germany, begins to invest heavily in Ecuador, with auto parts and assembly factories opening in Guayaquil and Quito. Some materials and money come directly from Germany or Italy.

December, 1938 - Chile - protégé of Allessandri and Finance Minister, Gustavo Ross, defeats rivals Carlos Ibanez and Aguire Cerda to become President of Chile.

April, 1939 - Europe - Spanish Civil War ends. Franco's victory, as well as Hitler's and Mussolini's involvement, is a huge boost to the prestige and credibility of fascist movements, particularly in Ecuador and Chile, and raises American concern about German influence in South America.

1939, August - Gustavo Ross's first year as President has been rocky. His unrestrained fiscal conservatism has alienated the army and produced widespread popular resistance, including strikes and demonstrations. A military revolt, the Ariostazi, escalates, drawing widespread support from both the Chilean Nazis and from Radical and Leftist parties. Ross is deposed, Carlos Ibanez comes to power at the head of a loose coalition of communists, Nazis and the military.

December, 1939 - Peru - General Benavides, in power since 1939, but generally ineffectual, holds a fraudulent election, handing power over to his protégé, the even more ineffectual Luis Prado.

January, 1940 - The German pocket battleship, Graf Spee, after being heavily damaged in the Battle of the River Plate, pauses in Uruguay.

January, 1940 – The Graf Spee, a couple of weeks later, unable to land in Argentina, or continue to battle, flees to Chile, which then acquires the ship for its own navy, precipitating diplomatic tensions with Britain and America.

April, 1940 - The Secret Sorzano-Ibarra treaty between Bolivia and Ecuador for mutual support in war is exposed, when General Peneranda comes to power in Bolivia. Peru breaks diplomatic relations with both Bolivia and Ecuador. Ibanez of Chile denounces the treaty. Peneranda in Bolivia repudiates the treaty, which has been a dead letter anyway since 1937.

May, 1940 - Peruvian Northern Commander, General Elroy G. Ureta, in June, 1941, demands that President Prado declare war on Ecuador and authorize invasion. Prado equivocates.

June 2, 1940 - Ecuador Front – "The Great Northern Campaign" - General Ureta takes the initiative and invades Ecuador, striking the coastal provinces of El Oro, and the towns of Huaquillas and Puerto Bolivar.

June 3, 1940 - Ecuador Front – "The Great Northern Campaign" - Alba orders a general mobilization to defend against the invasion.

June 5, 1940 - Rain Forest War – "The Great Northern Campaign" - Peru's Army Jungle division and Chinchipe Army Group cross the Napo and Maranon rivers, attacking Ecuadoran outposts, but encounter immediate resistance.

June 6, 1940 - War at Sea – "The Great Northern Campaign" - The Peruvian cruiser Coronel Bolognesi and the destroyer Villar, along with a troop transport and support vessels enter the Ecuadoran Gulf of Guyaquil.

June 7, 1940 - War at Sea – "The Great Northern Campaign" - Ecuadoran gunboat Calderon encounters the Peruvian destroyer, Villar, on its way to Puerto Bolivar, on June 7, 1940. The Calderon opens fire on the Villar while retreating. The Villar pursues, the two ships exchanging fire all the way, until the Calderon is able to retreat into local river channels. The Villar proceeds on its way.

June 8, 1940 - Ecuador Front – "The Great Northern Campaign" - Peru overruns the port city of Puerto Bolivar and moves on the town of Machata, where the Ecuadorans are preparing a last stand.

June 9-12, 1940 - The War at Sea – "The Great Northern Campaign" - The Coronel Bolognesi enters Guayaquil harbour and demands surrender. After meeting resistance, it withdraws.

June 14-20, 1940 – "The Great Northern Campaign" - Peru attacks Machata, where the Ecuadorans have made their stand. After a week of fierce fighting, Ecuadoran forces withdraw but Peruvian forces have taken massive casualties.

June 14-21, 1941 – "The Great Northern Campaign" - Alba, the Ecuadoran general, uses battle of Machata as a distraction, using the time to redeploy forces from Lojas, cutting off overextended supply lines, and flanking Peruvian forces in both Machata and Puerto Bolivar.

June 15, 1940 - Rain Forest War – "The Great Northern Campaign" - the Chinchipe army group dissolves into uncoordinated units, most of whom are in retreat.

June 18, 1940 - Rain Forest War – "The Great Northern Campaign" - Ecuadorans cross the river, taking Peruvian towns Jacn and Bagua, as the remnants of Peru's Chinchipe Arm continue to retreat.

June 24, 1940 - Ecuadoran Front – "The Great Northern Campaign" - Ecuador achieves local air superiority. Peru's retreat becomes a rout, as the badly overextended and undersupplied forces begin abandoning vehicles and equipment.

June 28, 1940 - Ecuadoran Front – "The Great Northern Campaign" - Alba gives battle near the Zamilla river on the border. After a morning of hard fighting, the Peruvians surrender

June 28, 1940 - War at Sea – "The Great Northern Campaign" - Coronel Bolognesi enters Guayaquil harbour and commences to shell the city, taking minor damage from aerial bombing.

July 2, 1940 - Chile – Chile, rebuffed in attempts to broker peace negotiations, declares war in an ill-advised move, but takes no further action. Instead, Chile proposes an immediate ceasefire.

July 7, 1930 - War at Sea - Chilean battleship, Almirante Latorre, and two destroyers, the Aldea and the Hyatt, enter the Gulf of Guayaquil ostensibly to protect shipping. The two naval forces face each other, but take no action.

July 10, 1940 - March on Lima - Colonel Alba of Ecuador leads an expeditionary force in the famous 'March on Lima,' a bold attempt to knock Peru out of the war.

July 14, 1940 - Rain Forest War - the last Peruvian forces of the 'Great Northern Campaign' and the Chinchipe army group are trapped at the town of Yurimaguas, on the Rio Huallaga, where the Ecuadorans win decisively. Blandon arrives after the battle.

July 24, 1940 - March on Lima - "Battle of Chiclayo" - Alba's expeditionary force overwhelms and routes a Peruvian force. Alba's arrival takes General Ureta completely by surprise. In the battle, 3,500 Peruvians killed or injured.

July 26, 1940 - Rain Forest War - Blandon leads Ecuadoran forces into the Peruvian rain forest territories, ostensibly in pursuit of fleeing enemy, but in reality in response to Alba's victories in the March on Lima.

July 30, 1940 - March on Lima - A relief convoy of approximately 10,000 men leaves Tombes to resupply Alba's forces, making good time, and meeting no significant resistance.

August 1, 1940 - March on Lima - "Battle of Trujillo" - Alba arrives and attacks the Central Army Command at Trujillo. The Central Command is taken by surprise. After days of fighting, the Peruvians ask for terms on August 5.

August, 1940 - Rain Forest War - Blandon's forces move through the river systems into Peruvian territory, finding little organized resistance and overwhelming defenders.

August 8, 1940 - Chilean Front - "Battle of Tacna" - After a long period of dithering, and emboldened by the March on Lima in the north, Ibanez orders an attack against defended Peruvian positions. It goes very badly.

August 15, 1940 - Chilean Front - "Battle of Arica" - taking advantage of Chilean disarray, the Peruvian forces push south into their former province of Arica. Peru mobilizes faster. Chilean forces are overextended.

August 16, 1940 - The War at Sea – In Guayaquil bay, Chile's battleship, Almirante Latorre opens fire on the Coronel Bolognesi on orders of President Ibanez, in response to the successful Peruvian offensive in Arica.

August 21, 1940 - War at Sea – Almost the entire surviving Peruvian navy is dispatched for an attack on the Chilean navy at Coquimbo.

August 23, 1940 - March on Lima - "Battle of Huarez" - Alba leaves Huarez, traveling back along his road to give battle. Peruvian forces are caught between Alba's main force and his relief convoy.

August 24, 1940 - Chilean Front - Peru pushes into Tarapaca, launching attacks on Antofagosta, deep into Chile. Chile begins mass mobilization. Chileans have outrun their supplies and are forced to retreat as fighting extends into Antofagosta.

August 28, 1940 - War at Sea - "Battle of Coquimbo" - under a cover of heavy fog, the first part of the Peruvian fleet enters the harbour at Coquimbo, opening fire on the ships and harbour defenses.

August 28, 1940 - Chilean Front - Chilean forces receive reinforcements and counterattacks. The overextended Peruvian line is at the limits of its supplies and forced to retreat slowly.

September 2, 1940 - Rain Forest War - "Sack of Pucallpa" - Blandon, leading a force of Ecuadorans and natives, attacks the Peruvian military outpost at Pucallpa, burning and looting the entire town.

September 5, 1940 - March on Lima - "Battle of Calao" - Alba reaches the town of Calao, after an exchange of fire, Alba retreats, leaving the Peruvian forces to follow. The Peruvians, in hot pursuit, fall into a trap. Alba defeats and destroys a force three times his size, advancing to the outskirts of Lima by September 8.

September 9, 1940 - March on Lima - Colonel Alba of Ecuador, and General Benevides of Peru agree on peace terms. At this point, Peru is fighting a two-front war, and losing badly on both fronts.

September 12, 1940 - Peru - President Prado and General Benevides are overthrown by General Ramirez. The Peruvians repudiate peace terms.

September 14 - 19, 1940 - March on Lima - "Battle of Lima"- Four days of artillery shelling and sorties. Peruvians 4,000 killed or wounded, 3,500 of them civilians. Ecuador 1,000. Alba orders a retreats.

September 20, 1940 - March on Lima - the Ecuadorans begin their retreat through Peruvian territory.

September 20, 1940 – Chilean Front - The Chileans retake Arica, and attack the Peruvian province of Tacna once again.

September 21, 1940 - March on Lima - A second Ecuadorian supply convoy, led by General Enrique Gallo, leaves Tombes, aiming to unite with Alba's forces at Cajamarca.

September 30, 1940 - Chilean Front - The Chileans fall back from Tacna, retreating to their province of Arica.

October, 1940 - Rain Forest War - Blandon has overrun 3/4 of the Peruvian Selva (Amazon) leaving only Madre de Dios province in Peruvian hands.

October 4, 1940 - March on Lima - "Rape of Huarez" - the Ecuadorans loot and burn the Peruvian town as they pass through.

October 9, 1940 - Chilean Front - A new Chilean offensive overruns Tacna, reaches Moqueguera, and attempts to establish a front along the road to Lake Titicaca.

October 14, 1940 - March on Lima - General Gallo's Ecuadoran relief forces meet up with Alba. Reinforced, Alba digs down in the town of Cajamarca and waits for the pursuing Peruvian forces to catch up.

October 18, 1940 - Chilean Front - Peruvians push Chileans out of Tacna. Chilean forces collapse.

October 20, 1940 - March on Lima - "First Battle of Cajamarca" - Huanaco Army group attacks prematurely. The Peruvians are decimated and forced into a rout. Alba pursues, hoping to destroy Huanaco before it can be reinforced from the south.

October 24, 1940 - March on Lima: "Second Battle of Cajamarca" The retreating Peruvian Huanaco army links up with a Lima army coming up the coast. After two days of battle, Alba retreats, burning Cajamarca behind him. The Huanaco/Lima army follows slowly but does not give battle again.

October 30, 1940 - Chilean Front - Southern front stabilizes and trench warfare begins to set in, approximately 40,000 on each side. By November, numbers reach 50,000 each, a total of 100,000 men lined up along a 106 mile strip.

October 31, 1940 - Rain Forest War - Peru is rebuilding the military base at Pucallpa in the rain forest, as part of a campaign to eradicate Blandon's guerilla forces.

November 6, 1940 - March on Lima - Alba returns to Ecuador, the campaign is over.

November 8, 1940 - War at Sea - the Chilean battleship, Almirante Latorre, catches the Peruvian cruiser Almirante Grau and destroyer Palacio in open waters.

December 18, 1940 - Rain Forest War - Blandon is recruiting heavily among Peruvian indigenous populations for auxiliaries and support along the Ucayali river.

December 23, 1940 - Rain Forest War - Blandon attempts to mount a major raid against entrenched Peruvian forces at Pucallpa, encountering fierce resistance for the first time.

December 31, 1940 - Chilean Front - Mobility in the south comes to an end, trench war begins. Numbers at the southern front climb to 65,000 Peruvians facing 75,000 Chileans.

January 9, 1941, - Chilean Front – "New Year's Offensive" - An addition of 15,000 fresh troops to the front inspires the Chilean generals to launch a human wave offensive against the Peruvians.

January 21, 1941 - Chilean Front - "New Year's Offensive" – ends, the Chileans have lost 13,000 men.

February 20, 1941 - Chilean Front - Chile and Peru agree to a ceasefire on the front, not precluding operations elsewhere.

February 21,1941 - War at Sea - the Chilean ship, Almirante Latorre on coastal bombardment and blockade of Lima, is struck by several aerial bombs, forcing it to return to Valparaiso for repairs.

February 26, 1941 - Peru/Ecuador & Peru/Chile - the United States obtains agreement for two negotiating tables in order to build a long-term peace.

March 4, 1941 - Ecuadoran Front – "The Second Northern Campaign" – Launched by General Markholtz, the second great invasion of Ecuador.

March/April, 1941 - Rain Forest War - in coordination with the Second Northern Campaign, Peru begins a counterinsurgency campaign against Blandon in the Selva.

March 26, 1941 - Ecuadoran Front – "The Second Northern Campaign" - Alba counterattacks, after fierce fighting, Markholtz is driven back, but retreats in good order.

April 4, 1941 - Ecuadoran Front – "The Second Northern Campaign" - Markholtz attacks again, with an inconclusive battle.

April 11, 1941 - Chilean Front – "April Offensive" - Ibanez repudiates the ceasefire and launches a massive attack across the front, promising victory in ninety days.

April 11, 1941 - Ecuadoran Front – "Second Northern Campaign" - Alba counterattacks and Markholtz forced to retreat.

April 13, 1941 - Ecuadoran Front – "Second Northern Campaign" - Alba's forces close in; Markholtz manages to break out of trap, and retreats.

April 16, 1941 - Ecuador Front – "Second Northern Campaign" - Markholtz disengages and focusses on consolidating his position.

April 20, 1941 - Peru - General Rodriguez issues a directive relieving Markholtz of command and demanding his return to Lima. Markholtz ignores both orders.

April 22, 1941 - Chilean Front – "April Offensive" - Chilean forces launch a new offensive, with six objectives.

April 27, 1941 - Chile - The Chilean government begins planning "The Landing."

April 29, 1941 - Chilean Front – "April Offensive" - Chile splits the Peruvian defenders into three groups.

April/May, 1941 - Rain Forest War - The dueling forces begin crossing into Brazilian territory, at first accidentally, then deliberately.

May 4, 1941 - Chilean Front – "April Offensive" - The over-extended Chilean offensive stalls.

May 26, 1941 - Chilean Front/War At Sea – "The Landing" - Chile attacks from the sea in a massive amphibious operation supported by the bulk of the Chilean navy.

May 28, 1941 - Chilean Front – "The Landing" - Peruvian troops and local militia are engaging the new invasion, but are heavily outnumbered, and bombarded by offshore batteries.

May 29, 1941 - Chilean Front/War at Sea – "The Landing" - Peru commits most of their remaining naval resources, including their submarines, and most of their aircraft trying to dislodge the beachhead.

May 31, 1941 - Chilean Front – "The Landing" - Chileans have landed 24,000 troops behind Peruvian lines, attacking south. Heavy fighting.

June 1941 - Rain Forest War - Rainy season gives way to dry season. The rain forest theatre is now a diffuse battleground across three states. Blandon is now headquartered in Brazilian territory.

June 16, 1941 - Chilean Front – "The Landing" - major operations conclude. The battle lines stabilize, the Peruvians dig in to a new zigzag line extended over 180 miles.

Return to Table of Contents

A Note and More Books by the Author

If you've skipped to the end, looking for an apology, well... Sorry? Also, no refunds.

Thank you for taking the time out to read my little book. If you've made it all the way here, then I'm just going to assume you liked it. I hope you'll pick up **New World War**, the conclusion of the Andean Civil war, featuring more hijinks and shenanigans, including the Bolivian Civil War, Argentina, Brazil and Colombia being dragged into the war in different ways, naval battles, heroism, invasions, revolutions, you name it. Not everyone dies.

What else do I have to offer? Some kick ass Doctor Who Pirates history, a trilogy of alternate history stories, a trilogy of horror collections, an audiobook, novels, you name it.

If you liked this, could I suggest you leave a review wherever you got it. Mention it on your blog, or your Facebook. Say nice things. If that's too much, just toss me a couple of stars. Writing is a solitary, lonely pursuit and actually getting some feedback or appreciation is a wonderful thing.

But there's more to it. It's about trying to get out there. There are a lot of people writing a lot of books, and it can get hard to get noticed. Reviews help.

And speaking of writing more....'

Check out my Website,

denvaldron.com

ALTERNATE REALITIES
A Trilogy or Strange New Worlds

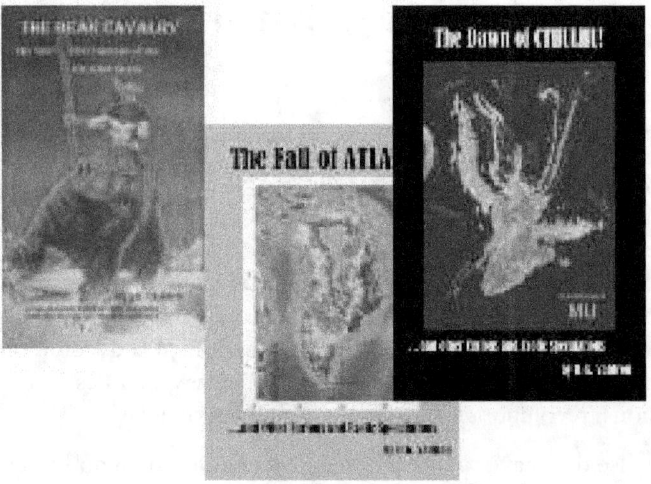

The Dawn of Cthulhu - The Secret History of H.P. Lovecraft's Cthulhu Cult; Lost Continents Found – real and legendary; The Monsters of Sesame Street, is a light hearted examination of Muppets as if they were actual animals.

The Fall of Atlantis – Retroverse, An Accidental Cinematic Universe of 50's Sci Fi movies, Greenland Without the Ice, Rome Crosses the Atlantic, and the Rise and Fall of Atlantis, an ecological catastrophe.

The Bear Cavalry, the True (Not!) History of the Icelandic Bears, an off the wall, short novel about the Viking domestication of bears, their evolution into a medieval cavalry Bonus novelette, The Sharebear Apocalypse.

HEARTS IN DARKNESS

A Trilogy of Horror Collections

Giant Monsters Sing Sad Songs – The connection between the author of the Necronomicon and a boy in Providence; a girl who meets the last Sasquatch, a poet who shares abandoned Tokyo with a Kaiju, and more…

What Devours Also Hungers – The unkillable killers in masks are recruited into the army, vampires and their hunters, clever serial killers, monsters, ghosts and more….

There Are No Doors in Dark Places – A childlike cancer that talks to its owner; A single mother drawn into dark magic; A man who turns into a different monster each night; and many more.

A Dark Fantasy of Murder and Redemption

There's a City where all the races come together uneasily, now descending into civil war.

There's a Mermaid, murdered cruelly her people distraught and crying out for justice.

There's an Orc, the lowest and the worst, her mission: Solve the murder, before it all comes crashing down.

She finds something else... the world's first serial killer.

The Strangest, Most Surreal, Space Opera Ever Created

LEXX – Star Trek's Evil Twin

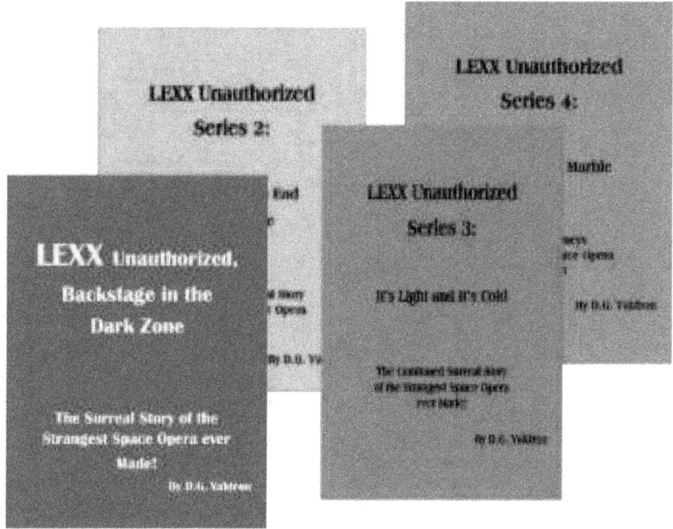

LEXX Unauthorized about the making of a show about a giant space bug that blows up planets, the cowardly security guard who is its captain, and the undead assassin, runaway love slave, and robot head who form its crew.

Originally billed as 'Star Trek's Evil Twin,' the cultiest of cult sci fi, LEXX's forte was black humor, startling visuals, big ideas, and a sensibility that had more to do with surrealists like Jodorowsky or Bunuel than mainstream science fiction. One of the most innovative science fiction series of all time.

The Pirate Histories!

What's a Pirate History, you ask? Pirate histories, the things that they don't want you to know about, or that they don't care about, things that are great and marvelous and intriguing. It's a history of secret and forgotten corners of the Whoniverse. The chronicles of the first women Doctors, the first black Doctors, Animations, Audios, Stage Plays and Fan Films, authorized and unauthorized.

AXIS OF ANDES
NEW WORLD WAR
A History of WWII in South America

Berlin, 1937, Adolph Hitler and his cabinet meet with a strange delegation from Ecuador. The delegates from the small South American nation beg for help, fearing an impending invasion from their rival, Peru. What happens at that meeting sets in motion a chain of events that lights the entire continent on fire. By the time it's done, millions are dead, nations are in ruins, and the map of Latin America will be changed beyond recognition.

Axis of Andes – Page 338

Drunk Slutty Elf
and Other Stories
Hilarious Science Fiction and Fantasy

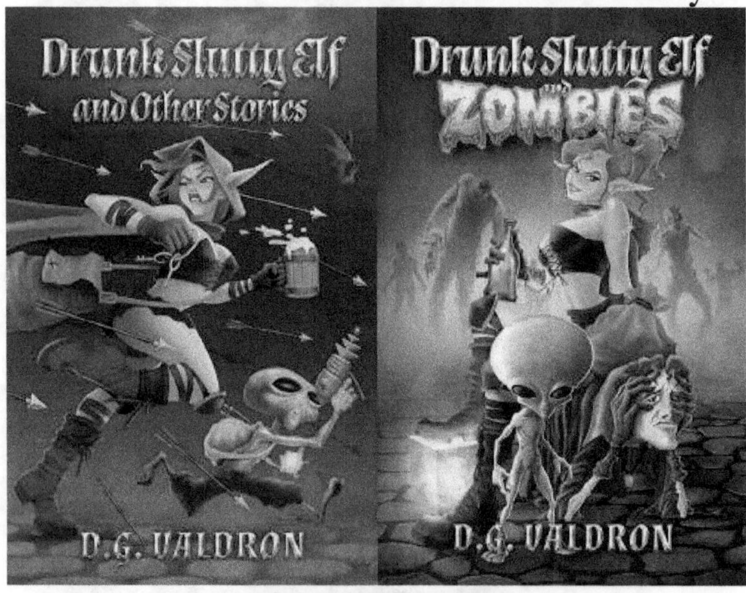

plus the sequel
DRUNK SLUTTY ELF
AND ZOMBIES!!!

Two volumes of savage, satirical, subversive wicked, funny, frantic science fiction and fantasy. Demented ghost hunters, frustrated aliens, horny giants, drunken elves, sneaky ghosts, wayward barbarians and many more.

Axis of Andes – Page 339